HELL TO PAY

Also by Garry Disher

HELL TO PAY

Garry Disher

SOHO
CRIME

Published by
Soho Press, Inc.
853 Broadway
New York, NY 10003

Library of Congress Cataloging-in-Publication Data

Disher, Garry.
Hell to pay / Garry Disher.
p. cm
ISBN 978-1-61695-395-9
eISBN 978-1-61695-396-6
1. Police—Fiction. 2. Murder—Investigation—Fiction. I. Title.

PR9619.3.D56H47 2014
823'.914—dc23 2014003808

Printed in the United States of America

10 9 8 7 6 5 4 3 2 1

to Jane Offor

HELL TO PAY

CHAPTER 1

ON A MONDAY MORNING in September, three weeks into the job, the Tiverton policeman took a call from his sergeant: shots fired on Bitter Wash Road.

"Know it?"

"Vaguely, Sarge," Hirsch said.

"Vaguely. You been sitting on your arse for three weeks, or have you been poking around like I asked?"

"Poking around, Sarge."

"You can cover a lot of ground in that time."

"Sarge."

"I told you, didn't I, no dropkicks?"

"Loud and clear, Sarge."

"No dropkicks on my watch," Sergeant Kropp said, "and no smartarses."

He switched gears, telling Hirsch that a woman motorist had called it in. "No name mentioned, on her way to view the wildflowers, heard shots when she pulled over to photograph the tin hut." Kropp paused. "You with me, the tin hut?"

Hirsch didn't have a clue. "Sarge."

"So get your arse out there, let me know what you find."

"Sarge."

"Could be someone's idea of a joke," the sergeant said, "and this is farming country, the sheep-shaggers like to take potshots at rabbits, but you never know."

IN WHEAT AND WOOL COUNTRY, in fact, three hours north of Adelaide, Hirsch's new posting was a single-officer police station in a blink-and-you'd-miss-it town on the Barrier Highway. There were still a few of these little cop shops around the state, the Department knowing not to call them one-man stations, not in this day and age, or not in print or in range of a microphone, but it didn't place female officers in them all the same, citing safety and operational concerns. So, single guys were sent to Tiverton (the wives of married officers would take one look and say no thanks)—often, or especially, guys with a stink clinging to them.

Like Hirsch.

The police station was the front room of a small brick house right on the highway, where flies droned and sluggish winds stirred the dusty community notices. Hirsch lived in the three rooms behind it: bathroom, sitting room with alcove kitchen, bedroom. He also enjoyed a parched front lawn, a narrow driveway for his own aged Nissan and the SA Police fleet vehicle, a four-wheel drive Toyota HiLux mounted with a rear cage, and a storeroom at the back, its barred window and reinforced door dating from pre-death-in-custody days, when it had been the lockup. And for all of these bounties the department screwed him on the rent.

Finishing the call with Sergeant Kropp, Hirsch located Bitter Wash Road on the wall map, locked up, pinned his mobile number to the front door and backed out of the driveway. He passed the general store first, just along from the police station and opposite the primary school, the playground still and silent, the kids on holiday, then a couple of old stone houses, the Institute with its weathered cannon and memorial to the dead of the world wars, more houses, two churches, an agricultural supplier, a signposted grain dealer down a side street . . . and that was Tiverton. No bank, chemist, medical practice, lawyer, dentist, accountant or high school.

He drove south along the floor of a shallow valley, undulating and partly cultivated hills on his left, a more dramatic and distant range on his right—blue today, scarred here and there by scrubby trees and shadows among erupted rocks, a foretaste of the Flinders Ranges, three hours further north. In the fashion of the locals, Hirsch lifted one finger from the steering wheel to greet the oncoming cars, all two of them. Nothing else moved. He was traveling through a land poised for movement: birds watched him from the power lines as if snipped from tin, farmhouses crouched mutely behind cypress hedges, and farm vehicles sat immobile in paddocks, waiting for him to pass.

Five kilometers south of Tiverton he turned left at the Bitter Wash turnoff, heading east into the hills, and here there was some movement in the world. Stones smacked the chassis. Skinny sheep fled, a dog snarled at a fence line, crows rose untidily from a flattened sleepy lizard. The road turned and rose and fell, taking him deeper into pretty but hardscrabble country, just inside the rain shadow. He passed a tumbled stone wall dating from the 1880s, a couple of massive perfect gum trees, a wind farm turbine. Someone had been planting trees up and down one of the gullies, to combat erosion. Then Hirsch remembered to check kilometers travelled since the turnoff, and wondered when he'd come upon the hut his sergeant was talking about.

He slowed for a dip in the road, water running shallowly across it from last night's storm, and accelerated uphill, over a peak and around a blind corner and jammed on the brakes.

A gum tree branch the length of a power pole lay across Bitter Wash Road. Hirsch switched off, his heart hammering. Close shave. Beyond the obstacle the road dipped again, bottoming out where a creek in weak, muddy flood had scored a shallow trench in the gravel, then it climbed to another blind corner. And in a little cleared area inside the fence and alongside the creek, was Sergeant Kropp's tin hut: corrugated iron walls and roof, mostly rust-colored, and a crooked chimney. He glimpsed trees and the suggestion of a green farmhouse roof on the flat above it.

Hirsch got out. He was reaching to drag the branch off the road when a bullet snapped past his head.

His first and natural instinct was to duck, his second to scuttle around to the lee side of the HiLux, drawing his service pistol, an S&W 40-caliber semiautomatic. His first *thought* was that Kropp's anonymous caller had got it right. But then, crouched there beside the grubby rear wheel, Hirsch began to have a second thought: two days earlier, some arsehole had placed a pistol cartridge in his letter box, and it occurred to him now that it hadn't been a joke or a threat, but a promise.

He weighed his options: call for backup; tackle the shooter; get the hell out.

Or the choice had been made for him. The cunts had trapped him where the road dipped between a canola crop and a stony hill. As soon as he showed himself—as soon as he got behind the wheel or clambered uphill to find the shooter or climbed the fence to run through the canola—he'd be shot. Meanwhile, police backup was in Redruth, forty kilometers away.

Hirsch's mind stopped racing and settled on one thought: the shooters were the very officers he hoped might back him up. They were not forty kilometers but forty meters away, up there on the hillside, positioned for a cross fire, their radios conveniently switched off. Redruth was a three-man station, Kropp and two constables, and when Hirsch had called in to introduce himself, three weeks ago, they'd called him a dog, a maggot. They'd mouthed *pow!* as they finger-shot their temples, grinned as they finger-sliced their throats.

Placed a pistol cartridge in his letter box when his back was turned.

Hirsch thought about it some more. Even if he managed to climb inside the HiLux again, the tree was still across the road, there was nowhere to turn around and they'd shoot him through the glass. Discounting a full-on, uphill assault, that left a zigzagging escape into the canola crop, a broad yellow swathe stretching to the smoky hills on the other side of the valley—but to reach it he'd first have to climb the bank and then tangle himself in a wire fence, and how much cover would the crop provide?

Hirsch began to feel jittery, a strange discordancy of his senses. He might have put it down to fear, but it was more a kind of illness. Some emanation from the wind farm? He was very close to one of the turbines. It sat on the stony hill where the shooter was hiding, the first of a ragged line stretching along this side of the valley, and the blades were cutting the air in a steady, rhythmic whooshing that reached deep in his guts. To Hirsch, it was all of a piece with ending his days where the world was unlovely, at the base of a scruffy slope of grass tussocks, rabbit holes and licheny stone reefs.

He glanced both ways along the road. He didn't know where the next farmhouses were or how much traffic to expect, or . . .

Christ, traffic. Hirsch cocked an ear, listening for vehicles he'd have to warn off, or protect, or mop the collateral blood from. Or fear.

Which raised the question: Why would the bastards ambush him here, within *cooee* of town? Why not somewhere more remote, like "out east"—as the locals called it. According to the calendar hanging above Hirsch's desk, "out east" was a region of undernourished mallee scrub, red dirt, nude stone chimneys, mine shafts, rock art, September wildflowers and one jagged hill named the Razorback.

September school holidays, wildflowers blooming . . . Hirsch listened again, imagining he could hear a busload of tourists trundling along Bitter Wash Road.

He risked a quick glance over the passenger door's windowsill.

The radio handset jutted from a cradle on the dashboard. His phone, a Motorola Defy, sat in a drinks holder between the front seats. He wasn't obliged to call the Redruth station. He could call Peterborough, Clare, even Adelaide . . .

The next shot came.

Hirsch froze, fingers on the door handle.

Then he relaxed minutely. He analyzed what it was he'd heard. Not a high-powered crack but something flat, puny, small caliber, dampened further by the huge sky above and the whoosh of the turbine blades. Hardly what you'd expect of a sniping rifle, and it had been accompanied by a weak howl as the bullet hit an obstacle—a stone?—and whanged away across the creek.

Nowhere near him.

A *second* ricochet came. He stiffened again, relaxed again. Not a ricochet, nor an echo, but a young voice saying *peeowww*.

Hirsch did what he should have done from the start and eyed the fallen branch. No drag marks in the gravel, no saw or axe cuts, excess foliage still intact. He eyed the tree itself. The wound was halfway up the trunk, and he recalled camping trips from his childhood, the teachers warning the kids not to pitch their tents under gum trees. All that sinewy health on the outside and quiet decay within.

Like the police.

He holstered his handgun and, hunching his shoulders a little, stepped into the middle of the road and dragged the branch into the ditch. Then he parked the HiLux on a narrow verge, leaving room for passing vehicles, and climbed the scabby hill to see who might have put him in his grave if his luck hadn't been running.

THEY DIDN'T HEAR HIS approach, the boy and the girl: the wind, the rhythmic rush of the turbine above their heads, their absolute absorption as one kid aimed a .22 at a jam tin on a rock and the other stood by to watch.

Hirsch knew he should pounce on them before they sent

another ricochet over the road, but he paused. The view from the base of the turbine was panoramic, exhilarating, and Bitter Wash Road was clear in both directions, so he took a moment to get his bearings. The broad valley, the vigorous crops, the road running up and down the folds in the earth. And that khaki smudge back there was Tiverton with its pale grain silos poking into the haze.

There was a farmhouse above the tin hut, the green roof clearly visible now, and on the other side of the road was a red-roofed house. Trees and cypresses hedged them in, shrubberies and garden beds and lawns, the usual landscaping out here in the wheat and wool country, but the green-roofed property was extensive, with a number of sheds, a set of stockyards and farm vehicles parked on a dirt clearing beside a haystack, while the red roof was small, faded, boasting only an attached carport and one small garden shed. Hirsch wondered at the relationship between the two properties. Maybe a farm manager lived in the smaller house. Or a "couple," a man to do the gardening, his wife to cook and clean. The shit work. Or maybe those feudal relationships no longer existed.

Hirsch shaded his eyes. The sun passed in and out of the scrappy clouds, a crow sideslipped above the road, sparrow-hawks hunted above the creek, sheep trotted, nose to tail, along a dirt pad on a nearby hillside.

Otherwise only the children moved, and Hirsch was betting they belonged to one or both of the houses. No school for two weeks, and, with the blessing or ignorance of their parents, they'd taken a .22 rifle out for some target shooting. The location was perfect: nothing here but grass and stones, sloping down to the creek, nothing with blood in its veins, yet you could pretend you were in a shootout with the bad guys, and when the rifle grew too heavy for your little arms you could prop the barrel on a rock.

Except that bullets strike objects and howl off in unexpected directions. Or you might forget where you are and take a potshot at a crow or a rabbit just when a policeman is stepping out of his HiLux to shift a fallen tree.

Yeah, well, wasn't this just great? A couple of *adults* he could deal with: clear regulations, clear offenses and penalties. But kids . . . He'd have to involve the parents; he'd maybe have to *charge* the parents. Hell to pay.

The children didn't hear him, not at first, not until, sidestepping down the slope, he skidded and fell. Now they heard him, his curses and the tock and rattle of stones tumbling over one another, Hirsch cursing because he'd frightened himself, torn his trousers and barked the skin on palm and elbow.

The children whirled around in shared alarm, mouths open, eyes shocked. They were caught in the act, and they knew it, but it was how they managed it that mattered, and Hirsch, forgetting his discomfort, was intrigued to see divergent reactions. The boy dropped his eyes like a beaten dog, already surrendering, but the girl grew tense, her eyes darting to the empty hill, the boy alongside her and possible escapes routes. She didn't run, but that didn't mean she wouldn't. The gaze she fixed on him was working it all out.

Hirsch held his palm up, not quite a warning, not quite a greeting. "Don't," he said mildly.

A faint relaxation of her limbs. She was about twelve years old, skinny, contained, unblinkingly solemn, with scratched bare legs and arms under shorts and a T-shirt, her hair dark and cropped at the shoulders and forehead. Scruffy, but she had the looks to light dark places.

Disconcerted, he eyed the boy. Thin, similarly dressed, he could have been her brother, but his hair was straw-colored, full of tufts and tangles, his pale skin was flushed and mottled, and where the girl seemed to look for the angles, he seemed ready to take orders or give up. But it was he who held the rifle, and he was practiced at it, keeping the barrel down, the stock in the crook of his arm, the bolt open. Hirsch counted five .22 shell casings glinting dully in the grass.

"My name," he said, "is Constable Hirschhausen. I'm stationed at Tiverton."

The girl remained expressionless but Hirsch sensed hostility, and he scratched around in his head for the best way to go on. One logical path was: "How about we start with your names?"

Her voice piping above the whoosh of the turbines, the girl said, "I'm Katie and he's Jack."

Katie Street and Jackson Latimer, and Katie lived with her mother in the smaller, red-roofed house that Hirsch had seen, and Jackson with his parents and older brother in the larger green-roofed house. In fact, Grampa Latimer lived on the property, too, in a house half a kilometer in from the road. "You can't see it from here."

Even Hirsch had heard of the Latimers. "This is your land?" he asked, indicating the hill they were standing on, the turbine above them, the ragged line of turbines stretching away along the ridge.

Jack shook his head. "Mrs. Armstrong's."

"Where does she live?"

He pointed to where Bitter Wash Road disappeared around a distant bend.

"Won't she be cross if she knew you were trespassing?"

They were puzzled, as if the word and the concept hadn't much currency out here. "It's the best spot," Katie reasoned.

Right, thought Hirsch. He continued to pick his way. "Look, the thing is, one of your shots went wild. It nearly hit me."

He gestured in the direction of the road. "I'd just got out of my car to move a fallen tree when I heard it go right past my head." Putting some hardness into it he added, "It's dangerous to shoot a gun so close to a road. You could hurt someone."

He didn't say kill someone. He didn't know if the severity would work. He didn't know if he should be gentle, stern, pissed off, touchy-feely or a full-on tyrant. He took the easy way:

"Do your parents know you're up here shooting a gun?"

No response. Hirsch said, "I'm afraid I'll need to talk to—"

The girl cut in. "Don't tell Mr. Latimer."

Hirsch cocked his head.

"Please," she insisted.

"Why?"

"My dad will kill me," the boy muttered. "Anyway he's not home."

"Okay, I'll speak to your mothers."

"They're out, too."

"My mum took Jack's mum shopping," Katie said.

They had all the answers. Hirsch glanced at his watch: almost noon. "Where?"

"Redruth," she said reluctantly.

Meaning they hadn't gone down to Adelaide for the day and would probably be home to make lunch. "Okay, let's go."

"Are you taking us to jail?"

Hirsch laughed, saw that the girl was serious, and grew serious himself. "Nothing like that. I'll drive you home and we'll wait until someone returns."

Keeping it low-key, no sudden movements, he eased the rifle—a Ruger—from Jack's hands. He'd disarmed people before, but not like this, and wondered if police work ever got chancy, out here in the middle of nowhere. He walked the children back over the ridge and down to the HiLux. The girl moved at a fast clip but the boy trudged with his spine and spindly arms and legs in a curious counterpoint, a kind of pulling back on the reins, and Hirsch saw that his left shoe was chunkier than the right, the sole and heel built up.

Catching Hirsch, the girl said, "You've got a hole in your pants."

THE KIDS STRAPPED IN, Katie in the passenger seat, Jack in the rear, Hirsch said, "So, we wait at Jackson's house?"

"Whatever," Katie said. She added: "You could be looking for that black car instead of hassling us."

The police were looking for hundreds, thousands, of cars

at any given moment, yet Hirsch knew exactly which one she meant: the Pullar and Hanson Chrysler. Rather than say the killers had last been seen heading for Longreach, in the middle of Queensland, over two thousand kilometers away, he said, "I doubt it's in our neck of the woods."

Katie shot him down with a look, swung her gaze away from him. "That's what you think."

Hirsch was fascinated by her. Dusty olive skin, tiny gold hoops in each ear, a strand of hair pasted damply to her neck and entirely self-contained. One of those kids who is determined, tireless, mostly right and often a pain. He tried to remember what he'd been like at that age. When it was clear that she didn't intend to elaborate, he slotted the key in the ignition.

"We saw it go past our school," said Jack in the backseat.

Slowly, Hirsch removed his hand from the key. Had some guy waved his cock at the kids? Tried to snatch one of them? "The primary school in town?"

"Yes."

"When was this?"

"Yesterday."

"A black Chrysler?"

"Yes."

"But what were you doing at school on a Sunday?"

"A working bee. Cleaning up and planting trees."

"Did this car stop?"

Katie shook her head. "It drove past."

"What time was this?"

"Nearly lunchtime."

Hirsch pictured it. The little primary school was opposite the police station, with a large playing field fronting Barrier Highway and the entrance, car park and classrooms reached via a side street. The speed limit was 50 km/h through the town, giving an observant child time to mark details. But what details had marked *this* vehicle out from the others that passed the school every day, the farm utes, family cars, grain trucks, interstate buses?

It was a black Chrysler, that was what. A car in the news, driven by a pair of killers.

Not a common car—but not rare either, and Hirsch argued that now. "I think those men are still in Queensland."

"Whatever. Can we just go?"

Hirsch glanced at the rearview mirror, seeking Jack's face. The boy shrank away.

"Suit yourselves," Hirsch said, checking the wing mirror and pulling onto the road.

Speaking of observant children . . .

"Did you kids happen to see anyone hanging around outside the police station late last week? Perhaps putting something in the letter box?"

They stared at him blankly and he was thinking the question beyond their ken when the girl said, "There was a lady."

"A lady."

"But I didn't see her putting anything in the letter box."

"Was she waiting to see me, do you think?"

"She looked in your car."

Hirsch went very still and braked the HiLux and said lightly, "When was this?"

"Morning recess."

Hirsch went out on patrol every morning, and someone would have known that. "What day?"

Katie conferred with Jack and said, "Our last day."

"Last day of term. Friday."

"Yes."

Hirsch nodded slowly and removed his foot from the brake pedal, steering slowly past the fallen branch. Seeing Katie Street peer at it, he had a sense of her mind working, putting the narrative together—his stopping the HiLux, getting out and hearing a stray bullet fly past his head. As if to check that he wasn't sporting a bullet hole, she glanced across at him uneasily. He smiled. She scowled, looked away.

Then she said tensely, "We're not lying."

"You saw a woman near my car."

Now she was flustered. "No. I mean yes. I mean we saw the black car."

"I believe you."

She'd heard that before, a doubting adult. "It's true!"

"What direction?"

She got her bearings, pointed her finger. "That way."

North. Which made little sense if Pullar and Hanson had been in the car she saw—not that Hirsch could see that pair of killers leaving their comfort zone to drive all the way down here to Daggy Sheep, South Australia.

Still sensing Hirsch's doubt, Katie grew viperish: "It was black, it was a station wagon and it had yellow and black New South Wales number plates, just like in the news."

Hirsch had to look away. "Okay."

"And it was a Chrysler," said Jack.

Feeling lame, Hirsch said, "Well, it's long gone now."

Or not, if it had been the Pullar and Hanson car. The men liked to target farms on dirt roads off the beaten track. Suddenly Hirsch understood what the children had been doing: they'd been shooting Pullar and Hanson.

He steered gamely down through the washaway and up around the next bend, to where Bitter Wash Road ran straight and flat for a short distance, the children mute and tense. But as he neared the red roof and the green, Katie came alive, snapping, "Jack's place."

A pair of stone pillars, the name VIMY RIDGE on one, 1919 on the other, the oiled wooden gates ajar. Imposing, but Hirsch supposed that a lot had occurred since 1919, for everything was weatherworn now, as if the money had evaporated or been spent on more pressing needs. A curving gravel driveway took him past rose-bordered lawns, oleander bushes and a palm tree, all of the road dust washed off by last night's rain, ending at a lovely stone farmhouse: local stonework in shades of honey, a steep green roof and deep verandas, in that mid-north regional style not quite duplicated elsewhere in the country, and sitting there as though it belonged. Hirsch eyed it appreciatively. He'd grown up in a poky terrace on the baked streets of Brompton— not that the miserable little suburb was miserable any longer, now the yuppies had remade it.

He pocketed his phone, got out, stretched his bones and gazed at the house. It was less lovely, closer to, careworn, the paintwork faded and peeling, a fringe of salt damp showing on the walls, a fringe of rust along the edges of the corrugated iron roof. Weeds grew in the veranda cracks. He didn't think it was neglect, exactly. It was as if the inhabitants were distracted, no longer saw the faults, or blinked and muttered, "I must take care of that next week."

The children joined him, Jack a little agitated, as though unsure of the proprieties. Hirsch contemplated phoning one or other of the mothers but mobile reception was dicey, the women were returning anyway, and a call from a policeman might panic them. So, how to fill in the time . . . He didn't think he should enter the house uninvited and didn't want to take advantage of Jack by suggesting it. And he didn't want to wander around the yard and sheds uninvited. Meanwhile, he needed to keep an eye on the kids.

Taking charge, he stepped onto the veranda and toward a huddle of directors' chairs. "Let's wait over here."

When they were seated he asked, "Who owns the twenty-two?"

"My dad," whispered the boy.

"What does he use it for?"

"Rabbits and things."

"Does he own any other guns?"

"Another twenty-two, a three-oh-three and a twelve-gauge."

"Where are they kept?"

"In his study."

Hirsch was asking the questions as if they were unimportant, keeping his voice low and pleasant, but he was scanning the dusty yard, taking note of the sheds, a scatter of fuel drums, an unoccupied kennel, stockyards, a field bin in a side paddock. A ute and a truck, but no car. A plow and harrows tangled in grass next to a tractor shed. A working farm but no one working it today, or not around the house.

"So anyone could take the guns out and shoot them?"

"He locks them in a cupboard."

Hirsch threw Jack a complicit wink. "And I bet you know where the key is, right?"

Jack shook his head violently. "No, honest."

"He's not lying," Katie said. "We used the gun that's kept in the ute. It's just a little gun, for shooting rabbits."

Little and overlooked and forgotten, thought Hirsch. Not even a proper gun, in the eyes of some people.

He was guessing the kids had done it a few times now, waited until the adults were out before grabbing the Ruger and heading down the creek for some target practice. Bullets? No problem. Small, overlooked and forgotten, they'd be found rolling loose in a glove box or a coat pocket or a cupboard drawer.

To ease the atmosphere, Hirsch said, "So, school holidays for the next two weeks."

"Yes."

A silence threatened. Hirsch said, "May I see the gun case?"

Jack took him indoors to a study furnished with a heavy wooden desk and chair, an armchair draped with a pair of overalls, a filing cabinet, computer and printer, bookshelves. It smelt of furniture polish and gun oil. The gun cabinet was glass-faced, bolted to the wall, locked. A gleaming Brno .22, a .303 fitted with a sight, a shotgun, a couple of cartridge packets, and an envelope marked "licenses."

Hirsch thanked the boy and they returned to the veranda in time to hear a crunch of gravel. A boxy white Volvo came creeping up to the house. It hesitated to see a strange vehicle, POLICE scrolled across the door and hood. Katie's mother at the wheel, reasoned Hirsch, and Jack's mother in the passenger seat, and he didn't know what the hell he should tell them. He removed the Motorola from his pocket. The shutter sound already muted, he was ready to photograph them—habit, after everything that had happened to him.

CHAPTER 2

VIEWED LATER, THE PHOTOGRAPHS captured on Hirsch's phone revealed women of his age, mid-thirties, and as unlike each other as their children. Katie's mother came into view first, slamming the driver's door and advancing on the house. She wore jeans, a T-shirt, scuffed trainers and plenty of attitude, throwing a glare at Hirsch as she neared the veranda. She was small-boned like her daughter, dark, unimpressed.

Jack's mother came trailing behind, leaving the Volvo in stages, closing the door gently, pressing against it until it clicked, and finally rounding the front of the car as if visiting strangers and reluctant to be a burden or disturb the air in any way. Hirsch wondered if she'd hurt her right hand. She held it beneath her breasts, fingers curled.

Meanwhile Katie's mother had stopped short of the veranda steps. She threw a glance at her daughter. "All right, hon?"

"Peachy."

"Excellent, excellent."

Hirsch experienced the full wattage of her gaze. He dealt with it by thinking, *Fuck this for a joke*, and sticking out his hand.

"Hi. Paul Hirschhausen, stationed at Tiverton." With a grin he added, "Call me Hirsch."

The woman stared at him, at his hand, at his face again; then, quite suddenly, her fierceness evaporated. He wasn't out of the woods, but did deserve a handshake. "Wendy Street," she said, "and this is Alison Latimer."

Hirsch nodded hello, Latimer responding with a smile that struggled to come in from the cold. She was tall, fair, subdued, pretty in a strained way, as if she had no expectations and understood disappointment. *But what do I know?* thought Hirsch. He could misread people as easily as read them, and bore the scars to prove it.

"Is something wrong?" she blurted, defeated expectancy in her face.

"Nothing too bad, but there is something we need to discuss."

Before he could elaborate, Wendy Street said, "You're new at Tiverton?"

"Yes."

"And you come under Kropp in Redruth."

"Yes."

"Fan . . . tastic," she said, dragging it out.

"Is there a problem?"

That might have been a shrug he saw. She grinned at his torn trousers, eyes briefly warm, brown and lustrous. "The kids beat you up?"

"Entirely my doing," Hirsch said.

"Uh-huh. So, you want to discuss something?"

Hirsch explained that he'd been heading out east, heard rifle shots, and thought he'd better investigate. For some reason, he elected not to mention Kropp's call.

"Oh, Jack," wailed Alison Latimer.

Jack stared at the ground. Katie stood with folded arms and stared out across the garden. And Wendy Street said, "You just happened to be passing, in your four-wheel drive, and heard shots."

Hirsch put a little harshness into it: "A tree was across the road. When I got out to shift it, a bullet flew past my head."

Okay?

It worked. The women were dismayed. They turned to the children, back to Hirsch, and after that he endured tides of apologies and recriminations.

"Look," he said, "no harm done. But I think the rifle should be locked away from now on." He retrieved it from the HiLux and handed it to Jack's mother. "I have to ask, is it licensed?"

Alison nodded. The rifle clasped a little awkwardly, as though her right hand lacked strength; she used her left to flip open the bolt. As she did so, a beautiful old-style diamond ring flashed a red spark as it caught the light. Then she gestured with the rifle, showing him the empty chamber. She was a lovely woman full of strain and privation, a woman who hated to be noticed and held herself stiffly, as though her joints had locked up. In a low mutter she said, "I can show you the paperwork if you like."

"That's okay," Hirsch said, knowing he should check but telling himself that he wasn't among criminals. "Look, you run a farm, it doesn't hurt to have a couple of rifles on hand, but keep them locked up so the kids can't get at them. No unsupervised shooting."

All through this, Wendy Street was casting tense looks at her neighbor. Alison, feeling the force of it, broke into tears. "Wen, I'm so sorry, I didn't know."

"Allie, I hate guns," Street said. She relented and touched the back of the other woman's hand. "Please, please, *please* keep them locked up."

"I will."

And to the children: "As for you two rascals, no more shooting, okay?"

"Okay," Jack said.

Katie didn't agree, she didn't disagree.

Wendy wasn't finished. She clamped her fingers around Hirsch's forearm. "Quiet word?"

Surprised, he said, "Sure."

She led him to her car and he stood there uneasily, waiting, watching the house, the other mother, the children.

"What's up?"

"I don't know you, I don't know if I can trust you."

There was nothing to say to that. Hirsch waited.

"I teach at the high school in Redruth."

"Okay."

"I've seen how Sergeant Kropp and his men treat the Koori kids."

Hirsch stroked his jaw. "I don't know anything about that. I'm new here. What's it got to do with Jack and Katie?"

Wendy took a breath. "Giving you the benefit of the doubt, I want you to know that Allie's husband is a bully. He won't handle this well when he hears about it, *and he's going to hear about it because he's mates with Sergeant Kropp.*"

Meaning, Hirsch thought, *she'll appreciate it if I keep my trap shut.*

"I assume you have procedures to follow," Wendy said bitterly.

"There are procedures and procedures," Hirsch said.

She assessed him briefly, head cocked, then gave a whisper of a nod. And promptly bit her bottom lip, as if thinking she'd gone too far, so Hirsch said:

"If Mr. Latimer is violent to his family I can refer them to a support agency. Sergeant Kropp needn't know."

The tension in Wendy Street shifted rather than eased. "What matters right now is the shooting business. If you have to report it, you have to report it—but I'd rather you didn't."

Hirsch gave his own version of an abbreviated nod. "How about we leave it as a friendly caution. It would have been different if someone had been hurt or the bullet had gone through the roof of my car." He paused. "Think of the paperwork."

He got a smile from her but it was brief, her big upper teeth worrying her bottom lip again. She cast a troubled look at the children, who stared back with trepidation, if not curiosity. They knew some kind of deal was being worked out.

"I don't know the *how*—I don't know where the gun was or where they found the bullets or whose idea it was—but I think I know the *why*."

A car passed by on Bitter Wash Road, tires crushing the short-lived paste of rainwater, dust and pebbles. Hirsch heard it clearly, and now he noticed the country odors: eucalyptus, pine, the roses, the grass and pollens, a hint of dung and lanolin. He realized his cut hand was stinging. All of his senses were firing, suddenly.

"Pullar and Hanson," he said.

Her mouth opened. "They told you about the car they saw yesterday?"

"Yes."

Wendy folded her arms. "It probably wasn't Pullar and Hanson, I know that, but the point is, they *are* scared. Ever since it started, Katie's been keeping a scrapbook. Jack has nightmares. The shooting is self-protection."

A burst of staticky squawks and crackles issued from the HiLux. "Excuse me," Hirsch said.

He reached in, picked up the handset, and it was Sergeant Kropp, demanding to know his current location.

"Poking around, Sarge," Hirsch said, watching Wendy Street return to the veranda. "No sign of anyone shooting a gun."

"Well, get your arse up to Muncowie. Make contact with a Mr. Ian Nancarrow, resident of Broken Hill, driving a white Pajero with New South Wales plates, somewhere on the highway there."

Hirsch scribbled the information in his notebook. "The reason?"

"A body beside the road."

CHAPTER 3

HIRSCH'S FIRST THOUGHT WAS: *Pullar and Hanson, the kids were right,* and he felt a queer kind of dismay mingled with excitement. "Suspicious?"

"Possible hit-and-run."

Hirsch made the mental adjustment: not Pullar and Hanson. "Nancarrow?"

"No. He claims he stopped by the road for a leak, saw a dead woman lying in the dirt." Kropp paused and added, "Doctor McAskill's on his way up there as we speak."

"I'm on it, Sarge."

Hirsch placed the handset in the cradle. The women and their children were watching him from the veranda. "Got to go," he called, climbing behind the wheel. He got a nod for his pains, a couple of halfhearted waves.

Pausing at the front gate, Hirsch entered "Muncowie" into the GPS. It directed him not back to the highway, as he'd expected, but further out along Bitter Wash Road, which eventually made a gradual curve to the north, smaller roads branching from it—one of which looped west onto the Barrier Highway a short distance north of Muncowie.

Shorter, Hirsch could see that from the map, but unsealed for most of the distance.

After twenty minutes, he found himself skirting around the Razorback, driving through red dirt and mallee scrub country, the road surface chopped and powdery where it wasn't reefed and ribbed with a stone underlay. Very little rain had fallen here last night; it was as if a switch had been flicked, marking the transition from arable land to semi-desert. Leasehold land, one-hundred-year leases defined by sagging wire fences, sand-silted tracks and creek beds filled with water-tumbled stones like so many misshapen cricket balls. You might find a fleck of gold in these creek beds if you were lucky, or turn your ankle if you were not. It was land you walked away from sooner or later: Hirsch saw a dozen stone chimneys and eyeless cottages back in the stunted mallee, little heartaches that had struggled on a patch of red dirt and were sinking back into it. Anthills, sandy washaways, foxtails hooked onto gates, a couple of rotting merino carcasses, a tray-less old Austin truck beneath a straggly gum tree, and weathered fence posts and the weary rust loops that tethered them one to the other. He saw an eagle, an emu, a couple of black snakes. It was a land of muted pinks, browns and greys, with the pale blue hills smudging the horizon, Muncowie on the other side. That was what he saw. What he didn't see, but sensed, were abandoned gold diggings, mine shafts, ochre hands stenciled to rock faces. A besetting place. It spooked Hirsch. The sky pressed down and the scrub crouched. "It's lovely out there," one of the locals had assured him during the week, waiting while Hirsch witnessed a statutory declaration.

He passed in and out of creek beds and saw a tiny church perched atop a rise. What the fuck was it doing there, this shell of a church? Calling to other stone shells, he supposed, left by the men and women who'd settled here and failed and walked away from it all.

Muttering, "I'm just a boy from the suburbs," Hirsch fought the steering wheel, the gear lever, the clutch. His foot ached.

Even the HiLux struggled, pitching and yawing inflexibly, taking him at a crawling pace through the backcountry. You had to hand it to technology, the GPS giving him the shortest route but blithely unaware of local conditions. It would take him forever to reach Muncowie at this rate, longer if he holed the sump or punctured a tire.

THEN HE WAS UPON the highway. MUNCOWIE 7, according to the signpost. He made the turn, heading south, the valley less obvious here, the highway striping a broad, flat plain. Driving down it gave Hirsch a sense of riding high above sea level, the sky vast and no longer pressing down, the hills a distant smudge on either side. Marginally worse crops, stock and fences up here, from what Hirsch could see, but better than the country he'd just passed through. More and greener grass, less dirt. It was as if he'd passed across the rain shadow again, moved from unsustainable life to a fifty-fifty chance of it. Not that he saw many signs of habitation, only a dusty ute driven at practically a walking pace, an old farmer at the wheel. Where did the geezer live? Hirsch could see no farmhouses close to the road, only gateways indicating homes back in the foothills of the blue range that stretched all the way to Wilpena Pound.

And then in the emptiness he saw another car. Black.

But not the black Chrysler.

Hirsch thought about it. In terms of timing, geography and logic, it wouldn't make sense for Pullar and Hanson to make their way down here. Travel two thousand kilometers in a notorious vehicle, away from terrain they knew? Hirsch couldn't see it. But he could see how the men might hunt in a place such as this, for they preyed on roadhouse waitresses on the empty highways, housewives and teenage daughters on lonely country roads.

IT HAD STARTED AS a vicious backblocks story, a Queensland story, which quickly went viral when Channel 9 muscled in, giving the killers a voice. Back in August a forty-year-old Mt. Isa speed freak named Clay Pullar and an eighteen-year-old Brisbane cokehead named Brent Hanson raped and murdered three roadhouse waitresses over a two-week period. Police managed to track the men to a caravan park in northern New South Wales, but arrived too late, and found a Canadian hitchhiker roped to a bed. Further sightings placed the men in Cairns, Bourke, Alice Springs, Darwin . . . Nothing definite until they broke into a farmhouse near Wagga, where they raped a teenager in front of her trussed-up parents and fled north with her to a property across the border and along the river at Dirranbandi.

Feeling pleased with himself, Pullar phoned Channel 9 on his mobile phone. He'd just managed to prove who he was when the signal failed, so Channel 9 dispatched a reporter and a cameraman by helicopter, which set down on the back lawn long enough to leave a satellite phone, and took off again, circling overhead. Pullar appeared, and even through the long pull of the camera lens he looked tall, gaunt, hard, insane. He grinned and waved, showing stumpy teeth, grabbed the phone, returned to the farmhouse, and began to explain himself. An exclusive, a live interview, you couldn't ask for better, think of the dollars rolling in, fuck the ethics, the public had a right to know. Fuck sense, too, for Pullar made absolutely no sense but was full of frothing lunacy.

The police took thirty minutes to arrive. They surrounded the house, jammed the signal, chased the helicopter away—and waited. Night fell. They tried to talk to Pullar and Hanson. After a few hours of silence it occurred to them to rush the house . . .

They found an elderly man and woman unconscious and the Wagga teenager naked and traumatized and no sign of Pullar and Hanson, who had fled, on foot, to a neighboring property. Here they stole a beefy black Chrysler 300C station wagon and by daybreak were hundreds of kilometers north, apparently heading for Longreach. An intelligent rape-and-murder team might have swapped the Chrysler for a less obvious car at the earliest opportunity, but Pullar, staying in touch with Channel 9, had said, "Man, this car has got some serious grunt."

HIRSCH SQUINTED. THE SUN was beating hard and the road shimmered with mirages, and now a collection of tumbledown houses appeared, set two hundred meters off the highway. MUN-COWIE the sign said, an arrow pointing to the little side road that took you there, to a place that seemed to have no function. Rusty rooftops, tired trees, sunlight breaking weakly from a windscreen.

Then Hirsch lost interest in the town. The Pajero was ahead of him, parked at the side of the highway, a man with his rump against it, dark heads showing inside the vehicle, behind tinted glass. He cruised to a stop, switched off and got out, stretched the kinks in his back. He could see the Pajero occupants more clearly now: a woman in the passenger seat, at least two kids in the back. Roof racks piled with roped-down luggage.

The driver, coming around to meet him, offered a huge paw.

"The name's Nancarrow, I called it in."

Powerful forearms, a nuggety chest, sun-damaged skin, sunglasses propped above a high, shiny forehead. A Broken Hill mine worker? "Heading south for a holiday," asked Hirsch, "you and the family?"

"Two weeks," Nancarrow said.

Hirsch strolled around to the front of the Pajero, eyed the bumper, the left and right panels. Dust, smeared insects, but no dents or blood. "You spotted a body?"

Watching him, Nancarrow said, "Down there."

The bitumen ran high here, raised a couple of meters off the pocked soil, the erosion channels. Grass tussocks and a couple of hangdog mallee trees were nearby, clinging to the rim of a shallow depression, and if you were a male and wanted to piss, that was where you'd do it. Two damp patches side by side in the dirt. *Father and son?*

As if in answer, Nancarrow said, "Me and my son went down there for a leak and saw her."

Hirsch glanced uneasily at the Pajero. Nancarrow noticed and said, "It's okay, he's little. I told him the lady had fallen over and the ambulance would come soon and take her to the hospital."

"Did either of you touch her?"

"Christ no. All I wanted to do was get my kid back to the car before he got too curious."

"How did you call triple zero? Is there a mobile signal here?"

"Nup. Dead. Zilch. I called from the pub."

Hirsch nodded and slipped in another question. "Do you know her?"

Nancarrow blinked. "What? Know her? Why would I know her?"

"Perhaps she was traveling with you? Your neighbor, babysitter, niece, a hitchhiker you picked up?"

"I know where you're coming from, and the answer's no. I stopped for a quiet leak by the side of the road and saw a woman lying there, end of story."

Hirsch nodded glumly. Maybe they'd know her over at the pub. "Thanks for reporting it. Thanks for waiting."

Nancarrow gave him a sad if crooked smile. It said "Sooner you than me, pal," and "Sorry I wasn't more help," and "Thank Christ I can go at last." And maybe even, "The poor woman, whoever she is."

HIRSCH NOTED THE MAN'S contact details and, when he was alone, grabbed the Canon stored in his glove box and stepped carefully to the rim of the depression, trying not to disturb the layers of dirt, pebbles and flinty stones. The dead woman lay a short distance in from the edge. He ran his gaze over the surrounding dirt. Last night's showers had left a speckled crust, meaning prints would show clearly. Hirsch saw no boot or shoe prints, no drag marks, but animals and birds had circled the body, leaving fine tracings behind them. A fox or a wild dog had gnawed at her forearm, a crow had pecked out the visible left eye. Ants had found her. Flies. Clearly she was dead, but Hirsch was obliged to check.

He took a series of photos first, the scene from all angles, then perspective shots: the body in relation to the road, a nearby culvert, the township on the other side of a stretch of exhausted red soil. Finally he stepped down into the shallow bowl, crouched and felt for a pulse. Nothing. Her clothes were still damp.

He straightened, stepped away from the body.

She was killed elsewhere and tossed down here from the road; she was struck while walking or hitching by the side of the road and fell into the hole; she fell from a moving vehicle; she was tossed from a moving vehicle.

She lay partly facedown, her chest to the ground but her left hip cocked and her legs slightly splayed, bent at the knees, as if she were running. Her right arm was trapped under her right hip, and her right cheek was stretched out in the dirt as if she were looking along her outflung left arm: looking blindly, Hirsch thought, remembering the eye socket. Maybe her other eye was intact, tucked as it was into the dirt. Very little signs of blood.

He took another series of photographs, taking in tight black jeans, a white T-shirt, a tiny fawn cardigan, bare feet in white canvas shoes. The T-shirt had ridden up to reveal a slender spine, a narrow waist, the upper straps of a black G-string. Bruising and abrasions. A silver chain around her neck. No wristwatch but craft-market silver rings on her fingers, and in her visible ear a silver ring decorated with a Scrabble piece in the letter "M."

That made Hirsch think about ID. He couldn't see a bag or wallet anywhere. If she was struck by a vehicle, and knocked or carried some distance, then bag or wallet would be further up or down the road. Time for that later.

He crouched, peering at the area of waist and spine between the low-riding jeans and the scrap of T-shirt, and saw a small manufacturer's tag on the G-string. Her underwear was inside out. He crab walked closer to the body and lifted the T-shirt: a rear-fastening black bra, fastened with only one of the two hooks.

None of that proved anything. It was suggestive, that was all. He could think of plenty of scenarios to explain it, some of them innocent. For example, she'd dressed in a hurry, she'd dressed in darkness, she was shortsighted, she was slapdash, she'd dressed in a cramped space, like the rear seat of a car.

Or someone else had dressed her.

He peered at her back, but couldn't read anything into the surface damage. Dirt on her bare ankles and arms, dirt on her cheek. But you'd expect dirt if she fell or was tossed by tires—or by hand—down a dirt incline. That was all he could tell. Dr. McAskill would do the rest.

Now Hirsch brought himself to examine her head. The eye socket stared at him as he stared at a small, fine-boned face, small, slack mouth, tiny teeth and a swollen tongue. A pert nose. A bruised, misshapen cheek. Something had hit the girl pretty hard, and he was thinking *girl*, not *woman*—the designation given him by Kropp and Nancarrow. *She's maybe sixteen*, thought Hirsch. *Somewhere between mid and late teens.*

Then he wandered along the road in each direction. He found a small fabric bag twenty meters from the body, strap and flap torn, still damp. He photographed it *in situ* and then fossicked around the contents. No mobile phone, but a wallet with $3.65 in coins, a tampon, tissues, chewing gum, a packet of cigarettes, disposable lighter, supermarket receipts. The only ID was a Redruth High School student card belonging to Melia Donovan, Year 10. A card under a clear plastic window confirmed the name and gave a Tiverton address.

So, fifteen? Sixteen?

HIRSCH WAITED FOR THE doctor to arrive. He wanted to walk across the highway and knock on doors, but couldn't leave the body unattended. He glanced at his watch: 1 P.M. A bus passed, heading north, PERTH on the sign above the windshield. A couple of cars, a handful of semis. Hirsch thought of their tires, their bull bars.

When a silver Mercedes appeared, twenty minutes later, decelerating, he stepped into the road, one hand raised. The car pulled in opposite the HiLux and an unhurried, neatly-put-together man got out, hauling a doctor's bag with him. He crossed the road, stopped when he got to Hirsch. "You must be Constable Hirschhausen."

"That's me."

The doctor stuck out his hand. "Drew McAskill."

He was about fifty, fingers of grey in his brown hair, dressed in a tan jacket, dark trousers, white shirt and blue tie. His hand was pale, scrupulously clean, untouched by the sun, hard labor or mishaps, which put him at odds with the men, women and children Hirsch had encountered so far in the bush. People out here were blemished a little: farm grime under fingernails, garden scratches, schoolyard scrapes, sun wrinkles, dusty trouser cuffs, tarnished watch straps and gammy legs. To top it off, McAskill wore gold-rimmed glasses, and the overall effect was ascetic.

The spotless hand was barely in and out of Hirsch's grasp. "I understand I'm to pronounce on a body?"

McAskill ran a medical practice in Redruth and was on call to the local police. In cases of suspicious death, he'd call in an official police pathologist from Adelaide, but otherwise he was there to save department pathologists a six-hour round-trip. "I'll show you," Hirsch said, turning to go, thinking with a hidden grin that this precise, fussy man was about to get dirt on his fine hands and clothes.

But McAskill surprised him. "Hold your horses."

Handing him the doctor's bag, McAskill returned to the Mercedes and took out a blue forensic jumpsuit and cloth booties. A car passed as he dragged them on, the driver and passenger gawking.

"Ready when you are."

Hirsch led the doctor along the road until they were adjacent to the body. "There."

McAskill nodded brusquely. "Not hidden, but you'd have to be almost upon her to spot her."

"Yes."

Treading carefully, McAskill edged around the rim of the depression, paused, and announced, "Melia Donovan."

"The damage to her face . . . You won't need DNA or dental records?"

The doctor was adamant: "No. It's Melia, without a shadow of a doubt."

Hirsch looked around at this broad, flat, sparsely nourished corner of the world, population about ten, and wondered how McAskill and the girl had ever intersected. He was about to ask when McAskill gave him the answer: "She came into the surgery a couple of times. You'd have met her eventually. She's a Tiverton girl. God knows what she was doing up here."

Now the doctor stepped into the hollow. He crouched, felt for a pulse, poked and prodded for a while. He took the temperature of the body, rolled it onto its back, flexed the arms and legs. "Well, I'm pronouncing death."

Hirsch scribbled time, date, location, names and circumstances in his notebook. "How long?"

McAskill shrugged. "Rigor is mostly gone. Animal damage. She's been here a couple of days at least."

"Since Saturday night, early Sunday?"

McAskill stood, frowned. "Possibly. The autopsy should establish time of death with more accuracy."

Both men gazed at the slack limbs. Hirsch crouched for another look at the thin, unformed, pretty face. The right eye was intact and showed petechial hemorrhaging. "How old is she?"

"Fifteen? Sixteen?"

Hirsch said carefully, "Family circumstances?"

"Only what I've heard via local gossip. There's no father on the scene. The mother's a drinker, succession of boyfriends."

"Siblings?"

"An older brother."

Hirsch jotted the names in his notebook. "What can you tell me about Melia?"

McAskill grimaced. "Pretty wild."

Hirsch pictured the girl's home life. He could see the patterns, the dimensions. No stability, older boys sniffing around, the mother's boyfriends, too. Maybe drugs and booze.

"But a sweet kid," McAskill said. "Struggled at school, wagged it pretty often—I'd sometimes see her hitchhiking in the middle of the day. Arrested a couple of times for shoplifting."

"Boys, men?" asked Hirsch.

"Who knows?" McAskill said.

He crouched again and rotated the head on its stem. "Broken neck." Then he lowered the head and palpated the flesh and bones of the torso, chest and spine. "Christ," he muttered, but didn't elaborate.

Finally he let her go and, still squatting on his heels, said, "Massive internal injuries. Broken ribs and spinal cord damage and no doubt some trauma to her major organs."

"She hasn't been punched?"

McAskill shook his head. "Nothing like that. If I were to hazard a guess I'd say she was run over."

"Run over, or knocked down?"

"I take your point. Indications are she was upright when it happened, and I'd guess the force of it tumbled her into the windscreen. I've seen it before."

"Facing away—hit from behind?"

"You'll have to wait for the autopsy, but my feeling is she was in the act of turning around."

"So no way of knowing if it was deliberate or not?"

McAskill grinned. "Got your work cut out for you."

He stood, brushing dust from his hands. "Would you like me to notify the family? I am their doctor."

Hirsch didn't think about it for long. "Thanks—though I will need to speak to them myself, eventually."

"Of course."

Both men looked up at the road, hearing a motor. "The hearse," McAskill said.

He turned to Hirsch. "As I said, she liked to hitchhike. Did it a lot, if that's any help to you. Anywhere, anytime. I even gave her lifts myself. Everyone did, just ask around. A sweet kid who sometimes had a bit too much to drink, tried drugs if she could get hold of them. I can see her staggering along the road with her thumb out, trying for a lift home, and you know the rest." He gave Hirsch a look, partly philosophical, partly distasteful, partly grieving.

"A lift home from *here?*" said Hirsch.

"That's for you to find out, sorry," McAskill said.

The doctor scrambled up onto the road to greet the hearse. Hirsch remained where he was, ruminating glumly. How did she get here? Had she been at the pub? A party at a nearby house? Someone brought her here, and later this same someone couldn't or wouldn't take her home, so she set out to hitchhike in the early hours and was struck by a vehicle which failed to stop. Or it wasn't an accident, she was killed elsewhere and dumped here.

He climbed up onto the road. The hearse driver and his offsider were dragging out a stretcher. McAskill was in his car, a mobile phone clamped to his ear.

WHEN THE HEARSE HAD left and he was alone, Hirsch turned to the HiLux, and the first thing he saw was a crack in the windscreen, a shallow crater and a couple of short tributaries, smack in the middle. Roadside gravel was his guess, flipped up by the tires of a passing car or truck. *Life on the frontier*, he thought, and called Kropp.

The sergeant was a couple—or possibly a hundred—steps ahead of him. "About time, hotshot. Melia Donovan, of this parish."

Hirsch waited a beat. "The doctor told you?"

"Finger on the pulse."

"You knew her, Sarge?"

A snake in his voice, Kropp said, "I been here twelve years, of course I fucking knew her. Even caught her shoplifting once or twice."

"Apparently she liked to hitchhike."

"Everyone knew that."

Hirsch waggled his jaw in thought. "We'll need to know if she was drugged or raped or beaten . . . Maybe some of her injuries aren't consistent with vehicle impact . . . Stuff like that."

"What, you're back in plain clothes?"

"Come on, Sarge."

"She'll be in good hands. McAskill will do the right thing by her."

Hirsch was doubtful. "Shouldn't the body go down to the city?"

"McAskill's been dicing and slicing for years."

"Okay. So who briefs the coroner?"

"Me, sunshine, all right? What I need *you* to do is stay put until the accident team arrives, then head on back to Tiverton and follow up on McAskill's visit to the family. Think you can manage that?"

"Sarge," said Hirsch.

But Kropp had already disconnected. Hirsch returned to the hollow. After a fruitless examination of the area of dirt that had been hidden by the body itself, he made a head-down search of the highway for a few hundred meters north and south, both sides, looking around for anything that might have belonged to Melia Donovan or the vehicle that had delivered her here or the vehicle that had killed her. Anything, he told himself, but preferably something like a fragment of glass indicator lens with the ID number intact. Nothing in the dirt verges, so he walked the bitumen surface this time. Still nothing, and no skid marks. From his work with crash investigators in the past he knew to look for dual tire skid marks, or the scuff marks that indicated loss of control, or the skip marks of a shuddering trailer.

Nothing.

So he ran crime scene tape around the area and sat down to wait.

LATE AFTERNOON BEFORE THE accident investigators arrived. Hirsch wanted to hang around, he wanted to propose his theories, but they ignored him, two men and one woman conscious of the dwindling light, the sun smearing itself across the horizon, long shadows playing visual tricks. They took their photos, measured distances, crouched and poked and grid-searched and marked up their diagrams.

"You're blocking the light," the female officer said, her tone indicating she knew exactly who Hirsch was.

CHAPTER 4

THE DONOVAN HOUSE REFLECTED 1960s small-town tastes and aspirations: squat, low, double-fronted, with scorched-looking bricks, stubby eaves, a tiled roof, a carport, floor-to-ceiling windows in aluminum frames. Now dimmed by the sun and hopelessness, it crouched in unmown grass, hedged by a rusty gas barbecue, a cracked plastic chaise lounge and a listing red Mazda. A fence line of crumbling bricks on either side separated it from the neighboring properties: a similar but spotless house, and a vacant lot. Hirsch waded through weeds to reach the front door, a cheap plywood thing, warped, the red paint losing against the elements. He knocked, waited, knocked again. A wind had picked up since the morning. It bent the trees and, out where the Bitter Wash Road pushed into the dry country, clouds were shouldering the Razorback.

"No offense, mate, but I'd leave it for now."

Hirsch turned. A blockish male shape at the shadowed end of the veranda, middle-aged, taking unhurried stock of him, quietly smoking a cigarette.

"Why's that?"

"McAskill gave her a sedative. The wife's sitting with her and I'm keeping the snakes away."

"Snakes?" Hirsch said, heading along the cracked veranda.

"One snake, a reporter for the local rag. I have to warn you he got a photo off Leanne and he'll probably sell it to *The Advertiser.*"

"It happens," Hirsch said, sticking out his hand, announcing his name.

"Wondered when I'd set eyes on you," the smoker responded. "Bob Muir."

Muir's hand was a hard slab thickened by years of manual labor, fingers like stubby cigars, but dry, warm and gentle as he shook with Hirsch. A square head with heavy lids over intelligent eyes. "Live next door," he said.

Hirsch nodded. They found themselves standing side by side, staring out at the miserable front yard and the HiLux at the curb.

"The doc said someone run over Melia?"

"Yes."

"Poor bloody kid."

Hirsch could hear muted sobbing inside, another voice murmuring, and said, "Maybe you could fill me in?"

"Go your hardest."

They walked a few paces into the front yard. In the better light, Hirsch saw a man with a few years on him, a man with a tough hide, barrelly torso and small backside, dressed in comfortable faded jeans and a khaki shirt. A mild-looking character with greying hair cropped short around the fringes of his big, genial skull. An unhurried individual, he drew patiently on his cigarette and got in first:

"McAskill said she was hitching?"

"Possibly."

Muir slid his gaze at Hirsch, taking on a calm, sardonic interest in what Hirsch wasn't saying. "Possibly?"

"Questions remain."

"Is that right."

"It's possible she was hitching and a vehicle hit her. All I can say is she was found lying in a hollow near the side of the road and not noticed until today."

Muir took the cigarette from his mouth. "Poor little cow," he said, turning to stare unseeingly across the quiet rooftops of the town, a flat skyline, interrupted by the grain silos at the railway station.

"Do you know anything of her movements over the weekend?"

"Not me."

"What can you tell me about her?"

"Known her all her life."

Hirsch brought out his phone, made to check the screen, waiting for the patient man beside him to go on.

"A bit wild."

"So I understand," said Hirsch.

"Not mean and nasty with it, a sweet kid in fact, just a bit unmanageable."

"What about her friends?"

"You mean boyfriends."

"And female friends." Hirsch paused: "Older friends."

"Older friends. There was a whisper she was seeing someone older, but they broke up. Me and the wife, there were times we wanted to step in, but you can't, can you."

"Any names come to mind? Friends, ex-boyfriends, anyone at all?"

Muir stared at him and finally said, "Good friends with Gemma Pitcher." He checked his watch. "Works in the shop, you might just catch her there."

Hirsch bought his groceries there, in the absence of alternatives, and recalled a solid pudding of a girl stacking shelves or sitting at the cash register. If asked to bet on it he'd say she was a lot older than Melia Donovan. "They're at school together?"

Muir shook his head. "Gemma left school two or three years

ago." Providing context he added, "There are only six or seven teenagers in the whole town, mostly boys, so it's not as if Melia and Gemma were spoiled for choice."

Hirsch nodded. No jobs, no nightlife. Net migration would be out of the district, not into it. "Were they close?"

"Thick as thieves, always off somewhere."

"How did they get around?"

"Gemma drives."

"Parties? The pub?"

Muir gave him a long look. "Wouldn't have a clue."

"Any other names you can think of?"

"I stay out of it, mate."

Muir paused. "Though come to think of it she did turn up one day last month with a black eye, said she'd been in a bit of a crash, said it was nothing."

Check accident reports, insurance claims, local panel beaters.

"Who else is in the family?"

Like a massive ship turning on the ocean, Muir stepped around to face Hirsch. "Mate, what brought you here?"

Hirsch frowned. "Melia Donovan. Her death."

"No, what brought you to *this town*?"

The vehemence was barely there but it registered. Hirsch put a snarl in his voice: "I was assigned here."

Muir stood close, crowding Hirsch. He was more animated, suddenly, and Hirsch could smell shaving cream, talcum powder, cigarette smoke and the heat of a day's work. Not unpleasant: decent smells, given off by a man who was decent but hot under the collar right now.

"I was thinking maybe you're a mate of Kropp's."

"And?"

"And Kropp arranged it so you'd get posted up here."

"Mr. Muir, what are you trying to tell me?"

But Muir had subsided, hands in his pockets, face turned away, muttering.

"Sorry, what?"

Muir said, very plainly, "Kropp and his boys like to take the Abo kids out into the bush, give them a good hiding and let them walk home."

"I don't understand."

Muir studied him, then finally nodded. "I guess maybe you don't. There are two kids in the family. Melia, white father, and Nathan, black father. Both are long gone."

He flicked his cigarette away. "Filthy habit."

Both men stared at the butt. Then Muir gestured at it, saying, "Maybe you should fine me for littering. And when you've done that, breathalyze me every time I leave the house. Then scream in my face for jaywalking."

"Why would I want to do that?"

"You wouldn't need a *reason*, not if you're one of Kropp's boys." Hirsch didn't want to get into it. "I'd better speak to this Gemma."

Muir gazed at him levelly. "Like I said, she works in the shop."

"Thanks," Hirsch said. He stopped. "Is Nathan inside with his mother?"

"Leave the poor bugger alone."

"I fully intend to," Hirsch said in his reasonable voice, "after I ask him about his sister's movements on the weekend."

Muir conceded that. "He's not home yet, but he's probably not far away. He and a mate of his work at the grain shed."

Hirsch nodded. Tiverton Grains, a collection of sheds in a side street near the pub. "I'll catch him tomorrow."

Muir, indicating the Motorola in Hirsch's fist, said, "You glued to that?"

And then he was crossing into the next yard, where a severely groomed grass lawn was bordered by garden beds splashed here and there with red, white, crimson, blue. A clean, older style Holden ute was parked in the driveway, Tiverton Electrics painted on the side. Hirsch glanced toward the rear of the property. He saw a large shed, door open, fuel drums, ladders, metal shelves and coiled wire inside. One neat house, one shabby, and that was a pattern repeated everywhere.

CHAPTER 5

ALMOST SIX O'CLOCK. HIRSCH parked the HiLux in the police station driveway, intending to walk the short distance to the shop. A minibus pulled in next door, REDRUTH DISTRICT COUNCIL stenciled along the side panels, half a dozen elderly people on board. The driver tooted, and here was Hirsch's elderly neighbor limping down the path from her house. Hirsch shot a glare at the driver. He took the old woman's arm, helped her mount the steps. "An outing?"

"A lecture at the old jail in Redruth," she said, "then dinner at the reform school."

Ruins dating from the 1850s and now tourist attractions. Hirsch said, registering that she was skin and bone, hoping his manacling hand hadn't bruised her, "Well, you belong in both places."

She cackled and they all waved and he was left in the exhaust gases.

HE WALKED IN THE other direction to the general store, an afternoon shadow tethered to his feet. Tennant's Four Square was an off-white brick building, long, low, the shopfront glass deep inside a corrugated iron veranda, with a petrol bowser at one end, secured by a bulky brass padlock, and a checkerboard of private post boxes at the other end. Nothing enticed shoppers but a dusty ice-cream advertisement on a sheet of tin and a board of daily specials. You couldn't see in: the windows were painted a greyish white. As Hirsch approached, an elderly man in overalls emerged with a liter of milk. Nothing else moved, not in the entire town.

The interior was a dim cave. The ceiling, pressed tin, was stalactited with hooks from the days when a shopkeeper would hang it with buckets, watering cans, coils of rope and paired boots. Refrigerator cases lined a side wall, shallow crates of withered fruit and vegetables the back, and in the vast middle ground were aisles of rickety shelving, stacked with anything from tinned peaches to tampons. The sole cash register was adjacent to the entrance, next to ranks of daily newspapers and weekly and monthly magazines and a little bookcase thumbtacked with a sign, LIBRARY. If you were a farmer or a gardener in need of an axe, sheep dip or nails and screws you headed for the far back corner. If you wanted to buy a stamp, you headed a couple of paces past the library.

No sign of Melia Donovan's friend, but Hirsch was pretty sure he'd been served by the woman seated at the post office counter a couple of times. She glanced up at him and hastily away, one forefinger poised above the keypad of a calculator as if she'd lost her place. A thin, pinched woman, full of burdens. "Excuse me," Hirsch said, his footsteps snapping on the old floorboards as he approached, "are you the shopkeeper?"

She whispered, "No," and nodded toward the dim rear.

Hirsch set out between the racks of groceries and found a small back room furnished with a desk, a fat old computer, filing cabinets, a swivel chair and a middle-aged man, tensely thin and neat. Pale, as if he lived in his office and let women and teenage girls serve his customers. When Hirsch knocked on the door frame, the man shot out of his chair. "Help you?"

"Paul Hirschhausen, I'm new across the road."

The shopkeeper reached out a long, thin, defenseless hand. "Ed Tennant. Thought I'd run into you sooner or later."

And without much joy in the anticipation, thought Hirsch, returning the shake. Tennant looked as sour as the woman in the post office.

"I just met your wife."

Tennant didn't reply to that. "What can I do for you?"

"I'm afraid this is not exactly a courtesy call."

"Oh?" said Tennant, a soup of apprehensions showing. Then he firmed up a little. "I thought it was all sorted."

Thinking he was forever at cross-purposes, Hirsch decided to play along. "Depends."

Tennant showed his teeth humorlessly, a stringy man fueled by nerves and grievances. "There was no need for Sergeant Kropp to send you."

"Right."

"I will give the Latimers some leeway, but they can't rely on shiny shoes and a smile to get them through forever. If they haven't got the money they shouldn't go shopping."

The wealthy Latimers were in strife? Hirsch stored that away for now. He held up a palm. "Actually, Mr. Tennant, I badly need to speak to Gemma Pitcher. I understand she works for you?"

"She's not here. What's going on? She got a phone call and burst into tears and left, said she'd be back tomorrow."

"If you could tell me where she lives?"

"Next to the tennis courts. Look, what's it about? Is she in trouble? You speak to me, first, all right?"

Hirsch hardened his voice. "Mr. Tennant, I'm not about to arrest or hassle anyone. But I do need to speak to Gemma."

"And I'd like to know what about," Tennant said, like a man of precise habits and concerns.

Hirsch sighed. "Her friend Melia Donovan has been killed. Now, can I go about my business?"

Tennant subsided. "That explains the phone call."

Hirsch was curious. "Did she say who called?"

"Nope." As Hirsch moved off, the shopkeeper added, "How did it happen, Melia? Another accident?"

Hirsch stopped. "She was found by the side of the road."

He could see the man picturing it, partly avid, partly horrified. He left the shop and went in search of the dead girl's friend.

ENCOUNTERED HER MOTHER FIRST. "She's that upset," said Eileen Pitcher at a peeling front door, the house peeling too, separated from the town's tennis courts by a line of overgrown cypresses.

Hirsch was tired. "Won't take a moment, Mrs. Pitcher,"

Gemma Pitcher's mother was tiny and aggrieved and didn't want Hirsch on her doorstep. "Wipe your feet."

She led Hirsch to a sitting-cum-dining room, semidark, a TV flickering and two boys crouched before it, thumbing Xbox controls. The dining table sat against the rear wall, and Gemma Pitcher was sprawled on a sofa, tissues in her fist, eyes damp. She was a plump eighteen, with a band of soft belly showing between the waistband of tight jeans and the scant hem of a T-shirt. Her navel looked sore to Hirsch, the flesh puckered around a thick silver ring. She wore her mousy hair long, a ragged fringe over her mascaraed eyes—the mascara leaking down her cheeks now that she knew her friend was dead.

Hirsch introduced himself, crouching so that his head was on a level with hers. "Do you remember me, Gemma? You served me in the shop a couple of times."

She shrugged.

Girls like this are shruggers, Hirsch thought, *and they fill the world.* "Are you up to answering a few questions?"

"No, she's not," the mother said.

"Gemma?"

"Don't care."

"Gemma love, you've had a shock."

"Mum, it's all right. You can go."

Mrs. Pitcher turned her hooked, distrusting features to Hirsch, scowled, touched Gemma's upper arm as if knowing she was beaten, and left them to it.

"Perhaps we could sit at the table?" Hirsch suggested.

"Whatever."

Gemma took one stiff dining chair, Hirsch another. She promptly lit up, using a pink disposable lighter. The three rings in the cartilage of each ear glinted as she snatched smoke from her cigarette and jetted it to one side. That was all the energy she could muster. Otherwise she was helpless, scared, a little weepy.

"'I don't know if I—"

"Won't take a moment. I'm trying to fill in Melia's movements on the weekend."

Gemma's knee jiggled. An old, habitual deflection of shame or guilt? Hirsch sharpened his tone. "Were you with her at any stage?"

Gemma didn't want to answer. Her eyes cut across to the hall-way door, her purple nails picking at the hard seam of her jeans. "Can't remember."

"Gemma. Yesterday and the day before. Were you with her or not?"

"Might of been. For a while."

"You went out Saturday night?"

Another shrug.

"You have a car?"

"Mum's car."

"You took Gemma somewhere?"

"I'm allowda."

"Sure, nothing wrong with that," Hirsch said, and he waited. It came: "We went down to Redruth."

"What did you do there?"

"Stuff."

"Pub? Friend's house? Café?"

"Didn't drink and drive if that's what you're asking."

"Did Melia drink?"

"Her mum lets her," Gemma said hotly.

Hirsch smiled. "It's all right, I'm not the underage drinking police." Which was a downright lie. "Which pub?" he asked.

"The Woolman."

"She was with you the whole time?"

"Friends and that."

"There was a group of you?"

Shrug.

"You stayed there the whole evening? You, Melia, your friends?"

Gemma launched into a blow-by-blow. They'd been joined by Nick and Julie but Julie's ex-boyfriend Brad showed up so Nick told him to get lost and there was a bit of a fight and Lisa, that's Jeff's cousin, she calmed them down and Gemma's boyfriend was like, let's go to the drive-in. It made no sense and Hirsch lost interest.

"Drive-in?" he asked.

"There's one in Clare."

"Melia didn't go with you?"

"I told you that."

"So she was still in the pub when you left?"

"I told you that."

"Was her boyfriend there? Ex-boyfriend?"

"What boyfriend?"

"Any boyfriend. How about the older guy she's been seeing?"

Gemma's gaze was sliding away at every question now, as if to escape her own evasions. "Don't know about no older guy."

"The one she was in an accident with," Hirsch said, guessing.

"On the weekend?"

"A few weeks ago."

"Wouldn't know."

"If you think of anything," Hirsch said, his voice on the far side of weary defeat, "give me a call."

◆　◆　◆

HE RETURNED TO THE Donovan house. Another car was there, a dinged-about Commodore. Melia's brother, thought Hirsch, or relatives, friends, and if Leanne Donovan was still sedated and the house was thick with grieving, there was no point in knocking on the door. He turned around and headed for the shop again, starving, thinking of dinner.

Hirsch's main kitchen appliance was his toaster, so he headed straight for the ready-made frozen meals. Almost closing time and the shop was relatively busy. He counted four women and two men in the aisles. Tennant's wife was at the cash register, Tennant hovering. He followed Hirsch to the freezer, watched as Hirsch selected a frozen lasagna.

"Gemma okay?"

"Bit upset."

"We all are," Tennant said, and Hirsch realized he'd sensed it as he'd walked through the store, a community atmosphere of fear and sorrow and whispers. Was the shop a clearing house of local gossip? "Shop's busy all of a sudden."

"It happens," Tennant said. "Can't complain." He looked with miserable triumph at Hirsch. "You're inviting a speeding ticket or a breathalyzer if you shop in Redruth, so business has picked up for me."

What the hell was happening in Redruth? Hirsch gestured with the lasagna. "Dinner."

"Your money's as good as anyone's."

A WHITE POLICE DISCOVERY was parked foursquare outside the police station. Hirsch didn't like that one bit. Hated it, in fact. No good would come of it, no sweetness or light. And so he ignored it, unlocking the front door and shoving through, admitting late afternoon sunlight, which probed briefly, illuminating the wall cabinet, its glass doors finger-smudged with country-town boredoms and disappointments. Checking automatically for envelopes that might have been slipped under the door, checking the message light on the answering machine, he entered his office, public notices stirring in his slipstream, a rose petal tumbling the length of the vase he'd placed on the counter earlier in the week. Time he picked another bunch. The town was half knitted together with rose canes.

As expected, footsteps came in hard on his heels, a bitten-off voice. "Constable."

Hirsch turned. "Sarge."

Kropp stood on the other side of the counter, a solid fifty-year-old with pronounced brows and short, receding hair. "Did you call Spurling?"

Spurling? Hirsch went blank, then remembered: the area commander, a superintendent, based at Port Pirie. "Not me, Sarge."

Kropp grunted. "Well he heard about the hit-and-run from somebody."

"And?"

"And he doesn't want any fuck-ups."

Hirsch waited, enduring Kropp's fury or whatever it was. The sergeant's nose had been broken and badly set sometime in the past. Now it seemed to steer him in scoffing and skeptical directions, his mouth a barely visible slash across the bottom of his face.

Hirsch said, "So you headed up here to see if I was fucking up?"

"Don't be a cunt, son. But, yeah—and to see you're settling in okay, your lovely new quarters."

Hirsch motioned to the stiff chair that faced his desk, but Kropp shook his head. "No thanks. Somewhere more comfortable, think you can manage that?"

Hirsch pictured his living quarters and doubted it. "Come through."

The connecting door led to a short corridor and a shut-in smell, no natural light, boxes hard against the wall. Edging past, Kropp said, "You've been here what, three weeks already? You're not going anywhere else, Sunshine, so you might as well unpack."

"Had my hands full, sir."

The corridor opened on to the cramped sitting room. "Get your wife to do it," Kropp said, stopping to give his meaty head a theatrical smack. "Oh, forgot, she left you, I seem to recall."

"Kind of you to remind me, Sarge," Hirsch said, his voice full of light cadences. He opened the curtains without improving anything. He switched on the overhead light. Dust motes floated. This was a loveless place and Hirsch sometimes found himself talking to the furniture in the dark hours. Dumping Saturday's *Advertiser* from one of the armchairs, he sat in the other, better, armchair. Kropp eyed the remaining chair and lowered himself as if freezing his sphincter muscle.

"Tea?" said Hirsch. "Coffee?"

The sergeant shook his head, thank Christ. "This hit-and-run. Anything leap out at you?"

"She was hitching home and a vehicle hit her. Or she was killed elsewhere and dumped. Until I know what she was doing there I—"

"What's this 'I' shit? Team effort. Oh, I forgot, you don't do team effort." Kropp leaned his forearms on his knees and stared at Hirsch. "Let the accident boys deal with the evidence and *we* will work out a plan of action to answer your questions about her movements, okay?"

"Sarge."

"Meanwhile I want you down in Redruth at noon tomorrow for a briefing."

"Sarge."

Hirsch waited, Kropp watching as if to chase him if he ran.

Then the man grinned crookedly and stood. "I'm off. That crack in your windscreen? Get it fixed." He paused. "Know why?"

Hirsch's mind raced. Roadworthiness? Then he guessed: "Anything we don't tolerate in the citizenry, we don't tolerate in ourselves, maybe?"

"Aren't you a sweetheart. Try Redruth Automotive."

Then Kropp was gone and Hirsch heated and ate his lasagna, so alone that he talked to the furniture.

CHAPTER 6

WHAT WAS WRONG WITH him? Those kids this morning had seen a woman hovering around his car. He dumped his dirty plate in the sink and hurried out to the Nissan with a torch, a rag, latex gloves and, after a moment's thought, a couple of evidence bags.

Started at the boot and moved forward: toolbox, spare tire well, under the boot carpet, then parcel shelf, under the rear seat, inside the door cavities, under the front seats, glove box. He found what he was looking for in an ancient, forgotten, unused first aid box, but continued his search inside the engine bay, just in case. Nothing there, so he returned to the first aid box.

An iPhone and a bundle of cash. First he photographed both items *in situ*, then removed them. Still some juice in the phone; it was an iPhone 5 in perfect nick. He scrolled through until he came to a screen showing the IMEI number, photographed it. The cash amounted to $2500 in hundred-dollar notes. He dismantled the bundle and photographed each note, twenty-five serial numbers. Finally he stowed everything in one of the evidence bags.

The time was six thirty. Hirsch returned to the shop, still

toting the evidence bag. Tennant had placed a CCTV camera above the petrol bowser. Might get lucky.

He found the shopkeeper switching off lights. Tennant frowned at the evidence bag. "You want a refund on your dinner?"

"Ha, ha. The camera above your bowser: does it work?"

"It works."

"Video or hard drive?"

"Hard drive."

"I need to see footage from last Friday, mid-morning."

Tennant was confused. "Somebody broke in? I'm not missing anything, and I would have known, I was here then."

With a "just routine" air, Hirsch said, "Someone put a note under my door, no big deal, something about a tax cheat, as if that's the police's business, but if the lens range and angle allows it, I might get an idea who left the note, and I can put a flea in their ear."

Stop babbling, he told himself.

"Tax cheat?"

"Not you," Hirsch assured the shopkeeper.

Showing doubt and irritation, Tennant took him to the back room and showed him the equipment and how to run a search. Wanted to hover, so Hirsch said, "Police business."

HIRSCH WAS IN LUCK: Tennant's camera had been angled to cover the bowser, but also showed the footpath and part of the police station. He saw a woman of slight build and above average height, shoulder-length fair hair swinging around her neck and cheeks, moving rapidly. No clear shot of her face, damn it all. Of course it helped that he rarely locked his old bomb, but she was in and out of his car inside a minute.

Hirsch found Tennant at the front door, anxious to lock up and go home. "Finished?"

"I need to buy a memory stick."

"Really? You found something?" Tennant said, intrigued,

unlocking a drawer, fishing around in it and coming up with an 8-gig version. "This do you?"

"Fine."

"I can show you how to transfer the footage."

"I'll be right."

So Tennant charged Hirsch twice what the device was worth and waited in a sulk at the door.

WHERE TO STOW THE phone and cash? If Internal Investigations officers searched his car now and found nothing, they'd tear the house, office and HiLux apart. And he knew and trusted no one here.

Hirsch walked around to the rear of the station, poked his head over the side fence, into the old woman's backyard. It was overgrown by weeds and roses, the little garden shed mute testament to her inability to keep up anymore. He clambered over the fence. Concealed everything in an empty paint tin, taking reasonable care not to touch it, disturb the dust that covered everything.

BACK IN HIS OFFICE, Hirsch dialed an Adelaide number.

"We need to meet."

Sergeant Rosie DeLisle said tensely, "You bet we do. In fact, I was about to call you."

Making Hirsch tense. "What happened?"

"You tell me."

Hirsch knew then that the Internals had some fresh hell in store for him: new evidence, a new slant on old evidence, something like that. Rosie had always been straight with him, ultimately gone into bat for him, but he'd always skated on thin ice, the sessions he'd had with her.

"I'm being set up," he said.

"Is that a fact," she said flatly.

"You show me yours and I'll show you mine."

"Not over the phone."

"That suits me. I can be in the city by ten."

"Tonight? No thanks. Tomorrow afternoon sometime."

"That works for me."

"Somewhere off the beaten track, Paul."

"I embarrass you," Hirsch said, meaning, *I taint you.*

"Something like that," DeLisle said. She named a winery in the Barossa Valley. "One o'clock."

"You think your colleagues don't visit wineries?"

"Not this one."

"Ah, somewhere exclusive," Hirsch said, "boutique. Are you sure you're not on the take?"

"Just be there, all right?"

TUESDAY MORNING, AND HIRSCH had things to do, places to be, before he attended Kropp's briefing in Redruth. He was on the road by 7:40, the sun smeared along the eastern horizon. A washed-clean day with vivid green on both sides of the road, the birds nesting or soaring. He lifted his forefinger to the oncoming cars, which didn't expect it from a cop. The morning was still. All movement seemed concentrated here, on the Barrier Highway, but he sensed the potential for movement away from it—in the birds along the wires, the cow paused in the act of chewing her cud, the farmhouses crouched behind cypress hedges.

Halfway down the valley he turned right, onto the road to Clare, the only town of a decent size in the area. It had an agency of his building society and it had a phone shop. He visited the building society first, withdrawing $2,500 in hundred-dollar bills, leaving himself with $164.65 until payday. Then he went to the phone shop.

Hirsch had bought his present phone there three weeks earlier, on Kropp's advice, Kropp telling him, "The first thing you need to know is we get shit mobile reception up here. As much as I welcome the idea of you stranded in the middle of nowhere with a flat tire and no signal bars, the Department would take a dim view, so get yourself a decent phone, all right?"

"Maybe the Department could spring for a satellite phone, Sarge."

"Don't push your luck with me, Sunshine."

What Hirsch remembered about the phone shop was the box of parts behind the counter: outmoded GSM phones, cracked touchscreen Androids, flip phones with loose keypads, scarred plastic cases, dead batteries, iPhones with the guts stripped from them.

He drove back to Tiverton with the cash and an old iPhone 4 that was stuck at the boot logo. Cost him $150, which he thought outrageous. Now he had $14.65 to his name.

Half expecting officers from Internal Investigations to jump him, half fearing to learn they'd already carried out their search, he reached into the Nissan, found the first aid box exactly where he'd left it, and made the swap.

CHAPTER 7

THEN HE PINNED HIS mobile number to the front door and headed back down the valley, reaching Redruth forty minutes later. Wheat and canola crops all the way, spread between the distant blue ranges, and finally signs of habitation and he was drawing into a town of pretty stone buildings folded through a series of hillocks. Copper had been mined here in the 1840s but it was a pastoral center now, the Cornish Jacks long gone, leaving behind flooded mine shafts, some cottage rows and a legacy of names like Redruth and Truro. Hirsch had explored the old mine when he first arrived, seeing bottomless pools of water an enchanted shade of blue, and mine batteries, sheds and stone chimneys sitting licheny and eroded on the slopes above the town.

Soon he was making a shallow descent to the town center, where the shops, a pair of pubs and a garage were arranged around an oblong square consisting of a statue to the war dead and a tiny rotunda on a stone-edged lawn. The building frontages were nineteenth-century but the hoardings and signage were purely modern, a mishmash of shapes, colors, fonts and corporate livery. Then he was through the square and entering an abbreviated side street, directed to the police station by a sign and an arrow. At the curb on both sides of the street were police vehicles: two 4WDs, Kropp's Ford and two patrol cars.

The time was 11:45. He parked and went in. This station was no converted house but a dedicated red brick building with a lockup, several rooms and a large rear yard, but inside its foyer-cum-waiting room Hirsch found a front counter like his own: scarred wood, wanted posters and community notices on the wall, a couple of desks and filing cabinets in the dim corners.

The counter was staffed by a middle-aged man in civilian clothing, an auxiliary support officer whose job it was to greet the walk-ins, hand out forms, take reports, do the filing. A dull, sleepy man, he gave off a quiver of interest when Hirsch gave his name. "Ah, Constable Hirschhausen. Through that door."

He pointed, and Hirsch found himself in a region of cramped rooms at the rear of the station: Kropp's office, a small tearoom, a briefing room, an interview room, storage area, files. At the end of the corridor was a steel door leading to the lockup. Drawn by voices, movement, a spill of light, Hirsch headed for the tearoom.

Which fell silent the moment he appeared in the doorway. Two men stared at him stonily: the Redruth constables, Nicholson and Andrewartha. Hirsch gave a face-splitting grin, just to rile them. "Hi, guys!"

Nicholson said, "Maggot," showing a mouth crowded with tiny teeth. He was fleshy and pink, his face squeezed and veiny.

Hirsch grinned again and turned to Andrewartha. Another from the porcine family, this one had moist, red budded lips that seemed poised to blow kisses. He stuck a stub of a finger to his temple, cocked his thumb and said, "*Pow.*"

"Good to see you, guys," said Hirsch, pushing through.

"Arsehole."

Two rickety plastic tables in the room, one strewn with paper cups, sports papers and skin magazines, the other bearing an urn and a percolator. Hirsch poured coffee into a paper cup. Nicholson jostled him.

"Whoops, sorry mate, clumsy of me."

Hirsch poured another cup. He grabbed a stale donut and ducked around Nicholson's tree-trunk form to stand beside the refrigerator, stashing coffee and donut on the top of it and fishing out his mobile phone. He angled the screen, he ran his fingers, not looking at the others but ready to fight if that's what they wanted.

Then, an alteration in the air, a tremor of awareness passing through Nicholson and Andrewartha, a subterranean nastiness and quickness. Glancing up, Hirsch saw a young female officer in the doorway, pink, tense, sprucely ironed.

"Morning."

Her voice was low and raspy, but a squeak of nerves ran through it.

"Did someone say something?" Andrewartha asked, cocking an ear.

"I didn't hear anything," Nicholson said. He flared his nostrils: "Hang on, there's a whiff in the air."

The newcomer flushed, but was game. "Maybe you've got a dose of hay fever . . . or a dose of something."

"Now, what *is* that smell?" said Nicholson. "Got it! Female hygiene product."

"You would know," Andrewartha said, jostling him.

Both men pushed past her into the corridor, their voices fading along it:

"They reckon she'll root anything on two legs."

"*Four* legs."

Leaving Hirsch alone in the room with her. She glanced at him without hope or interest. "Okay, give it your best shot."

Hirsch headed for the percolator. "Coffee?"

"Coffee and spit, right?"

"Or tea and spit, if you'd prefer."

He noted her name, Jennifer Dee, and waited inquiringly. She looked obstinate yet nervy, a slender woman of almost his height, with fine bones and sharp features on a narrow face, an impression of tightness reinforced by her hair, raked back savagely and caught in a short ponytail.

Meanwhile Dee was watching him, unblinking and intense. Abruptly a shift occurred, a kind of nervy humor surfacing as she said, "Weak black, no sugar."

"Coming up. Donut?"

She came nearer, moving awkwardly, a young woman of disproportionate parts and abilities, not yet comfortable with herself. Pretending she didn't know him when everyone knew him. "I could do with a sugar hit."

"Good thinking," Hirsch said.

He served her. They stood there a while. Swallowing sugary dough, Hirsch said, "You weren't stationed here when I checked in last month."

She shook her head. "Just started."

"They're giving you a hard time?"

"I can handle it."

As if responding to an invisible signal, they sat at the empty table. Hirsch swiped the top with his sleeve, the surface layer of crumbs, sports pages and boobs and tits giving way to carved initials and scorch marks, as if suspects and prisoners had sweated at it. Then he raised his cup, said, "Cheers," and a moment later Kropp was snarling from the doorway: "Both of you get your arses in the briefing room, and I mean *now*."

He was propped there glaring, one big hand on each upright of the door frame as if to stretch his chest muscles.

"Sarge," said Hirsch, echoed by Dee, as they grabbed their paper cups and plates.

They followed Kropp to the briefing room, where Nicholson and Andrewartha lolled in steel chairs, staring. But Hirsch had been stared down by experts. He blew a couple of kisses, then selected the chair next to Nicholson, who muttered, "Dog." Dee was obliged to sit beside Andrewartha. He scooted his chair away from her.

Kropp stood at the end of the table, slapping a white pointer against his thigh. "If you people are quite ready."

"Sarge."

"Let's get to it."

The sergeant propped his hands on the back of his chair, full of scowling impatience. "I've got a guy coming in from the accident squad, but until then here's what we know: sometime on the weekend a kid from Tiverton was killed by a hit-and-run driver up near Muncowie."

He straightened, turned to the board and wall map behind him, and touched the tip of his pointer to a photograph clipped from that day's *Advertiser*. "This is her, Melia Donovan. Some of you know her."

Nicholson nudged Andrewartha. "Some better than others."

"If you idiots could stop fooling around."

"Sorry, Sarge."

Kropp paged through a mess of paperwork on the table. "Got the preliminary autopsy here somewhere."

That was quick, Hirsch thought. A blowfly droned through the room, smacking the window behind him. He could hear the town out there, voices and car doors slamming and the hiss of airbrakes and a radio tuned to a breakfast show in the house next door.

Kropp looked up, frustrated. "Mr. Hirschhausen."

"Sarge?"

"Go to the file room, see if I left an A4 envelope in there. Marked 'Donovan autopsy.'"

"Sarge."

Hirsch saw but couldn't read the look on Dee's face. He winked at Andrewartha as he went out.

Went to the wrong door at first, almost opened it before he saw the sign pinned at chin height: YOU ENTER HERE WITH GOOD LOOKS AND THE TRUTH. YOU DON'T GET TO LEAVE WITH BOTH.

Meaning it was an interview room. The next door was marked FILES: he entered, spotting the envelope immediately, public service manila, flap open, angled across the top of a filing cabinet. He spotted the $100 note on the floor a moment later, when he was halfway across the room.

"Seriously?" he said.

Pocketing the note, he collected the envelope and handed it to Kropp in the briefing room. "Here you go, Sarge."

Seated again, arms folded benignly, he settled back to listen to Kropp.

Then smacked his forehead. "Almost forgot. Found this on the floor."

He contorted in his seat, turning onto his left hip and, sticking his right leg out, gained access to his trouser pocket. He fished out the $100, waved it, passed it to Nicholson. Everyone watched its progress down the table.

"It was on the floor?"

"Sure was. Should I take it to the front desk and log it in?"

"I'll deal with it," Kropp muttered.

Hirsch beamed in his chair, arms folded again. He bumped shoulders with Nicholson, gave a little nod. "Integrity test," he whispered.

"Get the fuck out of my face."

"Is that what you're calling it?"

Hirsch was having a high old time.

THE ACCIDENT INVESTIGATOR WAS a sergeant named Exley.

"If you find us the vehicle," he said, "we'll match it to the evidence."

Hirsch hadn't seen any evidence. "What evidence, Sarge?"

Spoiling Exley's flow. "All in good time. I've spoken to the coroner. She intends to visit the scene during the week and on Friday open an inquest. In all likelihood she'll immediately announce a recess, but it would help if we could report on the victim's last movements and meanwhile investigate local crash repairers and motorists with a history of driving under the influence."

Then he was gone.

Kropp was nettled; Hirsch could see it in his jaw, his whitened knuckles on the back of the chair. "The powers that be have spoken, so let's get to it. Constable Hirschhausen, your job is to interview family and friends, see what the poor kid was up to."

"Sarge."

"And have a poke around in Muncowie."

"Sarge."

Kropp gazed bleakly at Nicholson and Andrewartha. "Redruth Automotive. Given that you two simpletons work there in your spare time, I'll let you take care of that."

"Sarge," Nicholson said, swapping grins with Andrewartha.

Kropp looked at Dee sourly. "You can tag along if and as required."

"Yes, Sergeant."

"Yes, Sergeant," Nicholson said.

"Cut it out," Kropp said.

Hirsch waved his hand lazily. "Sarge, what's the story with the family?"

"Old story: single mum, two kids, separate fathers. What else is there to say?"

"Melia was done for shoplifting."

"She was. Slap over the wrist."

"I'd look at the brother," Andrewartha said, "Abo prick."

"Knock it off," Kropp said, weary.

"Well, he is."

Hirsch said, "Why would he run his sister over?"

"Why would he do anything? That's the point, there is no why."

"Thanks for clearing that up."

Kropp intervened. "She liked to hitchhike," he said, looking at Hirsch. "Bear that in mind."

"Sarge."

CHAPTER 8

EARLY AFTERNOON NOW.

Hirsch shot out of town before the others could interrupt him, heading south. He half expected Kropp to call him with some tiresome demand but his phone rang only once, a Barrier Highway motorist calling to report a spill of hay bales near Mount Bryan. "Try the Redruth police station," Hirsch said.

Better still, drag them off the road yourself.

Thirty minutes later he was at Tarlee, where he turned southeast into undulating country, giant silent silvery gum trees watching, and finally he was driving past vines and old winery names. Another thirty minutes and he was on a potholed dirt road leading up to Rosie DeLisle's tiny hilltop winery. Out of habit, Hirsch checked the cars parked there, slotted into bays delineated by old redgum sleepers. A mix of expensive German sedans and 4WDs. He didn't know Rosie DeLisle's car.

German refinement and his dusty, boxy police HiLux. No disguising that, but Hirsch disguised himself, tossing his tie, jacket and cap onto the backseat, stowing the gun belt in a briefcase, dragging on a denim jacket.

He found Rosie seated on a wooden bench at a wooden

table—more old redgum slabs—under a shade cloth, the fabric whispering and slapping in a stiff breeze from the valley. Severe rows of vines stretched down into the valley and up the other side, but here in the alfresco dining area there were beds of vegetables and herbs, the air scented and bees buzzing and one magpie warbling from a trellis. *There's money here*, Hirsch thought—obviously, given the cellar door prices he'd noted on his way in.

Rosie rose and stepped away from the table and pecked his cheek. Her movements were careful; her misgivings weren't about to evaporate anytime soon. And she'd already eaten, leaving a fleck of oily lettuce in a salad bowl and a crust of pizza on a chunky white plate.

"Started without me?"

"Starving."

Hirsch grumbled his way onto the bench opposite hers, stowed the briefcase at his feet and studied the menu. Salad, smoked salmon pizza, mineral water.

HE ATE, THEY TALKED.

When it all went wrong for Hirsch, he'd been stationed at Paradise Gardens, an outer Adelaide police station, an unwitting member of a corrupt CIB team headed by a senior sergeant named Marcus Quine. After the arrests, after the raid and the charges and the media frenzy, Rosie DeLisle had been the Internal Investigations officer assigned to question him. "One officer per corrupt detective," she'd told him at the time, "and we all swap notes at the end of the day, adding to our picture of what you shits have been up to."

"Nice."

And she told him to shut up. It was clear she thought he was scum. And then, days, weeks later, her mood lightened. *She trusts me*, Hirsch thought—*or, at the very least, is entertaining doubts.*

Finally she'd expressed these doubts to Hirsch. "Will you give evidence against Quine?"

"No."

She'd gnawed her lower lip, then confessed that she'd rec- ommended no further action be taken against him. "But my colleagues don't agree with me, and it doesn't necessarily let you off the hook."

Not off the hook to the extent that a whiff clung to him, and he was demoted and posted to the bush. And for all he knew, no one but Rosie and his parents had faith in him. And when Quine and the others were charged and punished—vari- ously sacked and jailed, with one senior constable committing suicide—it was asked why Paul Hirschhausen had got off so lightly. The answer was clear: he was a turncoat, a dog, a mag- got, and, for all he knew, no one but Rosie and his parents had faith in him.

And maybe I've lost Rosie, he thought now, noting a withhold- ing quality in her, misgivings shading her face as she drained her shiraz.

She slapped down her glass. "Sometime soon, maybe as early as next week, you'll be invited to police headquarters to face another round of questions."

"Invited."

"*Ordered*, Paul, ordered."

"Why?"

"To answer fresh allegations."

"Against me?"

"Yes. At the same time, Quine's not exactly been twiddling his thumbs."

Hirsch had heard it on the grapevine, Quine the master manipulator beating Rosie and her colleagues into exhaustion with a battery of freedom-of-information requests and demands for daybook entries, diary entries, files, notes, statements, records, reports, memos, emails, video and audio recordings, computer discs and memory sticks, and any and all correspon- dence, however vaguely connected to his twenty years in the employ of South Australia Police. A futile exercise if undertaken by anyone else, but Quine had got away with a lot for a long time and he might get away with this.

"He's saying the case against him is a soufflé," Rosie said.

Hirsch snorted. Soufflés were known to collapse, hard on the outside and nothing in the middle. "So what are these allegations?"

Rosie began to chip at a fleck of cheese on her pizza crust. Shapely hands, Hirsch realized. That was inconvenient. He dragged his eyes away. They'd had fun in bed, one night when it was all over, but love wouldn't do today, here under the sun. Yet he couldn't gaze upon vines and vegetable beds and other diners forever, so he watched Rosie struggle with herself. She was vivid and round and lit within, normally, her fine black hair flashing, her scarlet nails and lips avid for experiences. She was probably an affront to the men she investigated and treated seriously by no one.

"Anonymous tip-off," she said.

"Saying . . . ?"

She looked fully at him, eaten up, you could see it in her face and upper body. "No one will tell me anything, but I've *gleaned* they think you pilfered stolen goods from the evidence safe at Paradise Gardens. Apparently they have serial numbers."

"What kind of items?"

"No idea. Drugs? Cash?"

Her face twisted. She almost reached across the redgum and took his wrist. "Paul, they seem dead certain. Is it true? Will they find something?"

"Sure," Hirsch said, and he fished out his phone, pressed the photo gallery icon and handed it over. "Scroll through."

He watched a pretty forefinger flick the screen. "The first aid box in my car," he said. "The phone is an iPhone 5, and the cash amounts to two and a half grand in hundreds."

She continued to scroll. "Serial numbers."

"Yes. Phone and cash."

A twist of frustration. "It's all going to match, isn't it?"

"Without a doubt."

"Paul, tell me straight, did you pinch this stuff?"

"Fuck you, Rosie."

She slid the phone back across the table. "But who's going to believe you stumbled upon this? They'll think you took these photographs just in case, a weak attempt to say you were set up."

"Possibly," Hirsch said.

A young woman came by with a tray and a smile, a little frown when Hirsch bent his upper body over the phone. "Get you anything else? Coffee? Sticky date pudding's on special."

"Sticky date, please," Rosie said.

"Coffee," Hirsch said.

When the waitress was gone, tight black jeans winking at him, Rosie gestured at the phone. "They'll use this to discredit you. Quine has plenty of friends. Even the people I work with. You should have brought everything with you and logged it in with me."

Hirsch took up his phone again. "Got a little movie to show you."

He found the file containing the CCTV footage of the woman lurking around his car. Pressed PLAY and sat back to watch DeLisle's face.

She breathed out. "Quality's not great, but . . ."

"But it's clear what she's doing, and time and date are embedded in the original, and I have a statutory declaration from the shopkeeper whose camera took this."

"Who is it?"

Hirsch told her. "No idea."

"Kropp's wife?"

Hirsch went very still. He looked hard at Rosie. "It's not Kropp's wife, she's Thai, but one might ask why you mention his name."

DeLisle shut down. "I have my reasons. Could this be the wife of one of the others? Nicholson? Andrewartha?"

"One might wonder how you happen to know the names of everyone stationed at Redruth," Hirsch said. "You have been checking up on me."

Rosie DeLisle shrugged, a shrug that said volumes to Hirsch. Well, fuck them all. "When am I supposed to face the music?"

"You'll get an email."

"Not even a phone call."

"A phone call to ensure you got the email."

Hirsch would have to tell Kropp he wouldn't be available next week. "How long for?"

"Two or three days."

"How will they run it?"

"They'll say some irregularities have cropped up, no big deal, but we need your help sorting them out. They'll start by taking you through your history at Paradise Gardens CIB, let you explain everything away, the corruption, etcetera, etcetera, then just when you're feeling secure, hit you with the phone and the cash."

He could see the doubt was still there. He threw a twenty onto the table and left.

CHAPTER 9

HIRSCH WAS BACK IN Redruth by 4:30. Rather than drive through the town, keeping to the highway, he turned off, intending to reach Tiverton via the back roads that ran north and west of the town. A couple of properties on his watch list lay out there: an elderly farm widow and her schizophrenic son, and a farmhouse rented to a handful of kids who'd dropped out of city life and been accused of sabotaging wind farm turbines.

But his information was dated: the widow had died and the farm sold and the son taken in by a sibling, and the dropouts had returned to the city. Hirsch drove on, warm and slow from his lunch and the sun, and made the final turn back toward the highway. All of the roads out here were winding dirt nightmares like the Bitter Wash, so he wound down his window for a stay-alert breeze.

He came around a bend and a silver Lexus shot out of a driveway ahead, fishtailing as it gathered speed and spat pebbles at him, raised a choking dust cloud. He backed off, hoping the dust would dissipate, and then accelerated gradually. He was now twenty seconds behind the Lexus, the road otherwise empty, the air still, the dust dense, not budging. But the road coiled around the hillsides and dipped in and out of the erosion channels and so he glimpsed the Lexus now and then, before the dust intervened again. The driver was powdering along and Hirsch found himself muttering, "Too fast for the conditions of the road, pal. Slow down before you kill yourself."

Then about one kilometer before the Barrier Highway intersection, the Lexus sideswiped a guardrail. Hirsch saw the driver over-correct, the car shooting back to the center of the road, brake lights flaring, and he was pretty sure the driver had seen the HiLux behind him, a dim shape in the rearview mirror. The guy didn't stop but flicked around the next bend.

Fuck it. Hirsch accelerated, approaching the bend in careful stages, and found the Lexus in the middle of the road, doors open, the dust settling around it.

He braked, switched off, got out. So much drama, you'd expect an orchestra of panicky sounds, but the air was still and silent, only two hot engines ticking as they cooled. Then Hirsch's dust rolled over him and the stink of it was in his nose with his own diesel fumes.

When it cleared he saw a woman alight from the driver's seat, swinging one leg out of the footwell, then the other, emerging with the kind of fluttery relief you'd expect of a driver who'd had a close call. Or an actor.

"Oh, hello there. Whooh! My heart's going pitter-patter."

She walked the ten meters toward Hirsch, a flirty blonde full of smiles to turn your heart over. She was about thirty and, in a nod to spring, wore a darkish, short-sleeved cotton dress, knee-length over her tanning-salon, tennis player legs.

She toed the dirt cutely with her sandaled foot. Red toenails. "Talk about a lucky escape. These gravel roads are quite treacherous."

Hirsch smiled, nodded, clicked his tongue commiseratively.

"Sorry about the guardrail. Of course I'll pay to have it mended." She turned to eye the car. "My husband and I have insurance."

Now the husband was emerging, grinning like a madman, shaking his head at Hirsch, one bloke to another. "If I've told her once, I've told her a thousand times . . ."

"Oh, Mike," the wife said fondly. She rolled her eyes and turned on her smile for Hirsch, finger-hooking quotation marks in the air: "Drive according to the conditions of the road."

"Well, sweetheart, now you know firsthand what it means. Mike Venn," the husband said, sticking out his hand. "And this is Jess, my wife."

"Both of you, knock it off," Hirsch said.

Venn glanced at his wife, at Hirsch. "I beg your pardon?"

"You, sir were driving, and you swapped places with ol' Jess here."

"He did no such thing!"

"You've no doubt seen the drunk driving ads on TV," Hirsch said. "Every police vehicle is a booze bus. You can be breathalyzed on the spot."

The woman was astounded. "You think we've been drinking?"

"I can smell it on you," Hirsch said.

"A glass to celebrate a property sale, nothing more," Venn said.

The wife could have left it at that. Her nose was exquisitely and maybe even naturally shaped, and it quivered now, a terrier after prey. "What are you, some jumped-up little Hitler?"

"I'm sure if you run your mouth long enough I'll come up with another charge," Hirsch said. He fetched a couple of breath-test kits from the HiLux, picturing the drama playing out behind his back. She glares at her husband, he glares at her, fury, a touch of panic, a pantomime of *Make it go away* and *Who do we know?*

He returned stony-faced and gleeful. "Blow into this, please, sir."

"But I wasn't driving."

"Don't worry, I'm testing both of you. I can't have one drunk driver replaced by another, now can I?"

Both Venns registered over .05. Hirsch announced this, and asked, "Is there someone you can call?"

"Come on, we're clearly not drunk, and the road's not exactly crawling with vehicles."

"You hit a guardrail, sir, and you were driving under the influence of alcohol. It would be irresponsible of me to allow you behind the wheel again today. What if you killed someone?"

"*I* was driving," the wife said.

"Knock it the fuck off," Hirsch snarled.

The clouds were high and fat and white, the sky vividly blue, promising a change but glorious just now. Hirsch sought relief in the heavens, thinking there was no dust up there, only down here, where he walked. He mentally listed the charges among those available to him. Giving a false statement to police, driving a vehicle while under the influence, reckless driving, and so on.

He spelt it out to Venn, and asked again: "Do you have someone who can drive you home? In your car, preferably, for it's a hazard sitting here."

"You clearly don't know how things work in the bush," Venn said, hot in the face. "We give and take, live and let live, out here. We make allowances. It works."

Hirsch held up a warning finger. "Before I forget, how many demerit points do you have on your license, Mr. Venn?"

That shut his mouth.

"Mike *needs* his license," his wife said. "He's the Dalgety agent. He drives two or three *hundred* kilometers a day sometimes."

"If he knew he'd accumulated enough points to lose his license, why did he drink and drive?" Hirsch asked, telling himself he was a fool to get into it with them.

"The property market's quite depressed so we were thankful to steer a property sale to fruition," Venn said.

"And if you'd killed yourself? Killed your wife? Worse still, killed a kid on his bike?"

"All right! You've made your point. And my point is, my wife was driving."

Hirsch glanced curiously at Venn. "It's your intention to contest these charges before the magistrate?"

"Too right."

"You'll testify that your wife was driving."

"Sign a statutory declaration if I have to."

Hirsch turned to Jessica Venn. "You intend to perjure yourself before the court?"

She tilted back her nose, a woman forever intent on being disappointed or hard done by. "Not perjury. I was driving."

"If you continue with this," Hirsch said, "and your husband loses, then I will charge you with perjury there and then, and I hope you know it may earn you a jail sentence."

"You don't scare me, jumped-up little Hitler."

WELL, THAT WAS A gorgeous experience. Coming out just north of Tiverton, Hirsch decided to head on to Muncowie.

He found a town more depressed than Tiverton, but laid out like it, with one shop, one pub and a handful of houses on either side of an abbreviated grid of stubby, broad streets. About eight streets in total, four running east-west, four north-south. Small houses, some built of local stone, others of rusting corrugated iron in the old three-room settler style, the rooms running from the front to the back with a chimney on a side wall and a dunny in the backyard. Weedy yards, cars on blocks. Hirsch felt deeply fatigued.

The pub was long and squat, the dusty cream outer wall sitting dark and deep behind a vine-hung veranda. A tin West End Bitter sign rattled in the wind. A couple of panes in the fanlight above the front door were cracked and cobwebby. The veranda floor had once been painted red but the color had retreated over the decades, revealing glassy worn concrete—a good surface if you wanted to crack a head open.

He pushed into the pub, stepping from the concrete to creaky floorboards. Nail heads glinted brightly here and there, despite the curtained gloom of the front bar. The air was layered with stale beer fumes, cigarette smoke and the odors of rural work: diesel, petrol, grease, oil, sweat and animal odors, dung or lanoline or blood or all of it. Deeply ingrained and years old, guessed Hirsch, because the two old boozers and one publican at the bar didn't account for it.

They saw his uniform and the publican said, "Reckoned you'd be in before too long. Pour you a drink?"

It was said with a crooked eyebrow so Hirsch took a stool and rested his elbows on the bar and said, "Lemon squash."

"Lemon squash, lemon squash," said the publican as if the drink and its ingredients were beyond him.

"Or a Bloody Mary."

"That I can do," the publican said, sticking a glass under a spigot and flipping a lever. Lemon squash frothed palely into the glass. "Ice?"

"Hundred percent lemon squash."

The publican leaned back against the wall behind him, a small, narrow, beaming, efficient character, his arms folded arms above a neatly molded belly. "There goes my profit."

Hirsch took him in, seeing the kind of bustler who has virtually no personality beyond dishing up a patter of humor and inoffensive insults as he served drinks. He'd know your name and what you drank but you'd never learn a thing about him beyond the smile and the tight ship he ran. Possibly there was nothing to know. He'd have a history of pub management and ownership behind him, here and there around the state. You wouldn't know why he'd chosen to buy your local pub, or why it was time for him to move on again, or why he'd left the last one, and there'd be no point in asking.

Hirsch toasted the publican and the two drinkers, bleary old-timers in crumpled work clothes and whiskers, cigarettes smoldering in the cramped ashtray on the bar between them. They were halfway through tall glasses of beer that might have been sitting there for days, weeks. They weren't drinkers but drink nursers. And yarners.

They had questions and a few half-truths about the death of Melia Donovan so Hirsch filled some of the gaps, keeping his words, tone and delivery low-key. He was hoping to read some-thing in their responses, a tut-tut and a rueful head shake if they thought it just another tragic loss of a young life, or a flicker of something darker if they knew her or the circumstances of her death.

He got the former. "Poor bloody kid," they said. "Like to get hold of the mongrel what hit her."

"Does her name ring a bell?"

"Not to me," the publican said.

"Donovan," nodded one of the drinkers, precipitating a to-and-fro with his mate about who Melia's mother, father, uncles, aunts and cousins might have been, drawing pretty much on hearsay, it seemed to Hirsch, but one thing was clear, the lin-eage wasn't covered in glory.

"Did you see her in here on Saturday night or anytime Sunday?"

The publican gave a good impression of outrage. "A kid, you say? I don't serve no kids."

"She would have looked older," Hirsch said, and described Melia Donovan, her size, coloring, hair.

"Mate, we don't get that many kids in here. Maybe of a Satur-day we'll get a couple of young blokes in after the footie or the cricket, but they hardly ever bring their girlfriends with them or stay for long. They head up to Peterborough or across to James-town or down to Redruth, not the other way around."

"Arse end of the world," grinned one of the old-timers.

"So your first inkling," Hirsch said, "was when the bloke came in asking to use your phone."

"That's the size of it," the publican said.

Hirsch left his card on the bar. "If you see or hear anything, give us a call," he said, and went out to doorknock the town.

He got nowhere, heard nothing, and returned to the highway.

ANOTHER DEAD END IN Tiverton. There was no answer at the Donovan house, no Commodore, no battered Mazda in the driveway.

But Hirsch met Yvonne Muir, the neighbor who'd been comforting Leanne Donovan the previous day. "Yoo-hoo," she called, a thin, edgy figure where her husband was solid and comfortable, and she came across her yard and stopped at the side fence—but still in motion, her hands patting her hair, smoothing her dress, centering her necklace. She took a deep breath and said, "You're the new policeman. You met my husband yesterday." She added, in an expense of strength and feeling, "Has something happened?"

Hirsch shook his head. "A follow-up visit, that's all."

With an air of tiptoeing through the proprieties, Muir said, "She's at her mother's today. In Jamestown. Back tomorrow."

Hirsch didn't pursue it. "Have you known Mrs. Donovan for long?"

"Ten years. More."

"Are you friends, would you say?"

"Friends and neighbors. Are you sure nothing's wrong? It's not Nathan, is it? You leave that boy alone."

Hirsch was tired. Needing to cut through the thickets, he said, "Mrs. Muir, I'm helping investigate Melia's accident, that's all. A few questions and I'll be out of their hair."

"Please go easy on them."

It was an entreaty, yet with some steel in it. "Okay," said Hirsch carefully, inviting an explanation.

"That family's been through a lot," the woman said and she whisked back into her house.

HIRSCH SLIPPED HIS CARD into the doorjamb and walked back to the highway and the general store.

Inside, the air currents moved sluggishly, the day's warmth coming to a head. Two cars parked snout up to the shop veranda, two customers browsing with baskets hanging from their elbows. A teenage girl he didn't know was at the cash register, waiting.

Hirsch said, "Is Gemma here?"

Her lips peeled open slowly, she moved her head slowly.
"What?"

"Doesn't matter."

Hirsch made his way to the tiny backroom office. Since yesterday the space had shrunk: hard against the walls were bundles of unsold magazines, the titles torn away, and sundry cartons of cigarettes. Tennant was behind the desk; Eileen Pitcher in the only other chair.

"Well, look who's here."

Hirsch ignored the shopkeeper. "Mrs. Pitcher?"

Eileen Pitcher sat knees together, a cigarette in one rawboned hand, refusing to meet Hirsch's eye or return his greeting. He crouched where she couldn't avoid him. "Is Gemma at home, Mrs. Pitcher?"

The woman moved then, drawing powerfully on her cigarette. "All your fault."

"I don't understand," Hirsch said mildly.

"She was that upset last night."

"After my visit?"

She gave him a what-are-ya? look.

"Where is she, Mrs. Pitcher?"

"She's run off, that's where she is," Tennant said behind him.

Hirsch knee-creaked until he was upright again. "Did she say where she was going?"

Cigarette bobbing in her mouth, smoke dribbling up the curve of her cheek and into her narrowed eyes, Eileen Pitcher leaned over to fish in her cardigan pocket. The note was warm and read: *Mum I love you but I have to go away for a while don't worry about me I am fine I will ring you I need space I done nothing wrong remember that I love you your daughter Gemma.*

"Have you tried calling her?"

"Goes to voice mail."

"Mrs. Pitcher, is there anything we should be worried about here?"

"What do you mean?"

"Did she call anyone last night or this morning?"

"Wouldn't know."

"Did she pack a bag? Clothes, shoes, toiletries?"

"Course."

"Things you'd expect her to take?"

"Yes."

"What's going on?" said Tennant.

"I'm sure it's nothing," Hirsch said. "She's upset, it's only natural. But sometime soon I will need to have a chat with her about Melia's movements on the weekend."

"Thought you already done that," the mother said.

"It was a preliminary chat," Hirsch said. "I could see she was too upset to go on."

"My daughter doesn't know nothing about nothing."

"Of course not," Hirsch said. "Just a formality."

He glanced at Tennant. "If you could give me a moment with Mrs. Pitcher . . ."

The shopkeeper didn't like it. "I keep an eye on Eileen and Gemma. They don't need any aggravation."

"That's not my intention."

"Go easy, okay?"

"Mr. Tennant."

"All right, all right, I'm going."

When he was gone, Hirsch closed the door, crouched by the woman's knees again. "Mrs. Pitcher, is this Gemma's handwriting?"

Pitcher began to tremble full-on, her free hand plucking at her top button, ash falling from her cigarette. "Of course it is, what do you mean, are you saying she—"

"When did you find the note?"

"When I got home just now."

"Where were you?"

"I help out down the pub."

"Where was the note?"

"Kitchen table."

"Had Gemma locked up before she left?"

Pitcher jetted smoke across the room. "That girl never locks up, never turns off lights, never picks up after herself . . ."

"Was anything disturbed or out of place?"

"You're making me scared."

"Standard questions, Mrs. Pitcher."

"You think something's happened to her."

"Heavens, no," Hirsch said. "But there will be an inquest eventually and Gemma might be called and it would be good if we were all on the same page."

How many times in his career had Hirsch waffled on like that? It was part of being a cop, he supposed. "How about," he said, "you make me a list of her friends, anyone, family included, who she might visit or call. We'll contact them together."

"She's gone off in me car. Can't you put out a whatchamacallit, alert?"

"Do you wish to report it stolen?"

Pitcher worried at it. "Will that get her into trouble?"

"It might."

"No."

"Can you survive without a car for a few days?"

The woman slumped. "I'll need it eventually."

"For now," Hirsch said, "let's concentrate on those calls."

THEY USED HER KITCHEN phone.

The house was as airless as the store and laced with cigarette smoke and emanations from the kitty litter heaped inside the laundry door, which opened onto the kitchen. As Eileen compiled the list of names and numbers, Hirsch made the calls, figuring it was easier for people to deny her than a policeman. Fifteen calls, getting him nowhere.

Hirsch gave up then. Maybe her Facebook page would reveal her whereabouts. "Does Gemma have a computer?"

"One of those laptop things," Eileen said, taking him to a bedroom that was pretty much furnished by a floordrobe, movie posters and unmade single bed. Hirsch didn't bother stepping over the discarded clothes. There was a printer but no sign of a laptop.

He returned to the police station. The first aid box was missing from the boot of his car.

CHAPTER 10

HIRSCH GOT OUT OF bed at six-shitty on Wednesday, drained a coffee and exercised: stretches, then a walk around the town.

Tiverton seemed deserted. Perhaps country people didn't walk or jog? He took their point: they knew the place, worked hard at physical labor all day, so what was the point? A couple of passing motorists eyed him, curtains twitched and mad dogs raced as he invaded fences and hedges. He gazed benignly at the school, the little grain business along a side street, the Catholic church and the Anglican, various back and side yards, chook sheds, a skeletal horse on a patch of dirt. Galahs screeched in the gum trees and it occurred to him that he'd not been hearing the sounds of big city life these past three weeks. No traffic, no hoons with sound systems, no voices spilling from cafés. Only galahs in the trees.

Back in the office, he fired up the computer. One email, headed *Quine hearing*: starting Monday, Hirsch was obliged to present himself at the hearing into allegations of corruption against Senior Sergeant Marcus Quine and other detectives of the Paradise Gardens CIB.

Hirsch acknowledged, then fired an email to Sergeant Kropp, explaining the circumstances. *So I'll be in Adelaide all next week, sorry, Sarge.*

AFTER BREAKFAST, HE MADE another run at the Donovans' house. The tired Mazda had returned. He mounted the veranda, reached out his knuckles and knocked.

Nothing. He looked across at the Muirs', sensing their eyes on him.

Just then the red door screeched and a woman appeared, rounded, not plump, untidily beautiful, drawing a brush through damp red hair. Taking in Hirsch's uniform she said, "Rose said you'd dropped by."

As if he'd been an old friend passing. Hirsch removed his cap and said, "I'm very sorry, and I can't imagine what you're going through, everyone has such kind things to say about Melia, but I wonder if I could have a quick word with you and Nathan?"

He stopped, conscious that he was babbling. The door widened and he was hit by a front of stale warm air from inside the house, faintly laced with alcohol and dope. "Only if it's convenient. I could come back tomorrow."

Everything stopped. Leanne Donovan was very still in her doorway, her eyes clear and searching, then her hands moved, squeezing the end of a rope of the thick hair. Fresh out of the shower, her body was scented with shampoo and lotions and, despite himself, Hirsch was aware of her flesh beneath the green sundress.

"Nathan's not here."

"That's all right, I'll catch him another time. Could I come inside, do you think?"

Her voice came raggedly, "It's like a bad dream," and her eyes filled.

"Yes. I'm very sorry."

She dropped where she stood and might have slapped onto the cement front step if not for the doorframe and Hirsch grabbing her around the waist. "Let's get you inside. Would you like me to fetch Mrs. Muir?"

"That's okay."

Her legs found their strength and Hirsch eased her along a narrow corridor to a worn, dimly lit sitting room. A bulky old TV set dominated one wall, powered up and showing a detergent ad, splashing a bit of blue and red over the reflective surfaces—the glass cabinet against one wall, the glossy veneer coffee table. A lived-in room, with an empty wine bottle, an overflowing ashtray, a spill of lifestyle magazines, an image of Christ on the cross, another of Christ gazing soulfully past Hirsch's shoulder. But no grime or spills, and the only other furniture was a card table in the corner, crammed with a boxy old computer, a cheap ink-jet printer beside it. Communal computer? He settled Leanne Donovan onto a floral fabric sofa, but it faced the television set, which continued to paint the room, so he found the remote control and switched it off.

"Shall I make you a cup of tea?"

Leanne fiddled with a packet of cigarettes and a lighter. "I'm okay."

God, Hirsch was dreading this. "Before I start, were you told there'd be an inquest?"

Leanne nodded. "This coroner lady rang me, she said Dr. McAskill's finished the autopsy and I can have Mel back to bury."

There was a pause. A word you can't sweeten, "autopsy." It denotes a slab, knives, saws, fluids, the peeling back of flesh, the removal of organs. Hirsch said, "Do you have a day for the funeral?"

"Saturday."

"Would you mind if I came?"

"I don't care."

Another pause, and Leanne said, "Dr. McAskill said she must of been hitching."

Hirsch trod carefully. "Her injuries and the position she was found in do suggest that."

Leanne was very still and then she reeled and wailed. Hirsch waited. She swiped a sleeve across her nostrils and gasped, "Sorry, I'm okay, it hits me out of nowhere sometimes."

"Of course."

"I don't understand nothing of it. She was alone up there? Someone just left her to hitch home? Was she, you know, drunk?"

"She'd had a couple of drinks."

"Where was Gemma? She should of been looking after her."

"They went their separate ways earlier in the evening. Are you sure you don't want a cup of tea?"

"Everyone wants to make me tea. What I want is my daughter back."

"I understand. Perhaps we could start with what Melia had planned for the weekend."

Hirsch strained to hear the reply. "She didn't come home, the little devil."

"She usually comes home after a night out with Gemma?"

"She's a good girl."

"So you don't know what she was doing or who she was seeing in Muncowie?"

No reaction. Hirsch didn't know if the woman was taking it in or not, or had never taken an interest in her daughter's movements. "Mrs. Donovan? Does she know anyone up there? Did she mention a party she was going to, for example?"

No response, then, "Nathan's all I've got now."

"Did Melia have a boyfriend, Mrs. Donovan? Could she have been with him on Saturday night?"

"Maybe."

Hirsch felt his insides stir. "Can you give me his name? I'll need to speak to him."

She shook her head, her eyes weepy but alertness returning to them. "It was a secret. She didn't want to jinx it, you know."

"You didn't meet him."

"No."

Speak to her friends, Hirsch thought. Better still, speak to her enemies. If the boyfriend was an older man, married or single, or a farmhand, or from a town outside the district, he'd not be easy to find.

In a choked voice Leanne Donovan said, "It was a hit-and-run?"

"I'm afraid so."

"Would she of felt . . . Did she . . ."

"It was instantaneous, Mrs. Donovan," Hirsch said, reaching out to touch her wrist before he could stop himself. He saw her shrink away and knew she was watching a nasty movie in her head.

The voice rose. "She shouldn't of had to hitch home. Someone should of given her a lift."

"Yes," Hirsch said, understanding why Gemma Pitcher had left town. "We're still not sure of her movements after the pub in Redruth."

"She likes a good time out."

"Think back: did she say anything about her movements, anything at all? Did she mention anyone's name, for example?"

"Not to me," Leanne muttered, looking mad and incomplete.

"Did Gemma usually pick her up when they went out together?"

Leanne shrugged.

"They were together in the early part of the evening but later separated. Mrs. Donovan, I'd dearly love to know who she might have hooked up with. Have a think about it, will you, please? Ask around? Get Nathan to ask his mates?"

"They wouldn't know anything."

"I found her bag, but no mobile phone. Did she leave it at home?"

Leanne scoffed. "Her and mobiles! She loses them and I can't afford to buy her new ones all the time, plus she run up a huge bill last time."

"So she doesn't have one at present, she's not on a plan?"

"Not unless she paid for it herself."

Hirsch looked across at the computer. "What about Face-book? Email?"

"What about it?"

"Did she use the computer in this room, or have one of her own?"

Leanne shook her head. "We all use that one." Looking oddly shamefaced, she said, "Bob and Yvonne gave it to us when Melia started high school. It's their old one."

The sadness and poverty dragged at Hirsch. The Donovans lived on the margins, and a kid like Melia would want what others seemed to have, a regular connection to something large and attractive. "Would it be all right if I borrowed it for a couple of days? I'll give you a receipt."

He didn't tell her that he'd found a list of passwords in Melia's wallet, not that it would do him any good, for the befuddlement faded from Leanne Donovan's eyes. He could see the cogs turning: she saw dirty tricks, saw a greater darkness attending her daughter's death, quotation marks around the word "accident."

She shook her head adamantly. "We need it."

"Everything in confidence, Mrs. Donovan."

"Don't you need a whatchamacallit, warrant?"

I certainly do, Hirsch thought. "How about if I had a quick look at her Facebook page and recent emails? You can sit with me, watch I don't accidentally stray into anything private to you and Nathan."

"It doesn't feel right. I can't think straight and I don't think you should come here poking your nose in."

"You're quite right, Mrs. Donovan, insensitive of me."

"Yeah."

Hirsch climbed to his feet, feeling the weight. "Again, I'm very sorry about what happened to Melia. It's tragic," he added, meaning it.

"You'll never catch who did it. How can you? Long gone by now."

"We won't stop trying."

Leanne Donovan drew sharply on the last centimeter of her cigarette, scathing and focussed. "They might not even know they done it. Half asleep in the middle of the night, what was that bump? Must of been a rabbit, no big deal, no need to stop."

Hirsch conceded that she had a point. No more empty promises. "Is Nathan at work?"

"His boss gave him the week off."

"He works at the grain shed?"

"Yes."

"Is that his car in the yard?"

"Mine."

"How does he get around?"

"What is this? You think he run her over? Who the fuck do you think you are?"

Fortunately Yvonne Muir came darting in, she might even have been listening, and saved Hirsch from giving further offense.

HE SAID HE'D MAKE a pot of tea and hurried into the kitchen, ignored by the women, who were lost in hugs and weeping.

They're neighbors who habitually come and go through each other's back doors, he thought, filling the kettle. The window above the sink was laced with cobwebs in one corner, the insect screen clogged with dust, but he could see the backyard easily enough: a tumbledown chook shed, rotary clothesline with two stiff tea towels hanging from a wire, a rusted car body collared by weeds. A back gate to a laneway, some evidence of regular use indicated by the clear path through the patchy grass, the scraped dirt at the base, and Hirsch wondered if the girl had liked to slip out the back way at night.

Waiting for the kettle to boil, he peered at the refrigerator door, a dozen cards and photos held by cute magnets. A recent shot of Melia Donovan, looking vaguely scruffy in her high school uniform, and a family grouping: Melia, her mother, her brother. The brother had dark hair and skin. Hirsch removed both photographs, placed them faceup on the table, and took close-ups with his phone.

He heard a car pull up, doors slam, footsteps, and by the time he'd reached the hallway the boy in the family snapshot stood there, a slender form inside a black T-shirt and baggy jeans midway down his arse. He looked red-eyed and stunned, but the instant he noticed Hirsch's uniform, the distress faded to wariness, shame and anger.

Fear, too. Hirsch didn't have time to read it as another kid came in on his heels, a bulky ginger with pimples and weak stubble. He was alarmed to see Hirsch there, and Hirsch was about to hold up a reassuring hand when the kid raised a hand and said, "Catch ya later, Nate."

Nathan returned the wave. "Later."

The redhead shuffled away, out to a lowered Commodore that Hirsch recognized from earlier in the week. It complained away from the curb in a cloud of toxins.

Hirsch turned back to Nathan Donovan, who'd reached the door of the sitting room. Perhaps reassured that his mother didn't need him, or unwilling to intrude, he disappeared into one of the bedrooms.

Hirsch shook his head. He didn't want to distress the kid further, but did need to speak to him, and surely Nathan knew he wouldn't go away, or would soon be back if he did?

He followed the boy, knocking, entering. Nathan was already sprawled messily in the little room, on his back on the bed, arms flung wide, his huge dusty trainers trailing laces across the worn lino floor. This was his cave and he didn't move when Hirsch took another step into the room, and another.

"Nathan? My name's Paul Hirschhausen."

After a while the boy shrugged and examined the ceiling.

Hirsch regarded him, taking in the fine-boned, olive-skinned lankiness—attractive, but you had to look for it, under the scowls. "I know this is an awful time for you but I'm anxious to find the driver who knocked Melia over and I was hoping you might be able to help."

Too late, Hirsch wondered if saying "I" was a misstep. What did he have to offer? And would his saying "I" necessarily cancel his apparent ties to the despised Redruth police, in Nathan's estimation? There was silence and it grew and he was conscious of a kind of misery and defeat in the air.

"Just a couple of questions," he said gently. "For example, do you know what Melia's plans were last weekend?"

"Nup. Going out. She's always going out."

Hirsch said, "I've spoken to Gemma. She drove Melia to the pub down in Redruth but after a while she went to the drive-in with another friend and isn't sure what Melia's movements were. Do you know? Did you see her on Saturday night or Sunday morning?"

Nathan shook his head.

"Where did you go?"

"Pub."

"Where?"

"Spalding."

"With the guy who dropped you off just now?"

"Yeah."

Still Nathan was looking at the ceiling. "What's his name?"

"Who?"

"Your friend."

"Sam. Hempel."

"Would he know anything of Melia's movements?"

"Nah."

"Did you spend the night out, or did you come home?"

"Home."

"You didn't notice if Melia was at home or had been home and gone out again?"

"She does what she does."

"What about this boyfriend?"

"What boyfriend?"

"Older guy, apparently."

Nathan shrugged, said, "Dunno," and showed no other interest.

HIRSCH RETURNED TO THE sitting room.

"Did you see Nathan?" Leanne asked.

Hirsch nodded. "Unfortunately he doesn't know anything."

Leanne exchanged glances with Yvonne Muir. "Von thinks it would be okay if you looked at the computer."

Hirsch shot the neighbor a smile. "You can look over my shoulder if you like."

Both women demurred, as if fearing what they'd see. Hirsch sat himself at the old monitor, switched on the box and, waiting for it to boot up, smoothed out the paper slip from Melia Donovan's wallet. The machine was slow, and no wireless.

There were two passwords: the first gave him access to a file named *MelD* and it proved to contain a handful of school essays, saved emails, journal entries and photographs. He'd examined all of it within a few minutes. Nothing stood out, apart from several references to "Cool." A name? A concept? The second password gave him access to the Facebook page. He poked around in it. It revealed nothing of her secret life.

"Before I go, Mrs. Donovan, could you give me a list of Melia's school and town friends?"

That took a while, Leanne embarrassed because the list was brief and opened gaps in her knowledge. Hirsch returned to the station and started dialing. School holidays, so half the kids on the list were away. The others professed to know nothing of Melia's movements and were astonished that anyone would think they did.

THAT AFTERNOON HE BIT the bullet and called Kropp.

"What do you mean, missing?"

"She left a note, didn't say where she was going."

"Have you tried family? Friends?"

"No luck, Sarge."

"What's she scared of? What's she hiding?"

"Maybe she just feels guilty for not looking after her best friend, Sarge."

"Find the slag, all right? Drag her along to the inquest."

"Sarge."

"And what's this about a Quine hearing?"

"I have to attend, Sarge. All next week."

Kropp said nothing but what Kropp was saying was *dog, maggot.*

NEXT ON HIRSCH'S LIST was Dr. McAskill. "Sergeant Kropp gave me the short version, but I was wondering if there's anything to add."

There was a sense of the doctor drawing himself up on the other end of the line. "I don't feel comfortable having a side conversation about it."

Hirsch sighed. "The thing is, Sergeant Kropp has all of us working on it and it's my job to piece together the kid's last movements. So, anything?"

"I suppose you mean stomach contents?"

"It's a start."

"She'd not eaten much prior to death—a hamburger and chips some hours earlier—but she had been drinking wine."

"We'll need a toxicology report. She might have been drug affected."

"Are you telling me my job, Constable Hirschhausen?"

Moving right along . . . "I thought I saw petechial hemorrhaging in her remaining eye."

Another silence, then the stiff voice saying, "If a vehicle struck her and tossed her aside, flipping her into the bushes, one might expect a range of crushing-type injuries, wouldn't you say? And so, in and of itself, petechial hemorrhaging is not cause for suspicion."

"Fair point."

"It's a motorist you're looking for," McAskill said. "As I

suspected when I examined her by the side of the highway, she sustained severe internal injuries consistent with being struck and tossed aside by a largish vehicle."

"Going at speed? I didn't see any skid marks."

McAskill recited, "All one can say for certain is that the victim sustained severe external and internal injuries consistent with being struck by a largish vehicle."

"Truck?"

"I'd expect more damage. Possibly a van or a four-wheel drive."

"She wasn't punched? Struck with a blunt object?"

"If she were, and I doubt it, such injury or injuries were masked by the other injuries."

Treading carefully, Hirsch said, "Doctor, you say you treated Melia from time to time. I wonder if—"

"Hardly time to time. No more than a couple of times."

"For?"

"Earache when she was little, and painful periods, if you must know."

"I was wondering if she was sexually active," Hirsch said. "Perhaps you prescribed birth control."

"She wasn't a virgin, if that's what you're getting at."

"Were there signs of intercourse in the hours before she was killed?"

"I don't rule it out, but she sustained massive injuries in the center mass of her body, from groin to neck, consistent with the large, flat nose of a van or a four-wheel drive. Am I getting through to you?"

"So, no semen."

"Have you heard of condoms, Constable?"

"No one seems to know who her boyfriend was."

"No good asking me," the doctor said.

ON THURSDAY HIRSCH POKED around out east for a couple of hours, buffeted by warm northerly winds, returning via Bitter

Wash Road. Seeing the gates to Vimy Ridge reminded him of Katie Street and Jackson Latimer, their fear of Pullar, Hanson and the black Chrysler. *Be the good copper*, he thought, *check to see they're okay.*

A teenage boy answered at the Latimers'. He was about fourteen, solid, hair artlessly messy. Pimply, with one pimple raging at the cleft between nostril and cheek, and he could scarcely bring himself to look at Hirsch or get his words out. Craig, he said his name was.

"I was hoping to say hello to Jack. Is he in?"

"Nup."

"Your mum?"

"Nup, and good riddance."

Oh. So Hirsch said, "How is Jack?"

"Good riddance to him, too," Craig muttered.

Some school holiday thing, Hirsch thought. *She's taken the younger one to Adelaide or somewhere and the older one's been left at home; grounded, maybe.*

HE DROVE TO THE house across the road, parked behind the Volvo.

Approached the house and Katie Street called to him from a hammock on the veranda. She was full of a bright force today, not suspicion. "Poor you, finding Melia."

Hirsch sat on the warped boards, his back to a post. "Yes. Enjoying the holidays?"

"Yes."

"What are you reading?"

She showed him the cover wordlessly. *To Kill a Mockingbird.*

"Seen the film?"

"Yes."

She collapsed onto her back again and all he could see was a skinny leg hanging over the edge, a grimy, calloused foot. He heard her say, "Who's your favorite character?"

She wants me to say Scout, he thought, so he said, "Boo Radley."

"Huh."

But his answer satisfied something in her. She popped up again and looked at him. He said, "Is Jack okay? I thought you two would be playing."

Katie closed the book and swung both feet out of the hammock. She shook her head violently. "He's gone away."

"Oh."

Now she hopped to the veranda and sat with him. Sulking a bit at the dirt and grass blades between her toes, she said, "Have you come to see me or Mum?"

"Either. Both. Just passing," Hirsch said. "You haven't seen that car again?"

"No."

"There's no need to be afraid, those men are far from here and will be caught pretty soon."

There was silence and, "Me and Jack have been good."

Hirsch grinned. "Not too good, I hope."

"Really *bad.*"

"That's what school holidays are for. Your mum at home?"

"Somewhere. Mum!"

Nothing. "Where is that dratted woman? *Mum!*"

Hirsch laughed.

Pleased, Katie edged closer to Hirsh. "Have you ever arrested anybody?"

"Yes."

"Have you shot anybody?"

"Katie, the police don't generally go around shooting people."

"Me and Jack were careful that time you caught us."

Her face was tilted up, her fine hair framing her face, cropped at the level of her eyebrows and shoulders—a cap of hair. No freckles, olive skin, beautifully shaped lips. He could see Wendy in her.

"I know you were," he said, "but bullets can fly in unpredictable directions if they strike something, a rock. It's called a ricochet."

"I know what a ricochet is."

"Okay."

"*Mum!*" shouted the girl again.

Nothing, so she said, "Come with me," and led Hirsch along the side of the house to the wind in the backyard.

He halted. It was heart-stopping, seeing Wendy Street at a Hills Hoist set in the lawn, battling a great flowerhead of white sheets onto the line. They flung themselves about, enveloping, licking and taunting, flattening against her body and filling with air again. He watched her writhe and dance, fighting, feeling blindly for the pegs and the line.

"*See the tea towels fly!*" sang Hirsch.

She eyed him balefully. "Very funny."

She wore jeans and a T-shirt and patches of dampness, and crossed the grass toward him, drying her palms on her thighs. "Giving my daughter the third degree?"

"Trying. She won't break."

Wendy Street stopped a couple of meters from him and waited, giving him nothing.

"I've been out in the back blocks and thought I'd pop in," Hirsch said.

She nodded. It wasn't hostility she radiated, just wariness. She turned to glance at her daughter who, with a kind of tact, turned on her heel and disappeared toward the front of the house.

When she was gone, Hirsch took a breath. "Actually, I was wondering if you could tell me a little about Melia Donovan."

"Melia Donovan?"

Hirsch nodded. "An accident team's investigating the hit-and-run, and meanwhile I'm trying to get a picture of what she was like, as a way of tracking down her movements. Did you teach her?"

"Year 11 Maths."

"You teach Maths?"

"Don't look so surprised."

Hirsch grinned. "What was she like?"

"Sweet—when she bothered to attend school, that is. I had nothing to do with her outside of school."

"Any rumors?"

Wendy Street tucked a wing of hair behind her ear. "This and that, mainly to do with boys and partying and her mother."

"Anything specific?"

"No, you'll have to speak to others about that."

"Did you ever see older guys hanging around the school, waiting for her?"

"No."

"Do you know how she got to and from school?"

"There's a bus. It runs between Redruth and Muncowie."

"Muncowie. Was she friends with any of the Muncowie kids?"

"She wasn't friends with anyone. I don't mean she was friendless, I mean she seemed to have outgrown the kids at school, she didn't need them."

"So her friends were older? Older boys? Men? Can you give me any names?"

Wendy shook her head. "You don't understand, I don't know anything. Try a girl called Gemma Pitcher. She lives in Tiverton."

"She wasn't very forthcoming," Hirsch said. Feeling that he was on thin ground, he said, "Did Melia seem sexually active or experienced to you?"

"I'd hate to have your job. Look, I barely knew her, but I did wonder if she'd had too much experience, too soon. She wasn't knowing, didn't flaunt it, just seemed a bit lost and alone, if you know what I mean."

"Are the local kids into drugs? Binge drinking?"

"No more than city kids, and probably less, I wouldn't know."

Silence settled between them. "I popped in across the road," Hirsch said.

"Is that why you're here? Checking the kids aren't out target shooting? Checking their mothers haven't let them run wild?"

Hirsch said levelly, "I don't want them to feel afraid needlessly, and I do need to know about Melia Donovan, and I do need to patrol out east from time to time."

The tension slipped a little. "Fair enough. So you would have learnt that Allie has left her husband?"

That explained the teenage boy's manner. "Oh."

"She's in town at her parents'. Jack, too. Craig sided with his father."

"Permanent?"

"Seems that way."

BACK IN TIVERTON, HIRSCH saw his elderly neighbor wheeling her shopping cart into Tennant's. He ran to the backyard, vaulted the side fence and retrieved the iPhone and cash. Then he drove to Clare, hoping no one would call him to report a stolen stud ram or a cat up a tree. Entered the post office there and addressed the phone and cash to himself, poste restante, Balhannah, a town in the hills.

CHAPTER 11

FRIDAY, AND THE TOWN'S first inquest.

Hirsch's first inquest, and his first time inside the Mechanics Institute, a fine stone building two hundred meters from the police station. Wooden floors, wooden half paneling around the walls, pastelly blue paintwork, vases of flowers on solid wooden stands, pressed tin ceilings and photographs of prize rams and former councillors here and there. A staircase to one side, a corridor of meeting rooms—the Country Women's Association, he was guessing; the RSL; council chambers. A cardboard sign sat on a plain wooden chair outside the doors to the main hall: INQUEST HERE TODAY.

He stepped through, pausing to take in the vastness of the hall: high windows, more wood paneling, good ballroom dancing floorboards, and a stage at the far end complete with wings and a bushland scene painted on a canvas backdrop. Hirsch doubted that plays were still performed here, but the town did need an arena for the primary school concert, the New Year's Eve ball, the debutante ball, the strawberry fete, Liberal Party fundraising events. Below the stage was a table with a microphone and two chairs, a smaller table, chair and microphone stood to one side of it. The coroner and her assistant at one table, guessed Hirsch, witnesses at the other. And there was an easel, supporting a shrouded rectangular shape. Blowup photographs? Bird's eye diagrams showing the road and the position of the body?

The grandeur was spoiled by a dozen rows of metal folding chairs. Someone had been optimistic: the only onlookers—great gaps of empty chairs separating them—were Kropp, Dr. McAskill, one of the accident investigators, a reporter from the Redruth rag, the shopkeeper, the Broken Hill mine worker who had discovered Melia Donovan's body, and the Muirs, who were sitting with Nathan Donovan and his mother.

Kropp turned his massive head and jerked it at Hirsch: *Get your arse over here.* Hirsch complied. His shoulder brushed Kropp's, it couldn't be helped.

"Morning, Sarge."

"Correct me if I'm wrong, but you live a two minutes' walk away."

"Phone calls, emails."

"Speaking of emails, yours didn't say how long you'll be away next week."

"Could be a few days."

Kropp grunted. "At least we're not going through a crime wave." He paused. "So long as you're back by Saturday."

"Sarge?"

"Football final, so all hands on deck."

Hirsch got a kick out of that. "You mean Redruth actually comes alive? People on the street?"

Kropp turned quiet and nasty. "If there's any justice, someone might thump you."

"Looking forward to it, Sarge."

They were silent. Hirsch fiddled with his phone and stared at the empty tables. He knew he was here at the coroner's discretion. Today's hearing would merely establish the who, when, where and how of Melia Donovan's death, invite witnesses to come forward, and then adjourn until the police investigation was complete, and that might take months. Footsteps and a cadaverous man appeared, stiff-backed, grey-faced. "He was in the job," whispered Kropp, and Hirsch could see ex-policeman in the scowling figure, who halted beside the main table and called: "All rise for Her Majesty's coroner."

They stood, the air above them clanging, crashing, a symphony of cheap metal chairs sliding and colliding, and a middle-aged woman appeared in a whisper of fabric and rubber-soled shoes, her face kindly, apologetic, almost grandmotherly, a foil to the old cop. She gestured at them vaguely and they all sat and the man beside her boomed, "All mobile phones off, if you please."

"That means you," muttered Kropp.

Hirsch switched off, pocketed the phone.

The coroner remained on her feet, her hands moving folders around on the tabletop, and now she glanced out at the rows of chairs. She looked untethered to Hirsch, lost and adrift in the vast hall. *Sit*, he begged her.

She cast her voice over their heads, full, rolling, educated: "Thank you all for coming. You may be wondering at the choice of venue: quite simply, I wished to view the place where Ms. Donovan died, and I would welcome community involvement in the investigation into her death."

Leanne Donovan cried out. The coroner put her hand to her throat, opened and closed her mouth. Nothing further happened, but then Leanne and her son thrust back their chairs and stumbled out of the hall, followed by Yvonne Muir.

The coroner, unsettled, said, "I hereby formally open the inquest into the death of Melia Anne Donovan on or about Saturday the twentieth of September and I will presently adjourn these proceedings to enable the police to complete their inquiries and for any criminal prosecution arising to take its proper course."

She sat at last, removing her glasses. "What I must do today is confirm the identity of the deceased and the location, time and cause of death. Witnesses, including the pathologist and police members, will give evidence in regard to these matters and then my officer will give a brief summary of the circumstances, as far as these can be ascertained."

The coroner replaced her glasses. "I have made my visit to the scene of Ms. Donovan's death, and pray that opening the inquest here, her hometown, will encourage as many of her friends and family as possible to come forward and assist this court, and the police, to find the person or persons responsible for her death."

Kropp half-turned his huge head to Hirsch. Hirsch read the accusation: *We have you to thank for letting one such person do a flit.*

"Anyone giving testimony will be speaking under oath and may subsequently be required to make a formal statement to police. Of course, this is not to say you need see this morning's proceedings as in any way fraught with meaning and consequences. I wish merely to discover the truth."

Hirsch heard backsides shift on the cheap, thin seats. He didn't think anyone had anything to say, except to establish the groundwork and express grief.

Nancarrow was called first. He explained why he'd been driving south along the Barrier Highway and how he'd found the body. The coroner had no questions, and called Hirsch, who read from his notebook: times, the date, distances, the movement of personnel, the recovery of the body and plenty of cop speak like "female deceased."

"Then I remained at the scene until accident investigators arrived."

"Had a formal identification been made at this stage?"

"Dr. McAskill stated that he knew the deceased."

"You relied on his identification?"

Hirsch glanced around at Kropp. Kropp held his hands wide, so Hirsch returned to the coroner. "Sergeant Kropp is in charge of the investigation and will provide further detail in regard to this matter, but I do understand that he, like Dr. McAskill, knew the deceased and later viewed the body and had no reason to doubt Dr. McAskill's identification."

The coroner was scribbling. She looked up. "I am able to confirm that another method of identification has subsequently confirmed the visual identifications of Dr. McAskill and Sergeant Kropp, namely dental records. Constable Hirschhausen, you may step down. I call Sergeant Exley."

Exley summarized his team's findings at the accident scene: no tire tracks or skid marks, no identifiable fragments from the vehicle that had struck Melia Donovan.

"Was more than one vehicle involved?"

"If you mean, was she knocked over by one vehicle and run over by subsequent vehicles, there was no evidence at the scene to support or disprove that scenario."

McAskill was called. He confirmed identity, injuries and cause of death. "I submit that she was struck with some force by one vehicle, the impact sufficient to kill her and throw her body to the area where she was found. The locus of the impact was her right hip, arm and trunk, which might indicate that she'd had her back to the vehicle and was in the act of turning to face it when hit. There was also a massive injury to the head, which in my experience indicates that she was flipped up and into the windscreen or onto the roof of the vehicle before tumbling off the road verge."

"Were there indications of third party violence to the deceased apart from vehicle impact injuries?"

In other words, had she been choked, stabbed, punched, burnt with cigarettes, tied up, poisoned, raped . . .

"There were not."

"And the toxicology findings?"

"Indications of alcohol and cannabis use."

"Sufficient to cause disorientation?"

"In my opinion, and taking account of her slight body mass, yes."

Kropp was called. He confirmed identification and outlined

the police investigation. He also disclosed that Melia Donovan was an inveterate hitchhiker.

The coroner thanked him and, as he returned to his seat, said, "That completes the initial formal input. It remains for me to invite members of the community to step forward."

The chairs shifted minutely.

She waited, glancing keenly at their faces. "Very well, this inquiry is adjourned."

"All rise," the officer said.

"Fucking waste of a morning," muttered Kropp. "Find her slag of a friend, all right?"

"I'm in the city next week, Sarge," Hirsch reminded him. "The Quine inquiry."

Kropp screwed up his face at the floor, not looking at Hirsch.

CHAPTER 12

ON SATURDAY MORNING, HIRSCH attended Melia
Donovan's funeral. A service at the tiny Catholic church, followed by a procession of cars, lights on, to the cemetery on the
hill, a windswept patch of red dirt, busy ants and gum trees.
Everyone wept; the kids from the high school were inconsol-
able, Wendy Street attempting to console. Katie toed the dirt,
keeping company with Jack Latimer and his mother and a couple aged in their sixties. Maternal grandparents? Hirsch stood
well back. He felt sad, but didn't mourn. He watched, not wanting to appear that he was. Other than the schoolkids there were
men and women, young and old. He could not name a tenth of
the people there, but they all knew him. One or two nodded;
others glared. Bob Muir asked him to come to the get-together
afterwards, tea and cakes in the hall, but Hirsch declined.

THAT AFTERNOON HE WAS called to a farm contractor's property
a few kilometers outside the town. The man's work was largely
seasonal: plowing and harrowing, crop sowing, reaping, carting,
hay baling. He mended fences and bores, crutched sheep, put
up sheds, you name it, and leading Hirsch across a dirt yard to

a collection of implement, hay and toolsheds, said, "Feast your eyes on that."

The door to a small tin structure had been jimmied open, the wounds raw in the metal skin. "I was at that poor lass's funeral and come back to this. The bastards pinched me son's trail bike, plus some of me tools, a chainsaw, brush cutter, cans of fuel, saw, plane, pipe wrench . . ." He glared at Hirsch. "I bet I'm not the only one. The pricks were at the service. They clocked who else was there, and knew we'd be out for a couple of hours, the cemetery and the rest of it, and snuck off and robbed us."

Quite likely. It was a city crime but no reason why it wasn't also rural. Hirsch gave the man an incident report number for his insurance company, made no promises and returned to town. Where two more calls came in, people returning from the funeral to find broken windows, doors prised open, tools, computers and TV sets missing.

A *truck or a ute*, thought Hirsch, returning from the last call. In a land of trucks and utes.

FIVE THIRTY NOW, THE HiLux threw a long shadow as Hirsch returned to town, the fence posts and power poles striping the paddocks. He found a dusty Holden parked outside the police station, a woman piling out of the driver's seat, clutching a mobile phone. "Thank God. I tried calling the number you pinned to the door but I had no signal."

Hirsch recognized her from the funeral, the older woman with Alison and Jack Latimer. "Something wrong?"

She was comfortable, greying, grandmotherly, but in a state and wringing her hands. "It's my son-in-law. He's making a scene and I'm scared someone will get hurt."

"Lead the way. Is it far?"

She was already climbing into the Holden. "Better if you came with me, then I can explain."

Hirsch thought about it. Would he need anything from the HiLux? Would this end in a car chase? "Hurry," the woman said, so he slid into her passenger seat, belted himself in. "May I have your name?"

The woman shot away from the curb, no signaling or mirror-checking. Then again, Barrier Highway was always quiet. "Heather Rofe. Our daughter appeared on our doorstep during the week with her youngest, asking if they could stay for a while. Her marriage hasn't been the happiest so of course we said yes, but her husband keeps ringing her to come home, and a little while ago he turned up, yelling and swearing."

"Your daughter is Alison Latimer?"

She was astounded. "Yes. How do you know that?"

"We met briefly," Hirsch said. He paused. "Is her husband violent, Mrs. Rofe?"

A ragged sigh. "I'm not sure. Ray can be overbearing, needs to get his own way, I know that much."

Hirsch sat back as Heather Rofe swung the car into a short street beyond the Catholic church. Hirsch counted four houses on either side, the end house on the border of farmland. Eight old houses choked with cottagey shrubs and peeling gums, small-town houses that never opened the front curtains or spoiled the quiet. A beefy green Range Rover was angled outside the end house. The man on the path between the little gate and the front door was tall, solid, wound tight, dressed for a reconciliation in grey trousers, black shirt and a sports coat. A middle-aged man stood at the door, barring him.

Rofe pulled into the curb and Hirsch climbed out, adjusted his uniform cap and approached the house. He stopped at the garden gate, eyeing both men, who eyed him in return, the house-holder mostly unreadable but, sensed Hirsch, relieved—with an undertone of *I probably could have handled this.* Raymond Latimer was different, flexing his hands, a rampager not rampaging but wound tight as a spring.

"Gentlemen," said Hirsch.

Latimer ignored him. "Heather, you fetched the police?"

"Sir," Hirsch said, "your business is with me, now."

Latimer shook his head like a reasonable man pushed to the limit by fools. "You're not needed here. We can sort it out ourselves."

Huge, flexing hands. Hirsch watched the hands, the torso, for a hint of the man's intentions. Alison Latimer's husband was savagely shaven at this late stage of the afternoon, wearing his best casual gear. A big, practical man out of costume, but no joke, despite the tidy comb tracks raked across his skull. Regarding Hirsch with a kind of exalted fury, in fact, as if he'd never been challenged like this. Hirsch didn't feel trepidation, exactly, but an intense expectation. His fingers flicked over the equipment strapped to his belt. He gauged distances.

"You hear me? We can sort this. No need for the police. A civil matter."

"Ray," said Heather Rofe, "you were scaring us. I had to fetch the police."

"That's bullshit, Heather, and you know it."

Keith Rofe said, from the veranda, "Banging on the door, shouting and swearing, we felt threatened, Ray. You said some pretty terrible things."

"Heat of the moment. I only want to speak to Allie, then I'll be on my way."

"Not now, not today. Give her a chance."

"What about me? When's anyone going to give me a chance? That's the coward's way out, leaving home without talking it over with your husband. I think it's in everyone's interest if Allie comes home with me now."

"You're frightening her," Heather Rofe said. "You're frightening Jack, poor little boy."

Latimer put aside the fury. He shook his head and stomped out onto the footpath in a huge, martyred capitulation. "Unbelievable. A concerned husband and father tries to find a solution to a family difficulty and everyone gangs up on him and the police are called."

Heather Rofe slipped past him to join her husband. "Allie needs time, Ray, all right?"

"Time? A day? A week? What do you mean, time?"

"Time," Rofe said and pushed her husband ahead of her into the house. Hirsch sensed that the daughter and grandson were in there, peering through the curtains.

Latimer was about to climb into the Range Rover. "Sir, a quick word before you go?"

The man paused, taking a cold, summarizing interest in Hirsch. "You're the new cop. You can't do anything to me, Kropp's a mate of mine, all right?"

"I'm not fully convinced that you won't hassle these people again, Mr. Latimer."

Hirsch expected hostility. What he got was a grin. "I know all about you, you prick."

Hirsch waited. Waiting had become one of the chief conditions of his life. He waited right through a stream of oblique and wrathful abuse because he'd heard it all before. At the end of it he nodded, said "Sir," and walked past Latimer to enter the Rofes' yard. He heard the Land Rover drive away as he lifted his knuckles to knock.

Heather opened the door. "I can't thank you enough."

"Do you wish to take out a court order against him, Mrs. Rofe?"

She smiled. "That won't be necessary."

Hirsch gave her his card. "Call me anytime."

CHAPTER 13

"GOT CHURCH THIS MORNING?"

Hirsch's parents had church every Sunday morning. His asking was part of a pattern: he would call after breakfast, ask this question, catch up on what his sister was up to in the UK, ask after everyone's health, ask who his parents had seen lately . . . Every Sunday, and running behind the chatter were Hirsch's overpowering sense memories, aroused by their voices: the smell of eggs and bacon on weekends, his father's cigarettes, the play of light in the little hill towns above Adelaide, the stutter of the lawn sprinklers.

And their unspoken question: *Are you really bent, son?*

Then they'd sign off, but this time Hirsch said, "I should arrive sometime after lunch."

"Drive safely," his mother said.

TWO AND A HALF hours to Adelaide, then a quick climb into the hills, the road fast until he turned off for Balhannah. Cooler air up here, scented with spring grasses. He'd struck some Sunday-lunch traffic but the road was quiet now, lunchgoers sprawled at home or in cafés. Greenery pushed in on him from both sides, and he was woolgathering, not fully engaged, when the siren whooped.

A patrol car, in snarling white and martial black. A 90 km/h zone and Hirsch was doing 85. All his electrics worked: brake light, indicator light. No broken lenses. No failure to stop back there at the crossroads, no failure to give way. So Hirsch woke up pretty quickly, the daydreams dissipating like smoke.

If they wanted to pat him down they'd find the Beretta around his ankle and no paper to go with it.

He pulled over onto the verge and sat there, motor running, watching the rearview mirror. Two figures on board, but the angled windscreen gave him no more than shapes, heads and shoulders. Time passed and Hirsch felt for the pistol and tucked it against his thigh, under a flap of his street directory. They could have been calling it in, he supposed, but didn't seriously suppose it. Or they had their windows down and were gauging sounds, here above the plain, in the land of little hill towns and doubling-back, up-and-down roads. You'd soon hear a vehicle coming. If you were here to kill Hirsch, you'd want to wait until the coast was clear.

A car did come, an unmarked white Holden. Hirsch watched it crawl past, pull over and reverse until he was hemmed in. He cranked a cartridge into the firing chamber of his pistol, safety off.

Nothing happened, and then something happened. There were four men in the Holden, plain-clothed, and one of the rear passengers held up a mobile phone, waggling it at Hirsch without revealing more than a white shirt cuff under a dark suit sleeve and a shaven bullet head.

Was he to expect a phone call? Make a phone call? Hirsch took his Motorola from the dash cradle, clamped it against the windscreen, his way of saying, "Your move."

The Motorola screen, slumbering, woke with sound and light. Hirsch said, "Hello."

"Hello?" his mother said.

So Hirsch said, "Hello," wondering how the pricks had managed to network the call.

When there was no response, he said, "Mum, it's me."

She didn't hear him and her hearing was perfect, the line clear and her handset new, a cordless he'd given his parents last Christmas, so something else was going on. The next time she spoke—"Hello" and "Is anybody there?"—she sounded frightened.

"Mum!" shouted Hirsch, knowing it was futile.

"What do you want?" his mother was saying. "Why are you doing this to us?"

"Mum," Hirsch said, and there was a click and the man in the backseat of the white car waved two devices at him, phone and digital recorder.

"Brave," Hirsch snarled, "taking it out on my mother," but the white car was streaking away. The patrol car pulled out, too, pausing for a moment alongside Hirsch. A woman in the passenger seat. She shot him with her finger and then passenger and driver were gone, being juvenile with the siren again.

TWENTY MINUTES LATER HIRSCH said, "Have you been getting anonymous calls?"

"We didn't want to worry you, dear."

The house sat at the end of a quiet side street and was indefensible. No alarms or window bars, flimsy locks, a bedridden old woman on one side, a weedy paddock on the other, a plant nursery behind them. Hirsch prowled from window to window and tugged at his parents' blinds and curtains.

"You're making us nervous, dear."

"When did the calls start?"

"A few days ago," his mother said.

She worked for the ambulance service, a narrow, rangy, nail-nibbling woman used to dealing with drunks, addicts, the scared and the deranged. Her love for Hirsch was absentminded, as if she were not quite sure how she'd come to give birth to him.

Never mean or cross or negligent, just practical and distracted, and closer to his sister.

"Did you report it?" he said.

Hirsch's father cocked his head tiredly, a man as rawboned as his wife, still in his churchgoing pants and shirt. He was a farrier and had the dents, scars and arthritis to prove it. He said, in his mild rumble, "As soon as we give them the name Hirschhausen, what's going to happen, son, do you think?"

Saying plenty between the lines, Hirsch thought. "I think it'd be a good idea if both of you went away for a few days."

"Few days."

"Until the end of the week. Or sooner. As soon as I've finished giving evidence I'll call you on one of your mobiles."

His mother came and gave him a hug. It was there and gone. "I don't think that will be necessary, dear."

There was something about the main sitting room window. Hirsch crossed the room. He said accusingly, "New glass. Fresh putty."

"A brick," his father said.

"When?"

"Friday night. We found it when we came back from seeing a film in town."

"Had it repaired yesterday morning," his mother said.

"Why didn't you tell me?"

"We're telling you now."

"No, you're telling me because I noticed it now. And don't say you didn't want to worry me."

"Well, we didn't."

"Just a rock?"

"A rock would have been too subtle for us," Hirsch's mother said, "so it was accompanied by a note, in case we missed the point."

"Let me guess: 'Tell your son not to testify.'"

"Along those lines," Hirsch's father said.

His mother said, "'Tell your *cunt* of a son to do the decent thing and keep his trap shut.'"

GARRY DISHER   112

Hirsch had never heard his mother say the word and saw a glint in her eye. She was a bluffer, his mother, but under it he realized that she was worried, and he remembered her fear on the recorded phone call. Her manner was unchanged, her voice, but she was holding herself too tightly.

"Mum, please, talk sense into Dad. Go up north for a few days."

His parents owned a time-share apartment on the Gold Coast. School holidays were finishing so they might have the place to themselves.

"Do you think your pals would hurt us?" his father said.

"If it would hurt me, yes," Hirsch said, collapsing into an arm-chair, his body tired of the tension. Planted his feet firmly, held his arms out wide, a way of saying, *Am I getting through to you?*

The cuffs of his jeans rode up and his father saw the Beretta on his ankle. "Oh, son," he said, the color draining from his face.

Embarrassed, Hirsch stood until the cuffs draped over his shoes again. "A precaution."

"Pretty serious precaution."

"I don't know what to do," Hirsch said. "If I stay the week with you, as planned, I put you, not to mention the house, at risk. If I stay somewhere down in the city, I leave you here exposed. And if I stay with you I won't be around during the day. So I'm beg-ging you, take a holiday for a few days. Call in sick. When it's all over they'll have no more cause to threaten you."

"But they could come after you."

"I'll manage."

"Not if you get locked up, you won't," Hirsch's father said.

Inviting—*begging*—Hirsch to say that wouldn't happen, he wasn't a dirty cop.

Hirsch looked at his mother, she looked at her husband. "Karl," she said.

"Eva," he said.

❧   ❧   ❧

THEY WERE GONE BY late afternoon, a late cancellation on a houseboat based at Renmark on the Murray River. Meanwhile Hirsch supposed he was still a magnet. He didn't want to be killed in his childhood bed for his parents to find, so he booked into a pay-by-the-hour motel somewhere on South Road and paid for four nights in advance. The reservations clerk was troubled. He couldn't work Hirsch out, compared to the men and women who paid by the hour, the transients, but nothing surprised her in the end and she had low expectations of human behavior. It's just that Hirsch didn't look like a man with no expectations.

"Will that be cash or card?"

"Cash," Hirsch said.

And he had to turn around and hunt for a cash machine. He knew the transaction would trigger a record, but no one would know where the cash went after that. Unless there was a tracking device on his car. It did Hirsch's head in, all that thinking, and he almost forgot he still had to drive back into the hills first thing in the morning, collect his parcel from the Balhannah post office.

CHAPTER 14

MONDAY.

Hirsch arrived early and, marking time, saw Quine, Quine wearing the look of a man setting off on a raid, strolling in his languid, dangerous way toward one of the out-of-bounds corridors that filled police headquarters. You didn't mistake Quine for a teacher, surgeon or shopkeeper; he was a cop, tall, proprietorial, unimpressed, full of unschooled intelligence. Not good-looking—his features were too irregular—but the lopsidedness of his smile, when it appeared, rendered him attractive. Hirsch sank in his foyer armchair, hoping he hadn't been spotted.

But Quine stopped abruptly, seemed to sniff the air. He turned on his heel. And now he was cutting toward Hirsch, full of sharkish amusement. He halted. He grinned, no humor in it, his eyes like fractured marbles, his face constructed of harsh planes and shadows. He said nothing. Hirsch gazed at him blankly, then suddenly picked his nose, really sticking his finger in. Quine moved off again.

THEY GRILLED HIRSCH IN a room suited to savagery, a corporate blond wood and cream-walled kind of room, with a nondescript carpet, a side table holding a water jug and glasses, the scent of cleaning agents and aftershave. Two glum senior officers sat at the head of the room, facing down Hirsch, who sat alone at a small, centrally placed table, a briefcase containing his lap-top and the cash and the iPhone at his feet. He'd requested and been denied a lawyer: not necessary, just a few formali-ties, okay? And sitting in, ranged along the side walls, were a handful of officers from the various squads whose activities Quine had compromised in some way: drugs, armed robbery, fraud . . .

Rosie DeLisle was there, too, next to a woman who seemed tangled in distaste and fury, as if she loathed Hirsch. Short-haired, solid, gruff, a scoffing look on her face if he happened to catch her eye. He thought he knew all the Internals, but didn't know this woman, and shot Rosie a querying glance, *Who's your friend?* Rosie gave him a whisper of a shrug, as if it were none of his business, don't worry his pretty little head.

A prosecutor, maybe? Or someone from a specialist squad with some dirt on him, real or imagined?

ROSIE'S BOSS, AN INSPECTOR named Gaddis, asked the first question. He was thin and ferrety and perfect for the job, his long fingers tapping next to an AV control box. "What was your first impression of Paradise Gardens?"

Paradise Gardens was one of Adelaide's bleak new outer sub-urbs: cheap housing, struggling young families, a high welfare dependency but few welfare services, a volatile ethnic mix, job scarcity and nothing for the kids to do, including catch a bus or a train anywhere. But Gaddis hadn't meant the suburb, he meant the Paradise Gardens police station, which was dysfunc-tional. But what came first, the dysfunctional police station or the dysfunctional suburb?

"I was new to detective duties, sir, and had no clear expecta-tions."

Gaddis gave him a *stop stonewalling* look. "In an early interview you said you felt 'an atmosphere' soon after joining Senior Sergeant Quine's CIB team at Paradise Gardens. What did you mean by that?"

Hirsch thought he might as well give a straight answer. "Canteen and locker conversations would dry up whenever I showed my face," he said, "as if I wasn't trusted, and I wondered if they saw me as a spy."

Gaddis gave Hirsch a *poor you* look. "Did this atmosphere improve over time?"

"Eventually."

The other interrogator, a man who looked drawn, ill, said, "Please elaborate."

Conscious that he sounded a bit pathetic, Hirsch said, "At first the shunning was quite overt. I was rarely invited along on raids or to social events, for example, but left to man the CIB phones. That situation improved over time, but only to the extent that I was taken for granted, like part of the furniture."

"You were a junior officer, untried," Gaddis said, "and someone had to be on call at the station."

Nice try, Hirsch thought. He said nothing.

The other man said, "These social events: dinner parties? Barbecues?"

"Dinner parties, barbecues, strip clubs, four-hour lunches and nightclubs," Hirsch said.

Someone laughed. Gaddis snarled, "By nightclub I take it you mean the Flamingo?"

"Yes."

"A club owned by the brother of a Comancheros bikie gang member," Gaddis said, "so wouldn't you expect CIB interest in the place?"

"The Paradise Gardens CIB was only interested in sex and money: the girls in the back room, the pole dancers, the kickbacks and the Comancheros who bought the cocaine Quine had filched from the evidence locker."

"*Senior Sergeant* Quine," Gaddis said. He moved right along. "Presumably you did more than man the phones all the time. You performed some CIB duties?"

"Yes."

"Such as?"

"I helped to investigate minor crimes. Burglaries, noise complaints."

"When investigating one such noise complaint, did you accept a bribe of five-hundred dollars?"

"That is a lie," Hirsch said. "We were shorthanded and I was sent to look into an after-hours pub noise complaint. The publican offered me five-hundred dollars to turn a blind eye. My curiosity was piqued, so I accepted the money and immediately logged it in at the station, along with a written report. I then informed Quine, sorry, Senior Sergeant Quine. It's in my report."

"We have been unable to find that report, Constable Hirschhausen."

"Is that a fact."

Gaddis, at his oiliest, said, "You're not doing yourself any favors, taking that attitude."

Hirsch ignored him. "In addition to handing me five-hundred dollars, the publican took me into a back room where people were playing poker and roulette. I was invited to join in. I declined, saying I had another call to investigate. It's all in my report."

"Which no one can find. When you reported to Senior Sergeant Quine, what did he say?"

"He said, 'Big Trev offered you a bribe? Doesn't sound like him.' I then told Quine—"

"Senior Sergeant Quine."

"I then told Quine that we should raid the pub's gambling room. For all we knew, there could have been rooms set aside for prostitution. Quine said we needed to be better prepared, and suggested I see Big Trev again, wearing a wire."

"His name is Senior Sergeant Quine."

"He doesn't deserve the respect implied," Hirsch said.

Gaddis breathed out. "Did you go to the pub again, wearing a wire?"

"A week later. I was offered another five-hundred dollars. In fact, a weekly payment was suggested."

"You had this on tape?"

"Yes."

"You gave it to Senior Sergeant Quine?"

"I did."

The other man coughed. He was grey-faced and Hirsch couldn't read him. "What transpired?"

"He called me in two days later and said the equipment must have been faulty, all he could hear was static. I offered to write it up from my notes. He said, 'Yeah, why don't you do that,' and so I did."

"More paperwork that seems not to exist," Gaddis said. "Then what happened?"

"Nothing. No follow-up."

Gaddis smiled at him and pressed a button on the AV controls. Scratchy sounds filled the air. "Static. Clearly your recording didn't work, so why should there be a follow-up?"

"It did work," Hirsch said. He removed his laptop from his briefcase. He cranked the volume up and pressed play. The room heard his voice, and another voice saying, "Five hundred now and a hundred and fifty a week, whaddaya reckon to that?"

"Big Trev," Hirsch said.

Gaddis swallowed. "Has that recording been authenticated?"

"No."

"Formally lodged?"

"No."

"Then why—"

"Having determined that Quine was corrupt, I got into the habit of making two copies of everything," Hirsch said. "I have never deviated from that."

The grey-faced man glanced at Gaddis and back at Hirsch, so that Hirsch wondered if he had an ally here.

"Moving right along. In your year at Paradise Gardens did you not see a great number of successful CIB actions?"

"Yes."

"Robberies investigated, witnesses questioned, raids mounted, arrests made?"

"Yes," Hirsch said, and over Gaddis's attempts to ask a new question, added, "But more often than not the team returned empty-handed from a so-called 'sure thing' or flush with seized drugs and stolen goods which they never properly logged into the evidence safe."

Gaddis, tensely red, said, "More on that evidence safe later. What makes you so sure of these accusations, if you were manning the phones or whatever it was you were doing?"

"I got curious. One day I saw Detective Constable Reid make a call on his mobile before one of these raids that amounted to nothing. The next day he left his phone in the charger while he went to the pub, so I checked his call log. He'd called another mobile phone. After work I went to the address they'd raided and started calling the number. I heard a phone ringing and found it in a rubbish bin. The idiot who'd dumped it hadn't cleared any of his personal information: photos, texts, Google account, calls made, calls received. He'd been the target of the raid and Reid had tipped him off."

"Do we take your word for this?"

After all, Reid was dead. Facing imprisonment, he'd shot himself. *Not my concern*, Hirsch thought, and he held his briefcase aloft. "If you like I can show you screenshots of Reid's phone and the phone I found in the bin."

"Surely you gave this material to an Internal Investigations officer? Sergeant DeLisle, were you shown any of this material?"

She was slightly behind Hirsch and he heard her cough and shift in her chair, and to save her he said loudly, "Things have a habit of getting lost."

This must have seemed like an escape route to Gaddis. With a smirk he said, "Lost by Sergeant DeLisle?"

"No, not by her, by others under your command."

The man with the unhealthy skin said, "Getting back to these CIB raids. What happened when Senior Sergeant Quine's team *did* recover drugs and valuables?"

"It was never properly logged, sir. Partial descriptions, under-reported quantities, that kind of thing."

"Did you come to any conclusions regarding this?"

"It's my belief Quine and his mates would keep a portion of the drugs and the valuables and later sell them."

"To the Comancheros."

"The Comancheros preferred the drugs over the diamonds."

Someone laughed. The grey-faced man said, "Do you have proof that the squad kept aside stolen items for sale?"

Here Hirsch squirmed a little. Quine was a powerful man inhabiting a seductive world, and when the personalities are compelling and the stakes high, when you're adrift in life, you can be seduced. Quine was clever, appealing, he ran rings around defense barristers and made headline arrests of genu-inely bad people, and Hirsch—isolated, marriage failing—had felt himself drawn to the man for a while.

But could he confess wrong without losing rightness? "I attended a raid in which a large amount of stolen jewelry was recovered. I was later handed a Rolex watch from that haul."

"Did you sell it?"

"No."

"Did you declare it to a senior officer?"

"No."

"You kept it."

"In my locker," Hirsch said. "I didn't know what to do about it, who to turn to."

"You did nothing?"

"I made a note for my own files," Hirsch said, waving his

briefcase again. "Time, date, personnel involved, serial numbers and so on."

"You held on to the watch."

"Yes."

"It was found months later when your locker was searched."

"Yes."

"Tying you effectively to the other members of the team."

Hirsch said nothing. Gaddis said, "So the others trusted you by this time?"

"Not entirely, but they'd stopped thinking about me. I mean they were less cautious around me. I was part of the furniture."

"In the first inquiry," the grey-faced man said, "Senior Sergeant Quine's barrister excuses some of the squad's actions as 'noble-cause' corruption. Would you care to comment on that?"

Hirsch curled his lip. "It's a weasel word for fabricating evidence in order to get a conviction in cases where you know someone's guilty but can't prove it."

"Did you see Senior Sergeant Quine fabricate evidence in order to secure a conviction?"

"He boasted of it."

The pale man said, "We have statements from other sources that Senior Sergeant Quine also misplaced evidence or concocted false statements in order to protect his informants or the criminals he did business with. Can you speak to that?"

Hirsch wasn't sure what was going on. Gaddis appeared furious with his colleague, but said nothing. And who these other sources were, Hirsch had no idea.

"Sorry, no."

The grey-faced man sat back, a little deflated, but said, "You got into the habit of keeping meticulous records while serving at Paradise Gardens?"

"Yes."

"What things did you record and how were they stored?"

"Photographs and audio recordings," Hirsch said. "Lists, copious lists."

"Of?"

"Businesses that offered freebies. The quantities of drugs or valuables seized on raids versus the quantities later listed at trial. Vehicle registrations. Phone numbers. Plus my own recollections of events: what was said and done, by whom, and where and when, together with my doubts and suspicions."

"No one saw you do this?"

"No."

"It must have been well-hidden."

Meaning, the raid on the station and on his house had not uncovered anything—except the Rolex. "I used an Internet storage site," Hirsch said.

Then he had to explain how the system worked, and was asked by Gaddis, "Did you ever store material written by Senior Sergeant Quine?"

"No."

"Tape recordings of the things he or his team said?"

"No."

"Why?"

"The squad was preternaturally suspicious and wary. They rarely communicated by phone, paper or electronic means."

"So your records are limited."

"Yes, but—"

"It has been shown that Senior Sergeant Quine invested in restaurants, bars, home units, racehorses, the share market . . . Do you have similar investments?"

"I have a ten-year-old Nissan," Hirsch said, which raised a bit of a snicker here and there.

Gaddis said, "Tell the members of this hearing about your involvement with Ms. Eliza Ley."

Asshole. Hirsch swallowed. "She's a lawyer."

"A *drug* lawyer."

"I didn't know that at the time."

Eliza Ley was simply a pretty but harried-looking barrister he'd seen around the courthouse or visiting remand prisoners

from time to time. They got to talking. Hirsch found her appealing in a scatty kind of way. The gutter press intimated that she
was appealing in a big-breasted kind of way, but Hirsch had liked
her for her mind, too. They met for drinks a few times and then
later for sex. He'd not known until it was too late who she was,
and tried to explain this now.

"You were slow on the uptake?" Gaddis said.

"Yes."

"Your wife left you as a result?"

"We'd left each other long before that," Hirsch said. "But she
did move out as a result."

Gaddis was enjoying himself. "So you shared a drug lawyer's
bed and knew nothing about her?"

"Not until warned by the Drug Squad," Hirsch said.

He'd been sitting in the pub, minding his own business,
when two senior Drug Squad detectives, venomous with it, slid
into the booth, bookending him. "Eliza Ley," one of them said.

"What about her?"

They told him: cops in her pocket, a drug-dealer boyfriend,
sleeping with Quine, too, and photos to prove it. "You're getting
sloppy seconds, mate," one of the detectives said.

Gaddis was saying, "And you expect us to believe that you had
no idea who this woman was and what she was doing?"

"Not until it was too late."

"What precisely did the detectives tell you?" asked the
grey man.

"They'd noticed a pattern. If one of her clients appeared on
a possession charge, Quine would go into bat for him, appear
in court saying, 'We've misplaced that evidence, your honor,' or
'We have no objection to bail in this matter, your honor.' Also,
they'd raid meth labs only to find no drugs or equipment or
cooks or dealers."

"They believed Senior Sergeant Quine was passing on information?"

"Pillow talk," was how one of the Drug Squad officers had

put it, squeezing Hirsch's upper leg under the table, fingers like steel clamps.

"When in fact it was *you* passing on information," Gaddis said.

"That's a lie."

"You were advised to drop Ms. Ley?"

"Yes."

"What did she do or say as a result?"

In all honesty, Hirsch felt Eliza had been a little hurt that he'd stopped returning her calls. But he didn't tell Gaddis that. He didn't say that he'd grown more vigilant, changing his locks, buying the little Beretta, obtaining a silent phone number and a new mobile. And he absolutely stopped drifting into the grey areas of police work. When his cousin had asked him to run a number plate, citing a traffic altercation, Hirsch had refused. He also refused to protect a school friend from an irate creditor—and just as well, for the friend had proved to be a cheat and a liar.

Gaddis said, "We have mobile phone records showing that you made several calls to drug dealers."

"I've explained that," Hirsch said. "Ms. Ley made those calls."

Gaddis sneered. "When your back was turned I suppose? Lots of things happen when your back is turned, don't they, Constable Hirschhausen."

CHAPTER 15

THAT WAS MONDAY AND Tuesday.

On Wednesday Gaddis returned to the Rolex.

"Why was the watch given to you, do you think?"

"To implicate me and to make me one of theirs."

"And were you? One of theirs?"

"No. In their minds, perhaps."

And yet Hirsch had shared some of the squad's contempt for the weak, partisan and unjust nature of the courts, judges, magistrates and the justice system. He felt some sympathy with the notion of taking shortcuts, bending the rules, to obtain justice. Or at least punish. The feeling of us against them, an instinct to belong, had grown in him.

"You didn't wear the watch?"

"No."

"It merely sat in your locker, ready to be found."

"Yes."

Officers from the Internal Investigations division had raided the Paradise Gardens police station right on the morning shift change, nabbing staff going off and on duty. Those on sick leave were apprehended at home. The building was cleared, locks changed, computers and files seized. Then the place was searched. Drugs were found in gym bags, guns in the ceiling cavities, bundles of cash in the air conditioning vents. Previously missing files, tapes and evidence bags were discovered under different case numbers.

"You could have declared it. It's now known that the officer in charge of Paradise Gardens was not involved in the corruption. You could have gone to Internal Investigations."

"I didn't know who to trust. I believed then and I believe now that elements in Internal Investigations are supportive of Senior Sergeant Quine."

Gaddis said and did nothing, a quality of stillness that seemed like fury to Hirsch.

"Instead you started babbling your innocence once the inquiry began."

The initial inquiry sat for ten months. Hirsch had turned over his records, starting with his taped conversations with Big Trev, the publican, who'd already been named during the inquest. Hirsch was gratified to learn that the Internals already knew most things—that his material mostly confirmed that knowledge. He felt less like a dog and a maggot, he supposed.

And one by one, Quine's crew went down, committed to stand trial, until only Quine and Hirsch were left. But things got dirty. Hirsch received late-night phone calls, gravelly voices asking were his mother, sister, niece, in good health? He found 9mm shells in his letter box. A truckload of cement was dumped in his driveway. Breathalyzed three times in one week.

Dirty in court, too. Quine's barrister cited the Rolex and accused him of holding a grudge, turning on the other squad members because he'd not received his fair share of the loot. Hirsch thought that a bit self-defeating, for it implied the barrister thought his client guilty, but no one else remarked on it and soon other accusations were thrown at him: failing to call witnesses, losing crucial evidence, accepting bribes and gifts, leaking to the media. And those phone calls to drug dealers, made using his phone.

Meanwhile Quine remained on his feet while his squad fell into disarray. Two constables were jailed, two were committed to stand trial, a senior constable was on the run and the constable named Reid had shot himself. The only good thing to come out of it was a kind of wisdom in Hirsch. He'd grown to understand that police officers can drift over time, and it isn't always or entirely conscious but a loss of perspective. Real and imagined grievances develop, a feeling that the job deserved greater and better public recognition. Rewards, for example, in the form of more money, more or better sex, a promotion, a junket to an interstate conference, greater respect in general. Some of these rewards were graspable, others the thwarted dreams that drove their grievances. Cynicism set it. The bad guys always got away with it, and the media seized on the police officer who took a bribe rather than the one who helped orphans. So why not take shortcuts and bend the rules?

"Are you paying attention, Constable Hirschhausen?"

Hirsch blinked. "Sir."

"You'd like us to believe that you were tainted because you were an innocent member of a corrupt squad? That you naively supported a corrupt senior officer, not knowing the full extent of his corruption?"

Hirsch was wary. It was coming now. "Yes."

Gaddis was wearing a dark blue suit with a pale blue shirt and mid-blue tie today, the tie knot a fat structure at the base of his skinny throat. He wore gold-rimmed glasses and they glinted. He was a spotless man and at odds with the grey-faced man, who was yet to speak this morning and looked washed-out, badly shaven and creased. He sat unmoving, but Gaddis was full of motion, taking a box from the floor and crossing the room to where Hirsch was seated.

He spilled the iPhone and the bundle of cash onto the table.

"These items were found concealed inside your private motor vehicle late last week. Perhaps you can account for them?"

Hirsch took out a pen and poked at the phone, then the cash. "Never seen these before."

Gaddis was delighted. "Oh, really? You expect us to believe that?"

Hirsch shrugged. "Believe what you like: I have never seen these items before."

"Have a closer look."

So Hirsch stabbed the home button of the phone a few times and the screen lit up. "An iPhone 4," he said. He was having fun but didn't show it. "They had antenna issues, from memory." He peered at it. "Seems to be stuck on the boot logo. Maybe I could sell it on eBay, get a few dollars for it."

"Stop arsing about. For your information that's an iPhone 5 that was last seen in the Paradise Gardens evidence safe, along with the cash."

"Really? This is the latest iPhone?" Hirsch twisted around in his seat. "Anyone got a five? Anyone?"

Amused, Rosie DeLisle crossed the room, proffering her phone. Hirsch compared them. "See? The five is longer and thinner. This is a four. Easy mistake to make."

He shot Rosie a look as he returned her phone: *Hope he doesn't take it out on you.* She smiled, went back to her seat, and Hirsch turned his attention to Gaddis, seeing an alteration in the boss. He was shooting glances at a man standing at the back of the room. The man disappeared.

Hirsch smiled at Gaddis. "I mean, your investigators did check the IMEI number, right? Checked the IMEI of this phone against the one that was supposed to be in the evidence locker?"

Strangling his words, Gaddis said, "I would have thought the first aid box a strange place to keep a phone and two and a half thousand dollars."

Hirsch shrugged. "Like I said, I have no idea what these items were doing in my car, if indeed they were there in the first place."

Gaddis waved a folder at him. "My officers conducted a proper search, every stage photographed and witnessed, with no breaks in the chain of custody."

"Oh," Hirsch said. "Fair enough. So you'd have a record of all the serial number of each hundred-dollar note?"

Gaddis didn't bite. He froze, then left the room, giving off a *someone's fucked up* air. The grey man contemplated Hirsch. Fidgeting and murmurs. Then Gaddis came back. He said, "Are you pulling a swiftie on us, Constable? A dishonest man must expect dishonesty in others. You thought you'd embarrass the department by swapping the phone and the cash?"

"Well, you do investigate devious people, sir," Hirsch said. He reached into the briefcase, took out his laptop. "Like the devious person on this bit of CCTV footage. It shows a woman opening my car and leaning in. Don't know who she is. Your daughter, sir? Did you put her up to it? She's got your thin nerviness."

AFTERWARDS ROSIE DELISLE GRABBED him.

"You are such a smartarse. Gaddis is furious. He thinks you swapped the phone and the money, but knows he can't prove it, yet also knows you were set up." She gave him a twist of her mouth. "You come out ahead, don't you? I assume the cash they found is yours? You'll keep the original cash, change the hundreds each time you buy something? And you get the latest iPhone?"

"We'll see," Hirsch said.

Rosie shrugged. "You could be bent. You've got the gene. And the stink isn't going away anytime soon."

"Fuck them," Hirsch said.

"Another day," Rosie said. "Someone I want you to meet."

She grabbed him by the forearm, dragged him to where the other woman hovered, glum and hostile. "Paul, this is Inspector Croome."

Hirsch went very still. Here was some fresh hell, coming on top of being grilled by Gaddis for three days. "Of?" he said. All things would flow from knowing which department Croome represented.

Croome's eyes were like pebbles but less humane. "Sex crimes."

Hirsch flinched. He'd had his share of confused and confusing sexual encounters, but didn't think he'd broken any laws.

Rosie took pity. Her pretty hand rested on his forearm. "We'd like you to stick around for another twenty-four hours."

"Is that a request?"

"Not entirely," Croome said.

"So, an order," Hirsch said.

"Something like that," Croome said, handing him a slip of paper. "Be at that address noon tomorrow. Don't tell anyone where you're going, don't let yourself be followed."

CHAPTER 16

THROUGH WITH HUMORING HIMSELF, Hirsch relinquished the original iPhone and $2500 to Rosie, together with his photographs of them *in situ*, obtained a written receipt, and returned to his motel.

The next day he took a succession of short taxi trips to the parking area of a strip of shops in Tea Tree Gully. Through a door marked MAINTENANCE and up a flight of stairs. Knocked on the only door at the top.

Rosie DeLisle answered, leading him into a sitting room decorated in 1970s motel. "Nice."

"No it's not."

"Safe house?"

"Yes."

Croome was standing by the window. "Sit, please, Constable."

There were armchairs and a sofa free but Hirsch chose a stiff chair from the little corner dining table. With a glance at each other, the women joined him. "Inspector Croome has a request," Rosie said.

"Why the cloak and dagger?"

"Things will move easier and quicker if you sit and listen and shut the fuck up," Croome said.

She still thinks I'm bent, or a bit deviated, Hirsch thought. He said, "Language," and folded his arms. "Fire away."

"You're stationed at Tiverton."

Hirsch said nothing. She hadn't asked a question, merely stated the bleeding obvious, since that was probably his personnel file in her lap. Croome shot a look at Rosie DeLisle as if wanting her to run interference.

"Paul," DeLisle said, leaning her slender elbows on the table.

"Yes?"

"The inspector would like you to tell us about Sergeant Kropp and his crew."

The anger came on quickly, as it often did these days, but Hirsch expressed it coldly, a withdrawal. He didn't move or speak or act. When he trusted himself he said, "I'm not a spy. I'm not a whistle-blower."

"No one's saying you are."

"Everyone's saying it. And you're about to ask me to blow the whistle."

"Paul," Croome said, not having earned the right to use his first name, "we have a situation and no means of monitoring it."

"But sex crimes? Kropp and his boys?"

"I'll explain in a minute," Croome said. She was a little disordered, as if she'd expected plain sailing. "First, do you think you could paint us a picture, for want of a better term?" She glanced at Rosie. "Internal Investigations have received several complaints about the Redruth police but what we lack is context."

Hirsch stared at her. "Before I say or do anything I need to know if either of you are acquainted in any way, shape or form with Kropp, Nicholson or Andrewartha, or the new woman, Jennifer Dee. No bullshit, okay?"

"No."

"Never served with them?"

"No."

"You're not a second cousin or ex-girlfriend or ex-academy buddy with any of them?"

"No."

He glanced at Rosie DeLisle. "You?"

"Never met them, Paul, never served with them, no relationship with them, however tenuous."

Hirsch chewed on his bottom lip

Croome said, "Please, Constable, it's very important."

Hirsch liked her better now, marginally. "I can give you local gossip, that's all."

Croome's face said she'd noted the fancy footwork. If he was merely repeating gossip, he wasn't a spy or a whistle-blower. "Fair enough."

Hirsch gathered himself. "Look, they're not popular. Arrogant, heavy-handed, and this is a sleepy country town. It could be argued that Kropp has been there too long, has networked his way into it so thoroughly and has so much power, he tends to think of the place as his."

"Like Quine?" Rosie said.

Hirsch nodded. "Like Quine." He considered his words: "Kropp needs order," he said, "but he and the others overdo it with unnecessary speed and drunk-driving traps, on-the-spot fines, screaming in people's faces even if all they'd done was jaywalk."

Then he recalled the way Nicholson and Andrewartha had talked about Melia Donovan and her brother, and their treatment of Jenny Dee. He cocked his head at Croome. "If you're a female or black you're probably a bit of a target."

They fell silent. *Is Kropp another Quine?* Hirsch wondered. He pictured the full, frothing intensity of Quine, the stamp of his unimaginable expertise, but couldn't quite match Kropp with that. By the same token, hard men like Quine and Kropp could be found in police stations all around the country.

"Care to elaborate?"

Hirsch's instinct was to shut up. Impressions were dangerous if there was no substance to them. But impressions were all he had. "I don't have hard facts. I don't know any teenage girls."

"Yes you do," Croome said, and Hirsch didn't like the way she said it. He waited.

"Melia Donovan and Gemma Pitcher."

Hirsch waited. Was the older man in Melia Donovan's life a local copper?

"Paul," Rosie said, "it's been alleged the Redruth officers demand sexual favors of young girls in return for dropping charges they might be facing. Minor charges like shoplifting, drunkenness, possession . . ."

"So if you could get a bit closer to your colleagues," Croome said, "you–"

Hirsch ignored her and flared at DeLisle. "The term 'false pretenses' comes to mind. I've helped you people enough. Consider this meeting over."

"Paul," said Rosie soothingly, "there's someone we'd like you to meet."

Croome got to her feet and entered a short corridor at the end of the room. She tapped on a door, cracked it open, stuck her head in. Hirsch heard murmurs and then she was standing back and making a *this way* gesture with one arm.

A teenage girl emerged.

"There's nothing to fear," Croome said, gently ushering the girl to the sofa and settling her into it. Rosie left the table and sat beside her, giving the girl a smile of warm brilliance, then Croome sat, and now Hirsch had the three of them staring at him from the sofa.

"Paul, I'd like you to meet Emily Hobba."

Hobba looked barely fifteen but might have been older. She was pretty in an unformed, second-glance way, with a kid's open round face, long brown hair falling from either side of a ragged center part. Her frame was thin, almost bony, inside a lilac T-shirt, a scrap of floral miniskirt and half a dozen clanking bangles. She caught him looking and immediately gave him a lopsided smile. Startled, he struggled not to return it. It wasn't quite neutral, that smile.

And as if she'd promptly forgotten him, Hobba took out a mobile phone and in seconds was working it, texting crazily with a faint grin. Hirsch glanced at Croome, then Rosie, raising an eyebrow. They shrugged minutely as if to say, *It's the way it is, nothing we can do about it.*

Rosie placed a hand on Emily's forearm. Long, tanned, slender fingers. Hirsch looked away from them, concentrated as she said, "Late last year, Emily got involved in a . . ." she hesitated ". . . scene involving some other young girls and a number of men."

Emily lifted her head and said clearly, eyes bright and clear, "Sex scene."

"Indeed," Rosie said.

"The men wore masks, we wore nothing."

Hirsch thought he should chip in. "Where was this?"

Emily shrugged. "Here and there. People's houses. I mean, I was totally wasted, you know? Out of it."

"She means Adelaide," Croome said. "Inner suburbs, outer suburbs."

"Sometimes the country," Hobba said, anxious to put her right. "We'd be picked up in this big car and stay away a couple of days. Everything laid on, party, party, party. I'd be that sore."

The country. Hirsch said, "Where in the country, Emily?"

"How would I know?"

Hirsch frowned at DeLisle and Croome. Croome said, "Tell Paul what you saw in the newspaper."

Hobba brightened. "Oh yeah. Okay. Well, you know that girl what got run over, I reckernized her."

"Melia Donovan."

"I reckernized her."

"She was at one of the parties in the country?"

"That's what I said."

"Who else was there?"

Bored, Hobba said, "There was this one other chick."

"Was her name Gemma?"

"Dunno. Maybe."

Croome interrupted. "Emily nearly died of an overdose after one of these weekend parties. Someone dumped her outside a hospital in the Barossa Valley. It threw a little scare into you, didn't it, Em? She told a counselor and the counselor contacted us."

Hirsch looked to the girl for confirmation. She shrugged and gave him a whisper of a bat of the eyelids.

"What was Gemma's role?"

"I dunno . . . Anal? Golden showers? She did what we did."

"I mean, was there any sense that she recruited Melia?"

"Nup."

"How many times did you attend the same party as Melia Donovan?"

"I dunno, it's a bit of a blur, maybe only once."

"When was this?"

"What's with all the questions? Don't you believe me? He doesn't believe me."

"Em, it's all right, he's come into this new, he needs to fill in the gaps."

"Well he can stop with the questions."

Croome said, "Emily, I know it's a long shot, a lot's happened, but if you saw photographs of the men who might have been involved, would you recognize body shape, bearing, body language, do you think?"

Emily gave a teenage shrug. "I was like totally out of it. I just have this feeling of like black masks over their eyes and this one guy wearing a uniform."

Croome and DeLisle stared at Hirsch as if to say, *Now can you see why we want your help?*

Hirsch said, "He arrived in a uniform? You caught only a glimpse of it?"

Emily snorted. "He wore it like the whole time, like rubbing our faces in it. I need the loo."

She leapt from the sofa and disappeared into a room off the hallway. Hirsch watched her go. "How did Emily get involved? Did someone recruit her?"

"A girl called Lily Humphreys, they were in a youth training programme together," Croome said. "Humphreys got out first, took Emily under her wing when she was released. What that boiled down to was, 'Would you like to party with these cool guys I know?' Emily said yes. They did this a few times over several months, city and rural locations. Sex, booze, cocaine, probably GHB. Then one day Emily wakes up in a hospital in the Barossa Valley, sore and torn and bruised. She mends slowly, but starts to have flashbacks. They scare her. She puts them together with the state of her body and confesses things to a counselor who then gets in touch with us."

"Flashbacks."

"Men wearing masks, someone getting rough with her and another telling him to go easy, things like that."

"So speak to Lily Humphreys."

"Disappeared."

"Disappeared as in she's probably lying dead somewhere, or disappeared as in address unknown?"

"The latter. Packed all her things and hopped on a plane to the Gold Coast, according to Emily."

"When?"

"While Em was in hospital."

"She got spooked."

"Yes."

"It would be worth checking to see if Gemma Pitcher was in youth training with either of them."

Croome smiled. "One step ahead of you. Humphreys and Pitcher were there at the same time, but before Emily's time."

Hirsch glanced at Rosie DeLisle. "Gemma's disappeared. I've done all I can to find her, you've got better resources than I have."

"Sure."

Hirsch nodded his thanks. "What about Emily's parents? Siblings?"

"Paul, we're talking ex foster kids who shared a flat, no one looking out for them."

Hirsch nodded gloomily. "When did you learn about her?"

"Three months ago. We didn't know where or how to start the investigation, and then a couple of days ago she texted me to say she'd recognized Melia Donovan's picture in the paper as one of the girls at the party."

Hirsch fetched out his phone. "I have a snap of Gemma Pitcher. I could show it to Emily."

"Good idea," Rosie said. Then she gave Croome a look. "She's been in the loo a while . . ."

Croome blinked. "Oh, fuck."

She raced away, and when they heard thumps and drama, Hirsch and DeLisle ran to investigate. They found the sex crimes inspector on the bathroom floor, slapping the teenager's face, shouting, "What did you take? Emily! Wake up! What did you take?"

Brushing her away feebly, Emily Hobba said, "Gerroff me."

CHAPTER 17

HIRSCH HEADED BACK TO the bush that evening, wondering how he could appear to pass on information about his colleagues without passing on information about them. His head ached.

Ached again on Friday, all that paperwork, so that a run out into the dry country east of Tiverton was a relief. Then Kropp called him. "A little bird tells me you came out of the Quine hearing smelling of roses. No flies on you. But given that you haven't been sacked or jailed, may I remind you that your presence is needed here tomorrow?"

"Crowd control, I remember. Football hooligans."

"Just get your arse down here for an eleven o'clock briefing."

SATURDAY. HIRSCH SHOWERED, PULLED on his uniform and strapped his baby Beretta to an ankle holster. He drove to Redruth. Kropp said, "Nice of you to join us, Constable Hirschhausen."

Hirsch checked his watch. 11 A.M. "Am I late, Sarge?"

"In this job, on my watch, you arrive *early*."

"I'll remember that, Sarge," said Hirsch, giving Nicholson a winning grin. Andrewartha was there, and Dee, but Kropp had also brought in two constables from Clare: Revell and Molnar. Big men, stony, full of dim menace.

"Gents," said Hirsch with a wink.

"Stop arsing around and take a seat," Kropp said.

He'd pinned seven photographs to the board, head-and-shoulders shots of five white and two Aboriginal men. Four of the seven were young, three in early middle age. Sullen faces mostly, full of hard-won experience, men whose work, education, relationship and financial histories were paltry or nonexistent. Kropp's view of them was simple: slapping their faces with the flat of his pointer he said, "Behold the enemy."

Maybe so, thought Hirsch, *but how far removed are they from guys like Nicholson and Andrewartha?* Kropp's constables were just as young, poorly educated and lacking in work and life experiences. Equally clannish and suspicious of diversity. Attracted to police work because it's inward-looking, secretive and protective. And it licenses the art and craft of thumping other human beings.

"As I was saying, Constable Hirschhausen."

Hirsch blinked. "Loud and clear, Sarge."

"As I was saying, these magnificent specimens of Australian manhood are a nuisance when sober and an absolute nightmare when they get on the grog. Stir in a football premiership . . ."

And you get blood and broken glass.

"We have some long hours ahead of us, but I've secured overtime. Best-case scenario, the night proves to be a fizzer, but last year we had a glassing that resulted in permanent blindness in one eye, a full-on brawl in the Woolman, resulting in hospitalization, and a fatality when some kids had a drag race just out past the motel."

Here Kropp's voice cracked a little. Hirsch was curious. The guy seemed genuine, rising on his toes as he spoke, lifted by his emotions, as if the town were his and he its civilizing force.

Yeah, well, the Redruth sergeant was also a template for the hard men who ran fiefdoms around the state, men who'd turn evasive, verbose and arrogant if you tried to pin them down. But clever men, a witness-box headache to every judge, magistrate and defense and prosecution barrister in the land. How long had Kropp been here? Twelve years?

Kropp slapped the pointer down and folded his arms. "Questions? No, well get to it then."

Hirsch glanced at his watch: almost noon. The game wouldn't start until early afternoon, allowing time for a quick lunch. He glanced at Dee and mimed eating. She nodded.

"Aww," said Nicholson, catching it, "the first blush of young love."

Dee ignored him but went pink, looked down as she gathered her things.

Andrewartha got in on the act. Working a concerned frown onto his face he said, "I hope you're sexually responsible, Constable Hirschhausen. For your convenience, a protective sheath dispenser has been installed in the men's room."

"Nah," Nicholson said, "our boy likes to *feel* it."

"Then he's in for a disappointment," Andrewartha said. "Word is, he'll find a lack of tactile integrity, if you get my meaning."

"Totally do," Nicholson said. "She overused it at the academy."

"Yep."

"Look at Hirschhausen, cracking the shits."

"You're so funny," Dee said.

"We think so."

These clowns, Hirsch thought, *deserve to be informed on.*

AN HOUR LATER HE was patrolling the Redruth oval listlessly, watching for hotheads, just as he'd done years ago, a raw cadet.

Except he hadn't come full circle, exactly. For a start, here in the world of small towns and farms, the spectators were few and did their drinking and fuming in private, cocooned in cars parked snout up to a white perimeter fence. Once in a while a door would open and the occupant woud raise the tailgate or boot to rummage for another can of beer, but other than that they might have been at a church picnic. He recognized some of the Tiverton locals, including the Muirs, Tennant and Ray Latimer, who was there with his sons and a solid-looking older man. The boys' grandfather? Horns tooted desultorily, a woman knitted a baby's jacket, a man sipped Thermos tea, a dog pissed on a car tire.

When the wind came up, whipping a scarf from a car aerial, Hirsch retrieved it and handed it to the kid seated at the wheel.

"Thanks."

He peered in at the boys in the back. "Nathan?"

Melia Donovan's brother looked hunted, his dark eyes liquid in his dark face. The boy beside him was on Kropp's watch list. Sam Hempel sat beside the driver.

Hirsch straightened his back, saluted. "Enjoy the game."

"Yeah."

Hirsch turned to go and saw Andrewartha watching him.

"That figures—mates with the boongs."

Hirsch winked. "I'll put your name down for sensitivity training, shall I?"

"Fuck off."

Time dragged. Hirsch's feet hurt. The game didn't interest him even though the score was close, each side kicking too few goals, too many points. With halftime due, he headed for a van parked inside the main gate and bought four spring rolls. The woman who served him was Thai; he watched her fry the rolls in a spitting pan. Then the siren sounded and people poured from their cars, forming a line at the van window, a pulsing pressure point. Hirsch watched tensely, but nothing happened, the queue was orderly. The Latimers appeared, Jack giving Hirsch a tiny wave, Raymond a glare. The older boy was plump and hangdog, trying to appear unattached.

Then Kropp arrived in a police car, pulling up behind the Thai food van. He got out, bent his solid back into the rear

compartment, emerged with uncooked spring rolls and pack-
aged paper cups and plates. Hirsch watched him hand the bags
to the woman in the van, plant a kiss on her cheek and wave
goodbye. But he took his time leaving, striding like a general
down the queue of spectators, winking, geddaying, giving the
evil eye, shaking hands with Ray Latimer, ruffling Jack's hair.

Dee materialized at Hirsch's elbow, small and perky in her
uniform. "What would you call that? Crowd management?
Improving public relations?"

"Constable, please, a little respect. But who's the woman,
that's the real issue."

"Wife? Girlfriend?"

"Nice little sideline," Hirsch said.

"The woman or the spring rolls?"

AT THE FINAL BELL, Redruth was four points ahead and Hirsch
broke up a shoving match. Dee's shins were sprayed by spurting
gravel as she dodged an irate station wagon. Andrewartha got
into the face of a screeching woman. Nicholson and the other
constables whisked a man to the lockup.

And then it was all over. The scarf knitter and the old tea
drinker and the tired farming families were gone, leaving
only wrappers tumbled like scrapping birds as the wind rose.

"Don't get your hopes up," Kropp said, reappearing in his
police car. "Consider this the lull before the storm. By nine
or ten o'clock the troublemakers will be spoiling for a fight.
Meanwhile, grab yourselves a quick bite and then start making your presence felt."

Free hamburgers from the town's Greasy Joe, and at six
o'clock they split into two units and began to prowl the streets,
pubs and through roads of the town, Hirsch, Nicholson and
Revell in one car, Andrewartha, Dee and Molnar in the other.

Hirsch was happy to sprawl in the backseat and let Nicholson
drive. Up and down the streets, in and out of the town's three
pubs and car parks. The streetlights were barely adequate; few

cars were about. Hirsch wondered if life that evening was being lived on the side streets, behind drawn curtains, for the pubs were quiet. He felt he was encroaching whenever he entered a main bar or a lounge bar. Heads would turn away, registering not him but his uniform. It was an odd, alien feeling, standing on the sidelines while people enjoyed themselves.

At 8 P.M. he wandered through the Wheatsheaf Hotel while Nicholson and Revell had words with some kids hanging around the bottle shop. Ray Latimer was seated in a booth with a woman not his wife. She was tiredly pretty, dressed in black. Guessing that Latimer had sent his sons home with his old man, Hirsch nodded and returned to the car.

At 8:30 his mobile chirped.

"Hello?"

"*Mr. Hirsch . . .*"—the voice stumbled—"*. . . Hirsch . . . hawsen.*"

"Yes?"

"*This is The Dugout, concerning your eight o'clock booking.*"

"Sorry?"

"*Table for twelve, eight o'clock.*"

"I don't understand," said Hirsch, who did.

"*One of our busiest nights of the year. I'm afraid when you didn't show we allocated that table to another party.*"

"I'm afraid you've been duped."

"*We cannot issue a refund, I'm afraid.*"

"Forgive me," Hirsch said, "but I did not make a table booking. Someone is duping you."

"*You gave this mobile number. Party of twelve, eight o'clock, a twenty-dollar deposit.*"

Hirsch shook off the caller and pocketed the phone. "Trouble?" Nicholson wanted to know.

"Twenty bucks?" said Hirsch. "You guys wasted twenty bucks on me?"

"What are you on about?"

Hirsch folded his arms, got comfortable there in the backseat. "Didn't cost me anything, cost you twenty bucks."

❖ ❖ ❖

THE HOURS LENGTHENED. THE radio crackled from car to car, car to base, base to car. Hirsch glimpsed the other patrol car sometimes, outside a pub, nosing down a street. Otherwise he dozed. He'd been awake since dawn, his stomach heavy with the spring rolls and the hamburger. He wriggled to get comfortable. He'd had enough of this, the blanketing night air, the dew and the tricky half-light. Something had queered it for him—not here in the patrol car, exactly, but just out of range, in among the shadows. He supposed he was waiting for violence.

Nicholson and Revell talked while he dozed:

"How long's the sheila been with you?"

"Dee?" said Nicholson. "Couple of weeks."

"Nice tits."

"Get her pissed she might flash them for you."

"Is it true, she did the whole academy?"

"Top to bottom."

"Top *and* bottom."

The tires grumbled beneath them in the night.

Revell fished out his wallet. "Ten bucks says I do her before you do."

"Dork."

"I mean it," Revell said. "I saw the way she was looking at me."

Nicholson shook his head. "Let's make it interesting: who'll give her the first anal, first facial, first golden shower."

"You're on."

"Except are we sure she's worth ten?"

"Point," Revell said. He turned to Hirsch. "You in?"

"I don't gamble."

Revell stared at him a moment, turned away. "Scumbag."

They fell silent. The radio crackled, suspicious noises reported at 5 Truro Street. The car climbed out of the main street and up onto one of the town's little hills, where stone houses slumbered behind oleanders and ghost gums cracked the footpaths.

The old copper mine was a dark excavation on the adjacent hill, moonlight flaring on the depthless black water and pushing gantry and chimney shadows down the hill. The wind was higher here, a helpless whine in the pine trees. Revell got out, knocked, no answer.

He returned to the car. "No one in."

"Okay, shove a card under the door."

Hirsch stirred at last. "Shouldn't we check around the back?"

"Oh, it speaks," Nicholson said. "The place is dead, all right? Got better things to do."

"Let me check," said Hirsch, climbing out.

"Fucking Boy Scout."

Breathing in scented air from the garden beds, Hirsch strode through the gate to the side path and down it to the backyard. He was reminded of Grandma Hirschhausen's garden in Burnside, neatly cropped lawns, pansy beds, ivy trellis, a geranium in a cracked teapot, rotary clothesline. The screen door was ajar, a weak spill of light over the concrete steps, and just inside it, lumpy on the lino floor, her top half caught in the smashed glass that was the inner door, lay an old woman. Her stockings were this way and that and blood was pooling. *Tripped*, he thought, and a neighbor heard the glass break and alerted the police.

He called for an ambulance and a moment later a voice came through the darkness: "Yoo-hoo."

Hirsch headed for the side fence, where there was some light. "Yes?"

An old man's creaky voice said, "Is Crystal all right?"

"She had a fall. I've called the ambulance."

"That's good." Pause. "You're new."

"Temporary assignment. I'm stationed at Tiverton."

"I try to look out for Crystal," the neighbor said, "but it was dark and I suppose things are a bit rowdy tonight and I didn't want one of those policemen shouting at me for wasting his time."

A wobbly challenge in the voice, daring Hirsch to doubt him.

"My colleagues shout at people?"

"Great shouters. Quick to breathalyze you, too."

Hirsch returned to the old woman. Her breath was fluttery, her pulse slow, but he didn't think she was dying. But she would have if it had been down to Nicholson, the lazy shit. He heard a siren, went out to greet the ambos, just as a call came in: all officers, a brawl outside the Woolman. Well, he'd have to walk. Nicholson and Revell had abandoned him.

He was halfway down the street when he turned back. "If it's on the way, can you guys drop me off at the Woolman Hotel?"

"Yeah, sure, done, too easy," the ambulance driver said.

"You might even pick up some business," Hirsch said.

OWING TO THE BRAWL, the ambulance officers set him down on the opposite side of the town square. As Hirsch crossed it, passing the rotunda, where a couple of kids were sharing a bottle, he could hear shouts, see a jostling crowd, figures straggling away among parked cars.

Reaching the footpath, Hirsch broke through. Nicholson and Revell were back-to-back between two indistinguishable gangs of young men and women. Half crouched, batons extended, they were lunging and retreating, screaming, *Break it up, break it up.*

"Evening, gents."

"Took your sweet fucking time."

Hirsch waved his baton at one ragged clump and then the other. Derision greeted it, the women screeching, the men full of spit and jutting chests.

Just then Nicholson charged, shouting "Got you." Bodies retreated and a kid, backpedaling with Nicholson in his face, sprawled onto his coccyx. He cried out, and Hirsch recognized him: Nathan Donovan. Nicholson laughed. He began to strike the boy, landing meaty thumps with his baton. Revell joined him, booting Nathan's spine.

Nicholson paused, telling Revell, "I've got this. You go after his mates."

"Gotcha," Revell said. He lumbered away, down the side of the pub, not quite at a run and too heavy for it.

Just as Nicholson readied himself for another swing of the baton, Hirsch grabbed his arm. "That's enough."

"What?"

"You've made your point."

Nicholson shook him off. The mob didn't like it either. Raw voices called to Nicholson, "*Get the cunt.*"

"*Fucking Abo, smash his head in.*"

"*Fuck him up good, the black cunt.*"

Hirsch selected the brawniest Redruth local, a kid of twenty, and charged him, windmilling his baton, up into the groin.

The kid doubled over. His mates were shocked. "What did you do that for?"

"Piss off home," Hirsch said. "It's over for the night."

"Nikko," they said, "tell your mate to leave us alone."

Hirsch lunged; they retreated. One by one, they straggled away into the night.

He returned to Nicholson, who had a knee in Nathan's back, screaming into the boy's face, "You gunna behave?"

Hirsch grabbed again. "I said leave him alone."

Nicholson jerked away. "Get your hands off me."

"Let him go."

Nicholson stood. They were panting, Nathan prone on the ground. "You better have a fucking good reason . . ."

"There was no need to lay into him like that."

"Big fucking deal. You saw it, disturbing the peace, assaulting a police officer, inciting a riot."

"I didn't see that. They were retreating," Hirsch said. "There was no actual fighting, nothing damaged." He bent and hauled on Nathan's arm. "Up you get."

The boy complied, wincing.

"You okay?" Hirsch asked, seeing scrapes, a bleeding nose.

"Had worse from that bastard."

"Can you get home okay?"

Nathan shrugged.

"A lift with your mates, perhaps? Have they been drinking?"

"No."

"Off you go."

Nicholson was disgusted. "A true legend."

Hirsch ignored him. He could hear strained shouts in the night, disembodied and far away. He saw movements like tricks of the light, far back in the shadows. All of the tension had leaked away, and then Revell came stumbling in from the dark, holding an injured right hand, blood dripping from his elbow. Sounding astounded he said, "I went and fucking cut myself."

"What happened?"

"I need stitches, I think."

Hirsch fished for a handkerchief and pressed it against a gash in the man's palm. "What happened."

"Get off me," Revell said, jerking away. He shook his head. "Cut myself on a piece of roofing iron. Me best jerking-off hand."

Nicholson's disgust grew. "Another moron." He paused, computing rapidly. "This is what happened. We broke up a brawl. Someone pulled a knife and slashed you with it. He got away. Too dark and confusing to see who it was."

He shoved his chest at Hirsch's. "Are we agreed on that version of events, *Cunt*stable?"

Hirsch shrugged. "Whatever you like, but I don't see where it gets us."

"It gets our mate ten thousand bucks compensation, that's what."

"Hey, yeah," Revell said.

"No skin off my nose," Hirsch said.

"So long as we're on the same page."

They drove to the hospital, deeply fatigued now. The streets were deserted. The car made the hill climb quietly; even the radio was muted. Hirsch was lost to dreams, sprawled across the backseat in his regular position.

"Will they buy it?" Revell asked at one point. Hirsch barely heard him; had his eyes closed.

"Piece of cake," Nicholson said.

"Voice of experience."

"I'll tell you a story," Nicholson said. "I was with this chick, my car, she's driving—and she prangs it."

"Yeah, so?"

"Mate, no license."

Revell's light switched on. "You said you were the driver."

"Give the man a cigar."

IT WASN'T MUCH OF a hospital but performed minor procedures and offered a few beds. Sometimes kids were born here, and there was a small nursing home wing. Tonight McAskill and another of the town's doctors and handful of nurses were stretched to the limit, so the three policemen waited. The waiting room full, they leaned against a wall of the main corridor. A tiny surgery bustled at the end; neon lights buzzed; the white walls were blinding. Four men and a teenage girl were already seated in the plastic chairs outside the surgery, holding their heads in misery or pain. Some blood was evident, soaking through bandages. Nicholson loved it. He was like Kropp with the local populace: he strode up and down, full of badgering mirth, knowing them all by name.

Eventually Revell came out, bandaged, pale and grinning. "Good as new."

"About fucking time."

They drove down to the square, through pockets of waist-high night mist. Dew glistened on parked cars and here and there broken glass glinted in the gutters. Hirsch felt hollowed out. "Can't we pack it in? The town's dead."

"Not yet, boss's orders."

Hirsch closed his eyes. The tires rumbled through the night. Then the radio crackled: "*Get over to the motel, possible drunk and disorderly.*"

Nicholson swung the wheel and planted his foot. The town dwindled behind them and on its shadowy outskirts a Budget sign came into view. Nicholson slowed to a crawl, casting an eye over the cars parked in the motel grounds. Standard police procedure. Hirsch himself had done it a million times. It was like breathing. The place looked dead. He closed his eyes again.

Snapped them open when his tired mind caught up. The police car was adjacent to the motel entranceway and a pair of headlights was hurtling at them from inside the grounds. He cried out involuntarily. The other car struck where his left shoulder had been resting. He felt shocked, his head full of the percussive sounds and his fright.

A ticking silence, broken by Revell: "The cunt's only gone and run into us."

They got out, Hirsch obliged to scoot across to the other door. He blinked to clear his head, rubbed his sore shoulder, then shuffled around to inspect the damage. It had been an almighty bang, but all he could see was a Honda with a broken headlight and dented bumper, and the dented rear door of the police car.

Meanwhile Revell was jerking the Honda driver out of his car. "Bloody moron. You realize you hit a police car?"

"What?"

"Been on the grog, is that it? Judgement impaired?"

"What?"

The driver struggled, gaining focus, and Hirsch saw who it was. "Mr. Latimer?"

Ray Latimer, ignoring him, tried to attract Nicholson's attention: "Nick? Nikko?"

"Don't fucking move," Revell said. He turned to Nicholson. "You know this bozo, Nick?"

"Who you calling a bozo?" Latimer said, shrugging him off.

"Sir, stay where you are."

"I'm not at fault. Why the hell did you stop there? How was I supposed to avoid you?"

"Sir, I need you to calm down."

"I am calm."

Latimer craned his head around Revell's bulky shoulder. "Nick, for fuck's sake."

Nicholson had been standing back as if hoping it would all go away. He shook his head, disgusted, and came closer. "It's okay, he's not going to do anything silly."

"Tell this prick to get his hands off me," Latimer said.

"You're dreaming," Revell said.

"Fuck you."

"Just calm down, Ray, all right?" Nicholson said.

"I am fucking calm."

Nicholson, still disgusted, turned to Hirsch and gestured at the cars. "Don't just stand there, get this mess sorted."

"All over it," Hirsch said, reaching into the police car for the camera. He started snapping.

"The fuck are you doing?"

"For the insurance. For the report."

"Don't be a moron, just clear the bloody driveway, all right?"

"Keep your shirt on."

Hirsch climbed into the Honda, reversed it a few meters, metal shrieking, and got out. Suspecting radiator damage, he lifted the hood. The radiator had been pushed closer to the fan, but wasn't touching. No leaks. He took more shots with the camera, then photographed the damage to the police car. One of the rear panels was buckled and seemed to be touching the tire.

Finally he backed the Honda into a slot outside an empty unit, his attention caught by a spill of light from a neighboring doorway, then another, and another: guests, peering out at the racket. Catching his gaze, they retreated, curtains twitching.

One guest didn't. She stepped out of the light and crossed the dewy lawn in bare feet, wrapped in a bulky motel robe. Hirsch recognized her as the woman who'd been drinking with Latimer in the Wheatsheaf.

Closing in on the men at the street entrance, she called, "Ray?"

Latimer stiffened, slumped. "Oh, Christ. Finola, please, go back inside."

She stopped. "What's wrong? What happened?"

"Tell you later. Please, Fin, just go inside."

She came closer. "Did you have an accident?"

Hirsch pocketed the Honda keys and intercepted her, touched her forearm. She flinched. "Let's leave them to it," he said.

The tension went out of her and she let herself be turned around and guided back across the lawn to her doorway. *Number 6*, noted Hirsch. Behind them, the three men were shouting now:

"*Not fucking drunk.*"

"Sir, will you consent to—"

"*I was barely moving when I hit you. Get off me.*"

"Ray, I need you to blow into this."

Hirsch saw the woman into the room and hovered at the door. The interior was generic and held no interest, but the bed was a mess, an empty champagne bottle neck first in a bucket of ice. He turned his attention to the woman, who perched dejectedly on the end of the bed. A tousled forty, with a pretty but sundried face, the face of someone deeply fatigued or a drinker with her good looks accelerating downhill. An outdoors woman, he guessed, her tanned skin dark against the white of the dressing gown. The gown gaped; she was naked under it. Her clothes were heaped on a chair. As if reading him, she pulled the toweling close around her breasts and knees. Girlfriend? Pick-up?

"He was going out to find a bottle shop."

Hirsch nodded. Latimer's shouting had escalated, and she glanced past Hirsch, gnawing her lip.

"May I know your name?"

"Finola. Finola Armstrong."

The name rang a bell. "From Bitter Wash Road?"

"How did you know?"

"Have you been drinking, Finola?"

"I'm not much of a drinker." She paused. "What's that got to do with anything?"

"You might need to drive him home."

She looked at the floor. "What a god-awful mess."

"Are you okay to drive? Can I call someone to come and get you?"

"No! God no. Look, does anyone have to know about this? Can you leave my name out of it? I haven't done anything wrong."

"I'll see what I can do."

"His wife left him, you know. Moved in with her parents."

"I know."

"You know? How?"

Hirsch shrugged.

"I forgot—you're all mates. Do you need a statement?"

"Brief one."

Hirsch took it, then gave her the Honda keys and returned to the street. Latimer was swinging punches now, hitting nothing, Nicholson and Revell struggling with him, shouting at him.

Spotting Hirsch, Nicholson snarled, "For Christ's sake move our car out of the way."

"Don't know if it's drivable. Look."

They looked at the edge of the rear panel, resting against the tire. "Fuck."

Some of the bleariness went out of Latimer. He'd noticed Hirsch at last. "Look who's here."

Hirsch nodded hello. "Mr. Latimer."

Latimer shot out his fist. Hirsch swayed neatly away, too late, the hard knuckles spending their energy on his cheekbone.

He rubbed it. "Ouch. You want to explain that?"

Latimer took a boxer's stance, Revell jerking him back. "Moron." He glanced at Hirsch. "Well?"

Hirsch sighed. "Raymond Latimer," he said, and ran through the formal arrest statement while Latimer struggled and Revell swore.

"Do you understand these charges, Mr. Latimer?"

"You're arresting me?"

"Mate, it's already done," Revell said. "Weren't you listening? You've been arrested. You're spending the night in the lockup."

Meanwhile Nicholson was shaking his head. He scraped both palms down his cheeks tiredly. "How do we get him there if we can't fucking drive?"

"The others can come and collect us," Revell said.

Hirsch might have been invisible and irrelevant. He walked back across the lawn, knocked on the door to Number 6. Finola Armstrong had changed into her black dress.

"Mr. Latimer's been arrested."

"That figures. This's such a mess."

"He'll spend the night in the lockup. Without meaning to pry, what's your relationship with him? Will you stay the night and take him home in the morning? Go home and return for him? Let his family deal with it?"

Armstrong flushed. "That's really none of your business."

"Your headache, not mine."

Hirsch rejoined Nicholson and Revell, who had a hand on each of Latimer's elbows, Latimer trying to shake them off and shouting, "How about you call Bill Kropp, he'll sort this out."

"How about we add another charge, interfering with a police officer in the execution of his duty," Revell said.

"Fuck you."

Out of the night came a pair of headlights and a whooping siren, the other patrol car rocketing alongside them, tires scraping the curb. The passenger side window whined down and Andrewartha leaned out, full of humor. "Evening, gents."

"What took you so long?"

"Busy."

"Doing what?"

De Marco exchanged a grin with Molnar, the driver. "Showing Dee Dee the town."

Hirsch went still. He peered in. The backseat was empty. "What've you done with her?"

"Oh, she's on official police business," said Andrewartha, helping to bundle Latimer into the rear of the car. Nicholson and Revell climbed in after him, Nicholson winding down his rear window to say, "You stay with our car, okay? See if you can get it moving."

"Shouldn't I—"

No one wanted to hear what Hirsch thought he should or shouldn't do. He was alone, the road deserted and not much light leaking from the motel now. The street lighting was dim out here, blurred by mist. With a shrug, he returned to the police car and tugged on the lip of metal, feeling it move. A gap opened, he ran his hand along the surface of the tire. No damage.

Then he called Dee, and her voice in the barren night was far off and frightened. "Hey."

"Hey yourself. Where are you?"

"Middle of nowhere. Those pricks just left me here."

"Where? I'll come and get you."

He heard sounds on her end of the line: a squeaky gate, a knock on a door, murmurs. Then her voice was loud in his ear: "Apparently it's easier if I give directions rather than a street address . . ."

A minute later, Hirsch was heading northeast, crossing the dark town to a road signposted for Morgan, a town on the Murray River, on the far side of saltbush plains. Hirsch wasn't going that far. A hundred meters down it, he turned off. There were no pretty stone houses out here. This was a hardscrabble fringe, where people struggled on a couple of hectares of undernourished dirt, fibro dwelling and starved pets. Midnight and the sky was densely black. His headlights picked out Dee beside a rusty fence. She climbed in. "Thanks."

Hirsch planted his foot, headed back to the empty streets of the town. "What's the story?"

After a while she said, "Sex."

"Sex."

"Sex, sexism and sexual harassment."

"Okay," Hirsch said, drawing the word out.

"I can deal with the innuendos and crude suggestions. I had it all through training. But they wanted to have it off with a kid."

"How old?"

"About fourteen, pissed out of her tiny brain when we picked her up. When I say 'we,' Andrewartha nabbed her for jaywalking. Has anyone been charged with that in living memory?"

"In this town, yeah," Hirsch said.

"She was with a gang of kids, all of them a bit drunk but not doing anyone any harm. Andrewartha's plan was he and Molnar should take her home while I stayed behind and kept an eye on the friends."

She paused. "You should have seen the look on her face. And her mates. Fear, pure and simple."

"They knew what would happen."

"I'd say so."

Hirsch circled the town square, the lights misty and no movement anywhere.

"So I said no way, I was coming too, and when we got to her house I walked her to the door and checked someone was home." She snorted. "That's when they pissed off and left me."

Hirsch told her a little of his night. He was driving slowly; they were cocooned together in the warmth of the car. Out past the mine, back to the square, out past the motel. No sign of Finola Armstrong's Honda. Time dragged. The town was dead.

Presently Dee said, "You do know that I know who you are."

"Yep."

"So is this the new you or the real you?"

"Time will tell."

They lapsed into silence. Hirsch drove. And then at one o'clock in the morning, Sergeant Kropp came crackling over the radio: "Okay, boys and girls, call it a night."

❧ ❧ ❧

BACK AT THE STATION, Kropp took Hirsch aside and whispered fiercely, "The fuck you arrest Ray Latimer for?"

Hirsch had had enough. "So if your mates break the law they're allowed to get away with it?"

"That's not what I meant. He didn't have to spend the night in the lockup."

"Do him some good, Sarge. And it was Nicholson and the others who put him there. All I did was arrest him."

Kropp shook his head as if seeing life in all its stupidity. "The magistrate has offered to hear it at ten tomorrow morning."

Hirsch winced. Kropp smirked. "That's what you get for being the arresting officer."

"Sarge."

As if it pained him to say it, Kropp muttered, "We generally have a few beers after an operation."

Operation. "Great," lied Hirsch.

THEY FOUND NICHOLSON AND the others in the tearoom, herding Dee into a corner. "Come on, love, no hard feelings, stay and have a couple of drinks with us."

"In your dreams," Dee said.

"Don't be like that. You need to wind down, right? We've even got a bottle of woite woine in the fridge, if that's your fancy."

"Fuck off and goodnight," Dee said, inclining her head to drag the band from her ponytail, shaking her head to free the hair, free it to swing around her neck and over her cheeks, and at that moment, Hirsch knew he'd seen that precise set of movements in the recent past.

He reached out a hand. "You . . ." he said, wanting to say, *It was you who placed that stuff in my car.*

He didn't. She gave him a curious look and a smile half of gratitude for looking after her and then was gone out the door.

"Bitch," Nicholson said.

HIRSCH DISCOVERED THAT HE had a bottle in his hand. The hours passed and the Redruth policemen sprawled, bottles, pizza crusts and cigarette butts accumulating on the floor and the tearoom table. Two o'clock, three, the air so heavy, thick and male you could cut it with a knife. When the chairs couldn't hold them they slumped on the floor and sang "*We will, we will, rock you*." Nicholson and Kropp arm wrestled, tipping the table. The phone rang unattended in the front office. Andrewartha found a stash of pornographic DVDs and Hirsch watched, absorbed for about thirty seconds, the others slightly longer, catcalling the porn stars. They lapsed into talk and long pauses, then more talk, the pornography a forgotten flicker in the background. When the beer ran out, Kropp staggered to his car, returning with three six-packs. Ring-pulls tinkled, the cans foamed. It was the music of policemen winding down while a town sleeps.

And the others would say, "Drink up."

Hirsch would say, "Cheers."

The others would say, "Piker."

Hirsch had played this game before. He knew the moves. He swigged, burped, swiped his mouth with the back of his hand. He roared and laughed through until four in the morning, and presently the others forgot who he was, forgot his story.

In those deep hours, people will come and go, you'll scarcely register their movements, you'll lose track, but at some point it occurred to Hirsch that Nicholson and Andrewartha were gone, the pikers.

So he struggled to his feet. "Time for some shut-eye."

"The night is young," snarled Revell.

"It is somewhere, I'll grant you that," Hirsch said, grabbing his cap and his jacket and the belt load of crime fighting gear that threatened to do his back in. "Night, night, gentlemen."

Kropp waved a bottle at him. "Get your arse back here in time for court."

"Will do."

A COLD, STILL, SILENT, dampish pre-dawn, with dew beading the HiLux. Hirsch climbed in and worked the wipers and fired the ignition, then drove back through the square and out to the edge of the town with an agricultural rattle, the motor as stupefied as he was. He passed the Overlander Hotel, an antique store and two bed-and-breakfast joints, the high school, the latter arousing a mental picture of Wendy Street. He thought about Constable Dee. He thought about his love life, which had slipped away when it all went wrong for him.

NICHOLSON AND ANDREWARTHA BUSHWHACKED him on a slow, blind bend between Mt. Bryan and Tiverton, flicking into his slipstream from a concealed farm gate, giving the siren a bit of a whoop. Hirsch pulled over, switched off, powered his window down. "Guys."

Andrewartha grinned, waving a breathalyzer tube at Hirsch. "We have reason to believe, etcetera."

Hirsch feigned an itchy ankle to retrieve and pocket the little Beretta. A desolate spot out here, the highway a black ribbon, the moon pushing shadows across the valley. Dawn was staining the horizon and there'd be early farmers and interstate truckies pretty soon, but Hirsch wasn't taking comfort from that. How would they play it? *We stopped him for driving under the influence and he just went crazy.*

But first they had to arrest him and take his service pistol. Andrewartha's face-splitting grin said he knew Hirsch's breathalyzer reading would top .05. "If you would blow into this, please, sir. We need a steady, continuous exhalation, think you can manage that?"

"Right across it," Hirsch assured him, beginning to blow.

"Give it all you've got, pisspot," Nicholson said.

Andrewartha retrieved the tube for testing, still with his killer grin. The grin faded. He shook the tube as if it were a thermometer. "I don't fucking believe it."

"Point oh nothing?" Hirsch asked sweetly.

"We're conducting the test again."

Hirsch complied. He said, "Maybe both units are faulty. Maybe we should go back to the station and take a blood sample."

Andrewartha waited for half a dozen sour beats. "Just fuck off home."

Hirsch turned the key and drove sedately toward Tiverton. The patrol car trailed him for a few kilometers, a disconsolate white speck, until it turned off and Hirsch saw the red rear lights as it sped south again. A hint of the sun out east and Hirsch thought of Wendy and Katie Street out there, the sun touching them before it touched him. He thought of the tearoom back at Redruth, the sink, the pot plants, drowned in beer when no one was looking. "One step ahead, you pricks," he said.

CHAPTER 18

HIS ALARM SOUNDED AT eight on Sunday morning. Hirsch lay stunned, trying to process who and where he was. He swung his legs out of bed and planted them on the scratchy mat beside it. He yawned and stared at the floor.

It was no good. He showered, brewed coffee and drank it with toast on a licheny chair in the backyard, a Kumquat tree breathing down his neck, the filtered sunlight struggling to warm or encourage him. Then, still feeling pretty ordinary, he walked for thirty minutes, exploring the town, saying hello to the bony horse on its patch of dirt, a galah in a cage and an old codger squirting his roses.

"Lovely morning."

"Remains to be seen," the bloke said, and Hirsch thought that was about right.

NINE O'CLOCK NOW, A civilized hour. Hirsch, using his office phone, said, "Hope I woke you."

"You'd have to get up early," Rose DeLisle said. "What's up?"

"Overheard something last night," Hirsch said, telling her about Nicholson and the girlfriend who'd crashed his car.

"No license?"

"Which might mean she was too young," Hirsch said.

"Excellent. This is exactly what we want from you."

At once, Hirsch felt dirty. He felt cleaner saying, "And I know who planted that stuff in my car."

WHEN HE GOT TO Redruth there was no one in the lockup or the police station, so he walked around to the courthouse, a wood-paneled side room in the district council offices, wondering if Kropp had already released Raymond Latimer.

Not yet ten o'clock and court was already in session, the magistrate at a slightly raised table, the court reporter—a middle-aged woman—at a tiny corner desk, and Kropp sprawled with two of the overnight drunks on a bench in front of the public gallery, which at that hour on a Sunday was empty. Ray Latimer was seated at a long table across the aisle from Kropp, next to a natty suit. Lawyer, Hirsch guessed, taking in the briefcase and files. And something cute was going on between Latimer, his lawyer and the magistrate, a bit of humorous badinage about football grand finals, impossible long-range goal-kicking and high marks. Hirsch slid onto the bench beside his sergeant, barely covering a yawn.

The magistrate caught it. David Coulter, according to the nameplate, Coulter a twinkling butterball, a forty-five-year-old ex-small-town solicitor, already dressed for Sunday golf. "We boring you, mate?"

"Late night," Hirsch said.

He was the center of attention now, the magistrate, the lawyer and Latimer, all three smirking at him. But Kropp was seething. Hirsch edged away and made himself invisible.

Thirty minutes passed. The two drunks were fined. And now the court reporter was packing up, getting out of her chair, leaving with a little finger wave to the magistrate and the lawyer.

"Sarge?" murmured Hirsch. "What about Mr. Latimer?"

"Done and dusted," Kropp said. "Pleaded down to disorderly conduct and the minimum fine."

Hirsch checked his watch. "I didn't get here late, Sarge."

Kropp folded his arms and snorted. Some deal had been cooked up, but why was Kropp still seething? His mate had got off with a slap over the wrist, after all. So his beef was with the magistrate and the lawyer?

The courthouse emptied, leaving Kropp, Latimer and Hirsch. And Kropp didn't want to be there. He shook Latimer's hand perfunctorily, said through his teeth: "Well, you were lucky," and turned to go.

"Mate, what can I say? I was an idiot."

Kropp was almost to the door. He raised a hand.

Agitated, Latimer said, "Mate, wait, I was hoping you could give us a lift home."

"Ask Constable Hirschhausen."

Fuck, thought Hirsch, and now he was on his own.

Latimer's vigor and gloss had been worn to nothing by tiredness and a night in a cell. His clothing was wrinkled, chin stubbly, eyes bloodshot, hair in crazy tufts. But he lit up and looked keenly at Hirsch. "Could you? I don't know who else to ask and you have no idea how sorry I am about last night. I shouldn't have taken a swing at you."

"I'm not a taxi service. What about your wife, father, girl-friend, lawyer?"

Latimer shuffled his feet. "There isn't anyone. My father's taken the boys to the Jamestown air show, and obviously I can't call Allie. My lawyer's off to play golf with Dave Coulter and as for Finola, well, I might have done my dash there."

Hirsch was cranky. "I am leaving right this minute, all right?"

"Fair enough," Ray Latimer said. "Lead on."

Out into the sun, down the steps and into the HiLux, the town Sunday quiet and the air still. "Seatbelt," Hirsch snarled, but that expelled all of his energy and he let the 4WD trundle out of town, too tired to speed.

"Sorry about this," Latimer said.

Hirsch ignored him. Too tired to speed, too tired to speak.

"And sorry again for last night. I got stuck into the booze after our win."

Hirsch grunted, creeping through the empty town. Latimer, a stale lump beside him, ran commentary, swivel-necking as if he'd never been to Redruth before.

"Damn shame, Finucane's going out of business."

A white goods shop, CLOSING DOWN SALE pasted across the windows. Hirsch couldn't give a stuff.

"It's a heartache," Latimer said.

Hirsch wriggled his shoulders as if that would shut his passenger down.

"High costs, low returns," Latimer said. "When the man on the land struggles to survive, so do the local shopkeepers. There's nothing for the kids, no reason why they'd hang on, what with better money in the city and excellent money up at Roxby Downs or on one of the wind farms. You can't get shearers, shed hands or casual labor for love or money anymore."

Hirsch wanted to point to himself and say, "This is my caring and sharing face."

"Take my property," said Latimer. "Been in the family for generations and now we're barely hanging on."

And yet you keep buying things and not paying your bills. Feeling nasty, Hirsch said, "Why not cut back on the spending?"

Latimer continued as if he'd not heard him. "What with the economy and my wife . . ."

"How is she to blame?"

"A divorce will ruin me. My father and me."

"And yet you're giving her the grounds for a divorce."

Latimer snorted. "Am I a monk? Plus, you might not know this but she tried to kill herself last year. She's unstable, mate."

"Uh-huh."

"Says she wants fifty percent of what I own, plus child support? Where's the justice?"

Hirsch was tired. Latimer stank, stale alcohol leaching and cigarette smoke caught in the weave of his shirt. Flicking a switch, Hirsch dropped his window a few centimeters, wondering if he should monitor the man's movements for the next few hours. Keep him away from his wife. God he was exhausted.

"We're not made of money. We'd have to sell up if she goes through with it. A property that's been in the same family for generations."

"Uh-huh."

"Can't catch a break. The wind generators, for example. They put a line of them on Finola's property, but not ours. Rent worth thousands of dollars a year."

He's going to marry Finola Armstrong, Hirsch thought. Barrier Highway was quiet. He cared nothing for the oncoming and overtaking cars and farm vehicles, but Latimer would quiver alertly from time to time, tracking a family station wagon, a ute, a truck, remarking on the driver. Hirsch had no interest. He didn't care if so-and-so in the white station wagon was a good bloke, or whosiwhatsit in the red ute had cancer. He wanted to sleep.

"Next right," Latimer said.

Hirsch made the turn onto Bitter Wash Road, watched by a cow. Almost noon and he was starving. No rain for the past week and so for the next several kilometers, dust poured behind him and the steering wheel transmitted the surface corrugations to his hands. Then they were in the shadow of the wind turbines again, and shortly after that Latimer was pointing to his driveway entrance.

"Coming home to an empty house," he said, drawing his palms down his stubbled cheeks, a picture of desolation.

"Your father and the boys are at an air show?"

"They headed over there yesterday, after the game," Latimer said. "I've got an aunt lives in Jamestown."

The father is complicit in the son's philandering, thought Hirsch. The gravel complained under the tires as Hirsch followed the track between the lawn beds, shrubs and silvery gums. He pulled in opposite the flagstones leading to the veranda steps and the front door, and saw that the door was ajar before Latimer did. He touched the man's forearm, registering briefly strength and warmth through the creased cotton. "Did you leave your place open yesterday?"

"What?"

Latimer glanced wildly at the door and was out and powering toward the house before Hirsch could stop him. Up the steps and through the door. *Oh, fuck,* thought Hirsch, following him, but also thinking there should be a vehicle if burglars were still on the premises. He paused on the veranda, hearing Latimer stomping around inside, and glanced across to the implement sheds, the yards, the paddocks.

And there was a glint, sunlight flashing on a windscreen, down along the creek. Hirsch shaded his eyes. How would you get a vehicle down there? Was there an access gate, a farm track?

He stuck his head in, called to Latimer: "Anything? Damage, things missing?"

"Gun case is open. The twenty-two is missing."

Hirsch recalled that there were two .22 rifles: the Ruger used by the kids and the Brno in the gun case. So the Ruger was still floating around somewhere, still stowed on the window shelf of the ute, probably. That's what Hirsch was thinking as he trotted across the yard and slid between the wires of the fence. He spotted fresh tire impressions in the grass, and realized they followed a farm track concealed under the spring growth. The track ran beside the fence and then down an incline to the creek, and now Hirsch had a clearer view: the tin hut, some ancient quince, apricot and mulberry trees, and the small clearing where Alison Latimer had parked her Subaru.

He side-slipped down the bank to the edge of the creek. Reaching the car, he looked in: empty, a suitcase in the back, keys in the ignition. He straightened and ran his gaze in among the fruit trees, down into the reeds and pools of the creek, and

finally over the rusted hut. A shiver came over him. He was
spooked. What made him think of bloodletting?

He approached the hut and, rounding the end wall, found
Alison Latimer slumped against the rusted tin wall, half-top-
pled with a rifle butt between her thighs, her thumb caught in
the trigger guard. The barrel tip had been in her mouth, he
guessed, but she'd jerked as she died. It was not the Ruger but
the Brno. No exit wound; blood over her chin and inside her
shirt front. All in all, the stillness of death. Hirsch had seen it
before. But he advanced cautiously, keeping close to the undis-
turbed grass scratching the wall, and felt for a pulse. Nothing.
Some residual warmth, so death had been a few rather than
many hours ago. He reversed his steps and, keeping wide of
the body, took a series of photographs with his phone. He had
maybe a minute before Latimer arrived. Half an hour before
Kropp and the doctor and everyone else arrived.

He started with a series of establishing shots of the hut,
the grove of trees, the car and the creek. Then, closing in
on the body, he photographed the dirt and the grass around
it, the feet and legs, the rifle, the ringless hands holding it,
the bloodied chest and Alison Latimer's head. Then the same
sequence but side-on, first the left flank, then the right, as
Latimer came pounding down from the track above.

"What the hell are you doing?"

Said a moment before the penny dropped. He skidded to a
stop. "What the hell?"

Hirsch put a hand to the farmer's chest. "Mr. Latimer, you
can't—"

Latimer was full of trembling potency. "She might still be
alive."

"I'm afraid she's not, Mr. Latimer," Hirsch said, obdurately
maintaining the pressure, waiting him out. Slowly the quivering
chest relaxed. Latimer stepped back, mouth open in shock. He
took a ragged breath and said, "What am I going to do? How do
I tell the boys?"

Hirsch turned him away. "First I need to call it in, and then I'll help you phone your friends and neighbors."

"How do I tell the boys?"

"What time do you expect your father home?"

Latimer was slow, dull, staring at the ground. "Late afternoon," he said, rallying. "He'll have his phone with him."

They returned to the house, slipping and sliding on the grassy bank, Latimer babbling about his life now, the boys, emptiness and what might have been. "She was going to come home, I know she was."

Hirsch tuned him out. He trudged across the yard, a hand on Latimer's elbow. He felt mud paste to the sole of his shoes; there was a smear of it on one toe cap and his trouser cuffs.

And Alison Latimer's white runners had been pristine.

And the beautiful diamond ring: had she taken it off, a tidying act or a gesture from a woman about to kill herself?

CHAPTER 19

KROPP ARRIVED FIRST, ASKED for a rundown and elbowed Hirsch aside, then Dr. McAskill appeared to pronounce death, and Andrewartha and Nicholson showed up with crime-scene tape and hangovers. *Meaning Dee is holding the fort in Redruth,* Hirsch thought. All he could do was stand back and watch his crime scene—incident scene—be trampled over.

Then Kropp, still in management mode, began stalking up and down the creek bank, muttering into his mobile phone. Forty minutes later, a hearse arrived, ready to cart the body away, followed by a flatbed truck, REDRUTH MOTORS scrolled across each door. Hirsch watched it back up to the Subaru, two men hopping out, drawing on heavy gloves.

"Sarge, what are you doing?"

"What do you mean, what am I doing?"

"We need to preserve everything. We need crime scene people here."

"What does this look like to you? Suicide. A tragedy. No one needs to see it. I know the protocol, mister, I've called in Port Pirie CIB, they'll be here within the hour, and meanwhile that bloody car is in the way."

"But Sarge."

Kropp cocked his head. Hirsch heard it, too, a background rumble of vehicles.

"Get up there and make yourself useful," Kropp said. "Make sure no one wanders down here for a look-see."

Clambering up to the fence above the tin hut, Hirsch saw that a dozen cars, station wagons, utilities and four-wheel drives had poured in off Bitter Wash Road to jostle for room around the house and sheds. Jesus Christ. He began to run. Clearly some kind of phone tree had been set in motion, this past hour, neighbor phoning neighbor phoning football club member, churchgoer and Country Women's Association crony, and here they were, bringing cakes and casseroles and hugs and tears and nosiness.

And—if Alison Latimer had been killed at the house—trampling over a crime scene.

More cars arrived. Hirsch barged through the front door. But it was useless. At least thirty people were crowding the hallway, kitchen and sitting room, with more on the veranda or climbing out of their cars. "Excuse me," he said futilely.

He went in search of Raymond Latimer, finding him in a huddle with a dozen other people, enduring their embraces but aware of Hirsch, watching warily. Hirsch couldn't get through. He gestured; Latimer ignored him. And then the crowd moved and reformed and wouldn't budge, Latimer disappeared and Kropp was there, panting with effort, grabbing Hirsch by the arm. "The fuck are you doing?"

"We're losing evidence, Sarge."

Kropp dragged him through the room and out onto the lawn. "What evidence? You're upsetting people. Get your arse back down to the creek."

"Sarge," Hirsch said, and backed away, watching Kropp apologize, shake hands, pat backs, share the grief.

WHEN THE SERGEANT HAD merged fully with the crush of people, Hirsch made as if to head for the creek. Walking until he was screened by a clump of oleanders, he doubled back and entered the house by the laundry door. Another door led to the kitchen, where half a dozen women were getting in each other's way. "Need a quick word with Sergeant Kropp," said Hirsch amiably, not stopping to gauge their reactions but bustling by them to the hallway.

The door to the main bedroom was slightly ajar. He slipped through the gap and paused and scanned the room. Latimer hadn't made the bed; dirty clothes lay heaped on the floor and a chair; the wardrobe doors were open, drawers spilling socks and T-shirts. Only a few traces of Alison Latimer remained. Hirsch crossed to the left-hand bedside table. Nestled in a dusty patterned dish were Alison Latimer's rings: wedding ring and the engagement ring he'd noticed the day he met her.

Hirsch returned to the hallway. He left via the kitchen. He wasn't challenged.

HE WAS HALFWAY across the yard when he saw the Subaru. It had been dumped beside a haystack beyond the sheds. Hirsch was fed up with it all. He stumped out of the yard and was almost to the creek when he changed his mind and returned. This time he lifted the Subaru's tailgate and unzipped the lid of the case. Women's clothing. Badly folded, which meant a lot or nothing at all. There was no reason to suppose Alison Latimer was tidy. Meanwhile, no twelve-year-old boy's clothing. Hirsch closed everything and headed for the creek.

THE HEARSE DRIVERS SAT in the sun, smoking. McAskill was still bent over the body, and when he finally eased her away from the wall for the hearse drivers, she moved like a sack of disobliging logs.

Feeling Andrewartha and Nicholson give him the evil eye from the edge of the tape, Hirsch wandered down along the creek, thinking it a pretty spot for a house and orchard, except that it gave him the creeps. And he supposed it was prone to flooding, that's why the Latimer ancestors had moved to higher ground. Why had Alison Latimer come down here to die? Was it special to her? He gazed at the lichen, the fruit trees choking themselves to death, the choked rushes and hoof-trampled muddy verges. A good place to die.

He took out his phone, found a number in the contacts list, and dialed.

A voice lashed at his back: "Who are you calling?"

Hirsch whirled around. Kropp, slithering down the grassy slope. "Sarge, we need to take Mrs. Latimer's car to the lab."

"Do we?"

"I think so, Sarge."

"The poor cow shot herself. I'm sick of this," Kropp said. "I want you to piss off back to Tiverton in case someone reports a stolen lawn mower."

"Sarge."

"Dog," murmured Andrewartha and Nicholson. "Maggot."

ALISON'S PARENTS, THOUGHT HIRSCH when he reached the top. Everyone's wringing their hands over the husband and the boys, but what about her parents, her friends?

The yard being choked with mourners' vehicles, Hirsch was forced to steer a slow weave out of the yard, dodging a bulk fuel tank, heaped pine posts, haphazardly parked cars and utes. He was halted by a blue heeler, prone in a dusty pool of sunlight. He stopped; looked at the dog; willed it to move. Then he brapped the horn, and when that didn't work, got out, grabbed the dog by its collar and walked it to another patch of talcy dirt.

Climbed back into the HiLux and bumped along the driveway and immediately onto the lawn as a black Explorer shot in, followed by an unmarked Falcon, on a mission. He didn't recognize the suits in the Falcon but guessed they were the Port Pirie detectives, big men filling their seats and staring at him with the flatness and odium of policemen. But he did recognize the man at the wheel of the Explorer: the area commander,

Superintendent Spurling. As he waited for the dust to settle, Hirsch thought his irrelevance was pretty much fully under-scored now. He steered back onto the driveway and out through the gate and onto Bitter Wash Road.

It gave him a curious jolt to see Wendy Street standing beside her car in the driveway of the house with the faded red roof. The boot was open, stacked with bags of mulch, one bag out and in a wheelbarrow beside a narrow strip of unforgiving soil. She stopped what she was doing and gazed at him, and even at some distance he felt the force of her frankness, as if she'd caught him acting discreditably.

So he steered into her driveway, lifting his hand in greeting. "Lot of cars," she said when he got out, showing a little tension.

She doesn't know, Hirsch realized. *No one has phoned her.* He removed his cap and turned it absently in his hands. "Afraid I've got some bad news."

One hand went to her throat and she said, instantly, "Allie? He killed her?"

Interesting. Hirsch agreed that Alison Latimer was dead, but wrapped it up in some mealy-mouthed cop talk, finishing with, "There's no reason to suppose it was anything other than self-inflicted."

"Fuck off," Street said, her eyes filling with tears. "Beside the tin hut? No. She hated it there."

She gave a tearing sob and went slack, backing away from him and grabbing a veranda post. Using it as a prop, she low-ered herself, sat on the edge, her hands rubbing her thighs back and forth, back and forth, as if to bring herself back under con-trol. Hirsch waited.

She looked up. "Who found her?"

"I did."

Grim, intense, she said, "And where was Ray during all this?"

"Mrs. Street, he was in the Redruth lockup all last night and until lunchtime today. In fact, I gave him a lift home."

"Don't call me Mrs. Street. Has anyone told the boys?"

"That's all taken care of," Hirsch said, not knowing one way or the other. Surely Raymond Latimer would have called his father?

Wendy shook her head. "One can imagine the delicate way in which Raymond or his father might pass on the news: *Oh by the way, kids, your mum's shot herself.*"

"Aren't you being unfair?"

"Am I?"

"We have to give them the benefit of the doubt."

"You do, I don't." She bit her lip. "How do I tell Kate?"

Hirsch glanced toward the house, wondering where the girl was. "You'll know what to say."

"You think so?" Her eyes were full of tears, her arms folded to ward him off. "It's just terrible. I know he did it."

"Did you happen to hear a rifle shot this morning?"

"No, but there's always someone shooting something. Plus I was mowing."

A little Cox ride-on, parked beside the house, wearing a fresh chlorophyll skirt, damp cuttings in the tire treads. Hirsch glanced back at Wendy Street and saw that she was biting her bottom lip, something on her mind.

"What?"

"Katie saw that car again, that black car."

"Well, you can put her mind at ease: Pullar and Hanson stole a Holden the other day."

Then it dawned on him. "You think Katie sneaked the rifle out again and fired it?"

Wendy Street twisted in knots. "Could she have?"

And then her consternation disappeared, logic taking over. "No, she wouldn't do that."

"Exactly," Hirsch said. "All indications are, Mrs. Latimer shot herself. The gun was still in her hands when I found her."

Wendy rubbed her face. "This is just awful."

She was glancing across at the Latimers' as if she should head there but knew she might not be welcome. To divert her, Hirsch said, "Was Mrs. Latimer more than usually down lately?"

"You mean suicidal? No. She'd made up her mind to leave Ray. Get a divorce. She seemed freer if anything." She gasped. "Her parents!"

"I'm off to see them now."

Wendy was this way and that. "I should come with you, but I need to be here for Katie."

The youngest boy might need you, too, Hirsch thought. He nodded goodbye, seated his cap upon his head and reached for the driver's door.

"I Googled you."

Fantastic. Hirsch turned his blank face to her. "And?"

"And nothing."

"OUR DAUGHTER HAS KILLED herself, and you know how he informs us? By *phone*."

Heather Rofe was ragged, bleary, angry. Hirsch gently steered her back into the house, to the kitchen, where Keith sat dazedly, a solid man diminished, his decency more threadbare now. Man and wife, they'd been to church probably, best clothes on their backs. They'd made and poured tea but that was as far as they'd been able to take it.

"Is there anyone I can contact for you?"

Keith Rofe lifted his head. "Our other daughter's coming over."

Hirsch stood there, spinning his damn cap in his hands. He felt, and probably looked, like a storm trooper.

"How's he breaking the news to the boys?" Heather Rofe said. "Text message?"

All kinds of statements were issued via text message these days. *Your services are no longer required; by the way, your husband's having an affair; I want a divorce; here's a close-up of my pussy.* Hirsch said gently, "Alison spent the night with you?"

Keith Rofe didn't have the wherewithal to answer. He glanced helplessly at his wife, who said, "She was in bed when we left this morning."

"Church?"

"A christening," Heather said. "My niece's daughter, down in Gawler."

Two hours' distance. "What time did you leave?"

"Seven."

"So you were away half the day?"

Heather Rofe's tears welled and rolled down her cheeks. "We just got back."

"Did she tell you what she intended to do today?"

Rofe shrugged. "Sleep in. Rest. She offered to re-pot my geraniums."

"Didn't say anything about going out?"

"No."

"She's not a churchgoer?"

Heather struggled. She said, "Not lately."

"Can you think why she'd go to the tin hut?"

"No, she didn't like it there—and you're grilling me. I'd like you to stop."

Hirsch backpedaled. "Sorry, terribly sorry, that's not my intention."

"No, I'm sorry, I know you do have a job to do."

Hirsch rotated his shoulders in uneasy agreement. "One last question: was the house locked when you got back from church?"

"We don't bother, usually," Heather said. "Nothing worth taking, and we know everyone in . . ." Her voice trailed away.

"What?"

"It *was* locked. I had to fetch the spare key. Remember, Keith?"

"What?"

Hirsch tuned them out, letting his gaze roam around the kitchen and into the hallway and mentally retrace his route as he'd entered the house a few minutes earlier. He hadn't seen anything to suggest forced entry or a struggle, and how would he raise that question with them? "May I see her room?"

Heather Rofe fixed him with a level stare, still raw with grief but not about to lose herself in it. "Why?"

Hirsch did his uncomfortable shoulder rotation again. "I was wondering if she might have left some kind of goodbye."

"Like a suicide note. Well, she didn't. Last night over dinner she was quite chirpy. Not a hundred percent enamored with the idea of Jack spending the weekend with his grandfather, but a weight had been lifted from her shoulders over the past few days."

Heather gave in to the grief again. Hirsch moved to her. He placed a hand on each shoulder and, after the briefest hesitation, she let herself be consoled.

Hirsch waited, glancing over her shoulder at the husband, who was again staring sightlessly at the top of the table. Presently Heather stepped back and mustered herself and said, "Her old bedroom, down the passage."

A spare room now, all vestiges of the child and teenager removed. Hirsch surveyed it first and then began a search. The drawers yawned emptily, and all he found in the wardrobe was one wire hanger, a white bowls uniform in a drycleaner's bag whispering in the eddying air.

He popped his head into the adjacent room. An untidy bed, a child's pair of trainers on the floor, warm cotton pajamas poking from under a pillow, a laptop on top of the pillow, pasted with footballer stickers.

In the kitchen again, Hirsch said gently, "It seems Alison packed all her things but left Jack's here."

He saw the rapid assimilation in Heather Rofe's face. Instead of giving him her conclusions she said, "All right, how do *you* read it?"

Hirsch said, "Did she give any indication she wanted to thrash things out with Ray?"

"No."

"Leaving Jack here, where he wouldn't witness any nastiness?"

"Nothing like that."

They took it no further than that but Hirsch could see one scenario: Alison Latimer packed her bag, returned to the farm and had second thoughts.

❧   ❧   ❧

THE BLACK EXPLORER WAS waiting for him outside the station.

Hirsch parked in the driveway, liking this visit even less than Kropp's visit the day Melia Donovan was found. Choosing to ignore it, he stepped onto the little porch, his key at the ready. Well, that triggered movement. A door slammed and footsteps stalked him. He turned: Superintendent Spurling, in full uniform, a man of fifty with the bearing of an army officer and clean, slender hands and a narrow, ascetic face.

"Sir," Hirsch said.

"You know who I am?"

"Area commander, sir."

"I need a word."

Hirsch led the way into his office. Thank Christ Spurling was content to leave it at that.

"I'll get right to it. This afternoon I received a phone call."

Hirsch gave him a good, intrigued look. "Sir?"

"Anonymous caller, female, very brief: 'The husband did it.'"

Oh, hell, Wendy. "Well, sir, the thing is, he was in the Redruth lockup at the time."

Spurling grunted. "There will be an inquest."

Hirsch nodded his agreement.

"I need you to prepare a brief for the coroner."

The last thing Hirsch was expecting. "Sir, I'm new here."

"All the better."

The men stared at each other. Spurling broke first, saying, "And on the subject of phone calls, I've also been contacted about a different matter. Phone calls and letters."

"Sir?"

"Most were from good old Anonymous, but a handful were not. In particular, a nurse, a couple of high school teachers, a priest and the local ALP candidate. All from Redruth, all raising the same issue."

Hirsch waited.

"In a nutshell, the overzealous policing methods employed by Sergeant Kropp and Constables Nicholson and Andrewartha. Physical and verbal abuse, harassment, unwarranted speed and drunk-driving traps, etcetera, etcetera."

There the area commander stopped and stared.

Hirsch knew where this was going. All he wanted was to be free of worry and moral complications. "Sir?"

"Don't be dim. Is there anything to these claims?"

"Like I said, sir, I'm new here."

"Yeah, be like that. I've been hearing whispers for months now, and this afternoon I hear that Sergeant Kropp is best mates with a man who might have killed his wife."

"I haven't been here long enough to see any patterns or—"

Spurling snarled, "What, you're selective in which coppers you snitch on?"

"Is that why you called in to see me, sir? You think I'm a snitch?"

Has he been talking to DeLisle? Hirsch wondered. Meanwhile Spurling propped himself against the edge of Hirsch's desk and folded his arms. "Don't get smart. The alternative is a behavioral management audit. Is that what you want?"

Well, no. Audits were worse than ethical standards complaints. The latter obliged you to be interviewed, your house searched, even if the complaint were malicious, but an audit would prove to be more far-reaching. An audit of Redruth would mean an audit of the officers, the police station and all of its records, and it would mean an audit of Hirsch, and he was through with being poked and prodded by the Internals. He tried to understand Spurling, saw a man whose job required him to be political, clandestine, subtle. "The usual rumors, sir. Like I said, I'm new here and have yet to see—"

Spurling's disgust grew. He straightened abruptly. "All I'm asking, man to man, off the record, no comeback, is there any truth to the allegations that the Redruth officers are in any way overstepping the mark?"

Hirsch tensed himself. "It's not as if this is the inner city," he said. "We're not dealing with bikie gangs or ethnic clans."

Spurling headed for the little foyer. "Well that took you long enough. If you hear or see anything, I want to know about it, pronto."

He stopped at the front door. "Your fleet vehicle: get a new screen fitted."

"Sir."

"And it's filthy. Get it washed."

INSTEAD, HIRSCH GOT IT filthier, heading out along Bitter Wash Road again.

The Latimer house and yard were still choked with cars, but the Port Pirie detectives had been and gone, and in the meantime the Latimer children had returned with their grandfather. Hirsch found them in the main room, standing with Ray Latimer at the center of a constantly moving press of people. Without being sure of his intentions, he began to edge through to them, pausing to grab a sausage roll from a table crammed with sandwiches, sponge cakes, beer and juice bottles, wine flagons. The Latimer men spotted him and stiffened, acutely aware of his progress through the crowd. Why was that? They locked eyes with him, as if only they and Hirsch existed on earth and were a danger to each other. They betrayed nothing but stillness and vigilance, two powerfully made, big-jawed, proprietorial men.

Then Kropp was back in Hirsch's face, red, beery and emotional. "I thought I told you to piss off."

"Just seeing if you wanted a hand, Sarge."

"Is that a fact. I can read you, pal." He poked Hirsch in the chest. "You lay off, understand? That's an order."

Hirsch, glancing past Kropp, saw Raymond Latimer and his father watching the exchange. They didn't smile to see Hirsch get his comeuppance, didn't look relieved, merely affectless, leading him to wonder what vaunting disappointments and ambitions drove them.

"Well?"

"Sarge, if you must know, a few things bother me."

"Is that a fact."

"Mrs. Latimer had some odd bruises on her, Sarge. No mud on her shoes. What if this house is a crime scene? Or, if she was snatched from her parents' house, then *that* is a crime scene. The hut, the rifle, her car . . . We need prints, blood samples, tire impressions."

Kropp couldn't believe his ears, couldn't believe the cheek. "What the fuck are you talking about?"

Hirsch was distracted by an abrupt movement at the corner of his vision. He turned. Raymond Latimer had collapsed onto the sofa with his sons, Jack burrowing into his chest as if wanting to slip inside him, Craig shoulder-to-shoulder and looking stunned. All three looked reduced: damp, blotchy, all animation gone.

"Look at them," Kropp said. "*Look* at them."

"All I'm saying is—"

"The Port Pirie boys took all the samples and photos they need. Meanwhile you keep out of it. This is a peaceful community. You, son, are passing through."

CHAPTER 20

MONDAY BEGAN WITH KROPP on the line, in a mild froth. "Just been talking to the super."

Hirsch said nothing. He could hear yelling across the road, doors slamming: the school holidays were over.

"I'm warning you: the Latimers are decent people visited by tragedy, and Spurling or no Spurling, I'll have your guts for garters if you step out of line."

"Yes, Sarge."

"Why the hell he put you on it, I don't know."

"Sarge, I'm as surprised as you are."

"Arselicker."

Hirsch heard impotence in the sergeant's voice. "I'll tread lightly, Sarge."

HIRSCH PROPPED HIS FEET on the desk, notebook in his lap, not writing but thinking.

In his view there were three essential truths to police work: most crimes go unpunished; most crimes are solved not by forensics but chance, an admission or a word in your ear; and detection matters less than the piecing together of rumors, sightings, theories and random scraps of information.

Still, method mattered, too. Scrawling *Interviews* at the top of a blank page, he made a list: the Latimer clan; Alison's parents and sister; her doctor; her neighbors; her friends. Not knowing all of their names yet, that's how he listed them, by role and title.

Wendy Street should be able to help: friend and neighbor.

But he suspected he'd get mainly emotional, partial and impressionistic evidence from these people, proof of nothing, and it might very well lead him to one conclusion, that Alison Latimer took her life while the balance of her mind was disturbed, or however coroners liked it expressed these days.

Flipped over the page and made another list: *Formal Evidence*, namely the autopsy findings and forensics. What would her body, clothing, car, parent's house, own house, rifle and the tin hut reveal about her death?

Finally, gut impressions. He stared at the ceiling, formulating them in his mind. The death didn't seem right to him, or to her parents or Wendy Street. But were his guts listening to them or to his own rumblings? On the surface, there was little evidence to suggest homicide, plenty to suggest suicide. Alison Latimer knew how to handle a rifle, he'd seen it himself, and she'd made a prior suicide attempt. But no suicide note. But that didn't mean anything: plenty of people took their lives without explaining themselves. Meanwhile, what of her spotless shoes, the bruises, her thumb in the trigger guard? Why the tin hut, if it freaked her out? But those who might want her dead— her husband, her father-in-law, maybe even the older boy—had unshakable alibis.

Who else? A secret lover? Wendy Street might know.

Hirsch jotted scenarios:

She committed suicide.

She was snatched from her parents' house, subdued by force, taken to the tin hut and shot dead, the body and gun arranged to suggest suicide.

Ditto, but she was accidentally killed during the struggle and so on.

She was lured to the farm, or the tin hut, and killed by accident or design and the body and gun arranged to suggest suicide.

Alison Latimer was a slight woman, tall, but not frail. Could a woman have killed her?

And so Finola Armstrong's name surfaced again. Hirsch found her address in the phone book, locked up and headed out to Bitter Wash Road.

ARMSTRONG'S HOUSE WAS STONE with a wash of cement over it, painted white once upon a time but now mostly dust and mold. It sat among pine trees so high and cramped they robbed the sun, their needles starving the garden and choking the gutters. Hirsch had never seen such a miserable building, and wondered at the man or the woman, a couple of generations ago, who'd decided the pines and the cement were a good idea. The sheds on the other hand were in the open and expressed the busyness of a working farm.

Because the sun failed to penetrate, the place felt damp, and there was a hollow wind, mournful where it wrapped around the chimney, eaves and veranda posts. He was about to knock on the front door when Finola Armstrong appeared from behind a rainwater tank, removing canvas gloves. Hirsch stepped down from the veranda and eyed her carefully: jeans, a checked shirt, a scowl and an odor of diesel and silage.

She stopped a meter from his chest. "I guessed you'd be dropping by."

"Did you?" said Hirsch.

"Don't be coy."

"Fair enough. Perhaps you could tell me your movements after I saw you at the motel on Saturday night?"

Armstrong tilted her head, revealing a smear of chaff dust along her jaw that he itched to wipe away. "You'd like me to say

I went home in great turmoil, deciding that all my problems lay with Alison Latimer, and that I got up the next morning and did her in."

"Well, that would simplify matters. Is that what happened?"

"No."

"Do you think she was murdered?"

"Not for me to say, but I doubt it."

"What *did* you do after I left you on Saturday night?"

"Didn't stay in that dreadful motel, that's for sure."

"You went home?"

"I *was* in turmoil, but going home wasn't going to fix it. I went to my sister's."

Hirsch patted his jacket pocket for pad and pen, fished them out, clicked the pen, found a blank page. He could feel her eyes on him.

"Ready?" she asked, a glint in her eye. She gave him addresses, phone numbers and names: sister, brother-in-law, nieces.

"They can all verify, etcetera, etcetera?"

"They can." She tilted her head again. "Are you treating it as suspicious, the death?"

"Covering bases," said Hirsch blithely. "Preparing a brief for the coroner."

"Uh-huh. Bill Kropp thinks it's suicide."

Letting him know who her friends were. "Is that a fact? Getting back to Saturday night."

"I was upset. Cross. Couldn't think clearly. Told myself—not for the first time—that I should end it. So I went to the only person who'd listen and talk sense to me about it."

"After midnight."

"She's my sister," Armstrong said, the admonishment mild yet saying, *Don't you have someone like that in your life?*

"You stayed the night?"

"I stayed *two* nights. Got back this morning."

By now Hirsch had pretty much discounted her. She was a hard, brusque woman—notwithstanding her need of sisterly comfort—and seemed essentially truthful. A simple woman, even if her love life wasn't.

Or maybe in her mind it was. "What was your understanding of the Latimers' marriage?"

"Was I a slut, do you mean? Secretly sleeping with another woman's husband? He told me the marriage was over, she wanted a divorce."

"When did he tell you that?"

"Ages ago. The beginning of the year, when we first hooked up."

"Did Mrs. Latimer know about you?"

Armstrong shrugged. "We didn't shove it in her face, but yes, she did."

"Did she have words with you about it? Angry words, upset words?"

"I barely knew the woman. Don't get me wrong, I think her death's a dreadful thing, it's sad on all levels. Those poor boys. Her parents."

Hirsch nodded. "How did you get involved with Mr. Latimer?"

"We have an adjoining fence. There was a grass fire just after Christmas and part of the fence needed replacing." She shrugged. "We got talking."

"Grass fire."

"Passing motorist tossed a cigarette out the window? I don't know. Does it matter?"

"You got talking."

Armstrong revealed some feeling for the first time. "Look, he paid me some attention. I didn't go looking for it but it found me. It was nice."

"Will you continue to see him?"

"Mind your own business."

"How well do you know Sergeant Kropp?"

"Your boss, Sergeant Kropp? Is that the Sergeant Kropp you mean?"

Hirsch faced off the challenge with a smile. "Yes."

"He's mates with Ray."

"Is that a fact?" said Hirsch flatly.

Finola Armstrong was bored with him. "Got work to do," she said, walking away from him, her rear shapely, a smudge of engine oil on the seat of her jeans and one pocket torn. God Hirsch was lonely.

LONELINESS WAS MORE POWERFUL than his scruples, sensibilities and good manners. So was desire. And so it was that he slowed as he drew adjacent to Wendy Street's driveway. Nothing. No Volvo. Of course: the holidays were over; she'd be standing at the head of some classroom, pointing at the board.

CHAPTER 21

THAT AFTERNOON HE DOORKNOCKED the little street where Alison Latimer had spent her last few days alive. Had anyone seen Mrs. Latimer on Sunday morning, or at any time on Saturday? No one had. Had anyone seen an unfamiliar or a familiar but out-of-place car parked at or near the house at any time in recent days? Had anyone heard anything? Hirsch also invited speculations: all he got was some vague admiration of the Latimers and remarks on how Alison had done well for herself, only she'd suffered from depression in the past couple of years.

He left the Rofes alone for now.

THE WORLD TURNED OVER. On Tuesday morning Hirsch investigated the suspected theft of a hundred ewes. He found them in a neighbor's paddock, the neighbor apoplectic about the state of the complainant's fences. He calmed everyone down, returned to the town and called on the Rofes.

Heather answered, looking wrung out with grief. "You knocked on some doors yesterday."

"Yes."

"Learn anything?"

"Afraid not."

She shook her head, opened the gap in her front door. "Come and have a cup of tea with us."

Hirsch removed his cap and followed her through to the kitchen. Keith was there as if he were always there, still stunned, more rumpled. Heather gazed at him with a flicker of pity and irritation, told Hirsch to sit.

Hirsch drew back a chair. "I've been asked to prepare a brief for the coroner."

"Yes."

"I'm afraid I need to ask about Alison in a more formal context."

Heather turned from the sink, waved the wet spout of the kettle at him. "Formal context? Or formal *whitewash?*"

The spring sunlight lit her from behind, gauzy through the little window above the sink. Hirsch had never seen so many curtained windows before moving to the bush. He said, "There's no easy way to say this, but in the absence of foul play, everything will hinge on Alison's mental state in recent months—actual and perceived."

"Depends on who you listen to," Keith said, stirring at last. His wife moved to him, her thigh against one shoulder and her hand reaching around to his other. As Hirsch watched, some of the man's meekness and bewilderment evaporated.

"Right now," Hirsch said, "I'm listening to you."

"And we're biased."

"So are her husband and father-in-law," Hirsch said.

Keith cocked his head, then twisted around to share a silent communication with his wife. It seemed to say: *Maybe this fellow will listen.*

Heather said, "Alison, these last few days, was more buoyant than we've ever seen her."

Those intending suicide might be buoyant because they've come to a decision, Hirsch thought. "Uh-huh."

"A few weeks ago she inherited some money from a great aunt," Keith said.

"She began to see it as a lifeline."

"She wanted us to have some of it—"

"We said no, use it to start a new life."

Hirsch watched and listened: Heather, Keith, Heather, Keith. They'd been doing it all their married lives.

"May I ask how much it was?"

"A hundred and sixty thousand."

"Had she told her husband?"

"I don't think so," Heather said.

"He'd have made her pay it all into the farm," added her husband.

Hirsch thought it likely Ray Latimer *did* know about the inheritance. "Had she told him she wanted a divorce?"

"Yes."

"Was it a difficult decision for her?"

"Do you mean, she felt so awful she killed herself? Does that make sense to you?"

"How did Mr. Latimer take it?"

"He told her the only way she'd leave him would be in a box," Heather said, and stared at Hirsch, daring him.

"Did the boys know, about the inheritance and/or the divorce?"

Husband and wife glanced at each other. "She told Jack while they were here," Heather said. "Maybe Craig knew and didn't approve and so he stayed with Ray, we don't know. Certainly Ray poisoned the poor kid's mind against Allie."

Her eyes were wet with sorrow, misery and fury. Hirsch said, "I will have to talk to both boys sooner or later."

"If the menfolk let you."

Hirsch nodded that he pretty well understood what he was up against. "When Alison came here with Jack, did you think that was it, she was never going back?"

"Yes."

"Not even to thrash out the details?"

"Well, we told her to let a lawyer do that. But she hadn't been able to bring all her things with her. She would've gone back for the rest of her things at some stage."

"She didn't indicate that she'd do that on Sunday?"

"No."

"But what about Craig? She missed him, surely? Was she prepared to have the boys split up like that, Jack living with her, Craig with Ray?"

Husband and wife glanced at each other as if to acknowledge that nothing was neat. "We're sure Craig would have wanted to live with her eventually."

"Meanwhile his father would be poisoning his mind against her."

They shifted uneasily there on the other side of the kitchen table. Hirsch pushed it: "Wasn't it upsetting for your daughter, knowing she might have to challenge her husband for custody, knowing Craig chose him over her?"

"They were things that could have been worked out in time," Heather said.

Hirsch saw movement and a grey cat padded into the room. Spotting him it displayed apparent outrage, contempt and fear in one swift turnaround, its tail flicking as it fled the room.

"You have doubts," Keith said.

Hirsch didn't, not really. But he wanted to present a brief that would not be challenged at the coronial hearing, challenged by Kropp, McAskill or the lawyers that Leonard and Raymond Latimer would certainly bring to court with them.

"You say you found the door locked when you returned on Sunday?"

"We never lock it."

"But was Alison in the habit of locking it as she came and went?"

"No."

"Remember that she hadn't lived here for some time and was in the habit of locking her house at the farm," Hirsch pointed out, not sure if that were true or not.

Keith shook his head. "No."

"She arrived here with a suitcase?"

"*Two* cases, a big one for Jack, all his clothes and toys and school things, and a weekender for herself."

But why, thought Hirsch, *has she repacked? And why the larger case?*

"I'd like to go back to her previous suicide attempt."

Hirsch saw reluctance. They knew the earlier attempt to shoot herself gave credence to the view that this time their daughter had got it right.

"She'd been unhappy," Heather said finally.

"No light at the end of the tunnel."

"Ray and that damn father of his, they made her life a misery."

Rather than swivel his gaze—Heather, Keith, Heather, Keith—Hirsch sipped his tea. It was tepid. "In what way?"

"Ordered her around."

"Monitored everything she did, every trip, every dollar spent."

"And she got a creepy feeling if she was ever alone with Leonard."

Hirsch nodded. "I understand that she tried to shoot herself and Ray stopped her in time."

"Ray? No, his mother. Eileen."

"His mother?"

"She died late last year."

"Do you know the circumstances?"

Heather laughed. "You think they go around bumping off all the women in the family? Cancer."

"The circumstances of the suicide attempt."

Heather was patting her husband's shoulder absently. "Allie was in her car."

"At the tin hut?"

"No, she hated it there. Out in the paddock."

"Eileen was looking out her window and wondered what the car was doing there."

"The men were away at a clearing sale."

"She had a bad feeling and ran down the hill and found Allie just sitting there and talked her out of it."

"Sitting there with a rifle between her knees?" asked Hirsch.

Silence, and then Heather said, "This changes things. You think she finally did it."

Hirsch was noncommittal. "Tell me more about Eileen Latimer."

"Lovely woman. Life was no bed of roses, but she stood up to Leonard."

"Were she and your daughter close?"

"They were at the end."

"Allie nursed her in her final months."

"Did she feel it keenly when Eileen died? The only support she had within the family?"

"I know what you're trying to imply," Heather Rofe said, "and you're wrong."

Next, the Latimers. Hirsch spent the remainder of Tuesday and all of Wednesday attempting to make contact with Ray or his father. In between patrolling his district, delivering a summons, taking reports, signing statutory declarations and investigating the theft of a drum of diesel fuel, it was a time of frustration. The Latimers failed to answer phone messages or knocks on the door of either house, and had strangers running interference, telling him to come back next week or leave the poor beggars alone.

But then on Thursday morning Leonard Latimer answered when Hirsch knocked at the son's door. He wore the pastoralist's uniform of cream moleskin pants, elastic-sided R.M. Williams boots and khaki shirt; a bull of a man, with wide, sloping shoulders and a thick neck.

Hirsch removed his cap. "Mr. Latimer, my name is—"

"I know who you are."

Hirsch gave him a grave little nod. "First, may I say how sorry I am. I know you were fond of your daughter-in-law."

He knew no such thing, he just wanted to stir. And Leonard was stirred, his short grey hair bristled. "What do you want?"

"I was wondering if I might have a word with Raymond. Is he in?"

"Nope."

It might have been true. The family car was missing; silence, a sense of absence, seemed to come leaking out around the patriarch's large frame. Hirsch pictured the older man's life now, no daughter-in-law to bully or do his cooking and shopping.

"Then perhaps I could have a word with you?"

"I'm busy."

Leonard was dressed for town, not work. Did he work, get his hands dirty, track dust and mud over his daughter-in-law's carpets? Hirsch glanced at the man's hands. Stubby fingers, the nails remnant stubs, but that might have been his genes, not physical strain. "It won't take a moment," he said.

Leonard continued to scowl. His face had no other expression; it was the face his family saw day in and day out, seamed by long years of anger, irritation and solar rays. Pugnacious chin; barrelly chest; arms bowed as if bristling for a punch up. Keeping his own features open and pleasant, Hirsch moved one hand closer to the equipment hanging from his belt. "It's just that I'm preparing a brief for the coroner," he said.

"You? It should be Kropp."

"It's me," Hirsch said, shrugging as if to say: *Can't do anything about it, sorry.*

"We'll see about that. It needs someone senior. It needs someone who knows us."

Hirsch put some steel into his voice. "No, it doesn't."

Latimer seemed ready to throw a punch. But maybe that was his default position, for, without altering expression he said, "What do you want to know?"

"Perhaps you can tell me something of Alison's state of mind?"

A car passed by on Bitter Wash Road. Leonard cocked his head as if to identify the beat of the engine, then switched to Hirsch again. "She was a mess."

Hirsch got out his notebook and said, and wrote, "A mess." He looked up. "In what way, precisely?"

Latimer eyed the notebook. "In a way that caused her to shoot herself, what do you think?"

"She was depressed?"

"Depressed, agitated, anxious, suicidal."

"She expressed these feelings to you?"

"I could tell. So could Ray. So could the kids, for that matter."

"What if I were to inform you that others have said she'd been quite upbeat before her death?"

"That dyke across the road, you mean?"

"I've been told by more than one source that Mrs. Latimer was intending to divorce your son. Leaving home was the first step to doing that."

Nothing altered in Leonard Latimer's chemistry. "News to me."

"Your son didn't tell you? I'm astonished."

"I didn't know anything about any divorce talk."

"If Alison had divorced your son, how would that have affected business?"

"What do you mean?"

"Legal fees," Hirsch said, "settlement costs, alimony. You're already struggling, money-wise, can't pay your bills. You'd be forced to sell part of the farm."

"All academic now." Latimer said.

No satisfaction, slyness or triumph, just the bald truth. Hirsch opened his mouth for another question and heard voices within the house. Looking past Leonard's shoulder, he said, "Are Ray and the boys inside?"

"Leave us alone. We're grieving. And for your information the property's not struggling."

"Perhaps I'll pop in later."

"Perhaps you won't. The undertaker's bringing Allie home tomorrow and on Saturday we're cremating her."

They'd released the body? News to Hirsch. He pocketed his notebook. Away to the east a helicopter clattered into view, running along the line of wind turbines on the ridge. *Maybe it's partly down to the turbines*, Hirsch thought. None had been erected on Latimer soil, meaning no rental income. But in the nick of time had come news of Alison's inheritance—except that *that* rug had been pulled from under their feet when she announced she was getting a divorce and taking her money with her.

Leaving Finola Armstrong with her adjoining property and wind farm income.

Hirsch beamed at Leonard. "I expect your son will soon find arms to comfort him."

HIRSCH WENT BACK AND logged on to his email. He read the one from Rosie DeLisle first. *Letting you know that Jennifer Dee's father was best mates with Reid. The suicide hit him hard, so looks like the daughter decided to do something about it.* "But what are you going to do about *her*," muttered Hirsch.

The next email caused him to reach for the phone, dial the number for the Forensic Science Building in the city. Connected to a technician, he cited the reference number and heard the soft rattle of a keyboard.

"Got it," the tech said. "Point two two caliber Brno bolt action. What about it?"

Peering at his computer, Hirsch said, "Says here you found the victim's palm and fingerprints on the stock and the butt."

"Correct."

"Not on the barrel?"

"Correct."

"Wouldn't you expect her to grasp the barrel so she could place the end of it in her mouth? Wouldn't you expect to find prints there?"

"That's your concern, bud. I've known people to do all kinds of things when they shoot themselves. Me, I run tests. *Science.* Motives, impulsive behavior, they don't concern me."

Hirsch heard a young voice and pictured the guy: about thirty, breezy, loved his job, loved the science and the technology—but maybe he was crap at relationships. "Okay, but scientists speculate, right?"

"What's on your mind?"

"You've seen the photos?"

"I have."

"The victim's thumb is still inside the trigger guard, hooked around the trigger."

"Yeah, so?"

"How often would you expect to see that?"

"As against what?"

"As against the body going into spasms, jerking, arms flinging out."

"I see what you mean. But, a first time for everything. No two shootings are alike."

Hirsch moved on, rocking back in his chair and glancing out across the front desk to the community notices. "You found tiny amounts of gunshot residue on her hand and sleeve."

"Correct."

"*Tiny* amounts."

"What about it?"

"And none in her lap or on her thighs?"

"No."

"Wouldn't you expect to, if she sat on the ground with the gun between her legs?"

"Mate, I've seen everything."

"And that's your scientific conclusion," Hirsch said.

"I wouldn't want to get vague on you," the tech said.

Next, Hirsch phoned the forensic pathologist. She was slicing and dicing; she'd call back, the morgue assistant said. Hirsch waited. He should step outside and wash the HiLux before the area commander saw it again, but he waited.

She called an hour later. Thanking her, Hirsch said, "I understand you've released the body for burial."

"Correct."

The voice of a busy, short-shrift woman. Hirsch wasted no time: "Under cause of death you put gunshot wound to the head."

"Yes."

"You go on to say that foul play, accident and suicide are, quote, 'unascertainable.'"

"Correct."

"May I ask what you mean by that?"

"It means exactly what it says. I do not know if another party was present, I do not know the state of the victim's mind at the time of death, I do not know the choreography, for want of a better word, of her last few moments of life. She might have been enjoying the sunshine, idly playing with the rifle until a bunny rabbit came hopping into range and, in manoeuvring the rifle, accidentally shot herself. Or she committed suicide. Or someone staged it. Did she leave a note?"

"No."

"Like I said, 'unascertainable.'"

"But suggestive?"

"You know I won't speculate."

Please speculate, Hirsch thought.

Instead, the pathologist said, "I can't rule anything absolutely in or absolutely out. 'Unascertainable' does not mean the death wasn't suspicious or wasn't accidental. A gunshot to the head was the cause of death but an autopsy cannot ascertain the circumstances surrounding it."

"You've informed the Port Pirie CIB?"

"I have."

"And?"

"I have no idea what they'll do with it. I merely passed on my report."

"Okay, what about the marks on the body?"

"I found a subcutaneous bruise just above the collarbone when I peeled back the skin on the right side of her neck, and—"

"Suggestive of someone trying to throttle her?"

"You're jumping the gun. I can't ascertain what happened. And if you will let me continue, I also found a couple of tiny abrasions on her abdomen, a small bruise on one breast, a cut on the back of her left wrist, all trivial."

"Suggestive of . . . ?"

"A word you seem to like, Constable Hirschhausen. Suggestive of ordinary wear and tear from housework or gardening, for all I know, and so, again, 'unascertainable.'"

I hope that someone, somewhere, is ascertaining something, Hirsch thought. Before he could speak, the pathologist added, "On the other hand, when people die violently—when they shoot themselves, for example—or are in a heightened mental state, they mark or injure themselves. I've seen it in cases of anxiety and panic attacks, a need to wrench at upper body clothing, for example."

"But you've also seen women who have been forcibly manhandled."

"Yes."

"You can't ascertain that that happened in this case?"

"No."

"Anything under her nails?"

"No."

"Recent sexual activity?"

"No."

"What about *old* injuries?"

"She'd fractured her wrist at some point in the past."

"How? Could someone have bent it back, twisted it?"

"That I can't ascertain," the pathologist said.

"Toxicology?"

"Negative."

"Underlying medical conditions?"

"None."

"You've been a great help," lied Hirsch.

NEXT HE CALLED PORT Pirie, the lead detective reciting him the highlights of his report: "'. . . death consistent with a self-administered gunshot wound with further investigations pending'—meaning that's as far as we'll take it. Meaning you're preparing the brief, so it's your job to tell the coroner she was nuts. Sorry, balance of her mind was disturbed."

"But," said Hirsch, outlining his buts, concluding with the pathologist's claim of unascertainable.

"Exactly. It means foul play can be ruled out."

"No," said Hirsch, "it means that foul play *can't* be ruled out. In other words, foul play might be ruled in, if other evidence is found."

"Semantics," the voice from Port Pirie said, "and there is no other evidence."

THREE HOURS LATER, SPURLING was standing at the front counter.

"You rocking the boat, Sunshine?"

You came all the way down here to ask me that? "Sir?"

"My detectives can't see that any further action is needed on Latimer."

"So they told me, sir, but I need to be thorough."

"Oh, is that it? Do you have evidence of foul play?"

"No, sir. Not yet."

"When you do, *if* you do, I want to hear about it."

"Sir."

"Meanwhile, do you know a Wendy Street?"

"I have met her," Hirsch said carefully.

"And?"

"Schoolteacher, nice woman, widow, I think."

"Not the troublemaking sort?"

"I wouldn't say so, but I don't really know. Why?"

"She's called for a public protest meeting, police bullying in Redruth."

"Oh."

"Keep your eyes and ears open, all right?"

"Sir."

"And get that bloody windscreen fixed."

CHAPTER 22

FRIDAY MORNING, HIRSCH PARKED outside Redruth Automotive.

It was a sprawling place a couple of blocks from the motel, and "Automotive" was a catch-all term: you could buy a used car from the dozen tired vehicles in the side yard, fill your tank from one of three bowsers, diesel, unleaded and premium unleaded, get your oil changed or motor tinkered with in the workshop and, in a vast, silvery shed out the back, have your scratches, dents and crumples smoothed over.

That's where Hirsch found the boss. "Sergeant Kropp said you're the man to see about a cracked windscreen," he said, blinking as he stepped from drenching sunlight into shadows, air laced with chemicals and the stutter and clang of machinery.

Bernie Judd grunted, muscling past Hirsch to stare at the HiLux. Then he shook his head as if confirming worst fears. "She's stuffed, mate. Can't be repaired. I can replace it for you."

He was shorter than Hirsch, older, full of twitches and fury like a man who has sworn off cigarettes and alcohol. He glanced again at the windscreen, critically along each flank of the vehicle, then at his watch, Hirsch's uniform and finally somewhere past Hirsch's right ear. Stubby ginger hair on a bumpy scalp, fine gingery hair on his forearms and wrists, gingery freckles, grimy nails. A lopsided face, as though he held contradictory positions at once, condoner and judge.

"Take long to get one in?" Hirsch asked.

Judd jerked his head. "Got a good one out the back. Off a wreck, but not a scratch on it."

"Done," Hirsch said. "When?"

"Got things to do in town? Be ready in a couple of hours."

Hirsch handed over the keys. "We've been investigating that hit-and-run up at Muncowie. I guess the others have already asked if any vehicle has come in with—"

"Like I told Nicholson, nothing's come in."

Hirsch nodded philosophically. "Has he been working here for long?"

"Wouldn't call it working here. Him and his mate give me a hand now and then." He glared at Hirsch. "There a law against it?"

Hirsch shook his head. Plenty of police regulations, though. He peered into the dimness again, at the hoists, paint bays, drums, workbenches and two young and three slightly older men in overalls. The only vehicles in there were a farm ute patched with pink primer, a station wagon with a crumpled tailgate and a Honda he recognized as belonging to Finola Armstrong. "You do small jobs? My own car has a couple of dents."

"We do everything. Give you a good price," Judd said, staring at the silver watch face nestled in the ginger furze surrounding his wrist. "Would this be an insurance job?"

"Not exactly."

"Not exactly," Judd said. "Well, bring her in and I'll see what I can do."

"Fair enough." Hirsch turned to go. "Getting back to that hit-and-run: they reckon Melia Donovan was in an accident two or three weeks prior, older boyfriend. Know anything about that?"

"Not me. See you in a couple of hours."

"Wasn't Nicholson, was it? We were having a laugh the other day how his girlfriend crashed his car only she didn't have a license so he had to do some quick thinking."

A kind of stillness settled in Judd. As if Hirsch hadn't changed the subject he said, "Give me your mobile number. As soon as we've fitted the glass, I'll give you a bell."

HIRSCH WALKED.

First to a café, where the coffee was tepid and weak, the vanilla slice gluey and the conversations limited to the weather. It was going to be a long, hot summer. Not that anyone asked for Hirsch's opinion. Customers and staff averted their faces from him. His uniform worked to shut him off, and so, as he sipped and chewed, he tried to imagine how Wendy Street's public protest meeting might play out. He saw a big room, perhaps in the town hall, with Superintendent Spurling, a public relations inspector, a deputy commissioner and maybe Kropp himself seated at a large table at the head of the room, trying for smiles and patience and genial common sense. But the crowd would not have logic or patience on its side, only heat and hurt. One by one they would stand, awkward men and women who'd felt fine and flashing moments before but now, in the spotlight, tripped over their words and lost the threads of their accusations. A disordered atmosphere, the crowd blurting accusations that trailed into nothing or were overheated or roamed off the point, while Spurling and the others tried to smile and reassure and give everyone a fair go and water it all down with platitudes fed them by the public relations guy.

Where would Nicholson and Andrewartha be? Seated in the front row, solid and aggrieved, their uniforms too tight on them, their upper bodies so beefy they couldn't fold their arms with comfort—but wanting to, to show contempt or indifference. Their wives would sit with them, mirror images of their husbands, large, dimly intelligent, stubborn, sulky. Kropp's wife? She'd be out of sight somewhere.

Hirsch pushed his plate away. He left the café, strolled around the little square, bought the *Advertiser*, read it in the rotunda. Barely forty minutes had elapsed. He strolled into an op shop and immediately out again. Why did all op shops have an out of tune radio playing in the background? His fingers had itched to adjust the dial.

The little hillsides above the square beckoned and he found himself climbing narrow streets between stone walls dating from the 1850s. Jasmine scented the air, dense on back fences, and fake diamonds glinted where the sun struck the adzed stone.

Then down to Redruth Creek. According to a pamphlet in a plastic stand beside a plaque, huts had appeared along the creek in 1843, when Colonel Frome was surveying the northern reaches of the colony, but there was no town until 1850, when a shepherd, Alfred Tiver, spotted traces of copper oxide in the local stone. South Australia might have foundered if not for the mine. Twenty years later, the shafts were depthless blue pools of water that defeated the pumps, and the Cornish Jacks had migrated to other towns and mines, but not before the hillsides and flatlands had been denuded of trees, the timber consumed by the boilers or staked against the pressing earth deep under the ground.

"Huh," said Hirsch.

He crossed an iron bridge, guided by a map on the back fold of the pamphlet. Here near the bank of Redruth Creek was a square of miners' cottages with a common area in the middle, tiny tenement houses with undersized doors and windows set in thick blank walls. They didn't look the least Australian to Hirsch's eye but straight out of old Cornwall. Tourist accommodation now, according to the pamphlet.

Finally he followed the map to the museum halfway uphill from the town. It was a converted boiler shed, probably freezing in winter and stifling in summer but not so bad this morning. Upslope from it were great excavations in the hillsides, nude stone remnant walls and chimneys and deeply rusted iron frames and gantries. Hirsch stopped before entering. Below him the town threaded peacefully through the valley folds, a series of peaceful red roofs and oleander bushes. The hillsides looked bare. There was no wind. A hawk floated. There were no people about, no tourists or tourist buses in the car park or hikers approaching along the Heritage Track, which wound through to the mine from the ruins of the colonial-era jail near the creek.

He stepped into the museum, greeted curtly by an elderly man who turned the pages of a newspaper. The main display was a diorama of the copper mine. Miner's picks hung on the walls, together with shovels, brass telescopes, spears, boomerangs and woomeras. Old shop mannequins displayed mid-nineteenth-century trousers, jerkins, dresses, bonnets and shawls. Tables were laden with crockery and knotty green and blue glass bottles. Bentwood chairs. Lamps. An 1851 edition of the *Adelaide Observer*. And several pieces from more recent times: a pedal radio, an inky school desk, photographs of Army volunteers in 1917 and 1942 and of the cricketer Garfield Sobers visiting the primary school in the 1950s. Here and there were glass cabinets crammed with silver napkin rings and sugar bowls, christening gowns and porcelain shepherds. People would move house, or their old back-roads grandfather would die, and the museum would get anything that wasn't wanted, didn't work or couldn't be sold to a secondhand dealer. It wasn't quite junk and was even halfway interesting, but Hirsch's interest didn't stretch past fifteen minutes and he left, aware of the grouchy gaze of the curator, proof the town's hatred of Kropp and his boys was rubbing off on him.

HIRSCH WAS SAUNTERING BACK along the main street, draining a bottle of water, when his phone pinged: *Yr cars ready.*

He found the HiLux parked on the forecourt of Redruth Automotive, looking dusty and hand-printed with grease but with a spotless new windscreen. He entered the dimness of the panel-beating shed, benign, unprepared for the meaty forefinger that stabbed him in the chest. "Butt out of my business, all right?"

Nicholson. Hirsch went into a half-crouch.

Nicholson laughed. "What, you're going to try karate on me? You a martial arts expert now?"

Hirsch straightened. They were all watching from the shadows, the overalled men and Judd and a young woman he didn't recognize. Ignoring Nicholson, he said to Judd, "Keys in the ignition?"

Clearly Judd had called Nicholson and was expecting something else to happen, not this. "Er, yep, good to go."

"Don't fucking turn your back on me," Nicholson said. "Arsehole, sticking your nose in."

Hirsch tried walking toward the sunlight, but Nicholson confronted him, his big paw around the woman's forearm. "Meet Bree, arsehole. Bree, meet the cunt who dobs in his mates."

Hirsch said, "How old are you, Bree?"

"You prick, you absolute fucking prick."

The punch was fast and stone hard, winding Hirsch. He staggered, bent over and, presently, hurled the spring water over the floor and his shoes. He was a good target like that and Nicholson booted his backside.

"Nick," wailed the girl, "stop it."

Nicholson ignored her, dancing around Hirsch, aiming kicks. "Dog. Maggot. Slime ball. Bree's *nineteen*, arsehole. Old enough."

Hirsch found a spot of oily floor and sat, his back to the leg of a metal bench. Getting his wind back he said, "Bree, do you have a driver's license?"

"What the fuck is this?" screamed Nicholson. "Eh? You nuts? Butt out of my business."

The man's spittle flecked Hirsch's lapels and face. Hirsch swiped his forearm across his cheeks and mouth, the girl saying, "Nikko, don't, let's just go."

She does look nineteen, Hirsch thought, taking in the hacked about hair, skinny arms, a tattoo on one shoulder, rings here and there in her poor pink spongy flesh. She wasn't unlovely, just a young woman cowed by a bully. And he'd seen her before, he realized, serving food at the Woolman on the night of the football final.

Nicholson loomed over him. "Stay the fuck away from me and my girlfriend and my business, all right?"

WHEN HIRSCH CLIMBED TO his feet he ached, felt impotent and knew his uniform was a wreck. Judd and his employees had melted away. The air in the shed was superheated and dense and silent and the noon sun, a fat block of it angling a short distance in at the doorway, was lighting up dust motes. Hirsch walked stiffly into that light, out into the fresh air.

One of the panel-beaters stood beside the HiLux, dangling the keys. Hirsch expected taunts and contempt but what he got was, "Few things you should know."

"Yeah? What?"

"Bree's good people, doesn't deserve the hassle."

"I'm not going to hassle her."

The man nodded. He was narrow-faced, saturnine, slow and deliberate. "But Nicholson's another matter."

Hirsch waited. He placed a hand on the hot metal for support. He removed his hand again.

"Him and Andrewartha," the man said.

"I understand they work here in their spare time."

"The odd job, yes."

He was glancing around now as if he had eyes on his back, so Hirsch reached for the keys as if they were not having this discussion. He murmured, "Kropp's part of it, too?"

"Strictly behind the scenes. I will deny all this."

"Uh-huh. How much do I owe you?"

"Taken care of. We handle all the police repairs and servicing."

Hirsch put away his wallet. "Okay."

He knew enough now. Judd, getting all of the department's business in the area, probably overcharged and shared the excess with Kropp and his boys. The after-hours work would be cash in hand. And there were always crash scenes in the area, vehicles needing a tow, the police well-placed to advise distressed motorists about Redruth Automotive.

Hirsch nodded his thanks and climbed behind the wheel. The interior was baking hot. "Melia Donovan."

"What about her?"

"I've heard talk of a car crash, an older boyfriend."

"Can't help you."

OR WON'T. BY MID-AFTERNOON Hirsch was back in Tiverton, wielding a hose in the narrow driveway beside the station house. Squirted and swiped, trying to rid the metal of road dust and panel-beaters' grime. Presently he heard voices, high and sweet, cars and car doors slamming: school was letting out across the road.

He straightened his back to watch. Today, in the midst of spring sunshine and honest physical labor, and surrounded as he'd recently been by sudden death, he wanted reminders of innocence or blamelessness. Some kids were climbing into cars, others were kicking a football around, watched by a teacher who kept glancing at her watch. Then a figure separated from the others. Katie Street. She was coming to see him, he realized. She stopped, looked left and right along the empty highway, and ran across, halting abruptly on the footpath.

"Hello there," he said, glancing around for her mother.

"Hello."

"Waiting for your mum?"

Katie looked briefly stricken and confused. Grief, Hirsch realized. Until recently the person who'd dropped her off and picked her up from school most days had been Alison Latimer. Not only that, she'd been a regular visitor at the house across the road. Inevitably a closeness had developed. "Come and wait with me in the yard," he said.

She entered reluctantly, Hirsch making no big deal of it but turning off the hose and dropping the chamois in the murky bucket beside a back tire. "Would you like a drink? A snack?"

She did what kids do, shrugged elaborately, wanting the treats but not prepared to say so outright.

"I've got Coke and Tim Tams." Left behind by the previous tenant. He hadn't checked the use-by dates.

"Okay."

"Stay there."

He came back with two cans and the packet, both safe to consume. They sat companionably on the front step, where the sun warmed them as the world went by, what there was of it now that most of the parents had come and gone across the road. Hirsch eyed Katie surreptitiously. She chewed, brushed at crumbs, jumped when he crackled his empty can. Not to be outdone, she crackled hers.

Jack Latimer is off school for a while, he thought. *Meanwhile, I offer security until her mother arrives to collect her. Or she has something to say.*

It came finally, the voice almost a whisper: "I didn't shoot Alison."

"Good grief, of course not, no one thinks you did."

He didn't have the language or the know-how to explain a suicide to a child. Then again, why shouldn't she be told? And maybe she had been told. That led him to secondary thoughts: What if Alison Latimer had been shot in her car, then carried to the hut? Or shot in her house, ditto. Or shot at her parents' house, ditto.

Then Katie was up and running, out onto the footpath. "Mum! Mum!"

Wendy Street had been about to turn into the school when she caught sight of her daughter. She braked, swung the Volvo around and parked at the curb. Gazing hard at Hirsch, she got out, passed around the front of her car and clamped Katie against her thigh. "Hello, darling girl," she said, eyes busy, taking in the school, the dripping HiLux, the Coke cans and Hirsch, establishing a narrative from the evidence. "Sorry I'm late," she said. "Unexpected staff meeting."

She was inviting an explanation, and Katie sensed that. "I just came over to say hello."

"Did you."

"We had a treat. Coca Cola and Tim Tams."

Wendy shuddered. "Nectar of the gods. Well, I'd better get you home."

She was watching Hirsch intently, Katie glued to her side. "I understand you'll be briefing the coroner."

Hirsch acknowledged that he was, adding, "It would help if I could have a word with you sometime."

"Come for dinner," Katie said.

Her mother, nonplussed, recovered and said, "There you have it. Dinner. Six thirty—country hours."

CHAPTER 23

COUNTRY FOOD: LAMB CHOPS and vegetables.

Then at eight thirty, Katie in bed, they talked, Hirsch in an armchair, Wendy on the sofa, separated by a heavy rug on polished floorboards. Bookshelves to waist height lined three walls, with photographs, prints and one watercolor arranged in the spaces above. No television—that sat in a sunroom at the back of the house. Hirsch checked the book titles: biographies, photography, art, travel and a mix of good and crap fiction. No cookbooks, and none that he'd seen in the kitchen, thank the lord above. Vases, a couple of small brass gods from some trip to Southeast Asia.

Street was watching. An ironic flicker in her face and voice she said, "Pass muster?"

Hirsch gave her a faint grin. "Nice room."

"For an interrogation."

"A chat."

"A chat," Wendy said, and stretched her limbs and arranged herself along the length of the sofa. Hirsch was pretty sure she was having fun with him. Her gaze was sleepy with a hint of humor.

"Fire away."

Hirsch took a breath. "The popular consensus is that Mrs. Latimer committed suicide."

Wendy Street dropped her mild smartarse act. She swung upright, tears filling her eyes, a faint glistening in the dim light of the floor lamp beside her. "Can't we call her Alison?"

"Sure."

"And as far as I'm concerned, she *didn't* kill herself."

Hirsch shifted in his chair. "You were close?"

"Katie and I moved here four years ago and I met her pretty much straight away. We became friends. Walking distance from each other, and I think she was lonely."

"What can you tell me about her? Her health. Moods."

"I know what you're getting at. Look, now and then she complained of stiffness in her hand, maybe arthritis, and she said the wind turbines got to her, especially at night when an easterly wind was blowing. She'd wake up in shock with her heart pounding, she said, and suffered from sleep deprivation."

Hirsch thought of his own reaction to the turbines. "I had a strange feeling when I stood by one of the turbines the other day. Like I was seasick."

"Yet other people aren't affected. Katie and I sleep like babes. Which is not to deny what you and Allie felt. There's anecdotal evidence of a syndrome due to the noise and low-frequency soundwaves."

"Her husband and sons weren't affected?"

"No. But her mother-in-law was. These wind farms have split families and split communities. Ray and his father were dead set on getting turbines on the property and were angry when the company decided on Finola Armstrong's place instead."

"This syndrome: Could it have affected Alison so much that she'd take her own life?"

"No. Absolutely not."

"I can't overlook the fact that she made a previous suicide attempt."

"Look, when I first met her, Allie was timid and hesitant, but she opened up gradually and admitted things weren't great in her marriage and that she felt depressed. She'd have panic attacks and heart arrhythmia, get very down sometimes. I suggested she should speak to her doctor about going on anti-depressants, but she shied away from that. I think she was scared her husband would find out. Then about a year ago she was found with a gun as if she intended to shoot herself."

"Did she ever talk of suicide to you?"

"She told me once she wished she could end it all. At the time I thought she meant she wanted to get out of the marriage. I still think that. I don't think she was saying she wanted to kill herself."

"Why didn't she just leave? Ask for a divorce?"

"The boys, I suppose. And she was afraid, had no skills to speak of, no money, and there are no jobs for an unskilled woman her age around here."

"But she did walk out a couple of times, went to stay with her parents?"

Wendy struggled with her throat, trying to swallow. "Once late last year, and again last week."

"What did her husband do or say? Her father-in-law, for that matter?"

"I don't know. But Ray did say to her, all the time, 'The only way you'll leave here is in a box.'"

"She told you that?"

"Yes."

The statement sat there between them. "Did he hit her? Did you see evidence of it or did she ever mention it?"

"No, but she'd hold herself stiffly sometimes. Did the autopsy find any unexplained bruises on her body?"

Hirsch knew he didn't have to answer that. "No."

"I'm surprised. But let's say he *had* hit her in the past. What was she going to do about it? She couldn't report him to the police: he's *mates* with them. Footie club mates, what's more."

Hirsch said carefully, "And you don't have a high opinion of the Redruth police even if Mr. Latimer didn't have ties to them."

She shrugged. "They're bullies." Then her face altered, sharpened. "It can't hurt to tell you: I intend to call a public meeting about them—a protest meeting."

Hirsch said slowly, "Okay."

"I've been in touch with your superintendent."

Hirsch said, "Good."

She squinted at him, not satisfied, as if she suspected he already knew, so to deflect her he said, "How was Alison this past week? She left home again, like before, but did she seem downhearted about it?"

"The opposite. I can't describe it, upbeat, even elated, as if her eyes had been opened. She was going to ask for a divorce."

She hadn't been upbeat the day Hirsch met her but like a doll, stiff, cold, alien, powerless. He'd been in uniform, however, so she probably distrusted him, saw him as siding with Kropp, her husband, anyone who might want to put a halter on her.

"Did she tell you she'd come into an inheritance?"

"Of course. She knew it wasn't enough to buy a house in the city, but was enough to buy *time* somewhere, get settled, look for a job. Breathing space money. Running away money."

"Did her husband know about it?"

"Motive, right?"

"You tell me."

"He knew."

A child's troubled cough floated down the hallway. Wendy stiffened, head cocked, ready to take to her feet. There was no follow-up cough. She relaxed again, gave Hirsch a crooked smile, and said, "The Latimers are rich, right?"

Hirsch nodded cautiously. "They appear to be."

"Exactly," Wendy said. "*Appear* to be. But it's all tied up in land and equipment. The Latimers are big spenders. The biggest and best tractor, the biggest and best shearing shed, the biggest and best stud ram."

"Alison told you this?"

"It's common knowledge."

"What did Alison say about it?"

"She told me there was never enough household spending money. Always plenty for a new truck or another parcel of land, but she was never allowed to spend anything on the house. The fridge was on its last legs, the carpet needed replacing, the curtains had been there since the year dot. It did her no good to complain or beg. She said her father-in-law was a real control freak. He'd go through her supermarket receipts and ask why hadn't she bought no-brand tissues, why such expensive shampoo . . ."

"Ray put up with it?"

"Everyone did. Of course, Ray's been learning at his father's knee. He's like his dad, bad-tempered, a heavy drinker, a tyrant at home. Rarely has, *had*, a kind word for Allie. He used to snap his fingers to get her attention."

"I know the type."

Wendy shuffled forward on the sofa. "Look, everyone sees Ray as the life and soul of the party, community-spirited, an all-round good bloke. But in private it's a different story. Allie said he could be quite cold and indifferent to her side of the family, and he'd barely talk to her or the kids except to lay down the law."

Hirsch pictured Raymond Latimer standing over his sons and his small-boned wife, weaving threats around their ears, his voice low and insinuating when it wasn't raised, his big fingers twisting and flicking. The image came on strongly and felt real. "The other day Jack seemed frightened that I'd tell his father he'd been shooting the rifle."

"I'm not surprised."

"Do you think Ray hits his sons?"

"According to Allie, no. But he yells and browbeats them, especially Craig. You should hear him at football matches. The parent from hell."

"Everything comes back to football."

Hirsch said it lightly, but Wendy wasn't amused. "Football, cricket, tennis, in that order. And because Tiverton's too small to field its own teams, the locals gravitate to Redruth." She shot Hirsch a mirthless grin. "And that's how Ray Latimer became pals with your sergeant."

Hirsch returned the grin.

"The thing is," she said, "Ray was a district champion when he was young. A city team was going to sign him up. But he hurt his knee and the big dream came to nothing. Now he's trying to relive it through Craig. He keeps pushing the poor kid, but Craig's hopeless at sport, quite uncoordinated, and his heart's not in it. I bet he wishes he were still at boarding school where Ray can't bully him."

Hirsch noted that. "Boarding school?"

Another grin devoid of humor. "The official line is, Craig was homesick, but they pulled him out to save on school fees."

"We keep returning to money."

"Don't we. I think there *was* money, a generation or two ago, but Leonard and Ray have spent it all, there have been droughts, costs have risen, incomes have fallen . . ."

Echoing what Ray Latimer had told Hirsch. "Apparently they owe money here and there," he said, thinking of the Tiverton shopkeeper.

"I'm not surprised."

Hirsch tried to see all the angles, feel the atmosphere in the Latimer household. "So Craig was taken out of boarding school and now he's at Redruth High."

"Yes."

"How does he feel about that?"

"I see him in the yard and the corridors, looking lost and miserable. I've tried to talk to him, but he avoids me. Ray's influence, probably. I'm not kosher, a bad influence, a pinko, feminist rabblerouser who might put ideas in his head like I did Alison."

Hirsch gave her a crooked grin. "How does Craig get to school?"

"Hah! Exactly. Here I am, just across the road, willing and able, but he takes the bus."

"And life for Jack?"

"His bad foot saves him from the worst of it. He was never going to be a football champion. But I imagine he's just as browbeaten as Craig."

They fell silent. Hirsch said, "Tell me more about Ray."

"Well, he's a Latimer."

"Meaning?"

"The Latimer men have a certain reputation. The moment I moved in here Leonard dropped by to introduce himself, welcome me to the district. That's nice, I thought, until he backed me up against the fridge and touched my boobs and wondered if I got lonely with no man in my life."

"What did you do?"

"Shoved him away, told him I'd report him to the police, to which he replied, 'Good luck with that,' and I've had little to do with him since."

Hirsch bit his lip. "If you don't mind my asking, is Katie's father . . . ?"

"Died. Car crash."

"I'm sorry."

She shrugged but she also blinked. "Anyway, the fruit doesn't fall far from the tree. Before long, Ray made his move. Ray favors a more subtle approach. He likes the double entendre, the insinuation, the accidental shoulder or finger or groin contact. I'm expecting Craig to have a go next." She waved one arm agitatedly. "Sorry, scrub that."

Hirsch said, "Did, or does, Ray put the move on other women?"

"Is that a trick question? Everyone knows about Saturday night."

Hirsch held his palm up. "Country grapevine. Put it this way: Has he been at it for a while? Did Alison know about Finola Armstrong or his other women, if any?"

"Ray would *taunt* her. He'd stay out all night, come home without showering, take or make phone calls and not bother to hide what it was about."

"A sweetheart," Hirsch said. He tried to find his way into his next question. "What's your take on Finola Armstrong?"

"Well, it's easy to condemn someone, isn't it? I don't like her much, but that has nothing to do with her sleeping with Ray Latimer. I just don't warm to her. Too hard-edged and pragmatic. If it doesn't involve the seasons or the harvest or stock prices, she's got nothing to say for herself. But she is a widow, after all. She was left with a farm to run and has made a success of it."

"A practical woman."

Wendy laughed harshly. "If you mean she'd stage a suicide to solve a problem, I just can't see it. I mean, what problem?"

"Removal of her rival in love."

"So she could land Raymond Latimer? It's the other way round: Allie's death will solve *his* problem."

"Okay."

"Please, Hirsch, look closer to home. Ray and his father are seen as good blokes, pillars of the community, the local gentry, but underneath it, they're awful men."

She'd called him "Hirsch." He liked it. "But so far everyone with a motive also has an alibi."

"They paid someone."

Hirsch looked at her. Anyone else, he would have scoffed. The meal sat pleasantly in him and the light was warm and dim. Music played softly, an iPod on a random loop—The Waif's "Moses and the Lamb" right now, of all things. Hirsch, lulled by it, didn't want to go home.

The wicked gonna wail and weep . . .

Wendy said, "You didn't like it when I said I'd Googled you."

Hirsch stared at her, Wendy with her legs folded beneath her, her shapely feet resting along her thigh. There was a moment, but he let it run out like sand.

The savior coming with a sickle in his right hand.

CHAPTER 24

OCTOBER GATHERED ITS SKIRTS and raced past.

Alison Latimer's funeral attracted half the district and seemed to Hirsch an expression of confused grief and heartache, an occasion that sundered, not cemented, the community. He didn't see any hired killers lurking and a gritty wind blew and the ants still raced in the red dirt. The days were longer now and the sun had heat in it, and old farmers in the churchyard informed Hirsch that it was "going to be a long, hot summer," sniffing the air cannily. He dared not laugh. What did he know about disturbances of the bones, the air?

HE SETTLED INTO HIS small-town role of stern father, kindly father, father-confessor, bloke next door and go-to guy. All of the locals had his mobile number and some found a reason to call it. Or they knocked on his door if the HiLux was parked in the driveway. They wanted him to find their missing stock, sheepdogs, fence posts, fuel drums, motorbikes and mothers suffering from dementia. And he drove, sometimes 300 km a day, investigating thefts, introducing himself at remote farms, checking on the alcoholic shearer who had a history of violence, the intellectually disabled forty-year-old whose mother and sole caregiver had just died, the alternative-healing woman who'd threatened wind-farm workers, the schizophrenic who'd stopped taking his pills. He made a dash to Redruth with a gasping teenager whose asthma inhaler had run out and whose parents were in the city. He administered breath tests, doorknocked people who'd failed to renew their driving licenses or car registrations, had a quiet word with kids seen doing burnouts (once in front of the police station). He intercepted a ute with a stolen stud ram on board. Even helped an elderly couple get their shopping home. It wasn't all police work. One day he confessed to a mild fondness for tennis and found himself on the tennis club committee, where he was quizzed on any letter-writing or bookkeeping skills or experience he might have. He could have been everyone's mate, but the secret to being a cop in a small rural community—the secret and the pity—was not to let himself get too close to the locals.

Even if they'd let him.

THUS HIS LIFE SETTLED. What wasn't settled but ate at him were the deaths of Melia Donovan and Alison Latimer. While the accident investigators widened their search for a suspect vehicle, contacting crash repairers and hospitals, viewing CCTV tapes along Barrier Highway from Broken Hill to Adelaide, Hirsch kept the pressure on Gemma Pitcher's mother, extended family, friends and enemies. Had Gemma made contact? Phone calls? Letters? Emails? Anything on Facebook? Was there a favorite town or holiday spot she'd liked in the past? Old boyfriend? He phoned the far-flung contacts and visited those closer to.

He also called in on Leanne Donovan. He had nothing to tell her. She asked him not to come again.

THE REST OF HIS time was spent keeping others off his back.

DeLisle, Croome, Kropp, Spurling, Wendy Street, all wanting updates or action.

"I need to speak to Ray Latimer, Sarge," he told Kropp.

"Lay off a while longer. Let the family grieve."

"He's your mate. Ask him to phone me."

"Lay off, I said."

Wendy Street would call to say, "I've remembered something," and relate a bit of recalled conversation, something Alison Latimer had said about her husband. None of it proved intent, or that a crime had been committed.

AND SPURLING CALLED HIM regularly. Dropped in again one day, insisting he be briefed in Hirsch's sitting room this time.

"Like what you've done to the place."

Painted the walls, got a carpet cleaner in, replaced the curtains and light shades, hung a couple of Tiverton Primary School Community Art Fair watercolors: wildflowers somewhere out east, and the Razorback under boiling black clouds but shot by a bolt of sunlight.

"Putting down roots, sir."

"Sure you are," Spurling said.

The area commander settled himself on one of the tatty armchairs, tatty under a patchwork quilt cover from the same art fair. "Remember I asked you for updates on your Redruth colleagues?"

"Sir."

"I am yet to hear from you, Constable Hirschhausen. Why is that?"

"Been busy," Hirsch said, "and I haven't had anything to do with them lately."

Spurling grunted. "The Street woman's going ahead with her public meeting. No date set, but goodness, what a lovely experience that's going to be."

He stared at Hirsch. Hirsch held his tongue.

"Mr. Inscrutable. Where are we with the suicide? The coroner can't proceed until the police hand him a brief."

"The thing is, sir, I don't think it was a suicide."

"Here we go. All right, spit it out."

Hirsch expressed his doubts and frustrations: The car, the rifle, the trampled upon scene. The diamond ring. Alison Latimer's hand. The ballistic report, the pathologist's findings.

"You're light-on regarding evidence," Spurling observed. "Where's the car?"

"Sitting in the impound lot, as far as I know."

"May not be too late to have it printed and tested for fibers and fluids."

Hirsch shook his head. "I tried that. No joy. The windows had been left open, condensation had formed, too much time had elapsed."

"You took photos?"

"A couple of days earlier."

"Printed them out," Hirsch said, handing Spurling a folder.

The superintendent flipped through them, stopping occasionally, glum and unimpressed. "It had been raining from memory?"

"A couple of days earlier."

"Unexplained tire impressions, shoe prints?"

"Tires, no. As for foot traffic, half of Christendom traipsed over the area."

A pause. Spurling said, "Yet her shoes are clean."

"Exactly."

"I know what you're thinking, but in court they'll argue that people don't abandon their instincts. Here's a neat, tidy woman who, even though intending to shoot herself, didn't want to get dirty. She skirted around the mud, kept to the grass."

"Maybe."

"The same applies to the diamond ring. Didn't want it to get damaged or lost or lifted by light fingers. You say she knew about firearms?"

Hirsch shrugged. "Farmer's wife. Country woman."

"Not the most common way for a woman to kill herself."

"No. And look at this." Hirsch poked his forefinger on one

of the photographs. "See the way her thumb's still hooked inside the trigger guard?"

"That's hardly compelling."

"But she had a problem with that hand, a weakness, couldn't straighten her fingers or thumb very well. Meanwhile her prints are on the stock and butt, but *not the barrel.*"

Spurling said, "Again, not compelling. She did have some movement in that hand, yes? And it's not beyond the realms of possibilities that she held the rifle around the trigger area with her right hand and maneuvered the barrel tip into her mouth with the left hand holding the stock rather than the barrel."

"You'd be a good defense barrister, sir."

"Constable, I'm anticipating the questions that might get asked at the inquest—or at trial, if it gets that far, and it seems to me you don't have anyone in the frame for a crime."

Hirsch grunted. At the back of his mind was the thought that he'd paid too much attention to Wendy Street's viewpoint, sympathized because he was attracted to her. "Fair enough."

"And remember that brain injuries cause peculiar behavior. So does the intent to commit suicide." Spurling paused. "Was she checked for GSR?"

"A few flecks."

"There you go. She shot herself."

"It doesn't feel right, sir."

"Anything else on the body?"

"Some bruises and abrasions."

"Suggestive of . . . ?"

Hirsch shrugged. "Of being manhandled."

"Or of falling over, falling against the hut," Spurling said. "Get a second opinion."

"She's been cremated."

"Ah. Well, I suppose you can always get someone else to look at the pathologist's findings."

Spurling got to his feet. On the way out he said, "Get that flaming vehicle washed."

⟶ ⟶ ⟶

THE DAYS PASSED. IF Hirsch happened to be at the police station at lunch- or going-home time, he found himself watching out for Katie Street and Jackson Latimer in the schoolyard across the highway. Forty kids, ranging from five to twelve, and full of din and discord as they flowed out of the buildings and across the playing field or into waiting cars. Sometimes they were the town's only source of sound. He'd pick out Katie Street by her animation, a bright ribbon of movement and intelligence. He'd pick out Jack Latimer, stunned and lost.

Get that flaming vehicle washed . . . Hirsch was obliged to wash it once or twice a week these days, and one Friday in late October, as he sloshed and sluiced with sudsy water, the dust a stubborn film that reappeared in streaks and deltas whenever his back was turned, he heard Katie say, "Put some elbow grease into it."

Hirsch turned. "Care to show me how?"

"I will if you pay me top dollar."

She was full of life there in his driveway. Jack was with her, slow, dazed, hesitant, and it occurred to Hirsch that she'd dragged him with her in an effort to jolt some life into him.

As if I could help, he thought. "You only want me for my Tim Tams," he said, thinking *Christ, why did I say that?*

Katie toed a weed. "Can we wait here till Mrs. Armstrong comes?"

"Sure."

Finola Armstrong? Hirsch supposed it made sense. She lived not far from the children and there would be occasions—afterschool staff meetings, for example—when Wendy Street might be delayed. But why couldn't Ray or his father do the school run occasionally? Too busy? Women's work?

"You guys like a treat while you wait?"

Katie Street was game. She crossed the yard with a toss of her head.

"Make yourself comfortable," Hirsch said, indicating the

front step. He went in, came out with a tray of drinks and bis-
cuits.

But Jack Latimer was hovering at the gate, staring down the
road, seeming lost, as though unsure of the steps to take now.

"Jack?"

The boy stepped from his good foot to his bad, good foot,
bad. "What if she comes and can't find us?"

"Mrs. Armstrong gets a bit cross," Katie explained.

Hirsch could picture it: The impatience, stiffness and social
awkwardness of Finola Armstrong. Seeing the boy wither a little,
he joined him at the gate, risked dropping a hand on his shoulder. "How about it, Jack? Coke and a Tim Tam?"

But the high school bus was pulling up outside Tennant's.
Two girls and three boys alighted, their shirts half out, socks at
ankle height, shoes scuffed, hair this way and that, one girl tug-
ging her hemline from crotch to mid-thigh before her parents
caught her. The five moved off, one girl down a side street, the
other into the shop with two of the boys, the fifth to the end
of the veranda, beside the mailboxes. Craig Latimer. He looked
slumped, unhappy, wound tight, and Jack seemed to shrink further at the sight of him, giving Hirsch a glimpse of the great gulfs
in the family: the grandfather on the hill, the father at the bottom
of the hill or out wildcatting with his women, the older boy giving
off waves of anger, the younger boy waves of desolation.

Then Finola Armstrong's Honda came hurtling into town.
It stopped for Craig and was speeding the short distance to the
side street entrance of the primary school when Jack hobbled
out of Hirsch's gate, waving his arms.

Armstrong braked, U-turned, Jack stepping back to avoid it,
onto Hirsch's toes. "Sorry!"

He looked aghast at what he'd done. Hirsch clasped his
shoulders gently, a brief, bolstering contact, and nodded to
Armstrong through the side window of the car. Craig was in the
back. Jack joined him.

Then Katie was skipping past, crying "See ya!" and getting

into the front with Armstrong. She was a light in darkness, a ribbon of brightness, too good for her glum neighbors.

Hirsch decided to say hello. Walking around to the driver's window, he was watched by Armstrong, who scowled and with reluctance wound her window down. Not hostile, not wary, just affectless, a placid quality to her sun-damaged face.

"Helping out?" he said cheerily.

That's when her whole being altered. It was as if she thought him dim or uninformed. And that's when he saw Alison Latimer's diamond ring on one careworn, farm-chapped hand. She gave a secretive smile. "You could say that."

Hirsch gave her roof a little slap and stepped away from the car. Katie waved, the boys didn't. He returned to his yard and sluiced more mud onto the driveway, trying not to think too hard about what had just happened.

HIS NEXT VISITOR WAS Jennifer Dee.

She banged through the main door of the police station at the end of the first week of November, startling Hirsch in the act of taking down fly-specked public notices, tiny spiders under a couple of them.

"You bastard, I've lost my job because of you."

Hirsch stepped down from his stool before she kicked it out from under him. He eyed the door to his office, the door to his apartment, the front door. She was a slight, teary woman but fired up, and he didn't want to tussle with her in an enclosed space.

Yeah, but she'd brought it upon herself. "You were fired because you planted evidence on me."

"They showed me the tape, you can't even tell it was me."

Her eyes were red, she was trembling, perspiration dampness under her arms and at her neck. Hirsch said, "Would you like a beer? It's beer weather."

She blinked. "What?"

"Beer. Juice, tea, coffee . . ."

She actually stamped her slender foot. "Bob Reid died because of you."

"Bob Reid died because he shot himself in the head."

Perhaps no one had spoken to her frankly yet. She put her hands across her stomach as if he'd hit her. "Because his life was ruined."

"He ruined his own life. He let Quine corrupt him, and when he got found out, he couldn't cope with the strain."

"He only got found out because of you."

"Listen to yourself, Jenny. Are you saying it would have been okay for him to go on stealing and lying and perverting justice? Besides, Internal Investigations knew all about him before they spoke to me."

"You're lying."

She ran out and he didn't follow her. Living with her departing words is what his life would always be. It's what people believed.

CHAPTER 25

COULTER, THE CIRCUIT MAGISTRATE, rotated through the district every couple of weeks and at noon on a Friday in mid-November, a day dry and dusty, building in heat, Hirsch headed down Barrier Highway for the Venn drunk-driving case. On the outskirts of Redruth he noticed the first of several posters on power poles and crumbling walls: POLICE METHODS IN REDRUTH, VOICE YOUR CONCERNS and a date in December. He was surprised: Surely Nicholson and Andrewartha went around ripping them down?

Venn and his wife were waiting on the steps together with a man Hirsch recognized as the lawyer Ray Latimer had used the day his wife was murdered. He should have walked right on by but got his phone out, thumbed the camera icon and made straight for the little group, snapping as he went.

Stopping on the step below them—at a disadvantage, psychologically—he said, "I repeat my warning, Mrs. Venn: if you persist in claiming you were the driver, I'll arrest you for perjury."

The Venns were bright-eyed and bushy-tailed, well-dressed, people for whom nothing went wrong. Jessica Venn took a pace toward Hirsch on thin, stabbing heels, the tendons flexing in her toned legs. A fight! She was spoiling for it. "You jumped-up little—"

The lawyer touched her sleeve. "Jess . . ."

"Well he is."

Now the lawyer fixed on Hirsch, his eyes devoid of moral light. "Was that a threat I heard, Constable Hirschhausen? Directed at my client? As though I, an officer of the court, were invisible?"

"Perjury is perjury," Hirsch said. He stuck out his hand, not sure if the man would shake with him. "And you are?"

The lawyer was obliged to hunch over, reach down. The grip was firm, almost spilling over into a test. Hirsch took stock. They were of an age, the men who ran Redruth, he decided. Early to mid-forties, confident, smooth, full of secret knowledge. This one wore a costly grey suit, stiff white cotton shirt and a paisley tie. Paisley was coming back? No one had told Hirsch. A very clean man, dark-haired, buffed to a shine. Hirsch glanced down at the slender hand: a centimeter of white cuff, a hint of neat, black, expensive wrist hairs curling there.

"Ian Logan."

Hirsch had seen the man's ads in the *Weekly*. Wills, Trusts, Deeds, Conveyancing, Family Law. He said, "I don't know what your clients have told you but—"

"We'll thrash that out before the magistrate, shall we?" Logan said. He nodded at Hirsch's phone. "What have you got there, pictures of the crime?"

He chortled. He was fully alert, never still, taking in the passing vehicles and pedestrians, knowing the secret business of the town. Then he muttered, "Oh, fuck," and ushered the Venns ahead of him into the building. Curious, Hirsch glanced across the street. A young woman with a rope of blonde hair was parting the curtain beads at the entrance to the café fifty meters down the road. She stepped through, the beads briefly disturbed in her wake.

Then the court stenographer and general dogsbody stuck her head out and called Hirsch. He went in.

"WE MEET AGAIN, CONSTABLE Hirschhausen," the magistrate said.

What can you say to that? Hirsch nodded, said "Mr. Coulter," and glanced around the courtroom. No other cases were listed, but Kropp was there. No one else.

In the end, Hirsch had filed two charges, driving under the influence and giving a false statement to police. The damaged guardrail was a matter for the roads department; he'd sent them the details. Now, as Coulter announced the charges, he glanced at Kropp uneasily. Kropp had seemed pissed off with Coulter and Logan the last time Hirsch had been in this courtroom, and seemed so now.

Coulter was speaking. "Mr. Logan, your client has elected to contest these charges in court rather than pay the relevant fines and lose demerit points?"

"That's so, your honor."

"Very well. Constable Hirschhausen?"

Hirsch, with another glance at Kropp, gave his account of the arrest. He turned to Logan, expecting questions, but Coulter called Venn to the stand.

Venn, duly sworn, winked at his wife and grinned at his lawyer and explained that Hirsch was mistaken, it had been his wife at the wheel.

"I'd had a couple of drinks, your honor, and thought it best not to drive and risk endangering other lives."

"Drinks?" said Coulter. "This was the middle of the day."

His tone sounded wrong to Hirsch. It wasn't judicial indignation. It was as if he'd practiced his lines.

Venn said, "We had successfully negotiated a sale, your honor. Mrs. Elizabeth Jennings, who you might recall was widowed tragically two years ago and in the depressed real estate climate had been unable to sell her property. Until now."

"Of course. Fine woman," Coulter said. "Mr. Logan?"

"If I may, your honor, I should like to present a sworn statement made by Mrs. Jessica Venn, wife of the accused, in which she states that she, not her husband, was driving the car in question on the day and at the time and on the road in question."

The magistrate flicked his comfortable fingers. Handed the statement, he read rapidly, then stared at Hirsch, hunched and pugnacious. "Constable? Is this statement a true account of events?"

"I have yet to read it, your honor."

Coulter glanced at Logan, who fished another copy from his briefcase and handed it to Hirsch.

First: date, time, location and background circumstances. Then:

Mindful of his responsibilities, my husband elected not to drive and gave me the key. It was shortly after leaving Mrs. Jennings's property that I got into difficulties. Unused to the potholes, gravel surface, sharp bends and narrowness of the road, I inadvertently sideswiped a guardrail. Alarmed and upset, I pulled over as soon as it was safe to do so and attempted to gather my wits, whereupon Constable Hirschhausen appeared in his four-wheel drive. I got out at once to apologize and explain and, I must confess, seek reassurance and comfort and understanding. Instead, Constable Hirschhausen berated my husband and myself, falsely accusing my husband of driving and me of swapping places with him in order that he might keep his license and avoid a fine.

Witnessed by a notary public in Clare.

"Your response, Constable Hirschhausen?"

Hirsch stood. "Your honor, at the conclusion of this session it is my intention to arrest Mrs. Venn for perjury, and may I state that further charges against Mrs. Venn, and her husband, may be lodged at a later date."

He sat.

"Your honor, really," Logan said, getting wearily to his feet. "If it pleases the court, Constable Hirschhausen made threats to this effect on the steps of the courthouse a few minutes prior to the commencement of today's session. The threats were directed at my clients in my presence and there was no mistaking Constable Hirschhausen's intent. In fact, my clients and I felt most intimidated by the constable's words and manner."

Coulter swung his head, doing pretty convincing outrage. "Is this true, Constable Hirschhausen? Did you threaten Mr. Logan and his clients?"

"Your honor, Mr. and Mrs. Venn are making a mockery of this court. They—"

"You attempted to influence a witness so that she might alter her evidence before the court?"

"I attempted to help her avoid facing a serious—"

"I've heard enough," the magistrate said with a little smack of his gavel. "I find that Mr. Venn does not have a case to answer and is free to go. As for your conduct, Constable Hirschhausen, further action may be sought."

THERE WAS A BIT of gleeful backslapping on the steps outside the courthouse. Hirsch looked on gloomily, the sun warm but unrestorative. Then the steps cleared; cars whisked the Venns and Logan away. His day shot, Hirsch headed down the steps to street level, only to be stopped by Kropp growling in his ear: "Tell me they're wrong, Constable. You did not threaten to arrest the Venn woman for perjury."

Hirsch paused where he was, but decided he'd feel safer on the footpath than mount the steps again. "Not wrong, Sarge."

Kropp joined him and side by side they surveyed the town, which was doing nothing just then. The silence stretched; the bollocking didn't come. All was peace and silence and the sun beat down. Presently Kropp said, "Jenny Dee."

"Sarge?"

"She tried to do the dirty on you?"

"Apparently."

"I had nothing to do with that."

"Thought never crossed my mind."

They didn't mention the hundred-dollar note on the floor of the file room. A farm truck trundled through the town, hauling hay. Presently, Hirsch sneezed, and then the woman with the swinging ponytail emerged from the café and approached the two men. She lifted a hand to Kropp. "Sergeant."

"Linda."

They regarded each other. Kropp said, "You wouldn't be stalking your husband by any chance."

She gave him the ghastly, fixated grin of a stalker. "Heaven forbid."

"That's what I thought."

This was interesting. Hirsch looked on.

"Linda, meet Constable Hirschhausen. Constable, meet the ex-Mrs. Ian Logan."

A quick flash, a brief bit of fire. "I do have an independent identity, Sergeant Kropp."

"Of course. Forgive me."

"I'll forgive you when you take Ian's guns away."

"The court lifted the order, Linda, we had no choice."

She snorted. "You mean *Coulter* lifted the order."

Kropp said nothing, Hirsch taking it as assent.

She said with a sunny smile, "Like everyone, you were Coultered."

"Thanks, Linda."

"You're welcome. Well, I'll be off. Nice seeing you, Sergeant."

"A hundred meters, Linda."

The ex-Mrs. Logan waved negligently at the café. "I was no closer than a hundred and twenty."

"Excellent."

When she was gone, Hirsch put his head on one side. "What was that all about?"

"Old history. Logan put a restraining order on her."

"Why?"

Kropp in his brutal solid way turned slowly to face Hirsch. "You do know that I think you're a dog, right?"

"Sarge."

"But you're also a police member and you were just shafted by Coulter and Logan, so here's the story."

Hirsch watched Kropp gather himself, there on the footpath, under the early afternoon sun. "Ian Logan liked to thump his wife from time to time. Liked to forge her signature, too—banking matters, real estate contracts. Linda reported it, and when we heard he had this violent streak, we confiscated his guns. Shotgun, couple of hunting rifles. Anyway, she got screwed on the divorce and no action was taken on the issue of questionable documents and so he thought it okay to ask for his guns back. Filled out the forms, asked to be deemed, quote, 'a non-prohibited person in relation to a firearms application'—and Coulter approved it. Linda went mental and started hassling everybody."

"They're friends, Coulter and Logan?"

"I'll tell you what else about Coulter," Kropp said, as if Hirsch hadn't spoken. "Last year we went into bat for a wife and kids who were being bashed pretty regularly by the husband. She turns up to court on time, we turn up on time, Coulter doesn't. Apparently he turned up in Riverton. Redruth, Riverton, yeah, easy to confuse the two—if you were drunk or didn't give a damn. So Coulter races back here all pissed off, blaming everyone but himself, and refuses to grant an intervention order or let the woman read her victim impact statement. A week later, her husband hospitalizes her."

Kropp turned his bristly eyebrows to Hirsch. "And so on."

"The Bar Council?" Hirsch said.

"It's like the police force," Kropp said, plenty of nastiness in it. "The first rule is, look after your mates."

Fuck off. Far off down the street, Logan's ex-wife was climbing into an ancient Toyota. The motor caught, toxins belched.

"Nice-looking woman," he said.

"Married young," Kropp said. "Logan likes them young, quote unquote."

"Young as in . . ."

"Young," Kropp said.

Encouraged by Kropp's manner, Hirsch said, "I still need a word with Ray Latimer, Sarge."

"Lay off."

HIRSCH EMAILED SNAPS OF Venn, Logan and Coulter to Rosie DeLisle, using his phone on top of one of the town's seven hills, then bought a ham and salad roll from the café and drove slowly north. Tiverton came into view, the grain silo a stub on the horizon. The sky was huge and empty but faintly smudged out near the Razorback and then his phone came into range again.

Rosie DeLisle, saying, "You think these characters are involved?"

"Call it a hunch. Call it webs of influence and the fact that Ian Logan likes young girls."

"I'll see what I can find."

The next caller was Finola Armstrong, telling him that Craig Latimer was setting fires in the long grass next to her house.

CHAPTER 26

HIRSCH FOUND A FALLOW paddock inside the Latimer property line, consisting mostly of dying grass, red dirt and star thistles, except for a vivid smudge of sooty earth the size of a schoolyard hard against the fence. Dirty red hieroglyphics scored the blackness, the spoor of firefighters and their trucks. Only one truck and four men remained now, Tiverton volunteers mopping up, together with one hopeful neighbor with a drum of water, a Honda pump, a hose and a teenage son on the back. The Mt. Bryan truck had been and gone. Steam rose and hissed. Smoke wisped in the breeze.

"Could have been worse," one of the volunteers said.

Hirsch eyed the fence. Four charred posts, drooping wires, and a meter of blackness creeping onto Finola Armstrong's property. Another hundred meters and it would have reached her sheds, her house. He could see her car in the yard. Couldn't see the Latimers' house: it lay on the other side of a rise.

All those hectares and Craig Latimer comes to the boundary fence to light his fire? No sign of the boy or his father or grandfather. Carrying out some damage control somewhere? Presumably Jack was at school. What was Craig doing home from school?

Hirsch got behind the wheel again and headed back along Bitter Wash Road to the Vimy Ridge gates. Parked, and followed voices to the backyard, one voice bellowing, "I'll give you something to cry about, snivelling little wretch."

Latimer, panting, veins popping, swinging one huge paw in a backswing, the other clamped to his son's neck. Before Hirsch could act, the farmer had whacked the back of the boy's legs.

"Mr. Latimer!"

Latimer's arm froze at the top of another arc. He let it flop, straightened his back. "Stay out of this."

"If you strike your son again, I'll arrest you."

"You're joking."

"No joke."

"Know what the little shit's done?"

"That's what I'm here to find out."

"He was caught lighting matches and throwing them in the grass."

"Let him go."

Latimer shoved the boy from him, face wrenched in disgust. "You great sooky calf, get cleaned up and go to your room. I'm not finished with you."

"You are if you intend to hit him," Hirsch said.

Craig was mucousy, helpless. "Please, Dad, I didn't mean it. I was just—"

Latimer aimed a kick at him. Hirsch grabbed his arm. "I mean it, Mr. Latimer. Touch him again and I'll do you for assault."

"It's private."

"No it's not. It involves me, now. It involves Mrs. Armstrong. It involves the firemen. Is Jack at school?"

Latimer blinked. "What?"

"Is Jack at school?"

"Of course."

"Why didn't Craig go?"

"I thought he had. I thought Finola had taken him to the bus."

"Where's your father?"

"What's with all the questions? He's gone to the bank, if you must know."

Hirsch supposed it was possible the boy had heard talk of hard times, falling income, and decided a fire would bring in insurance money, but the more likely explanation was a lot simpler: family circumstances, recent and historic, had messed with his head.

Latimer was still panting. His hair flopped from heat and exertion, one wing of his shirt had escaped his belt and ash streaked his trousers and boots. He looked half-mad, in fact, and Hirsch stiffened in readiness—but then saw acceptance and good sense and self-pity come creeping back through the big frame and craggy head.

"Are you arresting Craig?"

"Should I?"

"He's just a kid."

"Let's go inside, make a pot of tea, have a talk," Hirsch said. He saw that he had ash on his shoe caps. He polished them on his trousers and promptly thought: *Why did I do that?*

DUST BALLS IN THE kitchen corners, a Corn Flakes packet on its side, a tide mark in the sink, newspapers piled on a couple of the chairs, unopened bills tucked between a pair of rotting apples in a cane basket. All of the love had gone from the room, the house, with the death of Alison Latimer, and it was possible that Finola Armstrong hadn't bothered to clean very often.

Watching Raymond slump at the table, Hirsch filled the kettle. He could see defeat in the heavy shoulders. Then as if sensing the scrutiny, Latimer lifted his head. "You don't know what it's like."

Hirsch sighed. Did he want to hear this? He pulled out a chair and sat opposite Latimer. Behind him the tap dripped and the electric kettle woke unwillingly. "Tell me."

Latimer swiped at his cheeks as if searching for a starting

point, as if there were many starting points. "My son hasn't been coping very well."

"With your wife's death."

"Before that. He didn't want to go to Redruth High but we had no choice, the Saint Peter's fees were crippling us."

"He found it hard to settle in?"

Latimer nodded glumly. "And then Allie moved out and he felt let down. Abandoned. And then she shot herself. Maybe he felt he was to blame, I don't know."

Latimer moved uncomfortably in his chair, continued: "It didn't help matters when Fin started staying over a few nights a week. I probably should have waited a bit. But it wasn't as if Allie and I had been getting on, not for years, really. Plus I thought it would be good for the boys, a woman in the house."

Hirsch didn't believe a word of it. "It was Mrs. Armstrong who caught Craig throwing lit matches into the grass."

Latimer shook his head as if still amazed. "The little bugger said he felt unwell, wanted to spend the day in bed, but when she went across to her house to do some chores, she spotted him in the paddock."

The kettle began tearing at the silence. It shut off. Hirsch got up and hunted for mugs and teabags. "Black? White? Sugar?"

"White and two," Latimer mumbled.

Hirsch smacked everything onto the table. The surface was streaked greasily, as if swiped at rather than cleaned. Latimer made no move to drink his tea. Hirsch sipped and realized the mug was greasy.

He said, "Ray, please don't hit Craig again. What he needs is counseling."

Latimer winced. "How much is that going to cost me?"

Hirsch stared. "You want him to go on lighting fires? What if someone dies?" Then he thought of the killer: "What if someone sues you for a million dollars? One of your neighbors, for example, or the wind farm company?"

Appalled, dismayed, Latimer brought his face back under control. "I'll get him some help. No joke. I mean it."

"Try the school. They'll have access to suitable counselors. So will the family doctor."

"McAskill," muttered Latimer.

"There you go."

A leaking tap got to Hirsch, drips falling with audible plinks. He pushed his chair back, stood, stepped across to the sink. The hot tap was dripping into a cereal bowl, which was piled atop three or four days' worth of cereal bowls. He twisted the tap handle, realising at once it was fully off. The washer needed replacing, and he recalled Wendy Street's words, that the Latimers spent their money on high end farm equipment and breeding stock, not the upkeep of the house. He returned to the table.

The farmer lifted his massive head and muttered, "Got to get that fixed."

"Yes."

"Is Fin going to press charges?"

"I've yet to speak to her."

"Is she going to sue for damages?"

"Like I said, I've yet to speak to her."

"Tell her I'll pay."

"Tell her yourself."

"Yeah, well, she walked out on me."

There was a thump from the distant reaches of the house. Latimer ignored it, but Hirsch was thinking *suicide.* He shoved back his chair and ran. Latimer caught on quickly. Both men clattered down the hallway, an unlovely passage through the house, the wind of their passing agitating another crop of dust balls.

The sign was a relic from primary school art class, CRAIG'S ROOM in colored wooden letters stuck to a board. Hirsch knocked and went in. Craig Latimer had washed inexpertly and dragged on clean clothes. He was handballing a slack football against the curtain, the ball punching the fabric and falling to the floor. Over and over again. He didn't register the alteration to the air, so Hirsch grabbed his arm. "Craig."

The tension went out of the boy. He slid to the floor, his back against the bed, his forehead on his knees. His shoulders heaved, strangled words leaked out of him.

"Stop mumbling," Latimer snarled.

Hirsch shot him a look and joined Craig on the floor. "She abandoned us," that's what the boy was saying, and Hirsch guessed that the father had said it first and the boy had learnt to recite it.

I'm out of my depth here, he thought. And then the bed slid away on the slippery floor, responding to the pressure of their spines. Nothing was satisfactory.

Hirsch swung around onto his knees. "Your dad and I thought it might make you feel better to talk to someone. Not me, not him, not your grandparents but a nice person who will listen and not judge."

His eyes crazy, the boy shrieked, "I'm not crazy."

"You'd better leave," Raymond said.

So Hirsch went next door.

CHAPTER 27

WHERE FINOLA ARMSTRONG TOLD him a little of her recent history.

"When Eric died, men came crawling out of the woodwork. I suppose they thought I'd be an easy touch."

"Did that include Ray Latimer?"

She shook her head. "His *father*, randy old goat."

They contemplated that. Armstrong said, "I think Ray was sniffing around a nurse at the time."

They were seated on a pair of frayed veranda chairs, behind an untamed vine. Hirsch caught glimpses of her yard and sheds and heat-stunned sheepdog and the dusty HiLux through the glossy leaves. Owing to the angle of the house, the burnt patch of grass and star thistles lay a few degrees out of sight.

He said, "But you got talking and things developed because there'd been a grass fire."

"Yes."

"And now we have another fire."

"Uh-huh. But that *first* fire," Armstrong said, "we blamed on a cigarette tossed out a car window."

Hirsch, his gaze alighting on the farm dog, saw it take a bite of the air and subside. A fly buzzed at its eyes. It snapped its jaws again. "Now you know better. You think it was Craig."

"I'm sure of it."

"But this time you caught him at it."

She nodded. "I'd just come back from dropping Jack off at school." She paused, shook her head in disgust. "More fool me. Why should I do the school run? Not my kids."

"You took Jack, not Craig?" checked Hirsch.

"He didn't show for breakfast and I didn't think it was my job to get him ready for school. I mean, he's fourteen and he's not my kid. Anyway, when I got back, Ray was sitting at the kitchen table, going, 'Did you think to buy milk? Did you pick up the *Advertiser*?' He wanted me to drive all the way back and get his precious milk and newspaper. Needless to say we had an almighty row and I stormed out." She shook her head. "Call it a temporary insanity. Can't believe I contemplated moving in."

Armstrong wore boots, jeans and a checked shirt. A practical woman, who for a time had had her head turned by a man whose sons were losing the plot and who might have arranged the murder of his wife. Hirsch said, "And meanwhile Craig's not in bed but out in the paddock throwing lighted matches on the ground?"

"I spotted him as I was driving in."

"Any theories?"

"Yes. He's fucked in the head, pardon my French. Last summer he learns he's not so special: his old man's broke and he has to attend the local high school. And this morning? Take your pick: His mother's suicide, my presence in his life, the way his father and grandfather treat him, life at school . . . All of the above."

"Have there been other fires?"

"Not that I know of." She stared at him. "That boy needs help, before it escalates. You can see how dry it is, and a hot summer coming up."

"Mr. Latimer said he'll find a counselor for Craig."

She snorted. "They all need it."

"In what way?"

"Craig's a pyromaniac in the making, Jack's just sad, the old man is a bully and a sadist and so is Ray. And lazy. He would sit around watching TV and drinking beer and expect me to cook and clean for him. I've got a farm to run. So has he, except he's stuffed that up."

Hirsch said, "His treatment of the boys."

"What about it?"

"Do I need to inform Children's Services?"

"A bit harsh," Armstrong said, but she bit her lip. "Ray's hard on them," she said, "but he's not negligent. Not really."

"Mrs. Armstrong, where's the ring he gave you?"

"You don't miss much."

Hirsch waited, and after a while Finola Armstrong said, "Like I said, the youngest boy is sad, and it turns out one of the things he's sad about is the fact that I was wearing his mother's ring."

She gave Hirsch a look, a crumpling of defenses. "I had no idea it was hers. I thought he'd bought it specially for me." She coughed and swallowed. "I challenged Ray. He said the ring was special, special to *him*, it had been his mother's ring. I gave it back. Couldn't wear it."

They each stared at nothing. Finola Armstrong broke the silence. "That was probably the beginning of the end. The other big thing was money."

"Money?"

"Something about his wife being due an inheritance but it hadn't been released yet and could I tide him over with a loan? Or better still, we could get married and amalgamate our properties into one big one."

"While you cooked and cleaned."

"Exactly."

Armstrong rubbed her palms on her thighs, embarrassed. "I know I went a bit crazy this year, you know, love is blind and all that, but at the same time I do have a head on my shoulders."

She indicated the house, sheds and farmland with a little sweep of her hand, and Hirsch knew she had survived, even prospered, using her own wits. She was a good farmer, a good manager. She was canny. A partnership with the Latimers would not have been canny.

"I've just been next door," Hirsch said, "and Mr. Latimer said he'd be happy to pay for the damaged fence."

"I should hope so. But I imagine he wants to know if I'll take further action. Tell him no. I'm well rid of that mob."

Hirsch got up to go. She said, her head at an angle, "One other thing: I was at my sister's when Alison Latimer died."

Hirsch agreed that she was.

"And Ray was in the lockup and his father was away with Craig and Jack."

"Yes . . ."

"It's just that Ray and Leonard kept reminding me of that, drilling it into me, as if it might be important." She shrugged. "That's all. Thought I'd mention it."

After a beat, Hirsch nodded. "Glad you did."

CHAPTER 28

HE RETURNED TO VIMY Ridge.

Kropp was there, waiting on the veranda, his police Explorer gleaming in the driveway. Hirsch said, "I suppose your mate called you?"

"Don't get on your high horse, son. The man's a mess. His wife, and now this."

Sounds from within, the wailing boy and the murmuring father. "Sarge, I'm dealing with it."

Kropp ignored him, stared out across the landscape to the Razorback. "You went to see the Armstrong woman?"

"Yes."

"And?"

"Not interested in pressing charges. Expects Mr. Latimer to pay for fence repairs."

Kropp nodded. "Okay, this is how it pans out. A passing motorist flicked a cigarette out the window, setting off a grass fire. Local units attended, and with the help of neighbors the blaze was quickly extinguished. That's the public face. Privately, the kid gets counseling, the blokes manning the trucks get a six-pack of beer each, and everyone's happy. All right?"

"How do you know I haven't already managed to negotiate most of that? You think because I'm a dog and a maggot I'm not also a good policeman? Fuck you, Sarge."

Kropp blinked. "I beg your pardon?"

"You heard."

Kropp looked amused. "Fair enough. Now, let me sit with my friend for a while. You head on back to town."

"I've still not spoken to Mr. Latimer about his wife. He won't return calls, he won't open the door to me, and I've had enough. No more bullshit from him, and no more from you, Sarge. It's been too long. And for Christ's sake, five minutes after his wife dies, he moves his girlfriend in? How broken up can the guy be?"

The men stared at each other. "The super asked me to prepare a brief for the coroner and that's what I'm trying to do," Hirsch said. "If interested parties refuse to speak to me, how does that look? It looks like guilt, it looks like having something to hide. I don't care that Ray Latimer is your mate, stalwart of the football club and all-round good bloke or that he suffered a tragic loss: I am not leaving until I've sat down with him and asked my questions."

After a gap in time, Kropp said, "I worked with Marcus Quine, you know. In the early days, Port Adelaide."

Hirsch said nothing.

"He got the job done."

Hirsch said nothing.

"But he did cut corners."

Was that an admission that Hirsch had got it right about Quine? He continued to watch the sergeant.

Who said, "But I don't care if a fellow police member swindles the Children's Hospital and violates a busload of nuns, you do not do the dirty on him."

Kropp didn't wait for a reply but banged his way into the house, calling, "Ray? You there?"

Surprised, Hirsch followed his sergeant, catching up just as

Kropp rapped his knuckles on the bedroom door, calling, "*Ray? It's Bill. We need a quiet word about Allie.*"

Hirsch grabbed his arm. "Sarge?"

"What?"

"Butt out."

Kropp shook him off. "What, you don't think I can do the job properly if a friend's involved?"

"Sarge, if you sit in on my interview with Mr. Latimer, my report will say so. If you say one word to, or for, Mr. Latimer during that interview, my report will say so. And what Superintendent Spurling or the coroner make of that, I can only guess, but it won't look good."

"You're a grade-A cunt, son," Kropp said.

"And proud of it, Sarge."

Kropp stomped out, a heavy man, brutally unhappy. The front door slammed. Hirsch heard the Explorer roar and kick up a little gravel.

LATIMER INSISTED ON USING his study, a dim, unloved cave, the lone armchair a long way from the desk. "Mr. Latimer," Hirsch began.

Latimer started talking. "No one will tell me when or even whether I'll get the inheritance. Do you know? If the inquest shows she shot herself while of unsound mind, that won't affect the inheritance, right? It's unrelated? Only I know some insurance policies won't pay out on a suicide, but this isn't an insurance policy, it's an inheritance. The state can't touch it, can they?"

Hirsch blinked. He was always meeting men and women who had the tact and emotional intelligence of a slab of concrete, but it always surprised him. "Mr. Latimer, you agreed to talk to me about your wife. I can't advise you on the legalities or otherwise of an inheritance."

But if you killed her I'll see you don't get a penny of it.

"I've got nothing to hide," Latimer said.

"Very well. What was Alison's state of mind in the last few weeks and months of her life?"

"Depressed. Irrational," Latimer said. His dark, hard man's good looks contracted. "Made our lives a living hell."

"In what way?"

"Didn't look after herself. The place was a mess. Forgot to cook or shop. Screamed her head off at us one minute and begged forgiveness the next. Then in the last few days this sort of calmness came over her. I can't describe it."

"She was happy?"

"I wouldn't say happy. More . . . like she'd come to a decision."

"A decision to leave the marriage now that she had an inheritance to fall back on."

Latimer shook his head. "That wasn't it. More like she'd decided to end it all."

"Not upbeat, happy, looking forward to the near future?"

"Who have you been talking to? That bitch across the road? She wasn't here, Allie's parents weren't here, you certainly weren't here. I was. Craig was. Ask him."

"And Jack?"

"You leave Jack out of this. He's just a little kid. He's not . . . strong."

Nor is Craig, thought Hirsch. "Did your wife threaten suicide at any time in the last weeks and months?"

"No. But she had tried once before."

Had she? Hirsch was having doubts. There was no direct evidence, only hearsay. "Was she depressed by nature?"

"Up and down."

"What was her relationship with your father like?"

Latimer bristled. "What relationship? What are you implying?"

You can't be too careful with your word choice, thought Hirsch. He spelt it out: "From all accounts, she had a close and happy relationship with your mother. She had a close and happy relationship with Mrs. Street across the road. That's what I mean by relationship. Was she close to your father or did they quarrel? I understand he's a . . . forceful man."

"My father loved her like she was his own. If she was nervy around him that says a lot about her, not him."

"Did he urge her to pay the inheritance into the business rather than leave the marriage?"

"My father's not the type to interfere like that. His view was I was well rid of her. She was splitting up the family, taking Jack away with her. Craig chose to stay with me."

"Well, did *you* urge her to reconsider? The farm's struggling, you told me that yourself. The inheritance would have helped carry you over until prices improved or the rains came."

Latimer curled his lip. "What do you know about farming? Look, we're not that far gone. It's all cyclical anyway. You wouldn't know that, being on a regular salary." He grinned crookedly. "Plus your other perks."

Hirsch bit. "*My* other perks? Or do you mean all police officers get perks?"

"You. I know all about you. Happy to belong to a crooked squad yet quick to dob the others in to save your own skin."

Hirsch smiled. "So your wife's inheritance *wouldn't* have been a godsend? Surely it would have eased the pressure? Craig could have returned to his boarding school. Apparently he was happy there."

"A hundred and sixty thousand dollars doesn't go far, not if you're on the land. All I wanted to do was save my marriage, not grab Allie's inheritance."

"But you just said she made your lives a misery."

"Only at the end, it would've blown over."

"If she did make your lives a misery, perhaps it was because you had other women."

"I still loved her."

"Really? You told Mrs. Armstrong *last year* that the marriage was over."

"I never said that. She misunderstood."

"You were quick to move her in."

"Not that quick."

Hirsch gave Latimer a scoffing look and let the silence build for a while.

"She's being magnanimous about the fire."

Latimer shrugged.

"She could have pressed charges against your son."

Latimer grew heated. "Didn't take her long to shoot through on me, though, did it? Didn't stay around once the shit hit the fan. And have you seen the condition of the fence? Half falling down, and I suppose she wants me to spend top dollar repairing it."

Hirsch was fascinated. "I think the engagement ring was the final straw."

"What do you mean?"

"She thought you'd bought it specially."

"It was my mother's ring. I can do with it what I like."

"You gave it to your wife."

"Of course. Then when she left me I got it back."

"She left it here when she went to stay at her parents'?"

"Yes."

"But she had a close and loving relationship with your mother and it would have meant a great deal to her to wear the ring."

"Who knows what went on in her mind. Can we stop now?"

"Returning to the inheritance."

"Do we have to?"

"At the start of the interview you seemed quite concerned that you might not get it. Why, if it's no big deal?"

"Of course it will help, I'm not an idiot. I've got two mouths to feed and no one to help me."

"What were your thoughts when you heard about the inheritance?"

Latimer looked dumb. "Nothing much."

"Well, did you think it would save the farm from ruin? Did you fear it would give your wife a measure of independence, give her the nerve to leave you? That wouldn't look too good, would it? Make you look a bit of a fool?"

"I don't have to listen to this. Why don't you just shove off and leave us alone."

"What time did you and Mrs. Armstrong go to Redruth the weekend your wife died?"

"In time for the footie. And I was with her until I got arrested. And I was in the lockup when Allie died, okay?"

Then Latimer's face altered, a look almost of glee. "Where are you going with this? You looking at Finola?"

"She's in the clear. But why are you pointing me at her? As far as you're concerned, your wife committed suicide."

"That's what I think, yeah. If you'd lived here with Allie, it's also what *you'd* think. But for some reason you've got it in for my father and me, probably influenced by that bitch across the road, so I'm indulging you, it amuses me."

"Did you break your wife's hand one day, Mr. Latimer? Bend her fingers back? Slam it in the car door?"

"Fucking get out."

HIRSCH COULD HAVE GONE home to talk to the furniture, but he said, "Mr. Latimer, where's the second twenty-two rifle?"

He pointed to the gun cabinet on the wall.

"What?"

"You have two such rifles: the one that killed your wife and one other."

"How the hell do you know that? You checking on my licenses?"

"A Ruger and a Brno. Where's the other one? In the ute? The shed?"

"Fucked if I know. Why?"

"Because your son is unraveling and might decide to shoot himself. Or you."

That got Latimer going.

They didn't find the rifle in the ute, the sheds, the car,

cupboards, wardrobes, under beds. Leaving one room still unsearched.

Craig Latimer was curled up on his bed, a damp, blotchy, unlovely lump of a boy, his meaty spine turned to them. Latimer sat, placed a big hand on an unresponsive shoulder. "Son? Where's the twenty-two we keep in the ute?"

Craig rolled onto his back. "I dunno."

"You haven't been taking potshots at tin cans?"

"Not me! Jack."

Latimer gaped. "Jack?"

"Him and Katie Street."

Hirsch stepped in. "Craig, where is your brother?"

"Staying with Allie's parents."

"Would he have taken the rifle with him?"

Craig scoffed. "Nanna wouldn't let it in the house."

"Perhaps your mum hid it."

"Why would the bitch hide it?" Craig said.

After a moment, Hirsch said, "Did your father teach you to talk about her like that? Perhaps she hid it because it wasn't being kept in a secure place."

He left, stewing. But the thing was, none of the Latimers could have killed Alison. They hated her, though. Given an opportunity to sweeten the memory, they hadn't taken it.

CHAPTER 29

ON A SUNDAY AFTERNOON in late November, Hirsch washing the HiLux again, maintaining standards, feeling stiff from yesterday's tennis, a new white Camry with Victorian plates entered town from the south. It slowed outside Tennant's store, braking next to the petrol bowser. A young man got out, rattled the nozzle. Hirsch knew Tennant locked it overnight and on Sundays and public holidays. Then the driver peered through the shop window, into the shadowy, closed, unlit interior. A young woman joined him. They pantomimed dejection, but that didn't last: Now they were looking around for a way out of their dilemma. And there was Hirsch a short distance away, a hose in his hand, the POLICE sign above his door. They climbed back into the Camry.

A moment later they were parked at the curb and stepping onto his lawn. Hirsch released the spray-gun trigger, dropped the hose, wiped his palms on his jeans and thought *backpackers*. The clue was in the backpacks like a pair of passengers on the backseat. Northern European? Tall, blond, lithe, sun-browned, clear-eyed, quizzical, fearless—on just about every count they were not locals.

"We are not having benzene," the boy said, his teeth white and straight. Board shorts, faded T-shirt, craft market sandals.

"Petrol," Hirsch said.

The girl said, "This is so. Pet-rol."

She was as tall as her boyfriend, vital, athletic, with cropped hair, tight shorts and a singlet top. Hirsch fell in love on the spot, looks and vitality and accent.

"The shop's closed, I'm afraid."

"We must be in Port Augusta for the famous Ghan and Pichi Richi trains," the girl said, mangling the words charmingly.

Hirsch had a mental stab at their movements. A few weeks or months traveling around and across the continent, hitch-hiking, taking buses and trains, camping, staying in hostels and cheap motels, some fruit picking and bartending and waitressing along the way. Hiring a car occasionally, like this Hertz Camry. The Ghan ran from Adelaide, with a stop at Port Augusta, on its 3,000 km journey to the Timor Sea, but it seemed they first wanted to ride the Pichi Richi train, a rickety little rattler that traveled a short distance near Port Augusta, where he supposed there was a Hertz agency where they could return the car.

"Please can you help us? The next town is too far for us and the last town is too far also. We are not having the petrol for these journeys."

Hirsch thought this was something they didn't prepare you for when they posted you at a one-man police station in the bush. He made a mental note to stock some emergency fuel, one jerry can of unleaded, one of diesel. A man of the people.

Bob Muir.

"I can take you to someone who might have some petrol."

"*Dank.*"

Dutch? He squeezed in with the backpacks—grimy, faded, unraveling—and directed them to the street where the Muirs and the Donovans lived.

Yvonne Muir answered. Eyeing the Camry and its occupants,

quivering to know, she said, "Bob's next door, setting up Leanne's new TV."

Hirsch paused at the Camry to explain where he was going, and walked across the grass to the Donovans'. Leanne opened the door, looking red-eyed, uncombed, a little awry in battered Crocs, tracksuit pants and T-shirt. She blinked at Hirsch, said, "Sorry, haven't had a shower yet," and led Hirsch through to her sitting room, where she collapsed into an armchair. A mug of tea steamed on a stool beside it, a cigarette burned in a saucer.

"Bob," Hirsch said, nodding at Muir, who was kneeling on the floor beside a wall opposite Leanne's armchair, a screwdriver sticking out of the rear pocket of his overalls.

Muir nodded, said "G'day," and returned to his task. He'd run coaxial cable along the skirting board to a large flat-screen television, which had replaced the boxy set Hirsch recalled from his first visit. The old TV sat with its face to the wall with a coil of old ribbon cable, disgraced, forgotten, ready for recycling. Ready for the rubbish tip, anyway.

The air was dense: Both Muir and Leanne had cigarettes going. Hirsch wanted to cough, wave the smoke away, open a window. "Need to ask a favor."

Muir, still on his knees, produced a Swiss Army knife, took up the cable end. He peeled back a couple of centimeters of black outer casing, revealing the inner sheath, core and copper wire. He hadn't a hurry in the world.

"Shoot," he said.

Hirsch told him about the backpackers.

Muir grunted. "Wouldn't be the first time. The last bloke always had a couple of drums on hand, one unleaded, one diesel."

"I'll remember that," Hirsch said.

"Go down the side of my place to the shed and you'll find a ten-liter jerry can. There's a forty-four gallon drum of unleaded against the back wall. How about I let them have twenty liters? Fifty bucks should cover it, get them a fair distance."

"Thanks, Bob."

Hirsch stepped over to the TV. "You won't know yourself with this, Leanne."

She smiled, tired, sad, thankful for small mercies. "Present from Sam."

"Nathan's mate?" said Hirsch, running his hand over the smooth flank. "Generous of him."

"He won it at the pub, but doesn't need it."

"Wish someone would give me a new TV," Hirsch said, peering into the gap between the rear panel and the wall. "All I've got is a little portable, lucky to get one channel, depending on the weather."

There was nothing to say to that. Muir was fastening a connector to the cable end, ready for the antenna socket. Leanne continued to watch him. Hirsch left them to it.

WHEN THE BACKPACKERS WERE gone and Bob had his fifty dollars—"Do I get a commission?" "How about a second channel on your TV?" "Done."—Hirsch opened up the office and hunted through the burglary reports, going back one year. Then he walked across to the Tiverton Hotel: Like the Muncowie pub on the outside but more appealing within. Dining room, main bar, side lounge, dartboard, snooker table, widescreen TV and no old-timers nursing beer.

And no raffle, not recently. Last Christmas, maybe? A ham.

Hirsch phoned a few other pubs in the area. Muncowie, Redruth. No raffles offering a TV set.

IT OCCURRED TO HIRSCH that he didn't know where Nathan's mate lived, and asking around would only alert him. But he did know where Sam Hempel and Nathan Donovan worked.

At eight on Monday morning he walked across town to Tiverton Grains, a collection of storage and processing sheds around a huge untidy yard, the admin area a cottage on a side street. Wracked with sneezes, he entered the main shed, a vast echo chamber, almost empty but for a few pallets, jute bags and nameless items of equipment. Thick air, thick with grain dust. Seeing no one, hearing a truck motor and voices in the back-yard, he continued through to a metal door in the back wall, stepping from dimness and scratchy air to drenching sunlight. The yard was a depressed expanse of fuel drums, rusted machin-ery, dead weeds and a broad patch of oily dirt that served as employee parking. Four cars this morning, including Hempel's lowered Commodore.

Hirsch headed across to an open tin structure against the back fence, a service bay. Inside it, nose out, was a grain truck, two overalls peering into the engine compartment, one of them saying, "Give her another go."

The motor ground over, didn't fire. With the hood up, Hirsch couldn't see who was behind the steering wheel, but he said, "Morning, gents," as he approached.

Sam Hempel and an older man straightened, turned. "Help you?" the older man said.

Hirsch drew nearer incautiously, and when he said, "I'd like a quick word with Sam," was punched in the stomach, Hempel waving his hand immediately, saying, "Ow, fuck," and running.

"Jesus, mate, sorry, don't know what got into him," the older man said, touching Hirsch as if he might get bitten, not sure what to do.

Hirsch, sucker punched twice in as many months, was too sore to run. Building up to a tormented shuffle, stomach muscles pulling, he followed the kid past the abandoned machinery and drums to the four employee cars. Hempel had vanished. Hirsch prowled between the vehicles, looking behind, under and into them, itching to look into the boot of the lowered Holden.

A whisper of cardboard or plywood against fabric, a soft booming sound, a sense of items shifting, compressing.

The rubbish skip.

Hirsch banged his fist against the metal flank. "Sam? Come on out of there."

After a while, "Leave me alone."

"Not going to happen, and you know it."

Hirsch waited. The morning was warm and still, the sun edging above the gums that marked the boundary between the town and the first wheat paddock. A vapor trail disintegrated as he watched it. Adelaide to Perth? Adelaide to Alice Springs or Darwin? He thought of the Dutch backpackers aboard the Ghan. Meanwhile Tiverton was silent, only a murmur in the background and Hempel trying not to disturb the rubbish.

"Sam? I promise I won't give you up to Sergeant Kropp and his boys, okay? But if I have to call them in, it will be taken out of my hands and I can't protect you, understood?"

He could hear the boy thinking.

"I know you're frightened. If you had your time over again, you wouldn't punch me. Assaulting a police officer is pretty serious, you know. Hell to pay. Maybe we can work something out."

"You promise you'll keep them Redruth jacks off me?"

"Yes."

"Particularly Nicholson?"

"Yes."

Still Sam weighed his options. Hirsch said, "That was a lovely gesture of yours, giving Leanne Donovan a TV set. She hasn't had a good trot, and it counts for a lot in my book that you did a nice thing for her."

Silence.

"Even though the set was stolen, it was still a kindness to a woman who needed it."

"She's good to me. And I felt bad for her because of Melia and that."

So bad that you went on a housebreaking spree on the day she put her daughter in the ground, Hirsch thought.

"I understand," he said. "But we do have to talk."

The load shifted, the metal skin boomed faintly and Hempel hoisted himself onto the rim of the dumpster, wild-eyed, oil on his jeans, hands and forearms. He was sweating, jittery and gave the yard the once-over.

"It's okay, there's only me here," Hirsch said.

Hempel jumped to the ground. His jeans slithered to his thighs. He tugged them up. "Where we going?"

"To the station for the time being."

"Not down Redruth?"

"No."

"I didn't mean to hit ya."

"I understand."

They were moving toward Hempel's car now, Hirsch shepherding and ready to grab, bolster, protect or brain the kid. "Keys?"

He lifted the boot lid. Two Blu-ray players, a Game Boy, a laptop, a media dock, a Samsung Galaxy phone still in its box. All on the list. Hirsch slammed the lid, said, "Get in," and drove out of the yard.

Down they went to the main road, passing the general store, into Hirsch's place of business, where Sam said, "If I tell yous who run Melia over, can I go?"

CHAPTER 30

HIRSCH WASN'T MAKING ANY promises. "First things first, Sam. Tell me about the burglaries."

They were in his sitting room, the front door locked to deter callers. He switched on the digital recorder, stating names, date and location.

Hempel, a forlorn shape in one of the armchairs, looked on in dismay. "Don't I need a lawyer?"

Hirsch got comfortable. "You've every right to one. But Sam, once a lawyer's involved I'll formally charge you. I will throw the book at you: Assaulting a police officer, resisting arrest, several counts of burglary, and I'm sure I can think of more charges. Then I will inform the homicide squad that you are a witness and maybe a suspect in the death of Melia Donovan. They don't mess around, those guys. They'll whisk you away and grill you for days and you won't see daylight for twenty years."

He paused. "That's if we go the formal route. You will still face charges, but I'd like to protect you from the worst of it, at this stage."

Hempel gnawed at his lower lip.

"So," Hirsch said, "the break-ins."

"It was me. I done them."

"But you were at the service in the church, with Nathan and his mother. I saw you."

Sam shifted, partly in agreement and partly in embarrassment. "I was like, you know . . ."

"Checking out who else was there."

"Yeah."

"You knew these people would be absent from their homes for a couple of hours."

"Yeah."

"Didn't Nathan or his mother wonder where you'd gone?"

"Said I had stuff to do."

"Where do you live at present?"

"At Nate's."

"And before that?"

"With me mum sometimes, with me mates, mattress on the floor and that."

Hirsch checked the recorder. Satisfied, he said, "I've been looking at burglary and theft reports for the past twelve months. There have been several similar break-ins: Farm properties over Easter, during the school holidays, Saturdays when people are playing sport. Was that you?"

Sam looked hunted. "Thought you wanted to know about Melia?"

"Was that you acting alone, or did you have help?"

"I didn't kill her!"

"The burglaries, Sam: Was that you acting alone or did you have help?"

"Me."

"Was Nathan ever involved?"

"Nate? No way. The cops are always hassling him."

"Making it difficult for you to operate."

"What?"

"Nothing. You stole quite a lot of gear in the past few months. The stuff in your car is the tip of the iceberg. Where's the rest?"

"Sold it."

"Bloke in a pub."

"Yeah."

"I'll need a name."

"Dunno if I could find him again."

Hirsch couldn't count how many times he'd had this conversation. "What did he look like, this bloke in a pub? Which pub?"

"Can't remember. Somewhere down Adelaide."

"You drive all the way to Adelaide to do your drinking? Don't answer that. Tell me why you gave Mrs. Donovan one of the stolen TVs."

"Like I told you, I felt sorry for her and that."

"Sorry how?"

"Sorry Melia got killed. A tragedy."

Hirsch gave him a look. "A tragedy. You're close to the family?"

"Yeah. Me own family's fucked."

"How do you know the Donovans?"

"Ever since I was in primary school with Nate. His mum let me doss down at their place when my mum was drinking or had a bloke over to stay."

"That's been a pattern for a while?"

"Years."

"So you'd known Melia since she was a baby?"

"She was kinda like my sister."

Sam had curled into the armchair. Fear, nerves and shame had shrunken him, it seemed to Hirsch. The kid's clumsy height and bulk counted for nothing. Here out of the light he was pale, very gingery, the hairs downy, no spring or verve at all.

"She was special to you?"

Sam shrugged.

"I've seen photos of her. A lovely girl. Beautiful, in fact."

Another shrug.

"But a bit wild, right?"

"I tried to look out for her."

"Like a brother."

"She's just a kid. She was just a kid."

"Old enough, Sam. So you looked out for her. What about Nathan and his mother? Shouldn't they have been looking out for her?"

"What can they do? I got more . . . I got more contacts and that. I go all over. The car and that. I hear things."

"Was it hard keeping your relationship with Melia a secret from her brother and her mother?"

Hempel's jaw dropped. "What? What relationship?"

"She infuriated you sometimes? Wouldn't do what you wanted? There was a bruise on her face dating from before she was killed."

"Fuck you. I never hit her, never touched her. I can tell ya who did."

"Maybe she hit her head when she was in your car? Was that it?"

Sam got out of the chair, no longer an unlovely ten-year-old boy in disguise. "I never done nothing to Melia."

"Sit down," Hirsch said in his whiplash voice.

Sam collapsed.

"Sam, were you the older boyfriend I've been hearing about?"

"What? No way."

"All right, try this. You kept an eye out. You know who she spent time with. Boyfriends, girlfriends."

"That's right."

"You saw her with an older man."

"Yep."

"Well, who, Sam?"

"That magistrate bloke, Coulter."

"Really? You know who he is?"

"Sure."

"How did Melia get involved with him?"

"She got done for shoplifting."

"He was the sitting magistrate?"

"Yeah."

"She caught his eye?"

"S'pose."

"They went out together?"

"You could say that."

"What would you say?"

"He took her to parties and that."

"Anywhere else? A film, a restaurant, the pub . . ."

"She was fifteen. How's he gunna do that?"

Hirsch nodded. "I had this girlfriend once, told me I wasn't good enough for her, wasn't making enough money, and who'd want to go out with a cop anyway?"

Hempel chewed on that. "You saying she said that to me?"

"Did she? Told you about her rich boyfriend, rubbed your face in it?"

"No."

"It can get under your skin, that kind of knowledge. No wonder you followed her around."

"I was lookin' out for her. Nothin' filthy like you're suggesting."

"You saw her with Coulter a few times, or only once?"

"Few times."

"He must be what, thirty years older than her?"

Sam shrugged.

"But loaded, right? Big house, flash car."

"I'm gunna get an apprenticeship," Sam said, as if announcing a path to riches.

"So you were hurt that she chose a rich man over you?"

"No, I'm just sayin', he's no better than me. Least I never killed no one."

Hirsch would come back to that. "Did she ever reveal to you, or anyone else, that she was involved with David Coulter?"

"Dunno. Prob'ly Gemma."

"Did she ever tease you about the affair?"

Hempel twisted about in his chair. "Tease me? Nah. Why? When I told her she was makin' a big mistake she told me to mind me own business, but that's all."

"What kind of big mistake?"

"I go, the guy's a creep, Mel, he's using you, he'll hurt you, you're not careful." A shake of the head. "Sure enough . . ."

"Did Nathan ever go with you when you followed Melia?"

"Like I said, he's a magnet to the Redruth cops."

Hirsch checked the recorder again. "Was Melia by herself when she saw Coulter, or did Gemma Pitcher accompany her sometimes?"

"Gemma was there a coupla times. Why?"

"How did it work? Gemma recruited Melia? Melia recruited Gemma? Or maybe Coulter recruited Gemma, who recruited Melia, or vice versa?"

"What are you on about?"

"The sex parties."

Hempel floundered, opened and closed his mouth. "Sex parties?"

"I have reason to believe that Gemma and Melia took part in sex parties with several men."

"I don't know nothin' about that. Explains a lot, though."

"Explains what?"

"Melia come running out of this house with nothing on, all upset, and—"

Hirsch held up a hand. "I need details for the tape. Date, location, times . . ."

Hempel swallowed and started again. "It was the night she was killed."

"Where."

"This house outside Redruth."

"Coulter's?"

"Don't think so. He lives over in Clare."

"You followed her and—"

"Coulter took Mel and Gemma to this house. I was watching, and then Melia come runnin' out, no clothes on, in a real mess."

"In what way a mess?"

"Cryin' and that."

"Where were you?"

"Behind this hedge thing."

"Not in your car?"

"Mel would reckernize it so I parked in the next street."

"Not peering through windows?"

"I'm not stupid."

"So you were watching and she came running out in distress. What did you do?"

"Happened so quick, I was gunna go and help her but Coulter come out. He was ropeable. He sees her runnin' down the street and he gets in his car and runs her down."

The silence ticked. Hirsch said, "Was it deliberate, do you think?"

"He was pretty pissed off."

"What happened then? Did anyone come out to see? Did you show yourself?"

"Me? No way. Bloody Coulter puts Melia in the boot and drives off."

"It was definitely Coulter."

"I reckernized him. I reckernized his car."

Hirsch looked at Hempel intently. "Were there other cars parked at the house?"

"Sure."

"Whose, do you know?"

"Sure."

"Perhaps you could tell me, Sam," Hirsch said, exquisitely patient.

"There was like Dr. McAskill's Mercedes. There was this white Lexus, Ian Logan's, and a silver one, that real estate guy. The Latimers in their Range Rover. Plus two BMWs—I didn't know who they were—and this Chrysler."

"Go back a bit: The Latimers? Both of them?"

"Yeah, sure," Sam said. He chortled. "And was Ray Latimer in big trouble."

"What do you mean?"

"Well, his wife was there, wasn't she?"

"At the party?"

Sam gave Hirsch a pitying look. "No, *watchin' the place*, like me."

"Behind another hedge?"

Hempel shook his head. "Parked up the road a bit."

Motive, Hirsch thought. "Tell me about the Chrysler."

"Dunno who drove it. From New South, but."

"It was a New South Wales car?"

"Yeah. Big black thing."

"Let's go back to Melia Donovan. Coulter drove off with her in the boot of his car."

"Yeah."

"What did you do?"

"I wasn't gunna stick around."

"What time was this?"

"I dunno, late, midnight, maybe."

"Sam, when we found Melia, she was fully dressed."

He shrugged. "Come runnin' out starkers but had all her gear with her."

Hirsch pictured it, the empty road in the moonlight, clumsy hands dressing a limp body before throwing it into a ditch. "Can you think of a reason why David Coulter would drive all the way up to Muncowie to dump the body?"

"Easy. I live there. Me mum does, I mean."

Hirsch closed his eyes. For want of a few key questions, he thought. And when he'd asked Leanne Donovan if she knew of anyone in her daughter's life from Muncowie, why hadn't she mentioned Sam Hempel?

Because her mind works literally, he decided. Sam was her son's friend, not her daughter's. "But what's the connection? What's it got to do with Coulter that you live there, or you did?"

"To frame me, what else?"

Makes sense, of a kind, Hirsch thought. If you were sick and devious. Melia told Coulter about Sam. Probably shared a laugh with him over the sad boy who had a crush on her.

"Saddle up: we're going for a drive."

⚬ ⚬ ⚬

THEY TOOK SAM'S CAR. The wrong people might know Hirsch's own car, and certainly the HiLux Hirsch drove. The Commodore was difficult to start and it stalled a few times and took a while to reach 90 km/h, at which speed it shook to pieces, so Hirsch backed off to 85. His seat sagged; dope, cigarette and beer odors clung to the fabrics, leaching out with body heat. A sun-faded dog nodded its head on the dashboard, the steering wheel belonged on a racing car and the fuel gauge didn't work. Take your hands off the wheel and the car drifted to the right. Correction: *leapt* to the right.

"Nice wheels."

"Piece a crap," Sam said.

Down the long, shallow valley between hills and crops to Redruth. The road shimmered. Hirsch had never seen so many mirages before this bush posting. A farmer stood in a corner of his wheat, rubbing a grain head between his palms speculatively, and then they were past and trundling along, waiting for the next little bit of rural business. "Soon be harvest time," Hirsch said, as if he knew.

Sam's bottom jaw peeled away from the top. It was entirely possible that he'd lived here all his life and had no sense of its patterns. A Pioneer bus passed, another farmer, this one kicking at a clod of dirt, crows along a wire, some dust out there in the blue-smudge hills.

Then they were passing through Redruth, Hempel directing Hirsch out past the motel and up a side street that became a dirt road leading up into one of the town's many hills. Over a rise, Hempel saying, "That one."

A little collection of newer houses far apart, semi-farmland, small garden sheds, clumps of ornamental and native trees and a couple of reedy ponds, mostly mud now. The house Sam indicated had a sign on a lean in unmown grass, FOR SALE: VENN REALTY.

That made sense.

The house itself was sizable, a pale brick structure about twenty years old, a little outmoded but solid, roomy, semi-secluded.

Hedges and shrubs.

Hirsch stopped the car. "Where were you hiding?"

Sam pointed. The hedge was a bulky stripe of dark green along the eastern flank of the house.

"And Mrs. Latimer?"

A gateway fifty meters west.

"You recognized her car, or did you actually see her?"

"Both."

"Did she see you?"

"Dunno. Don't think so."

"She didn't go inside, remonstrate with her husband?"

"What?"

"Sam, did she get out of the car and go into the house?"

"Not while I was there."

Spied on her husband, and a day or two later had gone to live with her parents. And a few days after that had died. Been killed. Had she had it out with Ray? *I saw you. I know what you're up to.*

"Where was the Chrysler?"

Sam pointed to the driveway, a grand sweep of gravel. "They were all parked along there."

"A big black Chrysler with New South Wales plates."

"Yeah," Sam said, rattling off the number.

CHAPTER 31

WITH SAM HEMPEL IN Adelaide, safe in the hands of Croome and DeLisle, Hirsch turned the car around and headed back to Tiverton. A five-hour round-trip. The afternoon shadows striped the crops, the highway, the hillsides. More birds on more wires. An air of waiting, of things drying, turning to dust.

It was late afternoon before he could begin tracking the black Chrysler. Called the New South Wales vehicle registry first, and was informed that the car belonged to one Daryl Metcalfe, a Broken Hill address. One fine for speeding, but not in the Chrysler.

Next Hirsch contacted the main Broken Hill police station, jumping through various hoops before anyone would talk to him.

"That car was reported stolen."

The logical question was, "By Pullar and Hanson?"

"What? No. Same kind of car, sure, but Pullar and Hanson haven't set foot in Broken Hill to the best of my knowledge. Plus their Chrysler was found burnt out near Townsville, wasn't it?"

"Okay, so . . ."

"So the car you're asking about was reported stolen here last week."

Last week? Hirsch tried to digest that. "Who reported it?"

Hirsch heard the clicking of keys. "Woman called Sandra Chatterton."

"According to the DMV it's owned by a Daryl Metcalfe."

"You have done your homework," the Broken Hill cop said. 'Chatterton is Metcalfe's daughter. She was looking after house and car while her father was overseas for six months."

That ruled Metcalfe out. But what other men did Chatterton have in her life?

Or maybe no one borrowed the car—Chatterton was another Gemma Pitcher and Melia Donovan.

"If it's the same car," Hirsch said, "someone was driving it in my neck of the woods back in September."

"And that's significant how?"

"A suspicious death." Hirsch thought about it and said, "*Two* suspicious deaths."

"Want us to look into it?"

"Have to clear it with my boss who will talk to your boss," Hirsch said.

AT SIX THE NEXT morning, Hirsch was in his Nissan, heading north along the Barrier Highway. No doubt he was breaching regulations, wearing his uniform and doing police work across the border, but he was pretty much fed up these days. Plus it might be days, weeks before requests moved through official channels, and the uniform would lend him some clout when he questioned Metcalfe and his daughter.

Three and a half hours, 350 kilometers, across an ochre landscape, under a vast sky. Eagles, stone chimneys silhouetted, an inclination to stone and grit, not dirt. Stone reefs, and smudges that were bluebush, saltbush, mallee scrub and lone demented ewes. A hawk diving, a crow watching. Road trains, trucks, cars and also emptiness ahead and behind, other than the shimmering lakes that dematerialized as the highway slipped beneath him, as the car ate up the kilometers. Hirsch didn't like any of it, exactly, but it felt less alien than it had when he first set foot out here. Not home, exactly, but a place vaguely familiar to him.

He'd never been to Broken Hill. It was both modern and old, bright and dull, smaller and richer and shabbier than he'd imagined. Plenty of dusty 4WDs and older sedans and station wagons on streets named for the mining industry: Gypsum, Garnet, Argent, Silica, Calcite . . . Not a lot of green in the garden beds but local colors: dusty reds and greys and olives. A baking noon sun.

METCALFE LIVED IN A low burnt-brick house with a blinding, unpainted, corrugated iron roof, mostly dead garden and empty carport. He was about fifty, a vigorous widower looking for some meaning in his life—or so Hirsch supposed, hearing him explain why he'd taken long service leave to spend six months working for a United Nations outfit in sub-Saharan Africa.

"My field's water: conservation, drainage, irrigation, well-sinking . . ."

"Uh-huh," said Hirsch. "And Sandra looked after the place while you were away?"

"She lives here," Metcalfe said, glancing at his daughter with a level of sadness.

They were side by side on a huge green leather sofa, sinking into it, you'd struggle to get out. Chatterton was a pixie, a wisp, very thin, her black hair cropped to a cap around her skull. Jeans, a scrap of T-shirt that showed her pale stomach. She looked no more than twenty, but Hirsch knew she was twenty-seven.

He smiled at her. "Someone pinched your dad's car just before he got back last week?"

She nodded, and Hirsch wondered if she didn't trust her voice.

Metcalfe patted her knee while watching Hirsch with suspicion. "Why are the South Australia police interested?"

Hirsch kept it vague. "A car matching the description was seen in the vicinity of an incident in the Redruth area."

"Wasn't me," Chatterton whispered.

Hirsch wondered about the surname. She took her mother's name? She was married? "I'm not suggesting it was you, I just need to eliminate the car."

"Consider it eliminated," Metcalfe said. "Sandy wouldn't have taken it out."

He had a sweet, benighted face, a large strong frame and sun-scorched skin. He'd probably never committed a crime in his life. The daughter was a different matter: Chatterton was full of methamphetamine twitches, sensations crawling under her skin. A malnourished wraith beside her big father, and not prepared to meet Hirsch's gaze.

"Sandy, what day did you discover the car was missing?"

"Tuesday, when I got home from work."

"She does odd jobs for the council," Metcalfe said.

"And you came home Wednesday?" Hirsch asked him.

"That's right."

"You reported it to the police, Sandy?"

She jiggled, blinked and managed a nod. Metcalfe patted her knee fondly, but there was tightness in him. "She's a good girl," he said. "But she's had a rough trot these past few years. Husband used to knock her around. Health issues."

Like addiction. She was barely holding it together and Hirsch thought she might fracture if he pushed. He smiled a smile that said he understood and hadn't come to judge. What he wanted to say was: "You sold your dad's car to buy drugs, right?"

Instead he said, "Did the neighbors see anything?"

Sandra Chatterton shook her head violently.

"Not her fault," Metcalfe said.

The stress was there in his voice, as if he feared the sky would fall in if he didn't hold it up, and he'd been holding it up for years and years and one day it would fall in, despite his best efforts. He rested his solid hand on his daughter's knee and, in his eyes, deeply recessed in their sockets, was pain.

The incontrovertible truth was that Sam Hempel had seen a

black Chrysler bearing Daryl Metcalfe's plates parked at a house in the mid-north of South Australia as far back as September. Katie Street and Jack Latimer had seen it, too, passing through Tiverton. And Katie had seen it again, a few days later, as if it hadn't left the district, or had returned.

"Do you know anyone down in South Australia, Sandra?"

She shook her head so hard the flat limp hair flew.

He said gently, "You've never been to parties down there?"

Another violent shake.

"What is this?" Metcalfe demanded, uneasy, his high forehead damp.

Then an alteration in him. He looked fully at his daughter, full-wattage regard and suffering and forgiveness. "Sandy?" he said, his voice a loving low rasp, pebbles slipping off a shovel.

It was enough to flip her. Her head dropped, her hands went to her ears. "I didn't mean it, I'm sorry."

"You sold the car to buy drugs?" her father asked gently.

"No, I swear."

"You owed people for drugs?"

"No!"

Hirsch was content to watch and listen. An old drama was playing out, the devoted father, the beloved daughter and her demons.

"I went on a trip," she muttered.

Metcalfe glanced at Hirsch as if seeking permission to continue. Hirsch gave him a nod.

"Where, sweetheart?"

"I wanted to see the sea."

Hirsch could understand that. He said, "The nearest water is Port Augusta?"

"I went there and then I went a bit further."

"When was this?"

Sandra Chatterton's knee jiggled. Hirsch could see the poor thin bone inside the fabric of her jeans. "My birthday."

The father looked pained. "Beginning of September."

"What happened, Sandy?"

"I ended up in Port Pirie."

A port can mean drug importation, Hirsch thought. A deal, a shiny big car as collateral. But when he thought about this particular port town, a kind of dread crept in, unrelated to Sandra Chatterton and drugs. He couldn't quite name it. "And?"

"I hooked up with these guys," she told her father, full of apology.

He patted her knee.

"I wasn't using, Dad, honestly. I've been getting my act together. But it was my birthday, and you know, you weren't around . . ."

"It's all right, sweetie."

"We got busted," Chatterton said.

Hirsch said carefully, "By the police in Port Pirie?"

"We were in this motel room, not making any noise or anything, not really partying or anything, and they came storming in."

"You were charged? Fined? Jailed?"

"One of the guys I was with I think was undercover, he just disappeared. The other one, he got six weeks."

"You?"

She squirmed. "Because me and Dad've got different last names and my ID shows my old address I couldn't prove I was driving Dad's car. Plus they rang the police here, who talked to the neighbors, who said Dad was overseas and the house was empty."

Voice and face said she'd spent her life feeling invisible and overlooked.

"They accused you of driving a stolen car?"

"Yeah."

"They confiscated it?"

"Yeah."

"Who did, Sandy?"

"There was this one guy there said maybe he could keep me

out of jail. I said 'I'm HIV positive,' so he wouldn't touch me."
She looked at her father. "I'm not, Dad, promise."

"Clever of you."

"What happened then, Sandy?"

"I hitched home."

Hirsch said carefully, "When this man said maybe he could
keep you out of jail, what was he proposing?"

Chatterton told him, her voice and delivery chopped about
but reaching an end point eventually. And, as she spoke, grow-
ing animated, Hirsch thought he could see what Spurling saw in
her, a gamine appeal.

CHAPTER 32

DURING THE THREE-AND-a-half hour drive back to Tiverton, Hirsch mentally outlined the case he'd present to DeLisle and Croome.

Melia Donovan first.

Melia was adventurous, suggestible, anxious to please, her head easily turned by a man with money and charm. The magistrate spent some time, money and charm on her, flattered her, let her drive his car, gave her a fun time: alcohol, cocaine, marijuana, sex, gradually introduced her to a group of men who liked to party with underage girls. Perhaps she caviled, so he held the shoplifting charge over her head, threatened youth detention.

Or he used Gemma Pitcher to bring Melia on board. Had the girls been friends before this? The age difference made it unlikely. Yet there were not many teenage girls of any age in the town, so maybe it was inevitable they'd gravitate toward each other.

Or Gemma recruited Melia Donovan of her own volition. To curry favor with the men? To share the sense of shame or degradation, if that's what she'd been feeling? To earn some reflected glory, Melia being the pretty one, the sexy one?

Hirsch would ask Gemma those questions—if he could find her, if she wasn't dead. The country out east was littered with mine shafts.

Something had gone wrong at the party—some abuse, some rottenness, one of the men overstepping the mark—with the result that Melia had grabbed her clothes and run. What had Gemma's reaction been? *Been there, done that, suck it up, Melia?* Or had she been sympathetic, even horrified, but too scared to speak out or intervene? Either way, she couldn't have expected or condoned what happened next.

HIRSCH REMEMBERED THREE THINGS about the day Melia Donovan's body was found.

One, as soon as Dr. McAskill had finished his examination he'd walked a few meters out of earshot and made a phone call.

Two, McAskill then drove to Tiverton, where he not only broke the news to Melia's mother but also made contact with Gemma Pitcher.

Three, Kropp had shown up.

Hirsch constructed a story around them. McAskill had been a witness to the incident between David Coulter and Melia Donovan, and he'd seen Coulter chase after her, so it would be natural for him to believe Coulter killed her. Coulter must have thought it would be ruled an accident and left it at that, but McAskill knew it was a problem for everyone. It needed to be contained. So he called Kropp. Kropp would know what to do. And Kropp promptly contained Hirsch by ordering him to stay put at the scene, giving McAskill time to contain Gemma Pitcher, possibly by threatening her.

Meanwhile it was arranged that McAskill would perform the autopsy: further containment. He could overlook evidence and skew findings. His pronouncements would be accepted.

THAT'S HOW HIRSCH SAW it as he headed south, the kilometers rolling beneath him and the sun beating down, the light permanently watery at the far extremes of the Barrier Highway but mica bright at the edges, broken-glass bright.

The story unrolled like the highway. What the men hadn't foreseen was a suspicious wife. Alison Latimer followed her husband, worked out what was going on and confronted him. *I want a divorce. I want half the farm or I'll see you in jail.*

Alarmed, Latimer told the others. They'd all go to jail if Alison Latimer contacted the police. And it would be Kropp she contacted—Kropp, her husband's mate—but police in Adelaide.

The only way out was to kill her. And the beauty of that was it solved the Latimers' money problems. The inheritance, no divorce payout, and one less mouth to feed.

She had a history of instability, so why not mock up a suicide? But who would have done it?

Clearly great attention would focus on the Latimer men, so they'd need unbreakable alibis. The old man's was easy: He'd take his grandsons away for the weekend. Meanwhile Ray would make a show of appearing with his girlfriend at the football final and celebrating afterwards, obnoxiously drunk, so drunk he's thrown into the lockup overnight and appears in court the next morning. Easy for Kropp and his crew to arrange, and the icing on the cake is Constable Hirschhausen, who has no stake in the matter, no relationship with Raymond Latimer, and will be Latimer's alibi for the later part of the morning.

So who abducted and then shot her? Not Kropp: he was in Redruth. Not Nicholson and Andrewartha, surely? They weren't reliable. McAskill? Coulter? Logan? Venn? Hirsch couldn't see it. He kept coming back to Spurling, a policeman, who knew about evidence and police procedures. And his seniority in the region would give him some control over the investigation and the information that flowed from it.

But he's a man of overweening ego. He can't conceive of making a mistake. He can't conceive that a man like Hirsch—disgraced copper—would start raising doubts on the very afternoon the body was found. Doubts about the victim's shoes, motives, position, car, weapon . . . *So the prick needed to contain and monitor me,* Hirsch thought, *and the best way to do that was get me to prepare the brief for the coroner.* Hirsch, a man demoted, friendless and new to the mid-north, ignorant of its ways and its secrets.

Spurling could have asked Kropp to prepare the brief, but there was always the chance that the press or someone in HQ would question the wisdom of that, argue that as a friend of the husband he'd be partisan. And the rumbles about Kropp's policing methods were widening, complaints were becoming public.

Managing Hirsch was a much better idea.

It was a pity for Spurling that McAskill couldn't have performed the Latimer autopsy as well, but there was no way the authorities would give a gunshot death to a small-town doctor.

Not like a hit-and-run.

Hirsch's phone rang in the car cradle. He pulled over, buffeted by the wind of a passing truck. He had one bar of reception.

"Where are you?" Rosie DeLisle demanded.

"Halfway between Redruth and Broken Hill."

"Can hardly hear you."

Hirsch tilted the phone. In the end he got out and walked along the miserable verge. "Is that better?"

Another buffeting truck, grit stinging him and a hawk slipping across the sky.

"Not much. Listen, don't talk, just wanted to fill you in. We had quite a chat with your boy—though his story is a bit all over the place."

"He's not the brightest knife in the drawer."

"What? Listen," Rosie shouted. "Just letting you know we've found connections between some of these heroes. Venn, Coulter, Logan and Latimer all boarded at St. Peter's College. Logan met McAskill when they shared a house together at university. There have been complaints lodged against all of them at one time or another. Several against Coulter, according to the Chief Magistrate. For example, he refused to grant a police application for a court order against a violent ex-prisoner who was stalking his wife, and overturned a protection order against some kids who were bullying another at school."

Hirsch thought he understood this aspect of Coulter. A crummy small-town solicitor, he'd developed a gorgeous sense of himself when appointed magistrate. No wonder Kropp disliked him. But what about Kropp?

"What about Kropp?"

"Don't know how he fits in," Rosie said. "But he has been there for at least twelve years. How are you doing on the Chrysler?"

Hirsch told her.

"Sorry, didn't catch a word of that. Call me when you have a better signal."

HIRSCH CLIMBED BEHIND THE wheel again. Nose down, the sun pouring through the glass, fatigue taking hold.

He tried to get inside Spurling's skin. A precise bureaucrat but a creep, a satyr, within. Huge ego. A man who selects and rejects, controls and judges. *He's been at it for a long time,* Hirsch thought, *and nothing's ever gone wrong, so he's grown complacent.*

He's been the area commander for a long time. As long as Kropp's been the Redruth sergeant? What's the connection between them? They're roughly the same age, so might have known each other since the academy. Or served together early in their careers and stayed in touch. Knew each other, knew the other's proclivities.

Hirsch saw the web of interests. Spurling and Kropp and his boys. Kropp and the locals—businessmen, football club members, the landed gentry. Hirsch still didn't know what the courthouse tension between Kropp and Coulter and Logan meant, but guessed he'd know once the arrests were made.

❦   ❦   ❦

FINALLY, THE CHRYSLER.

An out-of-state car, none of the locals knew it and it hadn't been reported stolen. The owner was overseas. Spurling could come and go without anyone saying, "Who's this?" Rather, people would think, "Interstate driver, passing through." After all, there were always New South Wales cars on the Barrier Highway, heading south for a holiday by the sea, heading north again when it was over.

Except that two children had seen the car and it had frightened them to death.

CHAPTER 33

LATE AFTERNOON NOW, HIRSCH sprawled upon his sofa in a T-shirt and baggy jeans, bare heels propped on the coffee table, laptop on his thighs. The plan was, send DeLisle and Croome an outline of his theory, give them time to absorb it, then follow with a phone call.

After that, it would be out of his hands.

The town was quiet, the highway, the school on the other side. Hirsch typed steadily, but before he reached the good bit, Spurling and the Chrysler, the desk phone rang.

Leonard Latimer, heat in his voice: "I'm scared Ray's going to do something stupid."

"Stupid how? Where are the boys?"

"Not here, thank God. Just come, will you?"

And the prick cut the connection. Hirsch gaped at the handset: catching flies, his mother called it.

HIRSCH WAS SHUDDERING HIS way over the Bitter Wash corrugations before he remembered his backup Beretta.

Idiot.

But he'd stopped work for the day, shed all of the cop

outerwear, shoving his uniform in the laundry basket, dumped the Beretta and his belt and service pistol and cuffs and baton and all that shit into his top drawer. He wasn't going to drag it all on again, not for the Latimers, so all he'd grabbed was his service pistol. Even in his T-shirt, jeans and battered Asics he was a cop.

Would he need to draw his gun? Maybe Raymond would do everyone a favor and shoot his old man and then himself.

That's if this emergency involved guns. Leonard didn't say, did he? Arrogant old shit. Arrogant old shit who doesn't know that I know he's about to be at the center of a major bust.

GLANCING AT WENDY STREET's house before he breached the Latimers' stately gateposts, Hirsch spotted the aged Volvo. No one in the garden or driveway or on the veranda. The old feeling crept through Hirsch: unfinished business.

He drove deeper onto the property. House and grounds had looked timeworn enough when he was last here, investigating Craig Latimer's pyromania; now the neglect was more apparent. The lawn, overgrown then, was dying. Wind debris—palm fronds, twigs, branches, plastic bags, seedling containers, a director's chair—hadn't been cleared. He steered around a bicycle dumped in the gravel. When he walked the crazy path to the veranda, he stepped over weeds, a cricket bat, dead snails. Meanwhile the gutters above him grew grass clumps and paint flakes peeled from the veranda posts. And a stalactite of bird shit hard against one wall, dropped from a swallows nest high on a light fitting.

God knew the miseries the place contained. Hirsch rapped his knuckles on the door.

LEONARD LATIMER ANSWERED AND he didn't look panicked. Glanced over Hirsch's shoulder at the HiLux and smiled.

"Come in."

Smiled because they'd got the drop on Hirsch. At the precise moment Hirsch stepped into the hallway, Superintendent Spurling came in hard on his heels, holding a .303 rifle, and Raymond Latimer came in on his flank, emerging from the front room with a shotgun.

Wasting no time, Spurling shoved him against the wall, disarmed him, patted him down, ankles included. So the Beretta wouldn't have done Hirsch much good anyway. "Supe?"

"Shut up."

Hirsch didn't. He glanced at Leonard, the only one not armed. "What, you're the brains of the outfit?"

The patriarch gave him the look he reserved for tradesmen. "Be quiet."

They stood there crowding him. Hirsch said, "Where's the Chrysler, Supe?"

Spurling blanched. "What?"

Hirsch kept his voice hardened and deliberate. "The Chrysler that was seen by various people when Melia Donovan died and again when Alison Latimer died."

Spurling's narrow face grew tighter. "Who else knows?"

"Internal Investigations."

Spurling chewed on that. "I don't believe you. And it changes nothing. I'll disappear the car, and everything else will have an explanation. Come on."

"Hang on," Leonard said, tetchy, irritated. "You were seen? Your car?"

"It's nothing."

"How do you know? What possessed you to drive such a distinctive car?"

"You think I was going to drive my own car? Or a police car? Get real."

"I'd be worried if I were you, Len," Hirsch said. "I'd—"

A BLOW TO THE head, thick, round and numbing. He was unconscious for about a minute, coming to on the parched lawn at the side of the house.

"Get up."

Hirsch made a show of it. Spurling booted him. "Get a move on."

On his feet now, rocky, Hirsch said, "Where are we going?"

"Shut up."

"What's the story going to be?"

Spurling drove the butt of the rifle into his stomach. He fell. They waited as he regained his footing. Began to prod him across the yard and beyond the sheds to the track leading to the tin hut.

"You're joking."

"Makes perfect sense, actually," Spurling said, punching again with the rifle butt.

The pain seemed to stab through Hirsch and lodge behind his left eye. He stumbled. They waited, Spurling saying, "Quit stalling."

The creek had retreated to a stretch of fetid mud between muddy pools, the edges dense with dying reeds. Sheep had tried to reach the water, churning the damper soil. A dead sheep floated in the largest pool and a live one struggled feebly to escape. No one but Hirsch noticed it.

He said, "You clowns aren't farmers."

"What?" said Raymond Latimer. They were on the flat area beside the hut's crooked chimney and he punched the shotgun butt into Hirsch's stomach. "What would you know?"

Hirsch got his breath back. "You've run the place into the ground. All that money poured into the latest toy, big shots in the district, you can't even pay your grocery bills, you're a laughingstock."

"Fuck you."

"You're pathetic the way you've always let your old man call the shots as if he were clever or deserving of respect." Hirsch tutted, shook his head. "You're just a sad little pedophile, that's how you'll be remembered."

Stretching it but, right now, goading these losers, driving a wedge between them, was all Hirsch had. What he got out of it was a bit of confusion and outrage and another blow to the guts.

Spurling looked on, irritated. "Do we have to do this? Why are you even listening to him? Get on with it."

"Yeah, get on with it, Raymond. Take orders, it's what you're good at. Spurling cleaned up your mess now it's your turn to clean up."

"I don't take orders from anyone."

"Just shut the fuck up, Ray. Stop listening. Put him out of his misery."

Hirsch ignored both men, gazing curiously at Leonard, the queer blankness in the man. "You must be proud of your boy, Len."

Leonard blinked, character, life, returning to his face, and they all saw it, a flicker that dismissed the son.

"Dad?" said the son. He looked at the shotgun as if it were a gadget beyond his figuring.

"Can't you idiots see what he's doing? Shoot him, Raymond, for fuck's sake."

"Yeah, take another order, Ray."

"Shut the fuck up," Raymond said, jutting his sulky jaw at the dry grasses.

"Come on, Ray," Hirsch said, "it's easy, just another staged suicide, and we know how expertly your wife's was staged. You'd think a cop would know how, but old Spurls here made one error after another. Let you down, didn't he? Maybe you'll do a better job, though why anyone would think I'd come out here and shoot myself with another man's gun, I don't know. Did you idiots think it through?"

"Yeah, we thought it through," Spurling said. "You're going down a mine shaft, hotshot. No one will ever find you."

"Same as you did with Gemma, right?"

"What? No. Don't know where she is."

"Yeah, right," Hirsch said. "Meanwhile they have all your names, guys. You three, Venn, Logan, Coulter, McAskill . . ."

Ray looked hunted. "Who has?"

"Sex crimes."

"He's lying," Spurling said.

"How does he know our names then?"

"Ray, shoot the prick, all right? You owe me."

The shotgun was a hot potato and Ray Latimer tried to shove it into his father's hands. "I can't, Dad. You do it."

"It was your fucking wife got us into this," Leonard said.

"*You* got him into it, Lenny boy," Hirsch said. "You knocked him around all through childhood, gave him sick ideas about sex and women so he'd go along with you and this other sick fuck."

"One of you kill him," Spurling said.

Ray Latimer continued to push the shotgun at his father, who backpedaled, saying, "The fuck are you doing? Grow up, you snivelling great calf."

"You must be so proud, Supe," Hirsch said.

Spurling, distracted and disgusted, said, "What?"

"The caliber of your fellow pedos."

"You don't know anything about it," Spurling said, watching the Latimer psychodrama. He glanced at his watch, yelled, "We haven't got all day. One of you had better come and shoot this cunt."

Hirsch was churning and thought he'd vomit. He swallowed, swallowed again and kept his voice even: "I suppose you've got Kropp running damage control. He'll send in a report about my mental state, plant some evidence, disappear my car."

Spurling frowned at him, half an eye on the Latimers. "What? Kropp? What are you on about?"

"Kropp's not involved?"

Spurling snorted. "Kropp's got nothing to do with any of this. The man's a disgrace."

"And you're not?"

One eye on the Latimers, Spurling said, "Some time in the next few weeks your HiLux will be found out in the dry country with an empty fuel tank. Your phone will be on the seat, flat battery. You wandered off, lost all sense of direction, no water, blazing sun, delirious, you probably fell in a mine shaft." He paused, smiled at Hirsch. "Meanwhile I'll poke around in your office files."

And manage the flow of information, Hirsch thought. *Paint me as corrupt after all, or off on an erratic course of my own, willfully misreading evidence, trying to atone for my crooked past.* He felt ill and drained and couldn't breathe and thought of Alison Latimer, her panic attacks and arrhythmia.

Spurling shouted, "What are you arseholes doing?"

Leonard and Raymond Latimer were enacting a strange, sad, wordless dance, the son pressing the shotgun onto his father almost as if proffering a gift and seeking an embrace, the father disgusted with him.

Then Leonard snatched the gun, shoved his son in the chest with it and swung it neatly to his shoulder, the bore swinging around on Hirsch.

A little voice crying from the rocks across the creek, "Stop it."

From Hirsch's point of view, it was a good thing that Katie Street then clarified her point by shooting Leonard with what he assumed was the missing Latimer rifle.

THE BULLET PUNCHED INTO the patriarch's belly and he *oof*ed in surprise and pain. He doubled over. He took one step back, and another, tossed the shotgun weakly away and lowered himself to the ground, taking the weight with his right hand. The collapse was slow, economical, almost graceful. All stared; no one said anything.

Ray Latimer moved first, starting toward his father as if wanting to give comfort but expecting to be lashed for it, and, too late, Spurling swung around on Hirsch with the rifle. But Hirsch wasn't there, he'd uncoiled from the starting block, leading with his shoulder. He took the superintendent full on, driving the air from his lungs. Hirsch heard the rifle crack in his ear, and then he was deaf, the bullet whining off over the rocks on the other side of the creek. Thinking, *I hope Katie kept her head down,* he began a dance for possession of the rifle as crazy as the Latimers' for the shotgun. He spun around and around with Spurling, spinning the man at the wall of the hut. He was young and he was fit; Spurling was a desk jockey. The superintendent smacked against the rusty metal and bounced off, limp suddenly. Hirsch snatched the rifle.

First he backed away until all three men were inside his field of fire. Then he called, "You can come out now."

Katie Street's spectacular impudence and daring had ebbed a little. She emerged edgy, ready to run, taking stock before picking her way across the creek bed. Now she was running toward Hirsch, stepping wide of Leonard Latimer as if he might still harm her. She reached Hirsch. She got as close to him as she could.

He hugged her thin shoulders briefly. "Where's the gun?"

She pointed across the creek at the rocks. "Over there."

"Just as well you pinched it."

She was a little indignant. "No one would listen to me about that car. Lots of times I saw it. Today I saw it go in Mr. Latimer's place." She pointed toward the Vimy Ridge gates.

"You've been hiding the gun all this while?"

She toed the dirt. "In my tree house."

"Listen, girlie," Spurling said, "this is a very bad man. Go and tell your mother to call the police."

"He *is* the police," Katie said, and Hirsch could feel her warmth pressing against his hip.

CHAPTER 34

TWO DAYS LATER, HIRSCH debriefed with Wendy Street over a glass of wine, Wendy holding her glass to the light a little crookedly, saying a little slurringly, "I have to say my daughter seems quite phlegmatic about shooting a man. 'Mr. Latimer was going to shoot Paul so I shot him.'"

"Just as well she did," Hirsch said. "Just as well she's not agonizing over it."

They were in the kitchen, late afternoon, Bob Dylan drifting from the speakers, *They're selling postcards of the hanging.* The sun, seeking a way in past the blind above the sink, lit Wendy's hair, the finer, flyaway strands so burning in the light that Hirsch wanted to reach out and tame them.

"A counselor's been offered, but I don't know that she needs one. What do you think?"

He almost answered, "You know her better than me," but that was too easy. He glanced at Katie, who was belly-down, chin-up before the TV set in the adjoining sunroom. "She's clearly suffering."

A twist of a smile, Wendy saying, "Joking aside, what if the enormity of it hits her one day?"

Hirsch took a chance and reached his hand out. Her hand was a warm claw under his. "All you can do," he said, "is listen and watch and not make a big deal about it if she raises the issue."

"Not make a big deal about it as in it's okay to shoot people or not make a big deal about it as in don't make her anxious and guilty?"

Hirsch was pretty sure she was smiling so he said, "Oh, the former."

Now she grew serious. "At least she didn't kill him. But what happens officially now?"

"She'll have to answer questions: where the gun came from, why she'd had it, why she shot it, that kind of thing. You'll be allowed to sit with her. Bring in a lawyer if you think things are straying into dangerous territory. But given her age and the fact the gun hadn't been secured by the owner and the fact she saved my life, then I don't think any action will be taken." He paused. "Ray, on the other hand, may face some kind of firearms offense in addition to everything else."

Katie wandered in. She stood close to Hirsch's chair, bumping her shoulder against his in absentminded affection. Wendy smiled at her. "Okay, sweetie?"

"Peachy."

And she wandered back to the TV.

Hirsch said, "You going ahead with the public meeting?"

"Sure. Superintendent Spurling won't be there for obvious reasons."

"They'll send someone in his place."

"The point is I want them to send someone in Sergeant Kropp's place—*and* Constable Nicholson's *and* Constable Andrewartha's. Despite everything that's happened, the situation in Redruth hasn't altered."

Hirsch nodded. Kropp had been strangely quiet. A few weeks ago—a few *days* ago—the sergeant would have been ranting on the phone for Hirsch to tell his girlfriend to back off. "Can I ask you something?"

Wendy Street tensed, slipped her hand out from under his, and Hirsch wondered, with sadness, if she were readying herself to rebuff him. He blushed. "I met you on a Monday, the second week of the September school holidays."

She still looked tense. "That sounds about right."

"Alison was with you."

"Yes. Where are you going with this?"

"Bear with me. On the *Saturday*—in other words, two days before that—she'd followed her husband to a house just on the other side of Redruth where several men, including her husband and father-in-law, were having sex with Melia Donovan and Gemma Pitcher and possibly others we don't know about."

"Yes . . . ?"

"As we understand it, she accosted Ray. He probably told his father, who told the others, and it was agreed she had to go."

"Didn't have anything to do with the inheritance after all," Wendy said.

"Icing on the cake, though," Hirsch said. "The thing is, I have a witness who saw Melia Donovan running from the house in distress, naked, carrying her clothes and shoes."

The tension hadn't ebbed. "And . . . ?"

"This witness said that David Coulter chased Melia in his car and knocked her down."

Wendy tightened against the air between them. "You think Allie should have said something?"

Hirsch said, "It's just that I'm surprised she didn't. Was she that browbeaten, or that single-minded about leaving her husband, that she'd fail to mention something like that?"

"How do you know she saw it? It was nighttime, she might not have had a clear view, she might already have left."

"True."

"All I know is, she was upbeat about leaving Ray and getting a divorce."

"She didn't mention that she'd followed Ray, had her suspicions confirmed, nothing like that?"

"No."

"She looked tense the day I met her. Scared."

"Wouldn't you be? She assumed you were a mate of Kropp's. We all did."

Hirsch winced.

"Maybe," Wendy said, placing her hand over his this time, "she did follow Ray, saw all the cars there, heard music or whatever and assumed he'd gone to a party. He'd always flaunted his other life, this was just more of the same, she felt ashamed and embarrassed and didn't tell me about it."

"You're probably right."

"What's Coulter saying? Did he admit to running over Melia?"

"Dunno, it's out of my hands."

"Gemma will know."

"If I can find her," Hirsch said, thinking of those mine shafts dotting the country behind the Razorback.

AND THEN ONE DAY Gemma Pitcher was seen in town. When word got through to Hirsch it was a Sunday, his day off. Wearing his board shorts and a T-shirt, he came knocking.

Gemma's mother answered with her sullen face, as if life was a disappointment, including her daughter's return.

Or maybe it's me, Hirsch thought. "Is Gemma in?"

"Are you taking her out?"

"I beg your pardon?"

The woman looked him up and down. "She's too upset to go out."

Hirsch shook his head, thinking that he should have worn his uniform. *Men, including policemen, came knocking on this door from time to time, asking for Gemma, so why should I be any different?* "It's a work matter, Mrs. Pitcher."

"I need her to help with dinner," grumbled the woman.

But she took Hirsch through to the sitting room, where Gemma was watching one of the Twilight movies, DVD discs and covers strewn around the TV set and across the carpet.

"Hello, Gemma," he said. "Movie marathon?"

Gemma was staring dazedly at the screen, as if she'd been doing it for half of her life. *Possibly she has,* Hirsch thought. Her mouth hung open, and she lolled rather than sat, dressed in a short top and tights, the fabric stretched to within a millimeter of tolerance and revealing her soft white belly.

"What?"

"Nothing," Hirsch said, watching the mother, who flashed him a look of bitterness and defiance before backing out of the room. Presently she could be heard in the kitchen, smacking dishes about in lieu of love or regard. Hirsch said, "Gemma, I need to ask you some questions."

"What for?"

Hirsch stared at her. "I have a better question: How come you're surprised I want to ask you some questions?"

Gemma looked at him blankly, as if astonished. "But it's all over, it was on the news."

Hirsch wondered how her mind worked. He sat beside her, sinking into the sofa cushions and against over-soft, over-round teenage flesh. He edged away hastily. "Gemma, obviously we have questions to ask you. You might have to give evidence in court. You might face charges yourself."

Beside him the girl was suddenly no longer soft but a dense, tight shape. She swallowed convulsively.

"Gemma?"

Full of tidal anxieties, her face sulky and damp, she said, "I done nothing."

"Gemma, I need to know who introduced Melia to this thing you had going with those men who have been charged, Coulter and Venn and Logan and the others. Was it you?"

"I didn't want her there. Who do you think they all preferred?"

The fifteen-year-old beauty, not the plain, bovine eighteen-year-old. "Did you try to dissuade her?"

"Huh?"

Hirsch sought inspiration from the stale air. "Did you try to convince her it was the wrong thing to do?"

"Her? Yeah, right."

"She was stubborn?"

Gemma snorted.

"You haven't answered the question: who got her involved?"

Her voice came, without conviction: "Mr. Coulter."

"How?"

"Me and her got done for shoplifting and he let us off and asked Mel out."

"Was she his girlfriend? Did they go out?"

"Yeah, but, you know, they had to keep it secret."

"For how long?"

Gemma heaved her heavy shoulders. "I dunno, a while. Few weeks."

"Just to be clear, they were having sex?"

Gemma couldn't believe he'd be so naive. "Like I said, they were goin' out."

"How long after he started going out with her did he ask her to one of your parties?"

The shoulders heaved again. "It wasn't like she went to lots of them."

"That first time, did you tell her what kind of party it would be?"

"No."

"You didn't try to warn her?"

"I would of got into trouble."

"With who? Melia?"

"No—Mr. Coulter. He said I had to hold her hand. He said he could still drop me in the shit because of the shoplifting and that."

"Was she shocked, upset, when she realized what was happening?"

Gemma snorted. "Not her."

"Did you give her a lift or did Mr. Coulter collect her or collect both of you?"

"Me."

"He couldn't let himself be seen with you?"

"Yeah."

"Getting back to that first party: She wasn't scared, nervous?"

"Mr. Coulter was there."

"But so were a lot of other men and they wore masks."

"What? No."

"They weren't masked?"

"Nah."

"Never?"

"No."

Emily Hobba had said the men had worn masks. *They changed their MO,* Hirsch thought, *or Emily had lied, not wanting to be asked to identify anyone.*

"These parties: I know you had sex with the men, but was there also music, dancing?"

"Sure."

"Alcohol? Drugs?"

Gemma slid her eyes to a forgettable corner of the miserable room. Hirsch said, "I'm not the drug squad. I just need to know more about the atmosphere of these parties."

"Like you said, dancing and drinking and that."

"And there was you, Melia . . ."

"Sometimes these other girls."

"I know about Emily Hobba and Lily Humphreys."

"So? Why you asking me, then? Deadshit."

"Apart from Emily, who were these other girls?"

"Dunno. They came with that cop."

"The party I'm mostly interested in is the last one. What happened?"

"Well, you know."

"No, Gemma, I don't know."

"I had sex and the others had sex."

"Melia too?"

"Sure."

"With more than one man?"

Gemma wriggled around where she sat. "I'll tell ya, all right?
She was with Mr. Coulter and then the others wanted to gang
her, all of them at once, including anal, and she got upset, all
right?"

"She ran out?"

"Said she was going to tell."

"Did David Coulter follow her outside?"

"Well, yeah."

"Did you?"

"I couldn't find her."

"She wasn't outside on the road or on the lawn?"

"That's what I said."

"Did you see Mrs. Latimer there?"

"What?"

"Never mind. What about Sam Hempel?"

"That loser."

"Was he there, Gemma?"

"Didn't see him."

"You don't sound surprised that I've mentioned him."

"He was always like sniffing around and that."

"He told me he was looking out for her."

"Yeah, right."

"The day I first asked you questions, why didn't you mention
any of this?"

"Get real."

"But your best friend had just died a terrible death."

"Doctor McAskill said don't say nothin' or I'd get in trouble.
Look what they done to Melia to shut her up. So when you go
asking me about Melia and some older guy I got scared."

"You ran."

"So?"

"I thought you were dead."

"Well I'm not."

"Where have you been all this time?"

"Me foster mother."

"You were in foster care?"

"When I was like nine."

Hirsch's checks had uncovered a juvenile record but not the foster placement. "She was nice to you?"

"Better than Mum."

"Tell me about Emily Hobba."

The big shoulders lifted to the fleshy ears. "We met in juvie detention."

"She had an older friend who got you involved in this party scene?"

"Yeah, so?"

"Just trying to form a picture, Gemma."

"I'm really tired."

"Before Melia was involved, you would sometimes travel all the way down to the city for these parties?"

"So?"

"Didn't your mother wonder where you were going?"

"I'm not a kid."

"Were you paid?"

She shrugged. "Got, you know, presents and that."

"Were you ever paid cash, Gemma?"

"I'm not a prostitute or nothin'."

"Why did the operation move to Redruth?"

"What?"

"Why did the parties stop occurring in the city and start occurring in the country?"

"There were these like whispers."

"Whispers?"

"Like we should take a break or not do it in the city."

"People were suspicious?"

"Suppose. Dunno, do I?"

Hirsch named all of the locals, and said, "Were these men new, or had they been attending the city parties all along?"

"Some of them, sometimes. It wasn't like every weekend or anything. I've only been to like six or seven parties, tops."

Hirsch thought about it. Even posted in the bush, a cop of senior rank would be in a position to hear about rumbles coming from sex crimes or any of the other squads. "If any of these men try to contact you, call me straight away."

Gemma shrank from him. "What?"

"We will need to speak to you again, but in the meantime perhaps you could stay with your foster mother again."

The girl looked frightened. "I thought it was over."

"Those men have been granted bail, I'm afraid. Strict bail conditions, but still . . ."

"Okay."

Hirsch took note of the foster mother's details then walked through to the kitchen and pointed out a few home truths to the birth mother.

CHAPTER 35

KROPP WAS WAITING FOR him at the police station, apparently dozing behind the wheel of a Redruth patrol car. Head tilted back, eyes closed, hands in his lap.

But he was quick to sense Hirsch. In a couple of economical motions he was out and onto the footpath as Hirsch slid his key in the lock. "Sarge," said Hirsch, one arm out to hold the front door ajar, giving the sergeant plenty of room.

"Constable."

They were chilly with each other. Hirsch opened the connecting door to his private quarters, again giving Kropp room, as if the pair of them might explode into violence if sleeve brushed sleeve, but Kropp shook his head. "Your office will do."

He took the plain wooden chair. Hirsch, a little tense now, swung into the swivel chair behind his desk. He didn't feel cowed, dutiful or deferential . . . What, exactly? Kropp had lost control of his men and was a dinosaur, a blind man, who'd forgotten who he was supposed to be and what he was supposed to do, but he wasn't bad in the way Spurling had been bad. Hirsch admitted that he felt a smidgen of regard for the man.

"You could have called me the other day," Kropp said. "I'd have done the right thing."

"Sarge," Hirsch said, thinking that no, he couldn't have called Kropp. The sergeant would have been compromised or at least Spurling and the Latimers would have tried to compromise him. If he'd revealed a flicker of doubt or hesitation, then Spurling or Raymond Latimer might have gone on the offensive.

And worse for me, Hirsch thought, *if Nicholson and Andrewartha had come along for the ride.*

Kropp saw the story in Hirsch's face and slumped and shook his head, all elasticity vanished. He drew one huge dry palm down over his face as if seeking comfort. Or erasure.

"It's a mess," he said.

Hirsch waited.

"Took my eye off the ball."

As if policing were a game. *Perhaps we can put everything firmly at the feet of football,* Hirsch thought.

"My officers let me down."

"You allowed it to happen."

A flash of the old quick surging power, Kropp snarling, "*You* going to lecture me about my conduct?"

They faced off, saying no more.

Kropp subsided again. "Your girlfriend's got her wish, there's going to be a public meeting, put-the-boot-into-your-local-copper."

Hirsch stared hotly at his sergeant. "Fuck you, Kropp. There were rumbles long before I arrived in the district. People complained to you personally and in writing long before they contacted police headquarters. And my girlfriend as you like to call her doesn't need any help from me to get a public meeting up and running."

"You're the one who dobs in his colleagues."

"Those officers stitched me up. They threatened my parents," Hirsch said. "They *frightened my parents,* cowardly shits."

"Like I said, you do not drop another police member in the shit."

"No matter what he's done?"

"No matter what he's done."

"If not me, then who? We let a rapist cop get away with it? A bully or a murderer or a thief?"

"What did I ever do to you?"

"You did it to yourself. People wanted me to spy on you but I didn't."

"Bullshit."

"*You did it to yourself.* They have files full of complaints, going back years. Internal Investigations, even Spurling. But I'll answer your question, what did you ever do to me . . . You didn't allow me to do my job. You interfered. You were partisan."

"You spied on me."

"I was asked to. There is a difference. And I didn't spy on you."

"You spied on Quine easy enough."

Hirsch said, "Quine was a criminal. He committed criminal acts. He corrupted junior officers and got them to commit criminal acts, and the Internals knew all about it, and now he's in jail."

"Hirschhausen, the holier than thou moralist."

Yeah, well, maybe a touch, sometimes, when the wind's in the right quarter, Hirsch thought. Which didn't make him wrong. "Quine set me up to take the blame. He threatened my life. He frightened my parents. This is news to you? You defend a man like that?"

"He's a colleague," Kropp said, jaw out.

"So anything's allowed? He's allowed to commit crimes? You're allowed to be a fuck-up? Because you both wear the uniform and swore the oath, that makes it okay?"

"I didn't fuck up."

"What was it you said, you took your eye off the ball? You fucked up, Sarge. You turned a blind eye to Nicholson and Andrewartha's bullying, their sexual assaults, their rapes. You turned a blind eye to their harassment of the female constable you were supposed to train and protect. You ran interference for morally bankrupt locals just because they belonged to your footie club. And meanwhile you were running some catering business in police time using your mail-order bride."

Kropp came out of his seat, red and frothing. "I *love* her. I treat her decent. And she was already living here, if you must know."

Fucked if Hirsch was going to apologize. "What was it, you came into town an outsider and knew you'd never be part of the fabric but pathetically let yourself think you could be, if you ingratiated yourself enough to people like the Latimers? You're a disgrace."

Kropp had sat again but was dangerously still, tendons standing out in his neck. "You're this close to a thrashing."

"Fine. Bring it on."

They faced off. Eventually Kropp said, "But if I did bash you up I might get a reprimand or something."

He's making a joke? Hirsch still watched for the explosion out of the chair.

Instead Kropp said, "I want you and me to take a little drive together."

"What, out east, some convenient mine shaft?"

"Mate, I'm not a killer—I'm a fuck-up and a disgrace, remember?"

NORTH ALONG THE BARRIER, into a day of rusty winds and black, staring birds dotted along the swooping wires.

"I've seen the forensic report on David Coulter's car," Kropp said.

"And?"

"The rear bumper and boot lid had been replaced at some point."

Hirsch nodded. "Melia Donovan backed into a tree. Few weeks ago."

"But the rest of the car is spotless," Kropp said. "No evidence it was used to run Melia Donovan over."

Hirsch chewed on that. "One of the others did it? Or Coulter used a car belonging to one of the others?"

"No. I checked. And if you eliminate Coulter and the others, what possibility are you left with?"

The road north swam in mirages, stretching to the dry horizon, the pink and grey hills. Hirsch was half fond of the place now. "Sam Hempel."

"Coulter sent him to jail a couple of years ago. Gave him six months."

"But I've seen his car," Hirsch said. "Even driven it. It's a mess, but I don't recall seeing any recent damage."

Kropp said nothing and they reached the signage for Muncowie. Kropp turned off the highway and onto a single vehicle track, two stripes of gravelly dust stretching to the hills. One kilometer, two, and they were out where the battlers lived in corrugated iron shacks set in dead grass and rusted car bodies, where cats slunk away and the dogs were nothing but ribs and a prick.

Pulling into a weedy yard, Kropp switched off and the air was still and hot when they got out and slammed their doors. The exhausted dogs watched them and no curtains stirred. A plate, knife and fork sat on a stump, a smear of tomato sauce blackening in the sun. A hand mower sat at the end of a stripe of cropped grass and would have finished the job if there'd been time and a will. A David Jones bag had been snagged by untamed rose canes; someone had coughed blood into the tissue Hirsch spotted beside a cane chair black with sun and water damage. And sure enough, he heard a woman hacking her lungs up inside the house.

"Sam's mother?"

"The father shot through long ago," Kropp said.

He didn't knock. He took Hirsch to the rotting sheds at the back, where nettles ruled and a rust-fretted Land Rover sat on weak tires. Slamming his meaty palm on the dented nose of the vehicle, he said, "If you'd done your job right, you'd have found this fine example of English automobile engineering registered to one Mary Kathleen Hempel."

Hirsch began to nod, recalling the unreliability of Sam's Commodore, a bitch to drive, hard to start. So he'd taken his mother's car. "Still got your copper's instincts, Sarge."

"Me, I'm going out in a blaze of glory," Kropp said.